Paul Finch is a former cop and journalist, now turned full-time writer. He cut his literary teeth penning episodes of the British TV crime drama, *The Bill*, and has written extensively in the field of children's animation. However, he is probably best known for his work in thrillers and crime. His first three novels in the Detective Sergeant Heckenburg series all attained 'bestseller' status, while his last novel, *Strangers*, which introduced a new hero in Detective Constable Lucy Clayburn, became an official *Sunday Times* top 10 bestseller in its first month of publication.

Paul lives in Lancashire, UK, with his wife Cathy. His website can be found at www.paulfinchauthor.com, his blog at www.paulfinch-writer.blogspot.co.uk, and he can be followed on Twitter as @paulfinchauthor.

By the same author:

Stalkers
Sacrifice
The Killing Club
The Chase: an ebook short story
Dead Man Walking
Hunted
Strangers

Ashes to Ashes

PAUL FINCH

A DS HECKENBURG THRILLER

avon

HarperCollins
PUBLISHERS
Since 1817

AVON

A division of HarperCollins*Publishers*
1 London Bridge Street,
London SE1 9GF

www.harpercollins.co.uk

A Paperback Original 2017
2

A catalogue record for this book is
available from the British Library

ISBN 978-0-00-755129-3

Set in Sabon by Palimpsest Book Production Limited,
Falkirk, Stirlingshire

Printed and bound in Great Britain by
Clays Ltd, St Ives plc

MIX
Paper from
responsible sources
FSC
www.fsc.org
FSC™ C007454

For Cathy, who has not just been my beloved wife for the last three decades, but also my best friend, my toughest critic, my staunchest supporter, my constant adviser and, in all things, my strong right arm.

Chapter 1

Barrie and Les saw customer care as an essential part of their role as porno merchants.

Some might laugh at that notion, given pornography's normal place in the world. It was all very well people pretending it was near enough respectable now, but the reality was that, even if you used porn, you tended not to talk about it. You weren't generally interested in building a rapport with the providers – you just wanted to acquire your goods and go (said goods then to reside in a secret compartment in your home where hopefully no one would ever find them). No, one wouldn't normally have thought this a business where the friendly touch would pay dividends, but Barrie and Les, who'd jointly and successfully managed Sadie's Dungeon, their street-corner sex shop for twelve years, didn't see it that way at all.

Certainly Barrie didn't, and he was the thinker of the twosome.

In Barrie's opinion, it was all about improving the customer's experience so that he would happily return. *Happily* – that was the key. Yes, it was about providing quality material, but at the same time doing it with a smile and a quip or two, and being helpful with it – if someone requested information or advice, you actually tried to assist, you didn't just stand there with that bored, bovine expression so common among service industry staff throughout the UK.

This way the customer would more likely buy from Sadie's Dungeon again – it wasn't difficult to understand. And it worked.

Even in this day and age, there was something apparently disquieting about the act of buying smut. Barrie and Les had seen every kind of person in here, from scruffy, drunken louts to well-dressed businessmen, and yet all had ventured through the front door in similar fashion: rigid around the shoulders, licks of sweat gleaming on their brows, eyes darting left and right as though fearful they were about to encounter their father-in-law – and always apparently eager to engage in an ice-breaking natter with the unexpectedly friendly guys behind the counter, though this was usually while their merchandise was being bagged; it was almost as if they were so relieved the experience was over that they suddenly felt free to gabble, to let all that pent-up humiliation pour out of them.

It was probably also a relief to them that Sadie's Dungeon was so neat and tidy. The old cliché about sex shops being seedy backstreet establishments with grubby windows and broken neon signs, populated by the dirty-raincoat brigade and trading solely in well-thumbed mags and second-hand videotapes covered in suspiciously sticky fingerprints, was a thing of the past. Sadie's Dungeon was a clean, modern boutique. OK, its main window was blacked-out and it still announced its presence at the end of Buckeye Lane with garish luminous lettering, but behind the dangling ribbons in the doorway it was spacious, clean and very well lit. There was no tacky carpet here to make you feel physically sick, no thumping rock music or lurid light show to create an air

2

of intimidation. Perhaps more to the point, Barrie and Les were local lads, born and raised right here in Bradburn. It wasn't a small borough as Lancashire towns went – more a sprawling post-industrial wasteland – but even for those punters who didn't know them, at least their native accents, along with their friendly demeanour, evoked an air of familiarity. Made it feel a little more welcoming, almost wholesome.

'Fucking shit!' Les snarled from his stool behind the till. 'Bastard!'

'What's up?' Barrie said, only half hearing.

'Fucking takings are crap again.'

'Yeah?' Barrie was distracted by the adjustments he was making to one of the displays.

When Sadie's Dungeon had first opened, sales had initially been great, but ever since then – thanks mainly to the internet, and despite the lads' conscientious customer-care routine – business had steadily declined.

'Don't get your undies in a twist,' Barrie said, determinedly relaxed about it. 'They're not that far down. We're doing all right.'

Though Les didn't share such airy optimism, he tended to listen to Barrie, who was undoubtedly the brains behind Sadie's Dungeon, and in Les's eyes a very smart cookie.

'Sonja, we're almost done!' Les shouted down the corridor behind the counter.

''Kay . . . getting dressed,' came a female voice.

Which was when the bell rang as the shop's outer door was opened. The breeze set the ribbons fluttering as a bulky shape backed in, lugging something heavy behind him.

Les turned from the rack of DVDs he was busy reordering. 'Sorry, sir – we're closing.'

The customer halted but didn't turn around; he bent down slightly as if what he was dragging was cumbersome as well

3

as heavy. They noticed that under his massive silvery coat he wore steel-shod boots and baggy, shapeless trousers made from some thick, dark material.

'Sir, we're closed,' Barrie said, approaching along the right-hand aisle.

Where Les was short, stocky and shaven-headed, Barrie was six-four and, though rangy of build with a mop of dark hair and good looks, he knew how to impose himself and use his height.

'Hey, excuse me . . . *hey, mate!*'

The figure backed all the way into the shop, the door jammed open behind him. When he straightened up, they saw that he was wearing a motorcycle helmet.

'Shit!' Les yanked open a drawer and snatched out a homemade cosh, a chunk of iron cable with cloth wrapped around it.

Barrie might have reacted violently too, except that as the figure pivoted around, the sight froze him where he stood. He wasn't sure what fixated him more, the extended, gold-tinted welder's visor riveted to the front of the intruder's helmet, completely concealing the features beneath, or the charred-black steel muzzle now pointing at him, the rubber pipe attachment to which snaked back around the guy's body to a wheeled tank at his rear.

Les shouted hoarsely as he lifted the counter hatch, but it was too late.

A gloved finger depressed a trigger, and a fireball exploded outward, immersing Barrie head to foot. As he tottered backward, screeching and burning, it abruptly shut off again, swirling oil-black smoke filling the void. The intruder advanced, a second discharge following, the gushing jet of flame expanding across the shop in a ballooning cloud, sweeping sideways as he turned, engulfing everything in its path. Les flung his cosh, missing by a mile, and then ran across the back of the shop, stumbling for the exit. But the intruder followed, weapon levelled, squirting out a fresh torrent of fire, dousing him thoroughly as he hung helplessly on the escape bar.

The suspended ceiling crashed downward, its warping tiles exposing hissing pipework and sparking electrics. But the intruder held his ground, a featureless rock-like horror, hulking, gold-faced, armoured against the debris raining from above, insulated against the heat and flames. Slowly, systematically, he swivelled, pumping out further jets of blazing fuel, bathing everything he saw until the inferno raged wall to wall, until the room was a crematorium, the screaming howl of which drowned out even those shrieks of the two shop-managers as they tottered and wilted and sagged in the heart of it, like a pair of melting human candles.

Chapter 2

The quarter of Peckham where Fairfax House stood was not the most salubrious. To be fair, this whole district of South London had once been renowned for its desolate tower blocks, maze-like alleys and soaring crime rates. That wasn't the whole story these days. It was, as so many internet articles liked to boast, 'looking to the future', and its various regeneration projects were 'well under way'. But there were still some pockets here which time had left behind.

Like the Fairfax estate, the centrepiece of which was Fairfax House.

A twelve-storey residential block, it stood amid a confusion of glass-strewn lots and shadowy underpasses, a textbook example of urban decay. Much was once made in the popular press of the menacing gangs that liked to prowl this neighbourhood, or the lone figures who would loiter on its corners after dark, looking either to mug you or to sell you some weed, or maybe both, but the sadder reality was the sense of hopelessness here. Nobody lived in or even visited this neighbourhood if they could avoid it. Several entire apartment blocks were now hollow ruins, boarded up and awaiting demolition.

At least Fairfax House had been spared that indignity. Darkness had now fallen, and various lights showed from its grotty façade, indicating the presence of a few occupants. There were several cars parked on the litter-strewn cul-de-sac out front, and even a small sandpit and a set of swings on the grass nearby, fenced off by the residents to keep it free from condoms and crack phials. Even so, this wasn't the sort of place one might have expected to find John Sagan.

A high-earning criminal, or so the story went, Sagan would certainly value his anonymity. Unaffiliated to any gang or syndicate, he was the archetypical loner. He wasn't married as far as the Local Intelligence Unit knew; he didn't even have a girlfriend, or boyfriend for that matter. He worked by day as an office admin assistant, and as such seemed to lead a conventional nine-'til-five existence. This, presumably, was the main reason he'd flown beneath the police radar for as long as he had. But even so, it was a hell of a place he'd found to bury himself in. It wouldn't appeal to the average man in the street. But then, contrary to appearances, there was nothing average about John Sagan. At least, not according to the detailed statement Heck had recently taken from a certain Penny Flint, a local streetwalker of his acquaintance.

Heck, as his colleagues knew him – real title Detective Sergeant Mark Heckenburg – was currently ensconced in Fairfax House himself, though in his case lolling on a damp, badly-sprung sofa on the lower section of a split-level corridor on the third floor. Immediately facing him was the tarnished metal door to a lift which had malfunctioned so long ago that even the 'Out of Order' notice had fallen off. On his right stood a pair of fire-doors complete with glass panels so grimy you could barely see through them; on the other side of those was the building's main stairwell. It was a cold, dank position, only partly lit because most of the bulbs on this level were out.

He'd been here the best part of the afternoon, with only a patched-up jumper, a pair of scruffy jeans, a raggedy old combat jacket and a woollen hat to protect him against the March chill. He didn't even have fingers in his gloves, or socks inside his rotted, toeless trainers. Of course, just in case all that failed to create the impression that he was a hopeless wino, he hadn't shaved for a week or combed his hair in several days, and the half-full bottle of water tinted purple to look like meths that was hanging from his pocket was not so wrapped in greasy newspaper that it wouldn't be spotted.

The guise had worked thus far. Several of the gaunt individuals who inhabited the building had been and gone during the course of the day, and hadn't given him a second glance. But of John Sagan there'd been no sign. Heck knew that because, from where he was slumped, he had a good vantage along the passage, and number 36, the door to Sagan's flat, which stood on the right-hand side, hadn't opened once since he'd come on duty that lunchtime. The team knew Sagan was in there – officers on the previous shift had made casual walk-bys, and had heard him moving around. But he was yet to emerge.

Heck was certain he would recognise the guy, having studied the photographs carefully beforehand. Purely in terms of appearance, Sagan really was the everyday Joe: somewhere in his mid-forties, about five-eight, of medium build, with a round face and thinning, close-cropped fair hair. He usually wore a pair of round-lensed, gold-rimmed spectacles, but otherwise had no distinguishing features: no tattoos, no scars. And yet, ironically, it was this workaday image that was most likely to make him stand out. In his efforts to look the part-time clerk he actually was, Sagan favoured suits, shirts, ties and leather shoes. But that wasn't the regular costume in this neck of the woods. Far from it.

And yet this was only one of many contradictions in the curious character that was John Sagan.

For example, who would have guessed that his real profession was torturer-for-hire? Who would have known from his outward appearance that he was a vicious sadist who loaned his talents to the underworld's highest bidders, and performed his unspeakable skills all over the country?

Heck wouldn't have believed it himself – especially as the Serial Crimes Unit had never heard about John Sagan before – had the intel not come from Penny Flint, who was one of his more trustworthy informants. She'd even told Heck that Sagan had a specially adapted caravan called the 'Pain Box', which he took with him on every job. Apparently, this was a mobile torture chamber, kitted on the inside with all kinds of specialist devices ranging from clamps, manacles and cat o'nine tails to pliers, drills, surgical saws, electrodes, knives, needles and, exclusively for use on male victims, a pair of nutcrackers. To make things worse, and apparently to increase the sense of horror for those taken inside there, its whole interior was spattered with dried bloodstains, which Sagan purposely never cleaned off.

Penny Flint knew all this because, having offended some underworld bigwig, she herself had recently survived a session in the Pain Box – if you could call it surviving; when Heck had gone to see her in her Lewisham flat, she'd been on crutches and looked to have aged thirty years. She'd advised him that there were even medical manuals on the shelves in the Pain Box to aid Sagan in his quest to apply the maximum torment, while its central fixture was a horizontal X-shaped cross, on which the victims would be secured with belts and straps. Video feeds of each session played live on a screen positioned on the ceiling overhead, so that the victims were forced to watch in close detail as they were brutalised.

As he waited there on the semi-derelict corridor, and took

another swig of 'meths', Heck recollected the initial reaction back at the Serial Crimes Unit, or SCU as it was officially known in police circles, when he'd first broken the story. Strictly speaking, a freelance torturer operating inside the underworld wasn't entirely within their normal remit, but it was anyone's guess how many people this guy had maimed and/or murdered. It was way too tempting a case to simply hand over. Even so, there had been understandable doubts expressed.

'Why haven't we heard about this guy before?' DC Shawna McCluskey wanted to know.

Shawna had grown increasingly cynical and pugnacious the longer she'd served in SCU. These days she never took anything at face value, but it was a fair question. Heck had asked the same of Penny Flint when he'd been to see her. The primary explanation – that Sagan was an arch-pro and that those he was actually paid to kill were disposed of without trace – was plausible enough. But the secondary explanation – that he'd mostly tended to punish gangland figures who'd betrayed or defied their bosses, and so those who were merely tortured and released again would be unwilling to blab – was less so. Contrary to popular belief, the much-mythologised code of silence didn't extend widely across the underworld. But then, Penny Flint had been the proof of that. From what she'd told Heck, she'd had no idea who Sagan initially was and had merely thought him another customer. She'd gone off with him voluntarily to perform a sex service, or so she'd expected. When they'd arrived at what she assumed was his caravan sitting on a nondescript backstreet in Lewisham, she'd had no idea what was inside it.

Perhaps if he'd simply beaten her up, Penny would have accepted it as justified punishment for a foolish transgression, but Sagan was nothing if not a meticulous torturer. In her case, after she'd recovered from the chloroform to find herself manacled and helpless, it had been deliberately sexual – the idea being not just to hurt her in a deep and lasting way, but to deprive her of an income afterwards. And that was too much to tolerate.

'Why is Flint tipping us the wink?' Detective Superintendent Gemma Piper, head of SCU, asked. 'What does she have to gain?'

'In this case I think it's personal, ma'am,' Heck replied.

'That won't cut it, Heck – we need specifics.'

'Well . . . she wasn't very forthcoming on the details, but she's got a kid now. A baby – less than one year old.'

'Bloody great!' DC Gary Quinnell chipped in. A burly Welshman and a regular attender at chapel, he was well known for tempering his sometimes brutal brand of law-enforcement with Christian sentiment. 'God knows what kind of life that little mite's going to have.'

'The first thing it's going to get acquainted with is the Food Bank,' Heck replied. 'By the looks of Penny, she won't be working the streets any time soon. Unless she can find some johns who like getting it on with cripples.'

Gemma shrugged. 'So she's got a child and suddenly she's lost her job. Perfect timing. But how does grassing on John Sagan help with that?'

'It doesn't, ma'am. But Penny isn't the sort to go down without a fight. She told me that if she isn't good for the game any more, she'll make sure this bastard's put out of business too.'

'So it's purely about revenge?' Gemma still sounded sceptical.

'Penny's an emotional girl, ma'am. I wouldn't like to get on the wrong side of her.'

It hadn't been a lot to go on, but it had been a start. Heck had touched other snouts for info regarding Sagan, but none had been prepared to talk. At least, not as much as Penny Flint. She'd given them the suspect's description, his home address, his place of work and so forth. In fact, just about the only thing she hadn't been able to deliver was the Pain Box, which he supposedly kept in a lock-up somewhere else in South London, though its actual location was his best kept secret. They'd searched hard, but no avenue had led to his ownership of any kind of vehicle other than a battered old Nissan Primera, which he'd owned since 2005 and which was parked outside Fairfax House at this very moment. Of course, it didn't help that Penny Flint didn't know the vehicle registration mark of the Pain Box. It had been late at night when Sagan had taken her to it, and, not knowing what was about to happen, she hadn't been paying attention to detail.

This was no minor problem.

Even the medical evidence proving that Penny had been severely assaulted was useless on its own; firstly, because there was nothing to physically link this act to John Sagan, but secondly, and mainly, because Penny valued her status as a cash-earning police informer, and had no intention of giving evidence herself – not in open court. The best they could do in this case was 'respond to information received from an anonymous tip' by stopping and searching the caravan for items intended for use in criminal activity, and then 'discovering' the many bloodstains inside it, which the forensics boys could later, hopefully, link to an extensive list of past crimes – in that event it wouldn't matter that Penny wasn't prepared to witness for them.

'We need that caravan,' Gemma said emphatically. 'We could raid his flat, but what would be the point? If this guy's as careful as Flint says, every incriminating thing in his life is stored in this so-called Pain Box.'

With regard to Sagan himself, it was highly suspicious

how clean he seemed to be. No criminal record was one thing, but his employment, financial and educational histories were also unblemished. The guy appeared to have led a completely uneventful life, which was almost never the case with someone involved in violent crime.

'What we've got here is a real Jekyll and Hyde character,' Heck declared. 'Openly a picture of respectability, deep down – very deep down – a career degenerate.'

'Inspired comparisons with cool horror stories don't make a case,' Gemma replied. 'We still need that caravan.'

Short of putting out public appeals, which was obviously a no-no, they'd done everything in their power to locate the Pain Box, but had still come up with nothing. However, when Heck went to visit Penny Flint a second time, now in company with Gemma, it was the prostitute herself who made a suggestion.

'Why don't I just piss the local mob off again?' she said. 'They'll send him to teach me another lesson, and you can nab him.'

'What are you talking about?' Heck asked her.

'Christ's sake, Heck, this is easy. After he finished with me last time, I was half dead, but still conscious enough to listen to his threats. "If I need to see you again, it won't end so well," he said. And he really meant it, I'll tell you.'

'Who paid him to do that to you?' Gemma asked.

'Don't be soft,' Penny snorted. 'I'm not telling you that.'

'OK, no names, but what did you do to annoy them?'

'Gimme a fucking break, Miss Piper –'

'Hey!' Gemma's voice adopted that familiar whip-crack tone. 'We're not here at your disposal, Miss Flint. Our job is to enforce the law, not pay off private scores. And we can't do that flying blind. At present we don't even know who you are, never mind John Sagan. So the least you can do is enlighten us a little.'

Penny glanced at Heck. 'You gave me your word I'd be immune from prosecution if I helped you out with this . . .?'

Heck shrugged. 'Unless you've done something very serious, we're only interested in Sagan.'

'OK, well . . .' She hesitated. 'Doing a bit of delivering, wasn't I?'

'Delivering what?' Gemma asked. 'Drugs? Drugs money?'

'Bit of both. You know the scene.'

'And let me guess, you were skimming?'

'What else?' Penny's cheeks reddened. 'Hey, you're looking at me like I'm some kind of criminal.'

Neither of the two cops commented, though both wanted to. Even so, she detected the irony.

'Don't get smarmy on me, Heck. Look at the state I'm in. I'm past forty. Even before that bastard Sagan tore my arse and pussy inside-out, how much shelf-life did I have left? Anyway, I thought I'd been careful. Thought no one'd notice me dip, but they did. And . . . well, you know the rest.'

'And you're seriously saying this firm would trust you with that job again?' Heck said.

'Yeah.' She seemed surprised he'd ask such a question. 'Sagan's a scary guy. They're sure I'll have learned my lesson.'

'And what you're proposing is to commit exactly the same offence all over again?' Gemma said. 'Even though you know what the outcome will be?'

'The difference is this time you lot'll be sitting on Sagan, won't you? You can jump on him as soon as he gets his caravan out.'

They were impressed by her courage – in fact they were quietly startled by it. Heck wondered if her desire for revenge was getting the better of her common sense, to which she merely shrugged.

'Heck – we both want the guy gone. The only way we

14

can make that happen legally is for you to catch him in the act with his Pain Box. This is the quickest and most obvious way to make that happen.'

'Miss Flint,' Gemma said. 'This time you may have pushed things too far. He could just shoot you through the head.'

'Nah. The firm I'm talking about like to make a show. Besides . . . Pain Box, gun? Why will it matter? Like I say, you lot'll jump on him first.'

It had sounded simple initially, but of course there were complicating issues. Even if Penny Flint *had* been prepared to testify in court, the fact that, by her own admission, she'd been stealing from an underworld bigwig would have made her an unreliable witness. It could even have allowed the defence to accuse the police of conspiracy for 'encouraging' her to steal again. It was all the more important, therefore, that the team write up their interest in Sagan as an anonymous tip-off, and go solely on any evidence they found inside the Pain Box, keeping Penny out of it altogether. Despite that, the risks of using a female civilian as bait would be extraordinary. Since the operation had gone live four days ago, Gemma had assigned a round-the-clock armed guard to her flat – all covertly of course, which had added an extra dimension of difficulty.

The same applied to the stakeout at Sagan's flat.

Thus far, in addition to slumping on this ratty old couch in his state of feigned inebriation, Heck had kept watch for another eight hours from behind a window in the empty low-rise on the other side of the cul-de-sac, and had spent half a day in the back of a shabby old van parked right alongside Sagan's Primera. Other detectives in the surveillance team had spent hours 'fixing' a supposedly broken-down lorry on the same street, while another one – Gary Quinnell of all people, all six-foot-three of him – had donned a hi-vis council-worker jacket in order to sweep gutters and pick

15

litter. The common factors had always been the same: damp, cold, the soul-destroying greyness of this place, and then the smell – that eerie whiff of decay that always seemed to wreathe run-down buildings. The word 'discomfort' didn't cover it; nor 'boredom'. Even their awareness that at any time they could be called into action – an awareness that was more acute than normal given that every officer here was armed – had gradually faded into the background as the minutes had become hours and, ultimately, days.

Heck shifted position, but in sluggish, slovenly fashion in case someone was watching. He hitched the Glock under his right armpit. It wasn't a familiar sensation. Though every detective in SCU was required to be firearms-certified, and they were tested and assessed regularly in this capacity, he for one had rarely carried a pistol on duty. But this was an unusual, open-ended operation which no one was even sure would bring a result. Gemma had opted for pistols purely for self-defence purposes, thanks to Sagan's deadly reputation – though again there was no certainty that reputation had been well earned.

And this lack of overall certainty was the real problem.

There was no way Gemma would commit so many SCU resources to this obbo indefinitely. She was on the plot herself today, having arrived early afternoon, and was now waiting in an unmarked command car somewhere close by. That wasn't necessarily a good sign – it might be that she'd finally put herself at Ground Zero to get a feel for what was going on, maybe with a view to cancelling the whole show. On the other hand, it could also mean that Sagan's non-appearance today – all the previous days of the obbo he'd gone to work as usual – might mean something was afoot. They knew he only worked at his official job part-time, so perhaps to maintain the impression of normality he would only indulge in his extracurricular activities on one of his days off.

16

Heck chewed his lip as he thought this through.

Penny Flint reckoned she'd dipped again into her employers' funds some four days ago. The retribution could come at any time, but if Sagan was a genuine pro he wouldn't respond with a kneejerk. He'd strike when the time most suited him – not that they'd want him to leave it too long. That could be inviting the bird to fly.

'*Sorry to break radio silence, ma'am,*' the voice of DC Charlie Finnegan crackled in Heck's left ear. '*But two blokes have just gone in through the front door of Fairfax House, male IC1s, well-dressed – too well-dressed if you know what I mean. Can't help thinking I recognise one of them, but I'm not sure where from, over.*'

There was a brief lull, before Gemma's voice responded: '*Be advised all units inside Fairfax House – we may have intruders on the plot. Could be nothing, but stay alert. Charlie, did these two arrive in a vehicle, over?*'

'*Negative, ma'am, not that I saw. They approached from Parkinson Drive, which lies adjacent to Fairfax House on the southeast side. I'm making my way around there now, over.*'

'*Roger that . . . PNC every vehicle parked, and make it snappy. Heck, you in position?*'

'Affirmative, ma'am,' Heck replied quietly – he could hear a resounding clump of feet and the low murmur of voices ascending the stairwell on the other side of the fire-doors. He checked his cap to ensure it concealed his earpiece. 'Sounds like I'm about to get company, over.'

'*Received, Heck . . . all units stand by, over.*'

The airwaves fell silent, and Heck slumped back onto his sofa, eyelids drooped as though he was in a drunken daze. The footfalls grew louder, the fire-doors swung open and two shadowy forms perambulated into view. In the dim light, Heck wasn't initially able to distinguish them, though from their low Cockney voices he could tell they were both males, probably in their thirties or forties.

'Q&A session first, all right?' one said to the other. 'Don't let on we know anything . . .'

For a fleeting half-second the duo were more clearly visible: shirts, sports jackets, ties hanging loose at the collar. And faces, one pale and neatly bearded – he was the taller and younger of the two; the other older and grouchier, with hang-dog jowls.

To Heck they were unmistakeable.

He held his position until they'd passed him, ascending the three steps to the dingy corridor and trundling off along it. He sat upright to watch their receding backs. Once they were out of earshot, he leaned close to his lapel mic. 'Heckenburg to DSU Piper . . . ma'am, I know these two. They're ours. DS Reg Cowling and DC Ben Bishop from Organised Crime.'

In the brief silence, he could imagine Gemma gazing around at whoever else was in the command car, mystified. 'What the hell are they doing here?' she'd be asking. 'How the devil did *they* get onto this?' He could also picture the blank expressions that would greet these questions.

'They're heading down Sagan's corridor,' Heck added. 'There'll be other villains living in this building, but if it's not him they're here for, ma'am, I'm a sodding Dutchman.'

'*Can you intercept, over?*'

'Negative, ma'am . . . they're virtually at his door.'

'*Understood. Heck, hold your position. All we can do now is hope.*'

Heck stood up, but slammed himself flat against the wall beside the steps, crooking his neck to look along the passage. He understood her thinking. If he went running down there and tried to grab the two cops, there was every possibility Sagan would open the door and catch all three of them. If he kept out of the way, however, it was just vaguely possible the duo had some routine business to conduct with the guy and might be on their way out again in a minute, with no one any the wiser about the obbo. That latter option was a long shot, of course. Like SCU, the Organised Crime Division was part of the National Crime Group. They didn't deal with routine matters. There was one other possibility too, which was even more depressing. Suppose Cowling and Bishop were up to no good themselves? Could it be they were here to see Sagan for reasons unconnected with police-work? If so, that would be a whole new level of complexity.

Heck squinted down the gloomy passage. The twosome had halted alongside number 36. They didn't knock imme-diately, but appeared to be conferring. He supposed he could try to signal to them, alert them to an additional police presence, but the idea was now growing on him fast that these two might have nefarious motives.

A fist thudded on the apartment door. Heck held his breath. At first there was no audible response, then what sounded like a muffled voice.

'Yeah, police officers, sir,' Cowling said. 'Could you open up? We need to have a chat.'

Heck breathed a sigh of relief. They weren't in cahoots with Sagan after all. But now he felt uneasy for other reasons. Given the severity of Sagan's suspected offences, this was a very front-on approach – it seemed odd the two detectives had come here without any kind of support. Did they know something SCU didn't, or did they simply know nothing? Had ambition to feel a good collar overridden the necessity of performing some due diligence?

The muffled voice intoned again. It sounded as if it had said 'one minute'.

And then two thundering shotgun blasts demolished the door from the inside, the ear-jarring din echoing down the passage. Cowling and Bishop were blown back like rag dolls. The impacts as their bodies struck the facing wall shook the entire building.

'This is Heck inside Fairfax House!' Heck shouted into his radio as drew his Glock. 'Shots fired – immediate armed support required on the third floor! We also have two officers down with gunshot wounds. We need an advance trauma team and rapid evac! Get the Air Ambulance if you can, over!'

A gabble of electronic voices burst in response, but it was Gemma's that cut through the dirge. *'Heck, this is DSU Piper . . . you are to wait for support, I repeat you are to wait for support! Can you acknowledge, over?'*

'Affirmative, ma'am,' Heck replied, but he'd already removed his woolly hat and replaced it with a hi-vis, chequer-banded baseball cap. Climbing the three steps, he advanced warily along the corridor, weapon cocked but dressed down as per the manual. 'Both shots fired through the door from inside number 36. Sounded like a shotgun. Both Cowling and Bishop are down . . . by the looks of it, they've incurred severe injuries, over.'

'What's your exact position?' Gemma asked.

'Approx thirty yards along the corridor . . . but I'm going to have difficulty reaching the casualties. They're both still in the line of fire, over.'

'Negative, Heck! You're to get no closer until you have full firearms support. Am I clear?'

'Affirmative, ma'am.' More by instinct than design, Heck continued to advance, but ultra-slowly, his right shoulder skating the right-hand wall. At twenty yards, he halted again. Neither of the shotgunned officers was moving; both lay slumped on their backsides against the left-hand wall. The plasterwork behind them was peppered with shot and fragments of wood, but also spattered with trickling blood.

20

Heck's teeth locked. In these circs, hanging back felt like a non-option. These were fellow coppers pumping out their last. He pressed cautiously on. And then heard a sound of breaking glass from inside the flat.

'Crap!' He dashed forward, only for a door to open behind him. He spun around, gun levelled. The thin-faced Chinese woman who peeked out gaped in horror. 'Police officer!' he hissed. 'Go back inside! Stay there!' The door slammed and Heck resumed his advance, radio mic to his lips. 'This is Heck – suspect's making a break for it through a window. It's three floors down, so I don't know how he's going to manage it. But his flat's on the building's northeast side, which overlooks Charlton Court . . . we've got to get some cover down there, over.'

Even as he said it, Heck knew this would be easier said than done. The surveillance team on Fairfax House was no more than eight strong at any time. Even with Gemma on the plot, that only made it nine – so they were spread widely and thinly. On top of that, though armed and wearing vests, they were geared for close target reconnaissance, not a gun-battle. No doubt, Trojan units would be en route, but how long it would take them in the mid-evening London traffic was anyone's guess. He slid to another halt as a dark shape appeared at the farthest end of the corridor, about twenty yards past number 36. By its size and breadth, and by the luminous council-worker doublet pulled over its donkey jacket, he recognised it as Gary Quinnell, whose lying-up position was on one of the floors above. The burly Welshman had also drawn his firearm, and was in the process of pulling on the regulation baseball cap.

They acknowledged each other with a nod. Heck lowered his weapon and proceeded, stopping again about five yards from the shattered doorway.

'Armed police!' he shouted. 'John Sagan, we are armed

police officers! There's no point in resisting any further! Stop this bloody nonsense, and throw your weapon out!'

There was no reply. No further glass crashed or tinkled.

They waited a couple of yards to either side of the front door. From this close range, it was plain that Reg Cowling was dead. His face had been blown away; in fact, his head had almost detached. However, Bishop, while wounded in the face, which was riddled with gashes and splinters, and the right shoulder, which resembled raw beefsteak through the rents in his smouldering jacket, was vaguely conscious. He was ashen-cheeked, but his eyes, which by some miracle had both survived, were visible beneath fluttering, blood-dabbled lashes.

'Bastard went for head-shots,' Heck said. 'Expected them to be wearing body armour.'

Penny Flint had told them Sagan was a pro. Here was the proof.

'This is Heck,' he said into his radio. 'Update on the casualties . . . both in a collapsed state and suffering extensive gunshot injuries. DS Cowling appears to be dead, DC Bishop is conscious and breathing – how long for, I can't say. We still can't reach them.'

Gemma's response broke continually and was delivered in a breathless voice, which indicated she was running. Before he could make sense of it, it was blotted out by another explosion of glass from inside the flat.

'He's going for it!' Quinnell warned. 'Must have decided the coast's clear!'

'I repeat, we are armed police officers!' Heck shouted. 'Throw your weapon out!'

With a third shuddering *BOOM!*, what remained of the front door was blasted outward. Again, DC Bishop got lucky. The shot was directed above him, so though he was bombarded by wreckage, he was spared further pellet-wounds.

A loud *clunk/clack* from inside signified that a fourth shell had been ratcheted into place.

'Pump-action!' Heck said.

More glass was struck from its frame. The detectives locked gazes across the open doorway, brows beaded with sweat.

'We can't just let him run,' Heck stated flatly.

Quinnell didn't argue the point.

Heck swallowed the apple-sized lump of phlegm in his throat, and wheeled partly around into the doorway, only his left arm, left shoulder and the left side of his head visible as he tried to pinpoint the target. Quinnell did the same from the other side.

But the immediate area, which was an actual living room, was bare of life.

There was no sign of the guy. None at all.

They were vaguely aware of plain, simple furnishings, of bookshelves that were empty, of bland pictures on the walls. But there were also doors to other areas, one on the left and one on the right. On the far side of the room stood three tall sash-windows. The left one had been smashed out.

'Doors first,' Heck said, running right, but finding only an empty bathroom. 'Clear!' he yelled, spinning back.

Quinnell had gone left. He reappeared from the bedroom. 'Clear.'

Heck darted for the left window, which had had to be broken because, by the look of it, Sagan had only been able to lift the lower panel several inches. He flattened himself against the wall, and risked a glance through it. Some twenty feet below, a figure in dark clothing – what looked like a heavy overcoat – and with the shotgun hung from its shoulder by a strap, scampered away across the tops of five flat-roofed garages standing in a terraced row. It was instantly apparent how he'd got down there. Some five feet to the left of the window, about six feet above it, there was a horizontal steel grating – the platform section of an old-fashioned fire escape. The fire escape stair dropped steeply down on the far side of that. There was no possibility of reaching either the stair or the platform by jumping. But the killer had prepared for this in advance by connecting a knotted rope to the underside of the grating, and looping it over a hook alongside his window, where it would hang down the apartment house wall unobtrusively. All he'd had to do when the time came was get a firm grip, unhook it so that it swung away from the window, thus preventing anyone in pursuit using the same method, and slither down to the garage roofs.

Heck peered dully at the hanging rope a good five feet away. He was vaguely aware of Quinnell appearing alongside him.

'Bastard!' the Welshman said, spying the dwindling form of Sagan as he reached the far end of the garages.

About sixty yards to the right of these, a uniformed police car swung over the grass into Charlton Court from the cul-de-sac at the front. Unfortunately, it was only a divisional patrol responding to the call that had just gone out, and it wouldn't be armed, which rendered it next to useless. Besides, Sagan had now jumped from the left side of the garage roofs onto Bellfield Lane, which led away at a much lower level. As well as the rugged, rubbish-strewn slope slanting down to this, there was a high mesh fence along its edge, which formed an impassable barrier for vehicles. Sagan made a rapidly diminishing shape as he raced away along the lower road. Still there was no sign of a Trojan unit.

'Check the casualties,' Heck said tightly.

Quinnell nodded, and went back across the flat.

Heck holstered his Glock and put his mic to his mouth. 'This is DS Heckenburg . . . urgent message. Suspect, John Sagan, is at large and on foot . . . male IC1, mid-forties, fair-haired, wearing glasses and a dark, possibly black overcoat. Currently escaping northeast along Bellfield Lane. Warning, Sagan is armed with a pump shotgun and more than willing to use it. For the cerebrally challenged, that means he's armed and dangerous. I repeat: John Sagan is armed and very dangerous!' He bit his lip, and added: 'In pursuit.'

'Hey, *whoa!*' Gary Quinnell shouted, as Heck climbed up into the casement.

The hanging rope was only five feet away. Heck knew there was a good chance he'd make it, but he also knew that if he stopped to think about this he wouldn't go any further. So he didn't think, just launched himself out, diving full-length – and dropping like a stone, maybe ten feet, before managing to catch hold of the rope. Several more feet of cold, greasy hemp slid through his fingers before he brought himself to a halt, ripping both his gloves and the flesh of the palms underneath. Doing his best to ignore the blistering pain, he clambered down and alighted on the garage roof nearest the building.

'Suspect heading northeast along Bellfield Lane!' he shouted down to the two uniforms who'd spilled onto Charlton Court from their patrol car, faces aghast at what they'd just seen Heck do. 'Spread the word!'

Without waiting for a response, Heck ran due north along the flimsy roofs, feet drumming on damp planks covered only in tarpaper, jabbering into his radio again, giving instructions as best he could. At the far end, he dropped onto all fours and swung his body over the parapet. He hung full-length and dropped the last five feet, before careering downhill through grass and clutter onto the road.

'Bellfield Lane heading northeast,' he shouted, hammering along the tarmac. 'Any units in that direction to respond, over?' But the airwaves were jammed with cross-cutting messages. 'Shit . . . come on, someone!'

As he ran, the vast concrete shape of a railway gantry loomed towards him. Above it, stroboscopic lights sped back and forth as trains hurtled between East Dulwich and Peckham Rye. Conversely, the shadows beneath the structure were oil-black. In normal times this would be a muggers' paradise, but Heck was armed, and besides the night was now alive with sirens – it was just a pity none were in the immediate vicinity.

Beyond the railway overpass, a sheer brick wall stood on the right, but on the left there was wire fencing, and behind that another slope angling down to a glass-littered car park. The fence's second section was loose, disconnected along the bottom, giving easy access to the other side. Heck swerved towards it – only to find that his quarry, neatly camouflaged in his all-black garb, had secreted himself flat at the foot of the waiting slope. The first Heck knew of this was the muzzle-flash, and the hail of shot that swept the wire mesh.

He threw himself to the pavement, rolling away and landing in the gutter – where he lay on his back, gun trained two-handed on the wall of fencing.

Until he heard feet clattering away again.

He scrambled to his knees.

A dark shape was haring across the car park below, at the far side of which a concrete ramp led down onto yet another housing estate, this one comprising rows of near-identical maisonettes. Heck slid under the fence and gave chase, stumbling down the slope until he reached the level tarmac, all the time trying to get through on his radio.

'Is no one fucking listening to me?' he shouted. 'For what it's worth . . . still in pursuit, suspect still on foot, still armed, opening fire at every opportunity. Heading west onto the Hawkwood estate. Listen, this is a built-up area with lots of civvies. Not many around at present, but someone's got to get over here fast. Over and fucking out!'

At the foot of the ramp, he vaulted a railing and ran along a boulevard faced on two sides by front doors and ground-level windows. Sagan was still in sight at the far end – a minuscule figure, which abruptly wheeled around, levelled the shotgun at its waist and fired twice. Heck was out of lethal range – Sagan was using buckshot rather than solid slugs – but instinct still sent him scrambling for cover behind a bench. When he glanced back up Sagan remained visible, but it went against all the rules to open fire in a residential zone like this. You didn't even need to be a poor shot; ricochets could go anywhere. To make matters worse, several doors had opened as curious householders peeked out.

Sagan darted left along a side-street. Heck vaulted the bench and gave chase, shouting at the onlookers as he did. 'Police! Lock your doors! Stay away from the windows!'

He rounded the corner and descended a flight of steps into a covered area. Sagan was visible again, framed in the exit on the other side. He let off two more rounds. Heck dived sideways, smashing through a decayed wooden hoarding and entangling himself in heaps of musty second-hand furniture. He fought his way out through a rear door and sprinted along an alley, hoping to head the bastard off – only to emerge into another car park.

Again, Sagan was waiting, shotgun levelled.

Heck ran low, scuttling behind a row of parked vehicles. Sagan blasted each one of them in turn, bodywork buckling, safety glass flying, before turning, ascending a flight of steps and dashing down a passage between faceless walls. Heck slid over the nearest bonnet and charged up the steps. He entered the passage, which was about fifty yards long; at the far end of it Sagan was rapidly reloading. Before Heck could point his pistol and shout, the bastard fired twice; ear-shattering detonations in the narrow space. This time, as Heck pitched himself down, he pegged off three quick shots of his own, which caromed along the passage, missing their target but sending him ducking out of sight.

Heck retreated around his corner, sucking in lungfuls of chill air. He risked a second glance. The passage still looked empty, but Sagan could be lying in wait, and once Heck was halfway along he'd be a sitting duck. He ran back down the steps, along a row of caged-off shops, and around the base of a tower block. He'd expected to find open space on the other side, but instead the shell of a derelict industrial building stood there.

Swearing, Heck panted the new directions into the radio as he set off running again. At the end of the factory wall there was a net fence and on the other side of that a deep canyon through which another railway passed. The London Overground, Heck realised, though at present it was a good twenty feet below him. He glanced right. The nearest route across it was an arched steel walkover about fifty yards off. A figure was already traipsing over this – slowly, tiredly.

Sagan.

The killer and torturer was an arch-pro. But he was also in early middle age. His energy reserves were finally flagging.

Heck took a short cut along a narrow defile between the factory's north wall and the railway fence. Initially he had to get through barbed wire, and then found himself negotiating thick, leafless scrub entwined with wastepaper and rubbish. Inevitably, cans and bottles clattered, causing such a racket that the figure on the bridge stopped and looked around – and began to run again. By the time Heck got to the bridge, there was no sign of him.

Exhausted himself, Heck lumbered up the steel staircase and over the top. A train thundered past below, a chaos of light and sound, illuminating the footway to its far end. There was a possibility Sagan could reappear over there – while Heck was hemmed between neck-high barriers of riveted steel. But that didn't happen. He made it to the other side, descended the stair to half way and halted, hot breath pluming from his body. Open waste-ground lay ahead, on the far side of which stood a cluster of dingy buildings: workshops, offices and garages, with an old Ford van parked at the front. Sagan was almost over there, moving at a fast but weary trudge – about sixty yards distant.

Heck raised his pistol and took aim, but he wasn't a good enough marksman to ensure a clean shot from this distance. Especially not at night. He continued down, and inadvertently kicked a beer bottle on the bottom step. It cartwheeled forward and smashed.

Sagan twirled around.

Heck scampered down the last couple of steps and veered sideways. Sagan strode back, shooting from the waist like a character out of a western, working the slide again and again, pumping fire and shot. Heck scuttled and crawled, but found no more cover than bits of rubbish and sprigs of weed.

At which point a third party intervened.

'Drop it!' came a fierce female voice. 'Do it now, or I'll shoot you, you bastard . . . I swear!'

Heck glanced up, to see a short, shapely figure in jeans, trainers, an anorak and a chequer-banded police cap, circling around from behind the van, her Glock trained with both hands on the back of John Sagan's head. The gunman froze, the shotgun clasped in his right hand, his left held out to his side.

'I mean it, you dickless wonder!' the girl cop shouted in a ringing northern accent. 'Drop that weapon now, or I'll drop *you*!'

Heck's mouth crooked into a smile as he rose to his feet. It was Shawna McCluskey.

Someone had heard his frantic transmissions after all. And if anyone had, he ought to have realised it would be his old mucker Shawna, who'd started off with him all those years ago in the Greater Manchester Police.

Sagan remained rigid. From this distance, his face was unreadable. Dots of yellow street-light glinting from the lenses of his glasses gave him a non-human aura. His right hand opened and the shotgun clattered to the floor.

'Keep those mitts where I can see 'em!' Shawna shouted, approaching from behind. 'You all right, Heck?'

'Never better,' he called, dusting himself down.

'Kick the weapon back towards me,' Shawna said, addressing Sagan again. 'Backheel it . . . *don't* turn around. And keep your hands spread where I can see them . . . in case you didn't realise it, you lowlife shithead, you're under arrest!'

Sagan did exactly as she instructed, the shotgun bouncing past her and vanishing beneath the van. Now Heck could see him more clearly: his black overcoat, a black roll-neck sweater, black leather gloves, black trousers and shoes, his pale face, the thinning fair hair on top, and those gold-rimmed glasses. Yet still the killer was inscrutable, his features a waxen, sweat-soaked mask.

'DC McCluskey on a lorry park off Camberwell Grove,' Shawna said into her radio. 'One in custody. Repeat, one in custody.'

But only now, as she angled around her captive, did Heck spy the possible danger.

Her Glock was trained squarely on Sagan's body, but side-on, the target's width had reduced and Sagan's left hand was suddenly only inches from the muzzle of her weapon – and it was with this hand that he lunged, slapping the pistol aside, and in the same motion, spinning and slamming his other hand, now balled into a fist and yet glittering as if encased in steel – a knuckleduster, Heck realised with horror – straight into Shawna's face.

Her head hinged backward and she dropped like a puppet with its strings cut.

'*Shawna!*' Heck bellowed.

But he was still forty yards away. He raised his pistol, but again had to hesitate – Sagan had dropped to a crouch alongside the policewoman's crumpled form, merging them both into one. Heck dashed forward as the killer flipped off Shawna's hat and smashed his reinforced fist several times more into her head and face. Then he snatched up her Glock and fired it once into her chest, before leaping to his feet and bolting towards the parked van.

Heck slid to a halt and fired. The van's nearside front window imploded as Sagan scarpered around it, returning fire over his shoulder, and proving uncannily accurate. Nine-millimetre shells ricocheted from the ground just in front of Heck. He fired back, but Sagan was already on the other side of the vehicle and shielded from view. A door slammed closed somewhere along the front of the building. Heck scrambled forward, but kept low. The killer was now indoors; he might have any number of concealed vantage points from which to aim.

'DC McCluskey down with head injuries and a possible gunshot wound,' Heck shouted into his radio, skidding to one knee alongside her, still scanning the grimy windows overhead.

In the partial protection of the van, Shawna lay limp. Heck tore open her jacket and gasped with relief when he saw the slug flattened on her Kevlar vest – it hadn't penetrated. However, her face was a mass of bloodied pulp, her splayed hair glutinous with gore. He probed for the carotid artery. Her throat was slick with blood, but at last he found a pulse.

An engine now growled to life somewhere inside. Fresh sweat pinpricked Heck's brow.

As he leaped to his feet, a pair of double doors some twenty yards to the left exploded outward in a shower of splinters and rusted hinges, and a powerful SUV came barrelling through. Heck backed away from Shawna's body to get a clear shot. But Sagan was already firing through the open passenger window, wildly, blindly. Heck let off one round before diving for cover, aiming at the SUV's front tyre but missing by centimetres. In the process he caught a fleeting glimpse of the vehicle's make and model. A Jeep Cherokee, dark-blue in colour with bull bars across the front, but with its headlights switched off it was impossible to make out the registration number. It was towing a gleaming white caravan, which tilted onto one wheel as the car swerved away across the wasteland, finally righting itself again as it accelerated into the darkness. Heck gave chase for several yards. He even got off one final shot, hitting the caravan's rear door, which judging by the lack of visible damage, was armoured. And then the target was gone, vanishing around the corner of a warehouse, the roar of its engine rapidly diminishing.

Heck got urgently onto the radio, relaying as much info as he could while rushing back to Shawna. As before, she lay perfectly still, and now the blood had congealed in her hair.

When he felt her carotid a second time, there was no pulse.

Chapter 3

Calum and Dean walked along King's Parade as if they owned it, which, to some degree, they did. There were bouncers on all the doors to the numerous bars and night-clubs; surly, brutish types in monkey suits, with gap-toothed grins and dented noses. But if Calum and Dean wanted admission, there was only a small handful who'd say 'no'. Most of the doormen, if they weren't involved with them professionally, knew about them by reputation, sufficiently enough to know that serious trouble was easy enough to come by in Bradburn without inviting it.

Not that, in a normal time and place, Calum and Dean were even close to being adequately attired to gain entry to any nightspot which held itself in reasonable regard.

The former, who was heavyset – more than was good for a guy in his early/mid-twenties – wore only a pair of grey shell-pants and grey and orange Nike training shoes. He'd removed his ragged pink sweater and now wore it draped across his shoulders, exposing acres of flabby, pallid flesh, particularly around the midriff, not to mention the usual plethora of tasteless tattoos. Whether he felt the evening chill was unclear. In all probability, thanks to his system being

33

overloaded with drugs and drink, he probably didn't think that he did, though if his body-odour permitted you to get close enough to appraise him in detail, you'd note that the small, pink nipples on his sagging man-boobs stood stiffly to attention.

Dean was no less dressed-down for the occasion. In his case it was blue and blood-red Nikes and emerald green tracksuit pants with white piping down the sides, a stained string-vest and thick gold neck-chains. Such bling was Dean's most outstanding feature, cheap and nasty though it all looked, especially the sovereign rings on his fingers and diamond studs in his ears.

The irony was that, despite all this, neither of the two lads looked especially menacing.

Calum's features were rounded and pudgy, with a small nose, a tiny mouth and button-like Teddy Bear eyes. If it hadn't been for the shaven ginger thatch on his cranium and his various nicks and scars, you could almost have said that he looked soft. Dean, on the other hand, was thin and weasel-like, but closer inspection would reveal that he was wiry rather than bony; he was certainly no weakling. Under his greasy mat of blond locks and between a pair of jug-handle ears, his face was also scarred, his features oddly lopsided, the mouth forever twisted into a weird, lupine grin. Dean didn't look soft; more like *strange*.

And yet they swaggered side-by-side through the Saturday night revellers thronging the pavements – the high-heeled, mini-skirted girls, the boys and men in polo-shirts and jeans – and if an alleyway didn't clear for them, they cleared one for themselves. This only involved pushing and shoving, but it was still early, not yet midnight.

It finally got tastier in the cellar bar at Juicy Lucy's, where a gold and crimson lightshow filled the crammed, sweaty vault with strobe-like patterns. They knocked back several more beers each, after which Calum decided that the teenager next to him had nudged his drinking-arm once too often. The lad was in the midst of smooching a shapely platinum blonde in the tallest shoes and tiniest, most figure-hugging dress either Calum or Dean had ever seen, but even so he got socked in the side of his kisser, and a real bone-cruncher it was.

Dean guffawed; he could have sworn that the way the blonde tart jerked her head back, he'd filled her mouth with blood and teeth.

At The Place, the door-staff again let them in without a word. They pushed their way through the dizzying throng to the bar. Here, an older guy with iron grey curls, a leather waistcoat over his flowery shirt and a large earring which looked ridiculous on a codger of his age, shouted an order to the barmaid louder than Dean did. So Calum yanked the surprised guy around by his collar and head-butted him, splitting the bridge of his nose crosswise. The guy's friends, all equally grey-haired and raddle-cheeked, crowded forward belligerently, and so Dean glassed one of them.

This incident looked set to turn into a right old fracas, and another punch was swiftly thrown, but this had nothing whatever to do with Calum or Dean – as usual in Bradburn on a wild session-night, when things kicked off they kicked off generally. It didn't matter for what reason.

Their next fight, if you could call it that, occurred on the corner of Westgate Street and Audley Way. There was a taxi rank there. Few were queuing yet, most brawling revellers choosing to stay out into the early hours of the morning. That said, one young bloke had hit it too hard too early, and now leaned against the taxi rank pole, being copiously and volubly sick.

Calum and Dean were passing at the time. They were several feet away, but Dean decided that several flecks of puke had spattered his already dingy, beer-stained trousers.

So they assaulted the guy together, Dean catching him under the jaw with a roundhouse, Calum kicking his head like a football after he landed on the pavement.

'Yeeeaaah, bro . . . goal!' Dean hooted. *'Great fucking goal!'*

*

Calum and Dean did all these things because they could.

There was no other reason. It gained them nothing except perhaps more notoriety.

But that didn't matter where Calum and Dean were concerned. It was a very personal thing for these two lads. It was about being who they were – *exactly* who they were. Expressing themselves in precisely the way they wanted to, with no one else doing anything to stop it.

But eventually even they had to draw the line somewhere. They'd been drinking since lunchtime after all, and were completely sozzled even by their normal standards.

They ambled away from club-land, the Saturday night hubbub fading behind them, the jaunty music gradually losing all definition, dwindling into a dull, distant, repetitive caterwaul.

In the Parish Church yard, they took a minute out.

This was a cut-through between shops and offices during the day, but now it lay quiet under the phosphorescent glow of a single streetlamp, which glimmered eerily on the flagstones where so many epitaphs had once been engraved and yet now were almost indiscernible through age. Bradburn Parish Church dominated the peaceful scene, its innumerable gargoyles jutting out overhead. To the right of it, the so-called Bank Chambers, a row of counting houses, brokerages and solicitors' offices, led away down an arched passage, the entrance to which was opaque with night-mist.

The sight of that reminded them both, even if only internally, that their bodies were rapidly cooling. Unconsciously, Calum scratched his itchy blubber before pulling his sweater back on. Together, they slumped down onto the War Memorial steps in the middle of the yard, Calum licking at the fresh but stinging notches on his knuckles. Before long, a soft snore issued from Dean's puckered, spittle-slathered mouth. Dead to the world, he'd tilted back against the orderly lists of heroic names inscribed on brass plaques around the base of the Memorial's obelisk.

'Dean! . . . *fuck's sake!*' Calum nudged him with his elbow. 'Gi' us a fucking smoke!'

Dean muttered in response, and slapped at his right hip pocket.

Calum rummaged in there and found a single crooked joint. It was half-smoked already and bent at a right angle. He straightened it out, stuck it between his lips and dug deeper into his friend's pocket, finding and discarding all kinds of crumby, sticky, manky crap, before retrieving a lighter.

And only then did he become aware that someone was standing in front of him.

Calum glanced up, vision blurring as his eyes tried to focus through the late-night gloom. The newcomer blotted out all light from the single lamp, casting a deep shadow over the lads. But he wasn't completely in silhouette. Calum could distinguish dark clothing and the bland, bespectacled features of someone he thought he'd spotted a couple of times in the bars earlier.

'Good evening,' the newcomer said.

'Who the fuck are you supposed to be?' Calum sniggered. 'Clark fucking Kent?'

'I've got a message for your boss.'

'Who the fuck are you?'

'Here are my credentials.' The newcomer jammed a black-gloved hand into his overcoat pocket, but when he brought it out again, it held a wadded rag, which, as he leaned down, he squashed against Calum's face, using his other hand to clamp the back of Calum's head, allowing no room at all for manoeuvre.

The young hoodlum tried to struggle, but what remained of his strength and awareness deserted him remarkably quickly.

'Now, don't breathe too deeply,' the man said, lowering him to the ground. 'I need you conscious again very soon. And *you* –' He turned to Dean, who, more through some basic animal instinct than anything else, was trying to shake himself awake. The newcomer reached for something he'd laid against the steps. It was half a pool cue, the slimmer end neatly sawn off. '*You* can have a longer snooze.'

He swung it single-handed. It clattered against the corner of Dean's skull, sending him half spinning into oblivion, but not entirely.

Dean dropped panting onto his hands and knees, blood spiralling down from his right temple, which suddenly felt as though it had turned to sponge.

'You, you fuck . . .' Dean stammered. 'You *fuck* . . .'

'Thick-skulled, eh? Probably should've expected that.'

The next blow came two-handed, down and then up, golf club style. *THWACK!*

Dean twirled over onto his back, head clanging like a bell, hands hanging flipper-like at his sides – in which prone, helpless posture the newcomer kicked him a couple of good ones in the face. But still, somehow, Dean – probably because he was insulated against real pain by his own inebriation – clung to consciousness.

'You not . . . not . . .' he gurgled bloodily.

'Thicker than average, eh?' The newcomer sounded impressed. 'OK . . .'

38

He re-wadded the rag he'd used on Calum, took a small bottle from his coat pocket, unscrewed the cap and tilted it over.

'. . . not know . . . who . . . we are?'

'Of course I do.' The newcomer knelt alongside him. 'That's the whole point.'

He crammed the foul-smelling, chemical-soaked pad onto Dean's broken nose and mangled mouth, and held it there for as long as he needed to.

Chapter 4

Heck skidded to a halt in the car park behind a line of Brixton shops, his tyres screeching so loud it sent several scrawny pigeons flapping from the surrounding rooftops. He jumped from his silver Megane and trotted up the outside steps to the concrete balcony serving a row of cheap and nasty flats on the upper floor. He hammered on the door to number 3.

Half a minute passed before a dull, muffled voice asked, 'Yeah . . . who is it?'

'Detective Sergeant Heckenburg. Open up.'

'Erm . . . what do you, erm . . . what do you want?'

'Do you want me to shout it at the top of my voice? Because I *will*.'

'Erm . . . hang on.'

'Never mind "hang on",' Heck growled. 'Open this soddin', piggin' door, or I'll kick it down.'

A chain rattled as it was removed, and the door opened. Penny Flint's younger brother, Tyler, stood there. He was weedy, pale and with a badly spotted face, particularly around the mouth. He had a mess of dyed-orange hair, and a single earring dangling from an infected lobe. He wore pyjama trousers, dinosaur-feet slippers and a ragged jersey that was three times too large.

'Thought it'd be you,' he said dully.

'Well, obviously.' Heck shouldered his way inside. 'No one else knows she's here. *Yet.*'

The colour scheme inside the flat was grey, grey and grey, with perhaps a hint of lime-green, which had faded almost to grey. The place was a tip: bare, damp-looking walls, tatty and disordered furniture, dirty crockery and empty beer bottles on a side table. It was cold for an April morning, so the electric fire was on full blast. It was too much really, but it didn't bother Penny Flint, who was slumped in an armchair and smoking an unfiltered cigarette, focused intently on morning TV, where Jeremy Kyle was putting a bunch of people just like her through their paces. She wore a thin dressing gown, while her long brown hair hung in ratty strands. The ashtray on her armrest was crammed with dog-ends.

In the corner, Alfie, her six-month-old son, lay snug in a rabbit romper suit, burbling to himself in his carry-cot. The baby was the only dab of real colour in the room, aside from Tyler Flint's ludicrous fake hair. Having checked outside that Heck hadn't been followed, Tyler had closed and locked the door again and now hovered in the background.

'Don't stare at me like that, Heck,' Penny said without looking round. 'You're making me nervous.'

'Nervous?' Heck retorted. 'You're lucky I'm not dragging you down to Brixton cop-shop by your knicker-elastic.'

She turned a face on him that had once been pretty but was now haggard.

'I'm not wearing knickers at the moment, Heck. I can't stand the pain they cause me. Or maybe I didn't make that clear enough the last time we spoke.'

If that was true, she was pretty scantily clad, her gown

finishing above the knee and her toe- and fingernails painted their trademark shocking-green. There was even a slinky gold chain looped around her left ankle. Her injuries weren't visible, but Heck had seen the photographs taken at the hospital, and they had spared no anatomical detail. If there was still any doubt, the pair of metal crutches propped against the back of her chair indicated that Penny didn't even yet figure among the *walking* wounded. His sympathy for her in this regard hadn't ebbed. But some things were unforgivable.

'You realise what you've done?' he asked her quietly.

'That wasn't what I intended,' she said.

'Intended or not, you tipped off two different police units about John Sagan, and you didn't have the good grace to warn either of them there were other friendly forces in the field. What did you expect was going to happen?'

'Look, I just wanted that bastard to go down. Wanted to make sure of it. It's not my fault if you lot don't talk to each other.' She turned back to the TV screen.

'You deceitful, self-centred cow.'

Her brother ventured forward. 'Hey, come on. She's been through –'

'Sit down, Tyler!' Heck jabbed a finger at him. 'Just being who you are and having the life you have is enough for *you* to worry about. Don't compound it by getting any more involved than you need to in a shit-storm like this.'

Mouth clamped shut, Tyler sank stiffly onto a chair.

'It's all right, Tyle,' Penny said, with more than a hint of the cocky belligerence which, up until now, had got her through so many years on the streets unscathed. 'I can handle Heck.'

'Oh, yeah?' Heck said. 'What you going to do, set me the same kind of trap you set for Reg Cowling?'

'I'm sorry 'bout what happened to Cowling. I actually liked him.'

'I sincerely doubt that, else you wouldn't have tipped him

off about Sagan but at the same time neglected to mention how dangerous the bastard could actually be.'

Penny said nothing. Just focused on the TV screen.

'You've got a sodding nerve,' Heck added. 'Blaming us for this. My boss logged our interest in Sagan with the top brass at Organised Crime, and with most of the CID offices in Southeast London. Everyone around here who mattered knew we were watching him. So you decided to go to one of the lower ranks, didn't you? What was it? Reg Cowling feel his days in National Crime Group were numbered? Perhaps he needed some arrests?'

She shrugged. 'Maybe.'

'Don't give me "maybe", Penny. Cowling was one of your official handlers at Organised Crime, wasn't he? Don't bother answering – I know, I checked.'

'What if he was?'

'Let me guess . . . he wanted something off the record? Something he could big himself up with? And you thought, "Bollocks to Heck and SCU. They're not making things happen fast enough. I'll tell someone who'll knock on Sagan's door straight away." But if I was a really cynical man, Pen, I'd say it was actually worse than that. I'd say you engineered this fuck-up deliberately. In the knowledge Sagan would run and bullets would fly. And that maybe, in the ensuing gunfight, he'd get zapped – by the police no less, so there'd be no comeback to you.' He peered down at her, but she refused to meet his gaze. 'Is that right, or is that right?'

'How could I have engineered all that, Heck? I'm a tom, not some criminal mastermind.'

'But you've got street-smarts, love. You always have had. And you knew Sagan wouldn't come without a fight. Just like you knew Cowling and his inexperienced sidekick would do something stupid like go in feet-first. Like you knew we were on the plot, armed . . . and that we wouldn't just stand by.'

'And still you couldn't take him,' she sneered. 'Two different teams and you both missed him.'

Heck shook his head. 'You know, Pen, I wish I lived in your world. Where real shithouse behaviour is measured only by the bloody inconvenience it might cause *you*. Not by guilt, or remorse, or regret . . .'

She glanced round at him again, wryly amused. 'You don't wish you lived in *my* world, Heck. You're quite happy in your own. Where you can go home at night and leave all this stuff behind you. Where if anything does go wrong, you've got an entire army one radio-call away. You really think it would satisfy me to see John Sagan in jail, in relative comfort, while me and Alfie are living on hand-outs, and the one thing that's ever earned me anything has turned to putty?'

'That was the deal we made.'

'Then more fool you.' She turned back to the television. 'Like I'd settle for seeing Sagan get life when the alternative was getting him shot down on the street like the dog he is?' Her smile grew tighter, thinner. 'At least that way I'd keep my respect.'

'Even more so if a few coppers died too, eh?'

'Like I say, Heck, that wasn't the plan. But if you need to take a positive from it . . .'

'The positive is seeing you for the conniving little mare you are. For your info, I'm having you scrubbed off the grass register!'

She turned again. The sneering smile had faded.

'Yeah, that's right,' Heck said. 'I'm gonna drive you into a normal, everyday life if it kills me. And to do that, I first need to ensure that no copper in Greater London ever makes the mistake of using you as an official informant again.'

'Well . . . cool. I lose half my income in one fell swoop, and now you're taking the other half too.'

'Try getting a proper job . . . you need to do that anyway

if you're gonna bring that kid up decently.' Heck's mobile chirped in his pocket. He checked it and saw a text from Gemma.

Shawna's come round. Meet at KCH

'Me – sat on a supermarket till!' Penny scoffed. 'You having a laugh, or what?'

'It could be worse.' Heck headed for the door. 'You could be lying on an intensive care bed, like a very good friend of mine.'

'I've been *there*.'

He glanced back. 'Or alternatively, you could be on a slab. Like Reg Cowling. You thank your lucky stars it's me you're dealing with, Pen, and not some other coppers I could name. Now, I'm pretty certain John Sagan's employers, these people whose identity you've so jealously protected, will already be asking lots and lots of questions about how the police discovered who the bastard was. You've already twigged that, else you wouldn't be hiding out in a shithole like this. But that won't be enough. They might have you marked as a tough chick who even gangsters shouldn't mess with, but you're still a flyspeck at the end of the day. So at a rough guess, love, I'd say you need to get yourself and, more importantly, your kid out of London. Right the way out. Right now.'

'Everyone I know is down here, Heck!' she shouted as he stepped out onto the balcony.

'Yeah,' he replied. 'Some of them might even miss you.'

'Piss off, you flatfoot bastard!'

Back in his car, he sat brooding. Penny had easily slipped the armed guard Gemma had posted at her flat the previous month. He'd spent the last two weeks looking for her before he'd finally learned she had a loser of a brother and had located her here in this scum-hole apartment. Cops who knew her less well than Heck might never have traced her, but the underworld would, and sooner rather than later. So it was definitely in her interest to skedaddle out of the capital as soon as possible. But if she didn't – and she was a silly, obstinate bitch – he didn't really intend to strike her off the grass register. Penny had long been one of his most reliable informers. He knew this indiscretion of hers had been a one-off. She'd never pulled a stunt like this before, and would be unlikely to do so again; Sagan had hurt her in a uniquely terrible way, after all – Heck understood her desire for revenge. On top of that, there might be even more she could tell him about Sagan – she clearly had her ear to the ground in the right places.

But then again, should this level of chicanery really go unpunished?

Another problem lay with the Organised Crime Division. While the Serial Crimes Unit were still officially heading up the enquiry into John Sagan – now entitled Operation Wandering Wolf – with Gemma herself as lead investigator, OC were still going ballistic about the shooting of detectives Cowling and Bishop and constantly harassing her with demands for information and requests to get involved. Gemma had resisted up until now because she didn't want a bunch of hot-headed cowboys compromising her investigation, though OC were well connected at Scotland Yard and the pressure was growing on her daily. At present, Heck's SCU colleagues were currently staking out Penny's empty flat in Lewisham. The trouble was that if he revealed her new hiding place, Gemma would go by the book, dragging her in and leaning on her hard. Penny would hold out – it was inconceivable that she'd admit she'd deliberately created that confrontation at Fairfax House. Do that, and the very least she'd expect was to be charged with obstructing an enquiry, but maybe with conspiracy to commit murder as well. Most likely she'd just clam up and refuse to offer anything further.

This whole thing was a confused mess, and he was torn with indecision.

The arrival of another text broke into his thoughts. Again it was from Gemma.

ETA?

He texted back:

10

He drove east along Coldharbour Lane, eventually pulling into the visitors' car park of King's College Hospital. Gemma was waiting for him, leaning against her aquamarine Mercedes E-class. By pure luck, he was able to find a parking bay close by.

She straightened up, hands stuffed into her overcoat pockets.

There were few more striking figures in Heck's life than Detective Superintendent Gemma Piper. Tall, only a couple of inches shorter than he was, athletic and good-looking in a lean, fierce, feline sort of way, she'd been a key fixture throughout his police service – as a fellow junior detective back in their days at Bethnal Green together, so many years ago now it seemed, for a brief time as his girlfriend, and more recently as his senior supervisor at the Serial Crimes Unit. She didn't look best pleased as he approached, but she rarely looked best pleased anyway. Gemma was renowned throughout the National Crime Group for her ultra-no-nonsense attitude. Anyone getting on the wrong side of her was likely to be mown down in the ensuing tirade. This was partly the reason she was known behind her back as 'the

Lioness' – her roar was legendary, though her famously unmanageable mane of wild ash-blonde hair was another reason for that, even if at present she was wearing it stylish and short.

'What've *you* been up to all morning?' she asked.

Heck pocketed his keys. 'I had half an idea how Bishop and Cowling might have got onto Sagan.'

'And . . .?'

'Didn't pan out.' It cut him to lie to her, but at present he had to make a finely balanced judgement call. She pondered that as they walked towards Intensive Care.

'Bishop's playing schtum,' she finally said. 'I mean, he's not all there at present. Still high on medication. But he reckons Cowling got the tip-off and didn't share the source.'

'The Devil protects his own,' Heck murmured, wondering if Penny Flint had any clue just how much luck she was enjoying.

Chapter 5

'Well, I got shot in the legs two years ago, along with getting my nose broken,' Shawna McCluskey said. 'Last year, I got suspended for serious disciplinary offences I didn't even commit, and now I wake up to find I got my brains beaten in over three weeks ago and that I've been lying in a coma ever since. Am I supposed to just carry on, ma'am? Is this all supposed to be in a day's work for me?'

Her eyebrows were still swollen and discoloured, covered by railway lines of stitching. Her nose, which had needed to be completely reconstructed, was buried under a pyramid of dressings and gauze. Her scalp had been partly shaved, so that numerous other lacerations could be sutured. She'd suffered extensive fractures to her left eye-socket and cheek-bone, and in consequence a perforated left eardrum, while the blow delivered to her chest by the point-blank impact of a 9mm bullet from her own Glock pistol had broken her sternum and three ribs. She currently lay at an angle, supported in an orthopaedic framework made from bars and straps, which looked more like a medieval torture device. She was also attached to a drip, which fed her a constant supply of painkillers. This might have been the cause of her slurred, frothy voice, or on the other hand that might have been down to her broken teeth. Once she was out of intensive care, a dental surgeon was going to look at her mouth.

'For two minutes back there I was technically dead,' she added. 'If Heck hadn't given me the kiss of life . . .'

Heck shrugged. 'I knew it was the only way I'd ever get any action with you.'

But the patient didn't smile.

'If you really want to collect your ticket, Shawna,' Gemma replied, 'I'm not going to try and talk you out of it. But I don't think you should make this decision hastily.'

'I love this job, ma'am . . . it's all I've ever wanted to do. But at present, I've not got much choice. I've no feeling at all in my left arm and left leg, much less any movement.'

'But if they've told you that'll be OK eventually . . .?' Heck offered.

'Eventually, yeah. But when's eventually? No one can say.'

'Shawna, come on . . .'

'Heck, I'm tired of getting hurt!' She said this with such force that it brought a cringe of pain to what remained of her pretty face. 'Seriously, Heck . . . ma'am. Me and Todd were looking to get married next year. He's now wondering if he'll be standing at the altar next to someone in callipers and a body-brace.'

'Why don't you look for a transfer?' Gemma said. 'Just take yourself off the frontline for a bit?'

'Yeah,' Heck said. 'Something with a community brief maybe.'

'At present, I'm not even fit to make cuppas for little old ladies,' Shawna replied. 'Mind you, might be a welcome change – going into a nice person's house to say hello and have a chat, instead of picking over their mutilated corpse.' If it was possible with a face as black and blue as hers,

Shawna blushed, turned sheepish. 'Sorry, ma'am . . . feel like I'm letting you down.'

'Why would you feel that?' Gemma asked.

'For not being tough enough to carry on.'

'Shawna, you've been with SCU what – seven, eight years? In that time, you've logged an impressive number of arrests and secured the convictions of some very nasty people. You've done your bit. So don't worry. If you really want to finish on a medical, it won't be a problem. I'll put the paperwork through and make any phone-calls necessary. But I recommend you think about it first.'

'I've already thought about it . . .'

'How long for?' Heck wondered. 'You've only been conscious half an hour.'

Shawna glowered at him, only for a fresh stab of pain to bring new tears to her bloodshot eyes. 'Half . . . an hour was long enough. Because if I took any longer, I might change my mind. And that'd be no good for me or Todd.'

Suddenly Heck wanted to ask if Todd Martindale was hanging around in the hospital somewhere, and perhaps if he'd visited Shawna before they had. Could he be the one who'd put her up to this? Heck didn't know the guy too well, only that Shawna had hooked up with him through a dating site a year and a half ago, and had finally, in her own words, found happiness. He certainly sounded the real deal. A divorced middle manager at a sports retail company, he was safe, stable and apparently considerate to her in every way. Hell, why shouldn't the guy raise questions about what Shawna did for a living? If he genuinely loved her, he'd be worried for her safety every day she spent in an outfit like SCU. Having initially felt hostile towards Todd, Heck now found himself warming to the guy even without having met him.

'The light duties option doesn't appeal?' Gemma asked.

'There's no such thing as a job for life in the cops any more, but with your record, Shawna, I'm sure I can swing something.'

'Permanent light duties, ma'am?' Shawna said. 'After SCU? That'd be even more likely to kill me.'

Heck understood that part of it, at least.

'It's better if I just make a clean break,' she added.

Gemma nodded understandingly. 'In the meantime, what work have you got outstanding?'

'Nothing that can't be picked up by someone else.'

'I'll take care of it,' Heck said. 'I'm at the Old Bailey for a couple of days from tomorrow, but I can sort it after that. Don't fret.'

'Shawna?' Gemma asked again. 'Are you sure this is what you want?'

Shawna took a deep, painful breath, and nodded.

'OK . . . well, it's your call. When you due to get out of here?'

'I've not asked, ma'am.' Shawna's eyelids fluttered, as if fatigue was overtaking her – as well it might, given the cocktail of drugs she was on. 'And I'm not bothered. Thanks for coming to see me, though. Sorry I've nothing better to tell you.'

They left, walking without speaking back to the hospital exit.

'You know she doesn't really want to leave?' Heck said when they arrived in the car park. 'She's probably just in shock.'

'Sometimes when you're in shock you get greater clarity of vision,' Gemma replied.

'I thought Sagan had killed her for sure. If he hadn't been panicking himself, he *would* have. He'd have put that bullet straight between her eyes.'

'Most normal folk would have thought they'd done enough damage cracking her skull open.'

'I think we can safely say there's nothing normal about John Sagan, ma'am.'

Gemma eyed him sidelong as they strode, appraising his pale, tense features, his taut body-language.

'We're going to handle this investigation professionally, aren't we?' she asked.

'As always.'

'We're not going to go looking for payback?'

'Do I ever, ma'am?'

'It's just that you seem, I dunno . . . edgy?'

'What can I say, ma'am. It's been a disappointing morning. For all sorts of reasons.'

'We're not thinking of going solo on this, are we?'

She halted and probed him with those penetrating blue eyes of hers. Heck smiled in response, which, from her expression, didn't look as if it reassured her much. Heck and Gemma had clashed several times in the recent past over his preference for working on his own, though he'd often argued that this stemmed from his either mistrusting those around him or finding them inadequate – he'd argued this point unsuccessfully, it had to be said.

'No chance.' He shrugged, walking on, as if it was ridiculous that she'd have any doubts. 'Shawna'll pull through. Plus, this time we're frying a much bigger fish. It isn't personal.'

'And I've told you *not* to. That would be even more of a reason, wouldn't it?'

He nodded. 'Lots of motivation to keep this one by the book.'

Gemma still looked unconvinced. It wouldn't have been the first time he'd soft-soaped her to try and buy himself extra leg-room. She knew perfectly well that Heck and Shawna were more than just work colleagues. They'd never been lovers, but they'd known each other virtually since the commencement of their two careers, and that was a huge thing in cop terms; on top of that, as fellow natives of the Northwest exiled in London, they'd drawn additional strength and comfort from each other's presence in that curious, indefinable way that only those of close heritage did when thrown together as strangers in a strange land.

'That's as long as the Organised Crime Division don't muscle their way in,' he felt it necessary to add, though immediately he could have kicked himself for saying this. Whatever your inner turmoil, you didn't give Gemma Piper conditions. It could literally be a red rag to a bull. But on this occasion – despite working her lips together tightly, as if she was strongly tempted to say something sharp in response – her reply was cool and measured.

'They won't. They're making a lot of noise at present, but they're also a bit shamefaced about blundering in on our operation. They know they're walking on thin ice.'

'Who's doing the shouting?'

'DSU Garrickson.'

'Garrickson, eh. For a minute then I thought it'd be some clueless, inept tosser.'

She glanced sidelong at him, and he raised his hands.

'I know, ma'am, I know. It's completely wrong and unfor-givable to discuss a senior officer in such irreverent terms. But wasn't Mike Garrickson the one you spoke to when you first logged with OC that we were looking into syndicate activity in Peckham?' Gemma's lack of response implied that it was. 'And it somehow slipped his mind to inform the rest of his team?'

'I expect he assumed that if they had any leads on new cases they'd have come to him before acting on them,' she said. 'And with some justification. Reg Cowling was out of order, Heck. He's the one who blew that obbo. No one else.' They stopped beside Gemma's Merc. 'Mind you –' she remained cool, but frustration lay visible underneath '– it would have helped if all I'd had to do was walk upstairs and tell them. Like I used to be able to.'

There was a time when all departments of the National Crime Group had been based in the same building at Scotland Yard, and very convenient it had been. As Gemma said, it was certainly easier back then to exchange intel. But cost-saving changes were under way all across the British police service. Though both squads still came under the umbrella of the National Crime Group, Organised Crime had been moved to new, state-of-the-art offices at London Bridge, while the Serial Crimes Unit had relocated to a somewhat less remarkable building at Staples Corner in Brent Cross. SCU had only been in place there a couple of months, and it still felt a long way from anywhere, though, situated at the heart of the North London transport infra-structure, it was actually well placed to house a national investigation team.

'Anyway,' she said, pointedly changing the subject – Heck was a devil for teasing out her true feelings regarding her fellow top brass – 'remind me why you're in court again?'

'Regina versus Wheeler.'

'Oh, yeah . . . that charmer.'

The previous spring SCU had arrested the so-called 'Wimbledon Rapist', a masked predator responsible for raping two young women and one schoolgirl at knifepoint after accosting them while they were crossing the Common early in the morning. The team had first homed in on local man Charlie Wheeler when his taxi was spotted on CCTV several times in the right area and at roughly the right time, but they only became actively suspicious when Heck noted that Wheeler never seemed to be transporting any passengers.

'He's banged to rights,' Heck said. 'Two days and he's topped and tailed.'

'Well, let's make sure. You can put all this aside until it's done.'

He nodded.

'Mark,' Gemma said, 'I don't want to fall out with you on this one.' She regarded him carefully, still spoke in that measured tone. 'Whatever happens, whatever Shawna decides, she's a grown woman, and if she leaves the job it's because she wants to.'

'Yeah, but . . . we owe it to her to get this right.'

'We do indeed. So we're onside, yes?'

'Ma'am, this was my case from the beginning. I *want* John Sagan, and not just for Shawna.' He shrugged awkwardly. 'Look, he could've tortured a hundred people for all we know. He could've murdered that many too. OK, they might be worthless vermin just like him, but that doesn't give him a free pass. In fact, we don't even know for sure that they're all worthless. He may not draw the line anywhere. What's to stop him targeting regular citizens if the price is right? Trust me, I'm giving no one any reason to kick me off this case.'

She nodded and climbed into her Merc.

And yet here he was, he thought, watching her reverse out and drive away – already withholding from her the whereabouts of the grass who'd deliberately set the disaster up in the first place. Whether protecting Penny Flint in this way was likely to pay any kind of dividend he simply didn't know. He just hoped he wouldn't have to wait too long to find out.

Chapter 6

Following one behind the other, Heck and Gemma crossed the Thames at Tower Bridge and cut northwest through the City, Shoreditch, Islington, Camden Town and Finchley, before heading west on the North Circular. It all sounded quick and straightforward on paper, but in midday traffic it still took close to two hours, and the new HQ at Staples Corner was a very unrewarding sight for those who'd had to fight through rivers of exhaust fumes and contraflows to get there.

It had previously been some kind of transport office, and it looked the part: a functional, flat-topped structure resembling three stacks of overlarge shoeboxes jammed unceremoniously together, its roofs covered with dishes and TV antennae. It wasn't exactly prefabricated, but it had the distinct air of something that had never been intended to last. Its once weedy car park had been tarmacked over, and, as a beefed-up security measure, the rusty metal fence that had formerly encircled it had been replaced by a tall perimeter of slatted, spike-headed steel. But its best defence was still its anonymity. It could have been any one of the thousands of nondescript semi-official buildings dotted across the

57

various boroughs of Greater London, blending perfectly into its drab but noisy location.

Heck and Gemma parked next to each other, and headed in through the personnel door, which was at the back. The ground floor housed the SCU garages, equipment and evidence store, and armoury. Admin and civvie staff were located on the first floor, while the detectives' office, or DO as it was known in the unit, was on the second. The Command Centre and Press and PR Suite were on the third. There was also a conference room up there, but that had now been co-opted by Wandering Wolf as an Incident Room.

It still felt like alien territory to Heck. They had only been in here a few weeks, having made the move from Scotland Yard in late February. Certain members of the team, who'd been assigned to enquiries elsewhere in the country at the time, were only just arriving and discovering their new workplaces. Two cases in point were DCs Andy Rawlins and Burt Cunliffe. When Heck entered the DO, they were arguing bitterly.

'What's going on?' he asked, pulling off his jacket.

Cunliffe and Rawlins occupied facing desks in a recessed bay, with a large, horizontal window directly behind them, though at present both were standing nose to nose.

Cunliffe gave his side of the story first, demanding to swap desks with Rawlins as otherwise the sun would shine in his eyes all day. Rawlins's response was to argue that if he was next to the window, he'd get vertigo.

'OK, here's the deal,' Heck said tonelessly. 'Burt, the sun is *not* going to shine in your eyes. You've got a motorway over the top to block it. And you, Andy, are *not* going to get vertigo! Now plant your arses where you've been told, and get some sodding work done!'

'This dump's crap,' Cunliffe muttered under his breath.

'Yeah, welcome to the rest of your career.' Heck turned

from the disgruntled twosome in time to see DS Eric Fisher amble in from the side-stair leading up to the Incident Room. Fisher had a pile of buff folders in his arms, which he slammed down on Heck's desk.

Heck regarded him blankly. 'What's this?'

Fisher was the unit's main intelligence analyst, and a permanent inside-man these days given that he was now in his mid-fifties with a waistline to match.

'You're taking Shawna's gigs, apparently.' He rubbed the lenses of his glasses with a handkerchief so grubby that it surely couldn't make any difference.

'Already?' Heck protested. 'I was just about to come upstairs.'

'Forget it,' Fisher replied. 'Apparently you're at the Central Criminal Court tomorrow?'

'Yeah . . . so?'

'So Gemma says there's no point you coming back on Wandering Wolf until you've been discharged from the trial. That means there's no point you coming back today either – so you can crack on with this lot. New referrals from Division. Yours plus Shawna's.'

There was a muted snigger from the direction of Rawlins's desk.

'This is all?' Heck said.

'Hey, there's a bigger pile on my desk if you want some of *them*.' Fisher sloped off towards his own corner of the room without awaiting a response.

Heck slumped into his chair, glowering at the tower of documentation. One of the least enjoyable aspects of working in the Serial Crimes Unit was trawling through paperwork forwarded to it from other divisions. SCU had a remit to cover all the police force areas of England and Wales, and had recognised expertise with regard to serial violent offenders – mainly murderers. If they weren't pursuing investigations they'd generated themselves or had been assigned to by the Director of the National Crime Group, SCU would provide operational, consultative and investigative support to other forces who might have uncovered evidence that they had a serial murderer or rapist on their patch. A national general order now ensured that details of all homicides or violent sexual attacks satisfying certain specified criteria (the 'weird and wonderful' as Heck tended to think of them) must be sent to the SCU office for assessment at the first opportunity.

Heck grabbed himself a tea before leafing through the top two folders on the pile.

At first glance either one might have heralded the arrival of a new kid on the serial killer block. A female torso had been found on a rubbish tip in Hull; it had been identified as belonging to a forty-year-old prostitute who had vanished two weeks earlier. OK, there was only one victim here (thus far), but immediately there were signs of excessive violence and bizarre post-mortem behaviour in the form of the dismemberment, while the aggrieved party had been a sex-worker – so that was three boxes ticked straight away. The second file described two homicides in the space of two weeks in Coventry. An elderly bag-lady had been found in a subway, her skull shattered by an estimated twenty blows from a hammer. Six days later, a homeless man was found brutally kicked and beaten in a backstreet some three miles away. He was alive when discovered, but died en route to hospital without ever regaining consciousness. That case carried the ultimate red flag in that already there was more than one victim.

Both these submissions required analysis, yet conclusions could never be jumped to.

Murder was rarely what it appeared to be at first glance.

It could be that the Hull prostitute had been a victim of domestic violence – apparently her common-law husband, from whom she was estranged but whom she'd fought with constantly while they were together, had dropped out of sight several months ago and his whereabouts were still unknown. Likewise, violent assaults on street-people were sadly common. The old Coventry woman had been a known heroin-user, but was not in possession of any drugs or drugs paraphernalia when her body was found, so the motive in her case might have been robbery. In contrast, the homeless male had a reputation for being an argumentative drunk, so he could have been beaten simply because he'd picked a fight with the wrong person.

Heck would need to wade through the directory-thick wads of affixed notes and photos sent down from the investigation teams up at Humberside and West Midlands before he could make a judgement. But before he had a chance even to start on this, his mobile rang.

The name on the screen was *Penny Flint*.

He walked out to the adjoining corridor before answering it.

'Don't take me off the register,' she said.

'Give me one good reason why I shouldn't.'

'I can still be useful to you, Heck.'

'Penny, you should be thinking about being useful to that kid of yours. Get your tail out of town before someone comes along and *really* damages it.'

'You want Sagan?' she said.

He moved to the window. 'However did you guess?'

'I've not lost track of him totally.'

Heck stiffened. 'What're you on about now?'

'He's left London.'

'Penny, you're in hiding. You're not talking to anyone if you've got any sense. How can you possibly know this?'

'I have my informers, just like you do.'

'You'd better hope yours are more reliable.'

'Do you want this intel or not?'

Heck gazed across the river of traffic flowing along the North Circular.

'What do you propose, Pen?'

'I give you info on Sagan's new location, and in return you keep me on the register and never tell anyone that I'm the one who set Cowling and Bishop up.'

The mere thought of this stuck in Heck's craw.

'Penny . . . a police officer died.'

'I told you, Heck, that wasn't the plan. It was Sagan who was supposed to die.'

'Tell me what you know and I'll tell you what it's worth.'

There was a lengthy silence at the other end, as she considered this. She knew Heck didn't trust her any more. The question was: did she trust him?

'He's gone north.'

'I need specifics.'

'Not at the moment. Not till I get what I want.'

Heck pondered. Though he was loath to admit it, it kind of helped him out. A good lead was something he could take straight upstairs to Gemma. It might also help him clear his conscience about the info he was currently sitting on.

'I'll need to tell my gaffer what you've been up to,' he replied.

'No way. They'll lock me up.'

'Not necessarily. If your intel bears fruit, chances are they'll make an executive decision to keep using you. And it's not like you pulled the trigger on Cowling yourself. All we have to say is that you tipped off your various police handlers. It wasn't your fault the OC guys decided not to tell anyone what they were doing.'

'No deal, Heck. I know your gaffer. Piper, isn't it? She'll chuck the fucking book at me.'

'Not if I can persuade her otherwise.'

'Sorry, no deal.'

'Listen, you stupid cow!' He checked there was no one else in the passage behind him. 'A copper died! And you're asking me to sit on vital information. Not just now but maybe for the rest of my career. If you seriously think I'm carrying that burden, you can forget it.'

'Heck —'

'Shut up, Penny! This is how we play. I'm going up to the Incident Room in approximately one minute's time. And I'm going to tell Superintendent Piper exactly what I know, namely that you contrived that clusterfuck. I'll probably get suspended for not telling her sooner, but even that's better than looking over my shoulder for the rest of my career on the off-chance you suddenly get tempted to spill the beans and drop me in it. The alternative is that I go up there with your red-hot tip and the mitigating circumstances I've just laid out. You don't have to be a genius to work out which'll be better for you.'

When Penny spoke again it was in a distinctly worried voice. 'Even if they don't lock me up, won't they at least take me off the register?'

'Not if you're giving us good stuff. Why would they? It'd be shooting themselves in the foot.'

'I don't want to go into protective custody or anything like that.'

He laughed. 'You'd be lucky. It's not easy selling super-grasses to the top floor these days. Anyway, it depends what you know.'

'Manchester,' she said sullenly.

'Manchester?'

'Somewhere in the Manchester area. That's where Sagan's parked himself. It's the usual thing. He's gone there as muscle, and he's getting well paid for his services.'

'Somewhere in the Manchester area?' Heck said slowly. 'Seriously? That's the best you can give me?'

'Christ's sake, Heck! I'm not his babysitter. I just hear things. He's in the Manchester area, and he's signed on for a firm who are in a bit of trouble. Jesus wept, you know his form . . . it's not like you won't know what to look out for.'

He didn't answer.

'So where do we stand?' she asked.

'Get out of London, Penny.'

'You deceitful bastard! You just said –'

'I said I'd put a good word in for you, which I will. But if you get out of London – like *now!* – I won't know where you are if they decide to pull you in as an accessory, will I? On top of that, I can't protect you from yourself, love. Whichever mob you've fucked over south of the river, they'll be looking for you as we speak.'

She gave a heartfelt sigh. 'How long do I have to duck out of sight for?'

'That's your call. If it was me, till the kid's eighteen at least. But either way, do it quick. And when you do, make sure I've still got a number I can contact you on.'

He hung up before she could argue further, and wandered back into the DO, halting in the doorway. Everyone was beavering away at their paperwork, but then Eric Fisher glanced up and spotted him. He arched a bushy eyebrow.

'I don't suppose we've had anything from the Northwest?' Heck asked, acutely aware that it sounded ridiculously vague.

Fisher sat back. 'Anything *what*?'

'Let's say, for the sake of argument . . . any recent torture-murders.'

Fisher remained blank-faced. 'Why do you ask?'

'For Christ's sake, Eric!' Heck approached him. 'Have we or haven't we?'

Almost theatrically, Fisher pushed an open file across his desk. 'Came in this morning.'

Heck picked it up and flipped through the various photographic images paper-clipped on top.

They were Greater Manchester Police crime-scene glossies, and they depicted two vaguely recognisable forms – naked males, by the looks of it – lying half-buried amid broken, mouldy furniture and other manky, rat-infested rubbish, and covered with filth and thick, clotted blood.

'Found by scavengers on a landfill,' Fisher added.

Heck flipped more pages, but barely saw the text. He knew already that he'd found what he was looking for. 'When did this happen?'

'March 24 or 25, GMP reckon. Seen the location, mate?'

Heck focused on the name of the Greater Manchester township where the double slaying had occurred. And it couldn't have hit him harder had it been inscribed on a house-brick.

Bradburn.

His home.

Chapter 7

'How long have you known about this?' Gemma asked coolly.

Heck, who was standing in front of her desk, made a vague gesture. 'Just since today.'

She tapped the pile of documents with a neatly manicured fingernail. 'This morning?'

He shrugged. 'Sort of.'

'Sort of.' She nodded and sat back. 'So let me understand this . . . when you told me earlier that this morning's lead didn't pan out, it was a barefaced lie? Is that what you're now admitting to me?'

She didn't look surprised by any of this, which, on reflection, he realised he ought to have expected. There was rarely any point trying to deceive Gemma Piper. Her will was iron, and she had a built-in bullshit radar.

'Ma'am,' he tried to explain, 'if I'd told you where Penny Flint was, you'd have *had* to act. You'd have her in custody by now, and we wouldn't have got this juicy titbit.'

Gemma remained calm, remarkably so given her infamously volcanic temper. She glanced again at the spillage of paperwork and crime-scene glossies. 'You think we wouldn't have assessed this at some point under our own steam and detected John Sagan's handiwork . . . without a hooker who's got a screw loose needing to show us the way?'

'Not as quickly, ma'am. This file was sent to SCU, not the Incident Room.'

Gemma said nothing else for some time, but perused the paperwork again.

Heck stood waiting, stiff-shouldered, feeling like a convict facing a hanging judge. They weren't in the Incident Room now but Gemma's own office, which conveniently was only located across the corridor from it.

'You take the bloody biscuit, Heck.' She glanced up again. 'Did everything I said to you back at the hospital go in one ear and trickle out the other?'

'No,' he assured her. 'I absolutely guarantee it.'

She spoke on as if she hadn't heard him. 'And of course, much as I'd like to kick you off Operation Wandering Wolf, I can't, can I?' Her voice rose, that old familiar whip-crack no doubt penetrating the closed door and echoing along the main corridor. 'Because the likelihood now is that we'll have to go all the way up to Bradburn, and you being a Bradburn native are probably the best weapon in that fight I could possibly have!'

That explained a lot actually, Heck realised. This time she needed him for more than his ability as a detective. But also, he couldn't help thinking that she wasn't giving him the total third degree because this latest little white lie of his had been well meant. Even the most productive police informants could be troublesome customers. You had to play it canny with them.

'So you want me to go up to Bradburn?' he said.

'I want you to sit down. We're not making hasty decisions.' She aimed a finger at him as he pulled up a chair. 'And don't think this means I'm not thoroughly pissed off with you, Heck! If it wasn't for the fact I've already lost Shawna from the team today, I'd be much more inclined to kick your impertinent arse all the way back to Division.'

Heck sat down while she read again through the GMP dossier. He glanced around her office, which, while it was larger than the cubby-hole she'd occupied back at the Yard, still didn't bespeak the rank of Detective Superintendent.

Gemma Piper was a conundrum to many who knew her: handsome and fiery, two traits that combined well when she fought her corner in this most competitive and male-dominated of environments. But at the same time she didn't routinely favour the trappings of power. She was forceful enough to pull rank any time she felt it was necessary, her bollockings were legendary, today's relatively painless session notwithstanding, and when she gave evidence in court or to a House of Commons Select Committee, she radiated strength and competence. But, possibly because she'd done her stint in the lower ranks, and had scrapped tooth and nail for every promotion she'd ever had, she didn't like to paint herself as an aristocrat of the job. Hence the Spartan décor and bare furnishings in this dull little room at the top of their dull new building.

'Four murders in Bradburn inside five weeks,' she said. 'Is that your hometown's normal strike rate?'

'Not when I lived there,' he replied. 'But times change.'

'Does *this* surprise you?'

She dropped another glossy onto her desk. It depicted two hunks of human-shaped charcoal laid side by side on a rubber sheet. This image had been inserted at the bottom of the file. Heck had only found it several minutes after seeing the pictures of the corpses in the landfill. It depicted the remains of two Bradburn porno merchants, Barrie Briggs and Les Harris, who early last March had been cremated alive in their own sex shop.

He pursed his lips and nodded. 'A bit, yeah.'

'It's pretty extreme stuff.'

'If what you're asking, ma'am, is: can I equate this kind of violence with the town I grew up in? . . . then no. We had crime. Of course we did – plenty of it, it was a rough old place. But there was a kind of moral focus in those days. At least in general terms. This is way off the scale in comparison, but I don't think these are normal times, are they? GMP Serious reckon Briggs and Harris were the first shots fired in an underworld war. The bad boys in the landfill – Calum Price and Dean Lumley – were probably retaliation.'

Gemma read more of the attached notes, this time concentrating on the latter two victims.

'Lots of form,' she said. 'Lots of it. For which they paid a very high price. Both castrated, eyes slit, tongues cut out, nipples scissored off, fingers removed with an electric saw. They finally died when a power-drill penetrated each of their brains through the left ear.'

Neither needed to give voice to what they both were already thinking: that, even given the two deaths by fire, this was a further escalation still, and to some tune.

'Put two and two together often enough, ma'am, and sometimes you get four,' Heck said. 'Those two torture-killings have got Sagan written all over them, especially now we know he's in the Manchester area. A war's erupted up there. A real one and Sagan's taken sides.'

'Taken sides or hired himself to the highest bidder?'

'Probably the latter. He doesn't have friends. But he does have chloroform.'

She glanced up from the file. 'Sorry?'

'You'll note from the post-mortem reports, ma'am, that both Price and Lumley's bodies contained traces of chloroform. Penny Flint told me that was how Sagan subdued her when she tried to fight back inside his caravan.'

'So chloroform's his signature?'

'One of them, yeah. Though this one, I'd argue, is the smoking gun. It makes sense that he would use it too. According to Penny, he's punished a lot of wayward underworld guys in the past. Some of them will have been pretty handy, and John Sagan's no Arnold Schwarzenegger. Chloroform would have helped him overpower them. Plus, it's not a long-lasting anaesthetic – would give him just enough time to strap them down, and then they wake up bang in time for the fun to start.'

'OK.' She spread out more paperwork. 'So what do you know about this guy?'

These particular notes originated from the GMP Local Intelligence Office, and referred to one Vic Ship, a notorious Manchester gangster who had been an associate of Briggs and Harris. GMP now believed him to be engaged in a power-struggle with the smaller Bradburn faction with whom Price and Lumley were connected. If Sagan had signed on for anyone up there, it was most likely to be Ship given that he was the bigger fish. Ship's mugshot in the file portrayed an overweight, brutal-looking guy in his midfifties, with pudgy, pock-marked cheeks, a small mouth and piggy eyes. His grey hair had thinned to the point where he was almost bald, and yet it was long enough to be greased back to his collar and fastened there with an elastic band. Distinguishing marks included a tattoo of a gorgon's head on the left side of his neck, and a jagged scar across the bridge of his nose.

'Never had dealings with Ship personally, ma'am,' Heck said. 'But way back when I was in GMP it was said he'd buried more bones than you'd find in the average brontosaurus room. And just skimming these notes, you can see that for yourself. Born in Whalley Range, which is Gangster Central. Lots of known previous for armed robbery, attempted murder, demanding money with menaces, supplying, you name it. He's the real deal. Likes violence and highly placed. By any standards, a player.'

'If Ship's genuinely the big time, why's he involved in an undignified scrap with a bunch of street-punks in a nowhere place like Bradburn?' Gemma asked. 'No disrespect to your hometown, Heck, but it's hardly Chicago or south-central Los Angeles.'

'True. But like most other nowhere towns in that part of the world, they'll have a voracious appetite for drugs, sex and contraband booze. Besides, Bradburn's probably only the battlefield-of-the-moment. I suspect what this is really about is Ship trying to firm up his control across the whole of the Northwest, which is a massive market. Other local elements will try to resist him in due course.'

Gemma scoured the documentation. 'Penny Flint . . . have we got everything out of her we can?'

'Sorry, ma'am. I just don't know.'

'If she's so keen to see Sagan go down, why didn't she volunteer the information about Manchester in the first place without you having to pressurise her?'

Heck had been wondering about this too. 'My reading is that she tried the police route first, but we blew it. This time I think she was hoping that whatever he's got himself into up north, that'd be the death of him in due course. She reckons prison's too good for Sagan. She wants him dead. That's why she tried to engineer that shoot-out.'

'And this is the person whose info we're basing a whole new line of enquiry on?'

Heck shrugged.

'These torture-murders?' Gemma said. 'Price and Lumley? How much was publicised?'

'Only the bare bones, as far as I can see. Names of the victims, confirmation there are sus circs. GMP Serious are sitting on the detail.'

'But people are not stupid, Heck. These fellas were known hoodlums, so it won't take long for the public to work out that these are tit-for-tat killings – probably in response to the fire-attack on the sex shop.'

'Sure,' he said, 'but nothing was given to the press about the use of chloroform or the extreme torture. So if what's concerning you is that Penny might have read all this in the papers and decided to spin us a line about Sagan to send us in the wrong direction, I'm pretty sure that's not what's happened.'

'Obviously we're going to have to go up there.' She dragged a pad from a drawer and started jotting notes. 'We'll keep the MIR here for the time being. But we need to liaise with GMP Serious, possibly about opening a subsidiary office in Bradburn.'

A former Greater Manchester Police officer himself, and knowing the macho culture that persisted in that corner – GMP were one police force whose approach to crime and criminals was proactive to say the least – Heck didn't think this would be quite so easy.

'I think we'll have to bring GMP in on it, ma'am,' he said. 'It was simple enough fending off the OC, but that was because their foul-up allowed all this to happen in the first place. Greater Manchester's Serious Crimes Division will be a different matter, and they'll consider it a right liberty if we just barge in and try to take over.'

'Story of our life, isn't it?' Gemma muttered.

'Seriously, ma'am. We're only after Sagan, but they've got this whole gangster war thing going on. They'll have wider priorities.'

Gemma stopped writing and tapped her pen on the table as she thought it through.

'Well, organised crime is not our specific field,' she conceded. 'So any help would be appreciated, I suppose. But like I say, Sagan's *our* case and I'm not relinquishing it. I'll go up there myself. See what I can sort out. In the meantime, Heck, you only need to think about convicting Charlie Wheeler. Join us in Bradburn when it's over.'

'Ma'am.' He nodded and stood up to leave.

'Unless that's a problem, of course?'

He glanced back from the door. 'Sorry?'

'You hate Bradburn, Heck. You can't stand going back there. You've told me a dozen times if you've told me once. It's got nothing but bad memories for you. You don't even like anyone who lives there.'

'I've probably mellowed a bit over the years.'

'Mellowed?' She smiled without humour. 'Heck, no one else in the job carries grudges as long as you do. Don't get me wrong – on one hand I agree that if we set up a new enquiry team in Bradburn, you should be in it for your local knowledge. But on the other, given your history with that place, perhaps it would be better if you were nowhere near.' She paused to let that sink in. 'We don't do emotions in SCU, as you know perfectly well . . . or we try not to.'

'Ma'am,' he replied, 'if tomorrow morning someone was to detonate a dirty bomb in the centre of Bradburn, the only reason I'd lose sleep is because it would prevent us getting our hands on John Sagan. My desire to bring to book a bloke who hurts people as his business is much stronger than any lingering dislike I may have for the hometown that shat on me.'

'That's fair enough, but is this something you actually *want* to do? And I'm asking you that as a friend, not your boss . . . maybe even as your ex. We could be up there quite a while. Do you think you could stand that? It's not like there isn't lots you can be doing down here.'

'I'll be fine. The past is gone.'

'If you say so.' She only seemed vaguely satisfied, though

she rarely gave a more positive response than this to any of Heck's glib assurances.

He opened the door. 'Any message for Penny Flint, in case she gets in touch?'

'Yes,' Gemma said distractedly, writing notes again. 'Tell her she's a bitch and she deserves locking up. And tell her that if she ever meets me again she needs to tread warily, because it might still happen.'

Chapter 8

April was supposed to be a spring month, Danny reminded himself as he plodded down the dank alleys of the Blackhall ward, heavy feet tramping the wet black cobbles. And, while it wasn't what you'd call bitter, it was a tad colder than it should be at this time of year, even late at night. His breath misted out in front of him as he stumped his way along. Danny hated cold weather, but then it didn't care much for him. A gangling six-foot-three and bone-thin, he felt it more than most, and his ragged denims and oily old military coat did little to help with that.

Of course, cold or hot, rain or shine, business was business – and it didn't stop for anything.

Not that Danny Hollister looked much like a businessman, or even someone who might be carrying money. And that was to his advantage at this time of night, though he always had a roll of cash on him and a stash of gear in his pocket.

He reached his normal pitch just after eleven. It was half-way down a narrow brick entry between two derelict warehouses alongside the Leeds–Liverpool Canal, whose water lay black and motionless under a thin film of oil.

Clapping his gloved hands together, Danny waited

patiently beneath the decayed stoop of a side entrance. It was a good position. He wasn't exactly hidden from the world; those who wanted to find him would do so easily. But the canal lay forty yards to his right, and an open cobbled backstreet forty yards to his left; if a patrolling cop turned in from either of those directions all he had to do was back out of sight and beat a retreat through the burned-out innards of the industrial ruin. But in all honesty, what were the chances of a patrolling cop showing up here? It was well known that they were understaffed to an epic degree. Course, if the Drug Squad came sniffing around, that would be more of a problem. But there was an open drain just to the left. Everything could go down there at a second's notice if it needed to. It was all cellophane-wrapped anyway, and Danny knew where it washed out again. He didn't see it'd be a problem. Such cops as were available these days surely had more important things to do. OK, Danny traded in crack and heroin as well as grass, not to mention a bit of China. It wasn't what the average Joe would call small potatoes, but for safety purposes he never carried massive amounts of the stuff. And Danny was a user as much as a dealer. If the time ever arrived, he'd shrug his stick-thin shoulders and say: 'I only shift enough to feed my own habit.' And he'd be absolutely sincere.

He coughed harshly. It hurt, the air rasping in his sunken chest. His head ached too – he always seemed to have a headache these days. And a cold. Snot spooled out from his sore-encrusted left nostril, and he wiped it with his skinny wrist.

An engine rumbled somewhere close by.

Danny stepped back into the recess, crooking his head right and left. There was no sign of anyone on the towpath, but the other way he saw that a vehicle had pulled up on the cobbled space beyond the entry. By instinct, his left hand burrowed more deeply into his pocket, fingers caressing the folded switchblade he kept down there.

The vehicle at the end of the alley had turned its lights off, but remained motionless. Danny watched it irritably. This happened on occasion. Middle-class kids looking to score would come down here nervously. Not wanting to get jumped on these mean streets, they'd get as close as they could in the car and then, ignorant of the protocol, would sit there waiting, engine chugging. With every passing minute, it was more likely they'd draw attention to themselves. The narrow backstreet they were parked on might feel like it was in the middle of nowhere, but actually it wasn't. A couple of hundred yards further up, another old warehouse had been changed into a nightclub. OK, it was only open on Fridays and Saturdays; there was no one there on weekday nights, but there was a small car park in front of it, and on the other side of that a grotty little pool bar which sometimes entertained midweek custom.

The fact the car was grey, or looked grey in the dimness, would reduce this risk a little. But even so, its occupants were clearly not for venturing down the alley.

Danny swore under his breath. He could picture them. A twenty-something couple. Probably both doing jobs they loved and at the same time earning good money. They'd have put street-gear on to come down here. Stonewashed jeans or Army Surplus, maybe hoodie tops, perhaps a baseball cap for the guy. But everything would be crisp and clean, with designer branding.

Danny loathed middle-class phoneys, but he could never allow himself to show it. Whatever their pretensions in life, they were still dopers, and dopers were his lifeblood.

But still the car sat at the end of the alley, swimming in a smog of its own exhaust.

'Shit,' he said.

These really would be silly little rich kids. They might not intend it, they possibly didn't even realise it, but it clearly came natural to them to get served. Well, this once – just this once, to get rid of the dickless fool and his bint before they attracted the entire town – Danny would wander down there. But once business was concluded, he'd give them some advice, spiced with a few choice swear-words of his own.

He ambled along the passage, hands in his coat pockets. Even when he reached the end, he couldn't tell for sure what kind of motor it was. It surprised him actually – it was an estate car, but it looked a bit grubby and beaten-up; not what he'd expected. Though perhaps this was the family spare; something they felt safer in down on the Blackhall ward, a bit more incognito. As he approached, its front passenger window scrolled down. Most likely this would be the guy. The girl would be behind the wheel, because he wouldn't want her dealing face to face with a criminal. Obviously not.

But then it all turned a bit unreal.

The window had reached the bottom of the frame, and yet no bearded or handsomely chiselled face appeared there. Instead, Danny saw a circular steel muzzle – a broad one, at least three inches in diameter. His mouth dropped open.

A bulky figure was visible behind the muzzle, hunched over from the driving seat. There was no one else in there, quite clearly. To operate this mechanism, one man was enough.

A fountain of white-hot flame spewed out.

One minute Danny's tall, thin body was uncomfortably cold, the next every part of him was ablaze with agony. He stumbled backward with such force that he bounced from the warehouse wall. At first, he was so agonised that he was unable to make a sound. But as his clothes fell away in charring tatters, taking much of the flaming, adhesive fuel

78

with them, he found his voice – in long, braying screeches. Only for a second jet to engulf him, lighting him head to foot, eating immediately into his scorched and vitreous flesh.

Danny tottered around like a burning mannequin. He blundered back into the dark alleyway, thrusting his way headlong, the dancing firelight shooting ahead of him and up the brick walls, his arms weaving glittering patterns. He didn't just feel the heat all over him, but *inside* him – inside his head even. Along with a pain he'd never known, a pain that clawed through his muscles and nerves and bones, shredding his very sanity it was so unbearable, and yet somehow he kept going, one unsteady foot following another, until he'd passed his normal pitch and was out at the other end, on the cinder towpath.

And now, in the reeling, tortured inferno of his mind, he realised why he had done this.

His brain was malfunctioning, but his body had made the decision for him.

He sensed the canal in front.

Staggering another few yards, he pitched down face-first into the water, a hissing cloud erupting behind him.

At first it was so frigid that it was like passing out of reality, and yet as well as quenching the flames, it served to numb him – to an extreme degree, to a point where he was able to flounder across the channel like a crazed fish. The semi-liquid flesh unravelled from his twisted limbs, but he threw himself forward until he reached the far side, where, with eyeballs seared beyond use, he thudded into a wall of bricks hung with tufts of rank vegetation. His blistered hands groped left and found an upright ladder, rusted and rotted in its moorings, but just about capable of holding his weight as he hauled his agonised form to the top of it, and there flopped wheezing onto another cinder path.

Danny's tongue had melted to a molten stub in the scalded

cave of his mouth, so he couldn't even sob let alone scream. His nose had gone, along with his eardrums and eyelids. He had minimal senses left with which to detect the armoured, helmeted figure that had clumped steadily after him down the warehouse alley, petrol tank sloshing in the harness on its back, and now came over the canal as well, footfalls louder on the metal footbridge some twenty yards to the left.

Even when the hulking, pitiless form came and stood right over him, the shuddering, mewling wreck that had once been Danny Hollister didn't know it was there. Thus it met no opposition, not even a protest, as it trained its weapon down, and from point-blank range blasted him with flame again, and again, and again.

Chapter 9

Heck didn't hang around at court to celebrate the conviction of three-times-rapist Charlie Wheeler, despite the bastard receiving the severe but appropriate penalty of three life sentences including a judge's recommendation that he serve no less than 45 years. While DI Dave Brunwick, who'd officially headed the Wimbledon enquiry, spoke to a bank of microphones and news cameras outside the front of the Old Bailey, Heck left via a rear door and hurried off back to Staples Corner, arriving there just around lunchtime, where he grabbed a quick sandwich before hitting the motorway.

Three days had now passed since Gemma had taken several other SCU detectives north to liaise with the Greater Manchester Police in Bradburn, but plenty more had happened since. To start with, there'd been another fatal fire-attack in the town. This time it was a drugs dealer called Daniel Hollister, another goon believed to have been on Vic Ship's payroll, and the *modus operandi* had been near enough exactly the same as that used in the sex-shop attack: the victim sprayed with some combustible accelerant, most likely petrol, while the delivery mechanism – quite literally a flame-thrower – had been clearly identified on this occasion because the armoured and helmeted killer had got caught in the act on CCTV, though the footage wasn't of the best quality. Only yesterday, Gemma, in company with DI Katie Hayes of the Greater Manchester Serious Crimes Division, had held a joint press conference at Bradburn Central police station to announce that a pre-existing investigative SCU taskforce, Operation Wandering Wolf, had now been expanded to tackle in full the escalating underworld war in the town.

Already feeling left behind by these events, Heck initially sped along the M1, not that he was looking forward to reaching his destination. As Gemma had intimated, there was no love lost between Heck and Bradburn, though in some ways it was quite illogical. Back in his youth, a major domestic crisis – not unconnected to his embarking on a career in the police – had put a deep rift between himself and his immediate family, which hadn't been easily bridged.

In truth, it hadn't properly been bridged even now, though Heck and his sole surviving close relative, his older sister Dana, were in regular contact and the tone was friendly enough. Dana's only daughter, Sarah, knew Heck simply as 'Uncle Mark' and though she hadn't been around in the bad old days and with luck had never been informed about them, she hadn't seen him often enough to forge any kind of real emotional bond with him.

So . . . no, Heck didn't particularly enjoy going back to Bradburn, but this would never stop him. It was true what he'd told Gemma: the past was the past as far as he was concerned; it was time to let bygones be bygones. In any case, he'd now lived almost as long in London as he had in Lancashire, having voluntarily transferred from the Greater Manchester Police to the Metropolitan Police at the age of twenty, shortly after joining the force. He didn't consider himself a Bradburn native any more. So why should it matter? More important than any of that was finding John Sagan, though it already sounded as if Gemma had succumbed to the inevitable and, to avoid putting out any GMP noses, had made her team available to launch a full-scale assault against *all* the mobsters who were making life such a misery up there.

By mid-afternoon, the traffic flow had increased, worsening noticeably when Heck hit the M6, forcing him to divert onto the toll-road at Coleshill. From there, the driving was easier so he was able to take a guilt-free break at Norton Canes Services.

Over a coffee, he perused the latest batch of paperwork emailed down that morning by the admin staff on Wandering Wolf.

This latest intelligence finally confirmed that the Bradburn feud was being waged between Vic Ship's Manchester-based firm and a breakaway crew who had once run Bradburn on Ship's behalf but now were looking to go independent. There was no evidence as yet, at least nothing firm, that John Sagan had hooked up with Ship, but if there was a retaliatory strike for the fire-attack on Daniel Hollister, which the taskforce was now nervously anticipating, and it involved torture *and* the use of chloroform to overpower the subject, it would be as good as a signature.

In the meantime, purely in terms of numbers and expertise, the contrasts between the two factions could not be more extreme.

As Heck had already seen, Ship headed a traditional inner-city crime family whose main areas of influence were tough districts like Whalley Range, Fallowfield, Rusholme and Longsight. According to the intel, Ship's crew dabbled in all the usual activities – pimping, loansharking, protection, drugs – and had a much-feared reputation. They could and would use serious violence if they deemed it necessary, and in the long term, even before this latest shooting war, were suspected of involvement in the murders of at least four rival gangsters. That said, on the whole it was believed that Ship's mob observed the old-fashioned laws of gangland etiquette in that mainly they messed with their own kind while the general public didn't even know they existed. This didn't make them Robin Hood and his Merry Men – they were high-level criminals, whose numbers and activities were on the rise thanks to a new infusion of Russian *boeviks*, which literally translated into English as 'warriors'. It seemed that Vic Ship, in his capacity as self-appointed Manchester godfather, had recently made contact with the Tatarstan Brigade in St Petersburg, a deadly cartel who had apparently been looking for an alliance in Britain to open new markets for their narcotics. If nothing else, the expectation of this hook-up was that Ship's crew would start to display a greater degree of viciousness. The Russian mob weren't slow to stomp on their opponents, and that would include policemen, judges, politicians, ordinary citizens, anyone. More to the point, with these Russian torpedoes in harness, alongside a merciless enforcer like Sagan, Ship's outfit ought to be more than a match for anyone if it came to a genuine gangster war.

As a result, Lee Shaughnessy – alleged head of the break-away group in Bradburn, and Ship's main rival in the town – could not have looked more out of his depth.

In contrast to Ship's brutish mugshot, Shaughnessy's official photo depicted a much younger guy, thirty at the most and remarkably unblemished by his chosen lifestyle. There wasn't a shaving nick to be seen, let alone a full-blown scar. In fact, with his neatly combed white-blond hair, grey eyes and refined, almost pleasant features, he was a boy next door, the guy you'd be totally happy with if your daughter brought him home. And yet his criminal record was ghastly. He was a Bradburn local, but he'd been in trouble all his life, with multiple convictions for burglary, robbery, car theft and assault. At the tender age of twelve, he'd raped and beaten the female warden in charge of the secure care-home where he was installed. All the credentials you needed, Heck supposed, to eventually work for someone like Vic Ship, though Shaughnessy had only come to the gang boss's notice in his mid-twenties while serving four years for attacking a police observation post opposite his house at a time when he was suspected of planning a post office raid – two under-cover officers were battered unconscious and fifty grand's worth of surveillance kit was smashed up.

But it was under Ship's tutelage that Shaughnessy had really blossomed. Acting as the Manchester mob's chief lieu-tenant in Bradburn, his brief had been to take charge of the local drugs trade, and lean on the pub and club owners for protection money – all of which he'd pulled off with aplomb. So much aplomb that he'd soon flooded the town's estates with heroin and crack, while there was scarcely a nightspot where he didn't have at least some interest. The readies had rolled in, but, perhaps inevitably, Shaughnessy had soon got tired of taking only a small cut when he could (and, in his mind, should) have been taking everything. So he'd recently broken away, taking many of Ship's Bradburn business inter-ests with him.

GMP were fairly sure the recent war had commenced with the murders, on Shaughnessy's orders, of the sex-shop managers and Ship loyalists Les Harris and Barrie Briggs, though there was some surprise that Shaughnessy had laid so open and violent a challenge at the door of the larger syndicate, especially as burning two men alive was an extreme punishment even by gangland standards – unless there'd been some provocation by Ship first which had not yet come to the police's attention. One theory was that this use of fire was intended to be exemplary – in other words a message for any other Ship soldiers still remaining in Bradburn. GMP intelligence officers also felt that such savagery would not be completely atypical of Shaughnessy's outfit, who were said to be wilder than the norm. Shaughnessy had achieved this by bringing together the worst of the worst in Bradburn's previously disorganised criminal underworld, recruiting only the most dangerous and unstable individuals: alienated, disenfranchised young punks who were more than willing to rip the world a new one to get what they believed they were owed, and now, under his guidance, would have the knowhow and the means.

As a footnote, Shaughnessy's mob were also well armed. Ship's crew produced firearms when it suited them, but only in certain circumstances. By contrast, Shaughnessy's crew carried guns as a mark of their manhood, a status symbol by which they would demand respect.

Heck shook his head as he perused this material.

Bradburn, his home and a former colliery and mill-town – turned into Dodge City.

It meant more drugs, more vice, more corruption, more opportunities for underachievers to break out of the poverty trap by embracing violence. On top of that, Shaughnessy's crew in particular were leaning towards *public* displays of aggression. In their eyes, profit and discretion didn't necessarily go together. To them, it was as much about status and bling and swaggering down streets that lived in terror of them. And looking further down the page, it became apparent where this attitude, and the guns, had come from. Because Shaughnessy's number two was another Vic Ship defector, a certain Marvin Langton. Heck had heard that name even in London.

Before joining Ship, Langton, a one-time pro boxer, had been a member of the so-called Wild Bunch, a mixed-race Moss Side posse. They'd almost exclusively been drugs traffickers, but they'd believed strongly in firepower and turf wars, and had become notorious in Manchester's poorest quarter for such American-style innovations as drive-by shootings, kerb-crunching – where the unlucky victim's open mouth was slammed down on the edge of a kerbstone – and gang initiation rites involving the random murders of everyday citizens.

Shaughnessy and his crew hadn't quite resorted to that just yet, but with Langton on the team how far off could it actually be?

The Wild Bunch had finally been taken down by GMP's Serious Crimes Division, but somehow Langton, who even now was suspected of having been a senior killer in their ranks, had slipped through the prosecution net. He'd signed on for a brief time with Vic Ship, but then he too had got greedy and had relocated to Bradburn to serve as Lee Shaughnessy's deputy. How long he'd be happy in that secondary role was anyone's guess, but for the moment at least he made a set of very nasty opponents even nastier still.

Heck was already wondering if Langton could be the lunatic behind the flamethrower. His mugshot depicted a tough-looking black dude in his early thirties. He was broad as an ox across the shoulders, and now in his post-sportsman days was inclined towards heaviness, though there was still something solid and virile about him. He had broad, even features, but wore his hair in a mop of dreads and his eyes burned with an odd metallic-grey lustre. His sneering half-smile revealed a single golden tooth.

As he folded it all away and finished his coffee, Heck was thoughtful.

Shaughnessy's lot were rough customers and no mistake. A real bunch of cowboys, but they'd still be meat and drink for Vic Ship's Russian assassins, not to mention John Sagan – as that pair of eviscerated losers in the landfill had discovered.

It was an unusual thing, he reflected, that all these animals were preying on each other and the only thing the cops actually needed to do was sit there and watch as they gradually and bloodily depopulated their own hate-filled world – but instead, SCU was going to intervene.

Damn right it was going to intervene.

Paperwork tucked under his arm, he walked back out towards the car park.

It would always intervene.

If it failed to do that innocent bystanders would get hurt, as they invariably did. And not all the bastards would perish anyway; some, most likely the very worst of them, would survive, stronger, meaner, wealthier, more deeply and widely feared than ever before.

No, the rule of law could never give way to the rule of chaos.

But more important than any of that, John Sagan was *not* going to die in some crazy midnight crossfire, or in a cloud of flame, or at the hands of Lee Shaughnessy or his brute-of-the-moment, Marvin Langton.

John Sagan was Heck's.

Chapter 10

As Heck pulled off the M6 onto the slip-road just after seven that evening, it was raining. It had been dry, mild and spring-like when he'd left London early afternoon, but he'd often suspected that the Northwest had a micro-climate all of its own. As he followed the main dual carriageway into Bradburn, passing the outlying estates, he saw leaves sprouting on hedges, gardens slowly turning green again. But what initially was drizzle had now become a downpour, the sky overhead as grey as lead, and none of that would help improve the atmosphere of a dump like his hometown. Though as Heck drove on, he couldn't help wondering if he was being a little hard on the old place; it was somewhere he'd enjoyed a happy and uncomplicated childhood after all. Even the early years of his adolescence had been fun – until the thing that had destroyed his family.

It struck him now that maybe this latter event, which had occurred when he was fifteen, had soured the place for him more than it actually deserved. Bradburn had never really recovered from the wholesale closing of its coalmines and mills during the 1960s and 1970s. These days, it was a tale of drab red-brick streets and multiple tower blocks, and here and there the relics of factories, most of them with boarded windows and chimneys that hadn't smoked in decades. But it was no more run-down than many other urban boroughs that once had depended on heavy industry and now were struggling to adjust to an age in which all that was history. There were *some* jobs here, but higher-than-average unemployment was an issue that never seemed to go away.

Heck left the dual carriageway to follow lesser routes through intermittent clusters of shops and houses, most on the shabby side. Every other pub he saw was closed, though of course in the twenty-first century that wasn't solely a Bradburn problem.

It was now half past seven, and Gemma wasn't expecting him at the Incident Room until the following morning. He was half tempted to stick his nose in anyway, just to grab himself an update, but as he hadn't yet found any lodgings, he resolved to sort that out first, and the most obvious port of call was his sister's house. He wasn't overly keen on the idea, but Dana would never let him hear the last of it if he arrived in Bradburn and didn't check in with her at the first opportunity. So once he'd penetrated the labyrinthine outer suburbs, he headed inward for what they'd always known as the Old Town, a large residential district lying east of the town centre.

He cut around this central zone, much of which was pedestrianised, via the Blackhall ward. This had always been the town's poorest quarter, and by the looks of it things hadn't improved. Its sordid streets appeared semi-derelict, while the lighting was dismal, the little there was of it leaching into smoky bricks and oily flagstones. Beyond Blackhall, Heck swung a left, following Riverside Way, which skirted along the edge of the River Pennington, passing numerous garages, scrapyards and workshops built into railway arches, and several more blocks of high-rise flats, before turning right onto Wardley Rise, which ascended gently into the residential parish of St Nathaniel's, or the Old Town, at the centre of which stood the teetering needle spire of St Nathaniel's Roman Catholic Church, known locally as 'St Nat's'.

According to a local newspaper, Heck's home neighbourhood had once 'summed up everything the old North was about'. It had a lively community, was strongly Catholic and therefore more orderly and law-abiding than a visitor might expect. It was also famous for housing St Nathaniel's ARLFC, created by Irish monks back in the candle-lit years of the nineteenth century to give local deprived youth an outlet for their aggression, and now one of the most successful amateur rugby league clubs in the whole of Northwest Counties. As a schoolboy star, Heck had represented its various junior teams with distinction. In every way, St Nat's had been picture-postcard Bradburn: parallel rows of slate roofs and brick chimneys, mills towering in the background. Grimy but picturesque, and also safe – tribes of kids playing on every street corner, mums and grandmas leaning in doorways, chatting idly. Of course that had been the way it *was*.

As Heck prowled these benighted neighbourhoods now, he scarcely saw a soul.

That might just be down to the rain and the fact it was midweek. Or alternatively, perhaps this district too had fallen onto hard times. Maybe muggers and street-gangs haunted its shadowy backstreets; or perhaps the escalating underworld violence in general was oppressing everybody.

That said, the Old Town wasn't exactly dead. Not quite yet. Here and there, streams of warm lamplight filtered through curtained windows, though none at all showed from 23 Cranby Street, the Heckenburg family home.

Heck pulled up in front and switched his engine off. The

tiny terraced house's front curtains were open, but the house itself stood in darkness.

He sat still, pondering.

Not much in Cranby Street had changed, except that there were fewer houses. At least half of them had been demolished at some point in the past, but down at the far end there was still open access through to the canal and the lock-gates, and on the other side the reclaimed spoil-land that had later been turned into the rugby league pitch where a juvenile Heck would score many of his tries. But that was so long ago, and so much had happened since, that it seemed hard to equate this desolate little backwater with the place where he'd spent his early life. And the fact that the house was still in his family made no difference.

Dana – Dana Black, as she'd kept her married name despite having long separated from her waster of a husband – was the sole occupant of number 23, along with Sarah, her sixteen-year-old daughter. Heck hadn't expected that they wouldn't be here. It wasn't quite Easter yet and the kids were still in school, so it had never entered his head that they could be away.

His gaze roved again over the sorry little façade. Like the rest of the street, number 23 only ever seemed to change by getting smaller. It felt incredible that all the Heckenburgs had once dwelled here together: George and Mary, the parents, and their three children, Dana, the eldest, Mark, the youngest, and in the middle . . . Tom.

It was a deep irony that the head of the Heckenburg clan, George, and Heck's older brother, Tom, had looked so like each other. Tom had been tall and lean, whereas George had been burly, but there were clear similarities: prominent noses, high, hard cheekbones. Of course, whereas George always stuck with the sober grey suits of his own youth, the sensible ties, the short, brilliantined hair, Tom had preferred the disorderly 'mophead' look of the late-80s rock scene (dyeing it straw-blond into the bargain), the tour T-shirts and stone-washed jeans with the knees torn out of them. Father and son had been worlds apart in so many ways. In fact, back in that era, Heck, who was younger than Tom by three years, had been the success story, the 'normal one' as his mum and dad would say. Mainly this was due to his star-athlete status at school, and because he and his mates were less a group of intellectual rebels, more a bunch of lads around town, which was something factory worker George Heckenburg could more easily understand.

But the real schism between father and eldest son had only come when Tom got into drugs.

Heck shook his head, deciding he was getting nowhere with such painful reminiscence.

Briefly, he rubbed at a crick in the back of his neck, which was stiffening fast, a result of the long motorway journey he'd just completed. He could certainly have used a warm bath right now, not to mention a hot meal, but it didn't look as if that was going to happen here.

That said, he at least had to check before resorting to Plan B. He climbed out into the wet and knocked on Dana's door. There was no response.

He retreated to the car and assessed the building again. The absence of light was very telling, not to mention the absence of drawn curtains or of a television left playing to itself – the kind of precautions an everyday householder would take if they'd just popped around the corner to the chippie. He glanced along the street. A few cars were parked, and there were lights in other windows. But it was improbable there'd be anyone living here now who'd recognise him. If anything, an unknown bloke of his age, wearing jeans, trainers, a zip-up jacket and hoodie, wandering around in the dark and knocking on doors would elicit fear rather than neighbourly assistance.

He climbed back into his Megane, glancing one last time at the house he'd used to call home.

*

With a crunch of brakes, Heck stopped on the car park to St Nathaniel's. Another place he'd once called home, albeit very briefly. Though it didn't feel that way now.

The towering religious edifice had been the focal point of this district since the Old Town was first built to house Irish immigrants shipped in as part of the Industrial Revolution. All Heck's life this had been the beating heart of Bradburn, though again he couldn't help but wonder how vigorously it beat in the twenty-first century. He hadn't encountered too many people in the past few years for whom spiritual succour was a high priority. He wasn't here himself for that reason. He had a more practical purpose in mind – to get directions to a decent billet, and maybe at the same time say hello to his late mother's younger brother, Father Pat McPhearson, who also happened to be parish priest at St Nat's.

Heck climbed out and looked the church over. Some parts of its venerable old structure were clad with scaffolding, while its windows were dark and doors locked – though that was no surprise at this time of night. Once, England's churches were left open twenty-four/seven, their interiors shimmering with candlelight so they could provide a haven for souls in distress whatever the hour. But now a church was just as likely to get robbed and vandalised as any other easily accessible building. Heck crossed the car park on foot to the presbytery, skirting around tins of paint and tools propped against its gatepost. It looked as if extensive refurbishments were under way, probably not before time, given the state of the two-hundred-year-old church.

The presbytery itself wasn't quite so old, perhaps dating from the late-Victorian period, but evinced the simple austerity of the ecclesiastical life: a narrow building, but tall, again built from red brick, with a steeply sloped roof of heavy grey slate. The fanlight above its large front door was filled with stained glass, as were sections of the two arched windows to either side of it. Both of these were curtained, but dull lamplight speared out.

As Heck rang the doorbell, he recollected the brief time he'd spent lodging here after his family had unanimously decided they didn't want an officer of the law living under their roof. He'd taken official police digs at first, but those had been in short supply back in the mid-1990s – most of the old section-houses were being sold off. So he'd soon finished up here. His uncle, Father Pat as the local school-children had known him, though equally bemused by his nephew's decision to join the force, had at least shown a spirit of Christian kindness. Heck had crashed in the pres-bytery's spare room until he could afford his own place.

'How can I help you?' came a terse Irish voice.

Heck had been so lost in his thoughts that he hadn't realised the door had opened.

An extremely short woman stood there – five feet at the most – with a truculent, weather-beaten face and thinning red-grey hair. Heck recognised her as Mrs O'Malley, his uncle's housekeeper. She'd filled out a little since he'd last seen her, which was roughly nineteen years ago. She'd been stocky before, but now was quite plump – an impression enhanced by the thick raincoat she was in the process of buttoning up with a set of stubby, ring-covered fingers.

'Erm . . . Mrs O'Malley?'

'Yes?' she said impatiently, as if this was something he should surely already know.

She'd been the official housekeeper here for the last

thirty years, but she clearly didn't recognise him. And it was hardly fair to expect otherwise. He hadn't changed too much in physical terms. He'd been six feet tall then and was six feet tall now. He'd been lean, weighing in at an athletic thirteen and a half stone, and was only slightly above that all these years later. But the smart police uniform had gone, along with the short-back-and-sides, and the unscarred, unlived-in face. It was tempting to say: 'Hey, it's me – Mark. I've come back to see you after all this time.' But Mrs O'Malley, who'd always been an irascible soul, was the last person he would ever have come back to visit voluntarily.

'There's no bed here,' she added, before he could say anything. 'The spare room's now a lumber room. You'll have to find one of the shelters down in town.'

Heck was a little surprised. OK, he was wearing jeans, trainers and a hoodie top, but none of it was tatty. Perhaps, if he was so easily mistaken for a hobo, he shouldn't have gone to all that trouble to dress down in Peckham.

'I'm looking for Father Pat,' he said. 'I'd just like a quick word.'

'He's not in.' She stepped out into the porch as she closed the door behind her. Its latch clunked home with an air of finality. 'He's making his evening rounds.'

These 'evening rounds' had been part of Heck's uncle's routine for as long as he remembered. Once the day's Masses had been said, Father Pat would visit the hospitals and hospices, then the homeless centres, then the houses of the sick and the bereaved and the down-at-heart. That wasn't the sort of thing you could wrap up in half an hour.

'OK.' Heck turned away. 'Thanks.'

'He might – just *might* – pop into The Coal Hole down on Shadwell Road,' she called after him. 'But only if he has a bit of time left.'

Heck glanced back and nodded. He knew where The Coal Hole was. Father Pat might be a priest, and a good one too, but he was occasionally partial to a small whiskey.

'If he misses you tonight, I'll be seeing him again in the morning. Who shall I say called?'

'Mark – his nephew.'

There was a long, cool silence, the woman's features inscrutable in the dimness. Finally, she said, 'Well, well . . . you wouldn't by any chance be in trouble again?'

Mrs O'Malley was another who'd disapproved of what Heck had done all those years ago. Descended from a long line of Irish Republicans, she'd disapproved of the British police in general, so she'd felt especially affronted by Heck taking up lodgings here.

'No, I'm not in trouble, Mrs O'Malley,' Heck replied. 'But you guys may be.'

'I beg your pardon?'

'*All* of you.' He walked on to the gate.

'If Father Pat asks?' she called again, now sounding a tad concerned.

'Yep,' Heck said over his shoulder. 'Him too.'

Chapter 11

Bradburn wasn't just known for being a grim town up north. It had also produced several celebrated sons and daughters who'd made an impact in the entertainment industry.

One of the most controversial of these – at least in his time – was Terry Bayber, a knockabout northern comic whose heyday was the late 1940s and early 1950s, but who'd mainly been famous back then for being irreverent and even 'subversive' according to one daily newspaper. Bayber's risqué routines were always aided and abetted by his busty, blonde and ever scantily clad girlfriend and business partner, Mavis Broom, 'Our Mavis', who was the recipient of endless light-hearted innuendo throughout his shows. Bayber's death in 1954, at the age of 55, was very premature, but his memory lived on, certainly on his home patch, where campaigners had lobbied from an early stage for a permanent memorial to him. Only now had this dream finally become reality, with Bradburn Council coughing up, and further donations coming from local businesses, to produce a seven-foot-tall bronze figure mounted on a plinth in the town's central Plaza.

But this was Bradburn, so things had not gone entirely smoothly.

There'd been considerable debate about the proposed grand unveiling, some officials expressing concern that on a rainy midweek evening there'd be a relatively low attendance. Others, however, argued that the recent gangland violence had frightened and depressed everyone, making them feel that they lived in a no-go zone, and that it could only be good for Bradburn to host some kind of event in the town centre, something lively and fun, something that would cheer people up and distract from the painful present by injecting it with a touch of nostalgia. As for the weather – that was a moot point. A bit of rain was easily tolerable for the average Bradburner, especially if they hired their woman-of-the-moment, Shelley Harper, to do the bouncy, blonde Our Mavis thing while she unveiled the statue.

Shelley Harper.

She'd been the town's official doe-eyed beauty for as long as most Bradburn residents could remember. A pageant winner from way back, and a mainstay of high-profile charity events, where she'd parachuted in wearing basque and suspenders or had run marathons in a thong and baby-doll nightie, the latter turning ever more suggestively transparent the hotter and sweatier she got, Shelley had always been one to catch the eye. But a recent television appearance had raised her profile dramatically, and on a national scale, even earning her the much-sought moniker 'reality TV star'.

Ever the willing lass, Shelley had signed up for the unveiling without hesitation, even though she'd never heard of Terry Bayber. Reflecting her recent TV success, the money would be marginally better than it used to be for events for this, though it still wasn't up to much. But, on the positive side, it wouldn't take long and would be easy enough work. All she had to do was pull some cord and a sheet would fall down, and if it was a little bit demeaning that yet again she'd be posing and preening while wearing next to nothing in the midst of goggling spectators, well . . . that was Shelley's stock-in-trade.

So she was there bang on time at the Town Hall that damp Thursday night of April 5, and, suited and booted, found herself ushered out into the middle of the Plaza, where, swathed in a heavy blue cloak, she was confronted by a lively crowd, mainly male, milling around behind the red velvet ropes and, though easily marshalled by a handful of uniformed bobbies in hi-vis doublets, so eager for the unveiling to commence – the unveiling of Shelley Harper as much as the unveiling of the statue – that they were shouting and hooting with impatience.

The mayoral party lined up alongside her in their overcoats and waterproofs, though Bradburn's actual Mayor, Councillor Jim Croakwell, who was currently at the microphone making a rather ponderous speech, was wearing his robes and chain of office, plus his tricorn, which, given his porcine shape, triple chins, roseate cheeks and gruff northern voice, made him look like some kind of Victorian beadle.

At least he isn't standing next to me any more, Shelley thought.

Several times already that evening he'd allowed his arm to steal around her waist under the pretence of fatherly protectiveness.

It wasn't very respectful, but there was nothing new in it.

In truth, she was under no illusions about her status here: she was no real VIP, and everyone in the Plaza knew it. She was little more than a bit-part actress and wannabe model. Shelley's glorious looks and figure and her flowing blonde hair were all for real. She was a natural-born stunner. But a variety of ill-advised career moves had served to limit her life's ambitions at an early stage. For example, an appearance on Page Three back when she was nineteen had led on to a much more explicit role as a centrefold in a less than classy girlie mag a couple of years later, and even if both those adventures had paid her well at the time, they'd detracted from her marketability in later years. So, on approaching her late twenties and fearing her star was waning, she'd embarked on several well-publicised affairs with other, somewhat less minor celebrities from the Northwest – one a locally born TV writer, whose married life was subsequently ruined, the other a Premiership footballer whose fabulous wealth had ensured that his wasn't – none of which had done her long-term reputation any good. This had been her career's last gasp, or so she'd thought at the time – fame for all the wrong reasons – yet now, ten years later (after doing a few other things she was even more ashamed of, though thankfully they remained private), she was suddenly in the midst of a personal renaissance thanks to *Bond or Break*, a satellite TV talent show in which the Z-list contestants had to endure extreme hardships as they trekked through the Amazon jungle, cooking their own food, sleeping under canvas and only able to bathe in rivers, lakes and waterfalls.

This latter aspect was where Shelley had come good, mainly because of the teeny string bikini she'd fortunately remembered to take along with her, and the fact that she was still in terrific shape. It didn't win her the contest, but it won her the hearts of male viewers, while her bubbly personality and determination to do well in the face of private accusations from one rival contestant that she was a 'cutie-pie airhead' won the admiration of women. She didn't cop off with anyone on the show either, which the dailies suggested meant that Shelley Harper had finally grown up and earned her widespread approval.

Of course her career hadn't exactly been relaunched. No sooner was she being talked about again than images from that infamous top-shelfer reappeared on the internet. But Shelley wasn't too concerned. This was, she understood, a brief second throw of the dice, which would get her back into the gossip columns for a short time, grant her a few unexpected earners here and there, and, if nothing else, make her 'Bayber's Babe' for 2017.

And why the hell not? She might be in her late thirties by now, but she was still the whole package. As eight o'clock came, she peeled off her cloak – to much ribald cheering from the crowd – and sashayed forward to stand alongside the veiled statue and its dangling cord. She boasted an impressive 36-24-36 figure, which fitted snugly into her sexy little showgirl outfit (the 'Our Mavis Special', as the organisers had referred to it). It was a bright-blue minidress, with a thigh-high hem and plunging neckline, and, trimmed with white tassels, it perfectly complemented her white fishnets and high-heeled white leather ankle boots. Shelley's flowing blonde mane shone to dazzling effect in the explosion of flash-bulbs.

Fleetingly, the attention switched away from her as she yanked the cord and the sheet rustled to the ground, exposing the glittering bronze form of Bradburn's very own cheeky chappie, standing in the guise of his personal favourite character, Wing Commander Porkins, complete with bomber jacket, flying helmet and monocle.

This was the moment when Shelley had to go that extra yard to win back the onlookers' attention. Because after all, if they weren't looking at her, what was the point in her being here? So she held her ground boldly, poised, pert, waving to the crowd, smiling gorgeously, throwing enormous kisses, shamelessly upstaging one of the grand old men of suggestive comedy, until gradually she became the focus again, everyone shouting and gesticulating back, and if some of those gestures were a little crude, and some of the comments a tad on the coarse side, what did it really matter if they desired her too?

The main thing was that she was back where she'd always wanted to be, in front of a mob of people who adored her. Whatever their preference, whatever their kink, *adoration* was the bottom line. They wanted her.

They idolised her.

They *loved* her.

Every single one of them.

Chapter 12

Heck felt no emotions as he stood on the corner of Shadwell Road and looked up at the grimy red-brick façade of The Coal Hole. Or perhaps he was just holding them in check, subconsciously restraining them. His dad's old local, the Hole had barely changed: the familiar image of a pithead flywheel framed on a cloudy sky still adorned the shield over the door; the two front windows were still frosted to half their depth, the words FINE ALES printed in an arch over the top of each; it was still basically an end-terrace, though now an end-terrace on the edge of a post-demolition wasteland.

How the Hole had avoided the wrecker's ball, Heck couldn't imagine, but somehow it had – a bewildering stroke of fortune, which might, under ordinary circumstances, have brought a tear to his eye. He'd lost count of the Sunday lunchtimes as a small boy, when he'd sat on the hostelry's back-step in his rugby scarf and bob-cap, listening to the jovial shouts from inside, smelling the mingled fragrances of alcohol and cigarette smoke, waiting with infinite patience for his dad to finally emerge, a clutch of workmates around him, so they could all set off to the match together. Or the Sunday afternoons afterwards, when the landlord would open the back door and allow the kids to come in with their dads and granddads. While the elders would drink and discuss the game, young Mark would spend endless happy hours clacking balls around on the snooker table, or sitting quietly at the back of the vault, a glass of lemonade and a bag of salted peanuts keeping him company while he carefully built armies out of dominoes.

Heck shoved the car keys into the pocket of his jeans, and went inside.

There was only a handful of people present now, most dotted at tables around the main taproom. The vault, which was accessible through an open arch at the far end, was empty, but a pool table now occupied the place where the snooker table had once stood. Otherwise, everything else was the same. The décor perfectly matched Heck's memories: coats of arms, sports trophies, sepia-toned photographs.

Heck ambled to the bar. When he got there, the pub landlord was a familiar face. Harry Philbert, a professional rugby league star of the 1980s, and apparently still content in his role as licensee of The Coal Hole, was silver-haired these days and paunchy. In his silk shirt and club tie, he looked hale, hearty and every inch 'mine host', but when he saw Heck he stiffened.

'Pint of Best, please,' Heck said, producing his wallet.

Philbert hesitated to pull the pint.

'Something wrong?' Heck asked.

'No, no.' Philbert blustered. 'Just . . . didn't expect *you* round here again.'

'I've been back once or twice.'

'First I've seen of you.'

'Well, funnily enough, Harry, you weren't number one on my catch-up list. Wonder why that might've been?'

Philbert reddened, clearly remembering that night all those years ago when he'd refused to serve the young off-duty bobby, telling him that he wasn't welcome in The Coal Hole any more. He cleared his throat as he drew the beer. 'Keeping you busy, is it? Your job.'

Heck shrugged, pushing his money across the bar.

'So busy you couldn't even attend your mum and dad's funerals?'

'Well, you know what, Harry . . . here's a funny thing. No one told me they were dead until they were underground.'

Even Philbert had the good grace to look shocked by that. 'Surely, your Dana . . .?'

'Apparently not.'

'Your Uncle Pat . . .?'

'I found it harder to believe in *his* case, but I'd imagine he was acting on the wishes of the recently departed.'

Philbert pondered this for some time, then, apparently finding it understandable, maybe even appropriate, nodded and pushed the brimming pint across the counter. Heck grabbed it and walked away. Not particularly looking for company, he avoided the tables where other customers were sat, and strode into the vault. He stood contemplating the pool table, wondering if he had the interest and/or patience to play a couple of sets. He supposed there was nothing else to do – it was anyone's guess how long it would be before his uncle came in, if he appeared at all. He placed his pint down and took a cue from the rack.

'Now, stranger,' a voice said. 'You not talking?'

Heck glanced sideways, surprised. He hadn't heard the woman approach. A minute ago she'd been seated in a quiet corner, drinking from a tall glass of coke while busying herself on a laptop. She'd caught his eye fleetingly: denim-clad and wearing a Motorhead T-shirt, but shapely with it, her thick dark hair hanging past her shoulders. He hadn't recognised her though.

Now however, up close, he did.

She was older than he recollected, obviously, his own age, but there was no mistaking that natural tan, those strong, even features. The mischievous smile settled all doubt. Kayla Green had been the apple of so many young lads' eyes during their school days, and a lass Heck had once known very well indeed – *intimately* well, as it transpired. Captain of both the school netball and hockey teams, she'd been, by turns, sporty, intelligent, spirited and wily, but at the same time funny, pretty and always flirtatious.

'Kayla . . .' he said slowly.

'Long time no see, Mark.'

For the first time in he couldn't remember when, Heck was tongue-tied. The coltish schoolgirl of his memory – his natural opposite number at the time, he having captained the school rugby league team – had been widely fancied, not just for her looks, but for her confident sexiness. Inevitably now, in her late thirties, she'd changed somewhat: she was curvier and less athletic looking, but, judging from her rock-chick attire and wild, raven-black tresses, her rebellious nature was as much to the fore as ever, and those entrancing violet eyes of hers hadn't lost an nth of their lustre.

'What're you doing here?' she asked, apparently fascinated to see him.

'Well . . .' He shrugged. 'I used to come in a lot.'

'I mean what are you doing here *now*? Don't you live in London?'

'Actually . . . I'm here to see my uncle.' That wasn't untrue, of course, but this didn't feel like the time to mention his job.

'Father Pat?' Kayla said.

'Yeah.' Heck was bemused. She knew his uncle?

'He'll be in soon,' she said. 'He's out on his rounds.'

'So I heard . . . is that common knowledge these days?'

Her mouth crooked into an impish smile. 'Meaning how

does a wayward lass like me from the Blackhall, who regularly drank you and the rest of the guys under the table, who finally led you astray one hot summer night and no doubt is still bad to the core, know anything about the comings and goings of the parish priest of St Nat's?'

Heck smiled too – probably for the first time all day. 'Something like that, I suppose.'

'Well . . . a lot's changed.' She cut a consciously prim pose. 'I'm a Eucharistic minister now.'

'*You* are?'

'*Hey!*' She gave his shoulder a playful slap. 'Don't sound *too* surprised.'

'Sorry, I didn't mean –'

'You *are* surprised though, aren't you?'

'Seriously, would you expect me *not* to be, a self-confessed villainess like you?'

It was strangely easy slipping back into the banter he'd once shared with her. They hadn't seen each other for twenty years or more, and yet it felt as if they'd barely been apart.

'Nah, I don't blame you,' she said. 'But listen, Mark – you going to grab a pew, or keep standing here like a spare prick at the wedding?'

Spare prick at the wedding? And she's now a Eucharistic minister!

It took all sorts, he supposed, following her to her table, where she pulled up a chair for him.

As he sat down, Kayla closed her laptop and moved it, allowing him room for his pint. She took another quick sip of cola, watching him carefully, almost expectantly. There'd always been an intense latent energy about Kayla Green, a lively schoolgirl allure that most of the boys in their year had found irresistible; she was much older now, but she still effervesced with it.

'Last I heard, you were . . .' Heck shrugged again, awkwardly.

'Well, to be honest, I didn't hear anything.' In truth, he had no clue how they'd left things between them. For all that it didn't feel as if they'd ever been apart, he couldn't pinpoint the last time they'd actually spoken.

She smiled again. 'Exactly what I expected.'

'I've lost touch, Kayla. Not just with you – with everyone, the whole town.'

'You've been back here now and then, though, haven't you – surely?'

'Only for flying visits. Sometimes on business. Couple of times to see Dana and Sarah. Don't suppose you know where they are, by the way? There's no one at home.'

'Could they be over at the Plaza? There's something going on in town. They're unveiling a statue – some old-time comedian, or something.'

'Can't think that'd be Dana's scene.'

'Not sure then. Your uncle should be able to tell you.'

'Yeah. On that matter . . .' Heck was still struggling to get his head round this idea that Kayla had found God. The girl he'd known had been a tigress in so many ways. She'd sink her claws into any guy she fancied and, without preamble, yank him out of line – whether he liked it or not (though he usually did).

'You're with him, Uncle Pat?' Heck said. 'I mean, not *with* him, but it's St Nat's where you're helping out at Communion?'

'Correct.' Still that mischievous smile.

He sat back. 'I can't believe it. I don't mean that in a negative way. It's not a condemnation of your former self –'

'Thank God for small mercies.'

'– but I *can't* believe it. Seriously. I mean, you're a modern girl, you're free-spirited, you –' he nodded at the brutal war-pig logo visible under her Wrangler jacket '– you still like metal.'

She looked amused. 'Ah, yes . . . the Devil's music?'

'I didn't quite say that.'

'The hell you didn't.' She grinned. 'Anyway, Father Pat's still a big Zeppelin fan, so if you're going to tackle *me* about it, you've got to tackle him too. But yeah, I like to think I'm an independent woman. I do my own thing.'

For some reason, he noticed there was no wedding ring on her finger. Not that this particularly meant anything in the modern age.

'But every so often bad things happen,' she was saying, still in a light and airy tone, though briefly Heck thought he detected a hint of seriousness underneath, 'and, well . . . people find different ways to deal with it.'

He nodded, wondering what that might mean exactly. Whatever this bad thing was, it must have been a doozy to turn the Kayla he'd known towards religion, especially in an age when faith registered on so few people's radars.

'Whatever works for you, I suppose,' he said.

'And what works for *you*, Mark?'

'Ohhh, hell, I don't know. I was raised a Catholic, just like you were. But I always . . . look, I just need something firmer to get hold of.'

'Ooh.' She sipped more cola. 'Is that me on a promise?'

He smiled. Still the same sassy Kayla, whatever her new religious convictions. Suddenly, he was tempted to ask if she was seeing anyone. Just come out with it, just be blatant. But even as a copper you didn't blunder straight in with unsubtle enquiries of that sort.

'What do you do with yourself?' he asked. 'I mean aside from helping out at the church.'

'I'm running my dad's business now.'

If Heck recalled correctly, Kayla's father had owned a car repair centre and body-shop somewhere in the town centre. 'You a mechanic these days,' he asked, 'or just the business head?'

'How about both?'

'Wow.'

'Full of surprises, aren't I?'

'So your dad? Is he . . .?'

Her smile only faltered a little. 'Passed on, I'm afraid.'

'Ah . . . sorry.'

'Mum popped her clogs when we were still at school, you'll remember?'

'Yeah.'

'Dad only went about ten years ago, but same thing. Too much booze, too many cigs. I was already running the garage for him by then, anyway. He'd been training me up. I'm a dab hand with a panel-beater, me . . . and an absolute killer with a blowtorch.'

Heck laughed. 'Nice to keep the family tradition going.'

'How about you? Aside from coppering, you still scoring tries for free on the RL field?'

Heck, who was in the act of sipping his pint, snorted froth. 'Gimme a break.'

'Why? You're not too old. You look fit enough.'

'No time for it now.' He put his drink down. 'No time for anything.'

'To be honest, I thought you'd have gone on to be a pro,' she said. 'You were good enough.'

'Nah,' he said firmly. 'I stopped playing when Tom died.'

'Oh, I didn't realise . . .' A shadow of regret crossed her face, as if it had only just occurred to her that this might be a touchy subject. Even so, she let the words hang – she was clearly intrigued to know more.

'Felt wrong to carry on doing sport,' Heck explained. 'Changed everything in our family, that, I'm afraid.'

'I suppose it would, yeah.'

'So I knuckled down to my A-levels instead. I'd been lax on the education front up till then.'

When Kayla smiled this time, it was softer, laced with a

111

genuine sympathy. 'I'm sorry all that happened to you, Mark. Must've been very difficult.'

Heck couldn't help wondering how much she knew. How much any of them knew, those friends and acquaintances who'd once peopled these terraced streets he'd called home.

At the time, it was common knowledge in their neighbourhood that Tom had rebelled against his family's old-fashioned blue-collar ethos by turning into a counterculture drop-out, and that in due course, having started off by smoking grass with his slacker mates, had slowly got himself into harder and harder drugs, which eventually had led him into petty crime, and finally into the hands of the police. It was also widely known that Tom had then been held on suspicion of being the 'Granny Basher', a brutal housebreaker who for several months had been terrorising the old folks of Bradburn. The Granny Basher's main motivation was apparently to steal, but he'd also quite clearly enjoyed the extreme violence he'd inflicted on his frail victims, most of whom had never really recovered afterwards.

Tom was innocent of that; of course he was innocent – he'd never once broken into a dwelling house, and even in those latter days, when he was constantly looking for his next fix, there wasn't a violent bone in his body. But, very conveniently for the hard-pressed CID unit who were hunting the Granny Basher, they'd suddenly found themselves with this lad in custody who'd been arrested by uniforms for breaking into the park café. That was a link to the Granny Basher crimes, of a sort . . . wasn't it? Moreover, while the physical similarities between Tom and the photo-fit of the main suspect were not conclusive, they were notable. It still shouldn't have been enough. But with a lack of professionalism bordering on the farcical, the investigating officers had begun bending facts to fit the thesis. This lad they currently had in custody for doing the park café – he didn't just look like the Granny Basher, they said, he *was* the Granny Basher. He was a junkie burglar scrote whom no one liked. OK, there was minimum forensic evidence, but this was back in '92 – it was only six years after the first ever use of DNA in a British murder investigation; that whole field of technology was in its infancy, so while there was nothing to indisputably place Tom at the crime scenes, there was nothing to place anyone else there either.

Anyway, the fact that there was no smoking gun was easily resolved.

Young Tom, eighteen at the time, was no tough guy, and all it took were a couple of fierce interrogations, two or three hairy-arsed detectives giving him a hard time, to break him down.

It's amazing what you'll admit to when you're strung out and desperate to shoot up.

Tom's eventual sentence was life imprisonment with a minimum tariff of thirty years. He would have been two years off his fiftieth birthday when he first became eligible for parole.

Oh, yes, Kayla would know all that, because it had totally scandalised the once respected family in this traditional working-class neighbourhood. She would also know that about one month later Tom Heckenburg would commit suicide in the prison shower, using a razor to slash his wrists and groin. She'd also be aware – as everyone was, because this had gone on to be an even bigger scandal – that only about three weeks after that, a couple of sharp-eyed Bradburn beat-bobbies had grabbed a notorious thief and mugger, Luke Gaskell, while he was leaving a Blackhall house by the back gate at three o'clock in the morning, wearing a freshly blood-stained sweatshirt and gloves. Inside the house lay the bludgeoned, half-dead body of the eighty-year-old widow who lived there. It seemed the real Granny Basher, though he'd taken the opportunity of Tom Heckenburg's arrest and conviction to lie low, hadn't been able to suppress his yearning for very long, and had finally been caught red-handed – literally.

But what she likely would *not* know was the reason why only three years later, Mark Heckenburg, Tom's once adoring younger brother, would go off and join the police himself. And not just any old police, but the Greater Manchester Police, members of whom had framed his sibling. Of course, it was highly possible Kayla would guess that this was why, two years after that, Heck had voluntarily reassigned from Manchester to London . . . because surely no one could be ostracised so much by their own family and not eventually flee from it.

'It's all in the past now,' Heck said, doing his best not to speak in the stony monotone these painful memories always seemed to keelhaul out of him. 'I've got other priorities now.'

'Yeah, I've read about you in the paper a couple of times,' Kayla said, bright-eyed again, smiling. 'That scary business in Surrey . . . that stuff up in the Lakes.'

Heck felt absurdly grateful that she was being mature enough to help him move the conversation on, and that she hadn't taken the opportunity to bluntly ask him – as so many others had over the years – what on earth he'd been thinking about when he'd gone and joined up.

'That's National Crime Group for you,' he said. 'It's not intentional. I just happen to be in the team that gets sent out to these nasty jobs.'

'And the next nasty one's here in Bradburn?'

'Well . . .'

'Come on, Mark. It can't be a coincidence that you show up here just when all these murders are happening. It was all over the local rag yesterday. They said a specialist Scotland Yard team's taken charge of the investigation. Is that not the National Crime Group?'

Kayla now spoke with a thinly suppressed smirk. She was ribbing him again – as if they'd already shared so much that it was only a matter of time before he'd give in and tell her all his secrets, and that if he didn't it was stingingly unfair on her.

'To be specific, it's the Serial Crimes Unit,' he said, playing along but not divulging any info that wasn't already in the public domain. 'I'm in SCU, and we have a lot of expertise where homicide is concerned. So, yes, it's true – we're helping out.'

She took another drink. 'I hope you have more luck than the bobbies up here have had.'

'We tend to trust to more than luck.'

'I'm glad to hear it. There's way too much crime in Bradburn these days.' She pulled a disgusted expression. 'More like a junkie sewer than the town me and you grew up in. Hasn't got an inch of its self-respect left. Maybe you should transfer back permanently, eh? It'd certainly keep you busy.'

'No, thanks,' he said. 'I like my roving commission.'

'Your what?'

'I like working all over the country. Stops me getting bored.'

Her eyes twinkled. 'So that's all it would take to keep you here? Stop you getting bored?'

Heck smiled again, unsure how to answer – even by Kayla's kittenish standards, this was a little bit forward. But then she glanced over his shoulder and registered a presence in the pub behind them. Heck turned.

Father Pat McPhearson had entered the taproom. All these years later, Heck's uncle still favoured a black raincoat and black trilby, though he removed the latter and hung it on a stand before walking to the bar, rolling his shoulders as though to loosen them. He wore his thinning grey hair longish and greased back, just the way Heck remembered it. The priest's angular face belonged as much on a weathered statue as a living man: all sharp bones, its features pitted, craggy and cut.

'Double Jameson's, Harry, please,' he told the landlord in the gruff Lancashire voice Heck had heard so many times echoing dramatically from the pulpit.

Kayla rose to her feet and walked towards him. Heck rose too, but waited by the table.

'Day's work done, Father?' she asked.

'Hopefully, love, hopefully.' He sipped blissfully from the amber spirit as he unbuttoned his coat, showing the black shirt and clerical collar underneath. But before he could say more, his eyes fell on his nephew, and the tumbler halted about nine inches below his mouth.

'The devil!' he said slowly.

Kayla smiled. 'Not quite, but I understand the confusion.'

'How you doing, Uncle Pat?' Heck said.

'Well, I'm . . . I'm . . . Bloody marvellous to see you!' The priest looked astounded. 'But I'm totally gobsmacked. I never knew you were coming up to visit us.'

He put the glass down, gripped his nephew's hand in both of his own and pumped it. From the big grin that split his creased, weather-worn features, it was clear he was genuinely delighted.

'He's only here on business,' Kayla warned.

Father Pat glanced from one to the other, briefly puzzled. And then the truth hit him.

'Oh, God in Heaven!' He grimaced as though in pain. 'These God-awful murders?'

'I'm afraid so,' Heck said.

Father Pat's brow darkened as he scooped up his drink. He shook his head vigorously. 'It's been non-stop since they started, one following another.' He imparted all this as though

116

Heck was likely to be in need of such information. 'There was one only the other night, down by the canal. It's getting so that people won't even go out. Not alone anyway. God help these tortured souls, that's all I can say.'

'We'll do what we can, Uncle Pat,' Heck said. 'I promise.'

'Well . . .' The priest broke from his reverie to briefly eye his nephew with curiosity, perhaps never having considered that his sister's youngest son might someday be their potential saviour. The moment passed, and he smiled. 'If nothing else, at least it's brought you back to us.'

'I don't think he's really come back to us,' Kayla said.

Again, the clerical gaze bounced quizzically between them. 'Do you two know each other?'

'I'll say,' she replied.

'We were at school together,' Heck said. 'But not to worry. I'll be up here as long as I'm working on the case. You'll see plenty of me, I hope.'

'Were you planning to stay at the presbytery?'

'I was half thinking about that . . . but not now. Seems my old room's unavailable?'

'Yes, unfortunately.' Father Pat frowned. 'We're having some work done at the church. Repointing, replastering, the gutters need fixing, the roof relining . . . I've also had the entire ceiling painted eggshell blue, with a few stars added. Sooner or later, I thought I at least ought to *try* to create an impression of Heaven on Earth.'

'First thing anyone would think of in Bradburn,' Heck commented.

'Your room's full of clutter as a result, I'm afraid.'

'Doesn't matter. I can find some other digs.'

'Have you got a key to Dana's house?' the priest asked. 'Because if you haven't, I've got a spare you can use.'

Heck tried not to show how wary he was of this suggestion. 'I don't think that'd be a very good idea, Uncle Pat.'

'Nonsense, I'm sure she'd expect you to stay there. She's abroad, by the way. Sarah's had a bad dose of flu and they're convalescing for a week in Malta.'

'Sarah's OK?' Heck asked.

'She'll be fine.'

'OK . . . good. Well, look, don't worry about me. Most likely my boss will have sorted somewhere for me. Probably at a local B&B.'

In actual fact, Heck didn't think this at all. Given the size of the operation Gemma was now heading up, it seemed probable that his sleeping arrangements would not be foremost in her mind. Which, he supposed – somewhat inevitably – brought him back to Cranby Street.

Dana was never unwelcoming – quite the opposite. But Heck had bunked there only once since leaving home in 1995 – and that had been a similar situation to this in that he'd had no other option. But on that occasion he'd had company, plus there'd been more immediate issues to deal with, whereas tonight he'd be alone, his mind no doubt swirling with unfettered and miserable memories.

Father Pat arched a bushy eyebrow. 'Dana won't be happy if you don't spend at least one night under her roof. And you know what a spitfire she can be.'

'Seems like the wrong thing to do without asking her permission.'

'Come up to the presbytery and get the key,' the priest urged him. 'They're back in a couple of days, anyway. If nothing else, you can tell Dana you tried but that it didn't work out.'

Heck pondered again. It was mid-evening now, and anyone's guess what standard of accommodation he'd be able to find in Bradburn at this hour. The town had long boasted its quota of cheap hotels and rooming houses, but they were poor quality for the most part. If memory served, there was a Travelodge or some such thing on the outskirts of the borough – that would be decent, but it would mean having to slog in and out of town every day. On the other hand, his sister's house in Cranby Street would be sparkling clean, the bedrooms tidy, the bedding fresh. There'd also be food in the fridge and booze in the drinks cabinet. In addition, it was no more than ten minutes from the town centre, so it'd be no problem getting to the nick first thing tomorrow.

'All right.' He nodded resignedly. 'Can't do any harm to crash there one night at least.'

The priest nodded too, and finished his whiskey. 'Bad times, Mark, bad times. I'm glad to see you, though.'

'Glad to see you too, Uncle Pat.'

Despite all the scepticism he held about this place, Heck meant *that* at least.

Over the last two decades he'd taught himself to live without the support network the average family might provide. This didn't mean that, deep down at some hidden emotional level, he didn't miss his relatives, and it wasn't as if his uncle hadn't at least offered him a berth in his early days as a Manchester copper, when his parents had shown him the door. OK, there was still some kind of discussion to be had about Heck's mother's death from kidney failure thirteen years ago, and why the priest had only informed him about it after she was buried. It was possibly understandable that Heck had never been asked to the funeral of his father, who had died with lung cancer four years before that – the old man wouldn't have wanted his 'traitor son' anywhere near and would probably have made his wife and her brother swear to this while he lay on his deathbed. But once Mary Heckenburg had gone, surely Father Pat could have exercised his own judgement? Heck wasn't sure what the explanation was there, but that was a conversation for another time. Now, it would only serve to sour the mood.

'So who do you think's responsible for these crimes?' the priest asked, collecting his hat from the stand.

Heck was noncommittal. 'Anyone's guess at present.'

'Gangsters fighting over the drugs trade, isn't it?' Kayla said. 'That's what the papers are saying.'

'The papers are theorising,' Heck replied. '*We've* got to go where the evidence takes us.'

Father Pat shook his head again as though the whole thing still baffled and revolted him. He buttoned up his coat. 'Do you want me for anything, Kayla?'

'Not especially,' she said. 'Just wondering when you'll next need me.'

'Sunday's fine. Usual time.'

She nodded and smiled, and then turned to Heck as he finished the last of his beer.

'This is for you.' She handed him a small card. He saw that it was a business card. It referred to the company she'd taken charge of, Greenways Autofix, but it also included her personal contact details, her email address and mobile phone number, both of which she appeared to have circled in biro. 'I'm sure you're not going to be working every single hour while you're up here, Mark,' she said. 'I mean, you're bound to have some recreation time that'll need filling . . .'

'Erm . . . I hope so, yeah.'

She winked, sat back at the table and reopened her laptop.

'You ready?' Father Pat asked, pulling his hat on. 'Follow me up there, if you like.'

Heck nodded, waved at Kayla – she returned the gesture with a simple waggle of her fingers – and he went out with his uncle onto the rain-wet pavement.

Heck glanced again at the business card, vaguely bemused.

A lot of water had passed under the bridge since he and Kayla had been kids, but even so he remembered the good times they'd had, one glorious June evening in particular when they were sixteen and had lost their virginity to each other in a tent in a wooded section of the park. Shyly for sure, and clumsily . . . but eventually very successfully, and God, it had been fun. Over the following couple of years he'd occasionally seen Kayla for a smooch and fondle – in discos or at house parties. But they'd never officially dated, most likely because she hadn't seen much more in him than a school jock who long-term wasn't going anywhere. Things were different now, of course, though perhaps not as much where Kayla was concerned. She'd been quite a catch back in the day. Now, as he'd noted, she was more buxom, more womanly, but still a beauty – that raven hair, those violet eyes.

'I take it you and Kayla were more than just school friends?' Father Pat said, unlocking the door to his battered old Volvo.

'We had a brief thing.' Heck slid the card into the back pocket of his jeans. 'Which, to be honest, is all my relationships with women have ever seemed to amount to.'

'Just so you know – Kayla's been through some tough times recently.'

Heck was amused by the tone of reproof.

'I'm here to work, Uncle Pat,' Heck reassured him. 'Not mess with people's heads.'

'I'm not trying to judge you, son. It's just that I've got to know Kayla quite well, and she may seem very strong and together, but underneath all that she's probably a bit more vulnerable than you may think.'

'No worries.' Heck dug out his own car keys. 'Like I say, I'm only up here as long as I need to be. Not one second longer.'

121

Chapter 13

Shelley Harper couldn't wait to get away from the reception in the atrium at the Town Hall. Mainly so that she could evade the groping hands of Councillor Croakwell.

It was a rather splendid affair, but somewhat incongruous inside the tall, glass-roofed chamber with its purposely functional steel-girder reinforcements and encircling walls made exclusively of red brick, and frescoed with photographic images celebrating Bradburn's industrial heyday: coalmines, mills, canal barges, sooty streets thronged with hard-faced working folk in flat caps and shawls. There was much shouting, guffawing and clinking of glasses, and a lot of tactile contact from Councillor Croakwell as he wheeled Shelley back and forth, introducing her to sundry colleagues, the vast majority of whom seemed to be elderly men, all wide-eyed with admiration, loudly acclaiming the beauty she brought to these 'otherwise dull proceedings', and congratulating her profusely on her choice of attire, which apparently was 'suitably saucy'!

At Councillor Croakwell's behest, she'd left the Our Mavis suit on for the party.

'It doesn't leave much to the imagination, my dear, but it could be worse, could be the same suit you wore for that lads' mag all those years ago, eh – your birthday suit!'

Shelley smiled bravely through it all. But it was increasingly difficult. One guy he introduced her to was a real creep: Max Griddle, or something to that effect. He could have been anywhere between seventy and ninety, and was tall but pale and cadaverous. He leaned on a cane with a silver ram's head at the end, and wore a rather old-fashioned suit: pinstriped and double-breasted, with a waistcoat. It hung on his emaciated frame like empty canvas, its shoulder panels patterned with dandruff from his lank white hair. His eyes were hidden behind impenetrably brown-lensed glasses, and his large, wet mouth was curved in a rictal grin, revealing overlong ivory teeth.

He said nothing, simply gazed down at her as the introductions were made and Shelley gave a dutifully flirtatious curtsy. He still said nothing when Croakwell confided in him that Shelley was a local lass of whom they were all very proud. But when he added that she'd 'been around and knew the ropes (heh heh heh!)', Griddle's smile widened and tightened.

That was bad enough, but following on from this – and there seemed to be so many more people to meet – Shelley was increasingly aware of the Mayor's hand creeping down her shoulder to her upper left arm, and then to the small of her back, which was exposed. Clearly, it was time to leave. There was nowhere else for that hand to go. Its grip was getting firmer too – it wouldn't be shaken off easily when it finally landed somewhere it really wasn't supposed to.

Only at around ten o'clock, and after much difficulty, promising she'd be back for further functions at the Town Hall, was she able to extricate herself from the increasingly drunken throng. With a sigh of relief, she hurried down the stairs to one of the basement passages. There was a storage room down there where she'd been able to change earlier.

She re-entered it and opened the cupboard where she'd left her jeans, jumper, training shoes, coat and bag. She quickly checked that everything was there, only to hear an explosion of gravelly laughter from the corridor close behind – it sounded like Jim Croakwell.

Shelley's heart sank. Surely the randy old goat hadn't followed her? Did he really think she was so grateful to be put on that podium tonight that she'd give him a reward?

The average man on the street would be amazed how many male VIPs genuinely believed they cast such an aura that pretty girls would drop everything, literally, just to be with them. But Shelley had been around enough fêtes and festivals of this sort, usually in her scanties, to know that this happened with alarming frequency.

She stuck her head out of the storeroom and glanced left and right along the dimly lit corridor. Two figures were visible at the far end, about fifty yards away. Both clutched glasses of wine, but looked to be engrossed in conversation. Their loud, Bradburn-accented voices echoed back to her. Whether they were aware she was here was unclear, but this didn't mean she was out of the woods. One of them could be Croakwell – he was portly enough, while the other seemed to be thin. God forbid it was Croakwell and Max Griddle. What could be worse?

From this distance she couldn't tell for sure who it was, but she suddenly didn't like the idea that she was about to get undressed in here. It wasn't a proper dressing room; there was no lock on the door, and there'd be nothing to stop someone poking his head in at just the wrong moment. Deciding that she wasn't going to take the chance, Shelley pulled her coat on over the Our Mavis costume, folded her clothes into a bundle and shoved them into her bag and, grabbing her car keys, left the storeroom, heading hurriedly in the opposite direction.

She reached an outer exit-door without incident, thankfully slipped through and closed it behind her.

She was now in the labyrinth of alleyways at the back of the Town Hall. This place was even more dimly lit than the basement corridors, but at least the rain had eased off, plus her Renault Clio was just around the next corner. The problem was that when she got there it had been clamped.

Shelley stood rigid, mouth sagging open in shock and outrage.

She'd been told she could park here by a Town Hall official when she'd first arrived. It was a proper parking zone, recessed back from the narrow side-street.

She bustled forward, her pin-point heels clicking on the tarmac. Her Clio was the only car left here now – it stood alone alongside a row of wheelie-bins – so there was no mistake. She squatted down to look more closely, wondering if it was some kind of joke. It was too dark to see much, so she fished her mobile phone out and activated its light. The phone's battery was fading fast, but in the short time she had before the light winked out, she was able to see the wheel-clamp more clearly. It looked solid. She touched it. It *was* solid, fixed in place. And yet . . . curious, she looked more closely. It actually seemed rather crude and – was it possible? – homemade. It was constructed from grey unpainted metal and rough along its edges. Weren't these devices usually yellow? Moreover there was no company logo on it, no telephone number.

When she stood up and checked, no accompanying paperwork had been tucked under her windscreen wiper.

Suddenly Shelley felt vulnerable.

She glanced over her shoulder. The alleyway receded into shadow and silence. No voices could be heard from anywhere nearby; the town centre would now have cleared of course – it wasn't yet eleven o'clock, but it was a weekday.

She decided she'd go back into the Town Hall, but then she remembered that the door she'd used was an exit, not an entrance. She wouldn't be able to get back in that way. She'd have to work her way round to the front of the grand old building, and that wouldn't be quite so easy. She'd need to walk back to the main road and follow the pavement around, which would take about fifteen minutes. There might be a short-cut from here, but this whole area at the back of the Town Hall was a rabbit warren of passages between garages and workshops. It would probably be easier to head back to the road and get a cab. She could then go straight to the police station, and, when she arrived, if she needed to open her coat and bat her eyelashes, she would – anything to find out what was going on with that phoney clamp.

But was it phoney?

She stared down at it, wondering. It didn't matter. She'd have to contact the police anyway, because as things were she had no idea who to pay the fine to. She pocketed her keys, slung her bag over her shoulder and set off along what she assumed would the quickest alley out of here. She also tried her phone again, to see if she could make a call, but the battery had finally expired. Frustrated, Shelley shoved it into her pocket – just as she saw a figure stepping out of sight ahead of her.

She halted, wondering if her eyes might have deceived her. She was currently between a high brick wall on the left and a single-storey lock-up on the right. It could have been an effect of the poor lighting, but it really had looked as if someone – a large, heavyset someone – had quickly shuffled out of her field of vision.

She thought about creepy Max Griddle again, though it couldn't possibly be him.

'Oh, God.' She shuddered. But no, it couldn't be him, he was too thin. Unless he'd sent out some kind of henchman to ambush her, and that sounded a bit unlikely. After all, who was she – apart from 'a local lass who knew the ropes'?

A dark entry yawned next to the lock-up. It was narrow, dank, and she had no idea where it led to. But as long as it led away from here . . . She turned down it, walking as quickly as she dared in the near-complete darkness. Ten yards in, the passage passed beneath a brick arch. Beyond this there was a roof of girders and rotted planking. Shelley found herself in a tunnel so narrow her shoulders brushed along either wall, but the thought of what might lie behind kept her going, plunging through intermittent patches of blackness and light as gaps appeared overhead. Shelley was a woman of the world and didn't feel easily threatened, but this was different. Some bloke wouldn't be hanging around in a maze of darkened passages like this for any good reason. Then there was the issue of the homemade clamp. The more she thought about that, the less encouraging it was.

She stopped a couple of times to listen, though she was quite sure the secondary set of footfalls she kept hearing were echoes of her own. She glanced over her shoulder, able to see all the way back to the section of passage beyond the roof. It was obscured by late-evening gloom, but she could see enough to tell that there was nobody there.

Relieved, she continued on. The real issue was where to go next. She reached a T-junction. Slightly broader alleyways led left and right, the left one trailing away between rows of garages, the right one curving out of sight around higher, older buildings. She hurried that way first – only to halt about ten yards on. An open door had appeared a few yards in front, at the side of some dark, nondescript structure. The door wasn't wide open; it stood ajar by several inches, which, even if the building was derelict, seemed odd at this time of night. Unable to shake the impression that it would be too easy for someone waiting on the other side to simply pounce out on her, she backtracked, turned and headed the other way. As she passed the T-junction, she glanced left, peering down the entry that had brought her here – and, about forty yards along it, saw a figure standing perfectly still beneath the rotted plank roof.

She didn't stop to make sure, just strode on – and, as soon as she was out of view, began running. The echoes of her heels resounded so that it was impossible to tell if someone was chasing her. Garage doors flitted by, made from timber, with peeling paint on them and grimy, cracked windowpanes. Again, it would be so easy for one of these to suddenly swing open and someone to spring out.

She wheeled around the next corner, breathless – entering a paved yard.

Initially she was horrified. Was it a cul-de-sac, a dead-end? A warehouse towered over her on the left. On the right stood the rear wall of another civic building, more recently built than the Town Hall but with darkness in all its windows. Then she saw a barred gate in the opposite corner. She hurried towards it, dreading that she might find it padlocked. Thankfully, it swung open – but with a shrill squeal. She slid through, closed it behind her and fumbled around its jamb to see if she could find a bolt. But if there ever had been one, it had fallen off now. The gate was old, rusty flakes coming away like scales.

She hurried on, digging her phone out, hammering its keypad, but it remained lifeless. She was now between buildings so long boarded-up and disused that it was impossible to say what they had once been. Town centre dereliction was a real problem in Bradburn. She rounded a corner into another passage, this one wider than before – you could easily get a car or van along it. For some reason this gave her heart. She slowed to a walk, mainly because she was concerned that in these boots she was likely to turn an ankle.

Another ten yards on, she came to an abrupt halt.

A figure was standing just ahead on the right side of the way, very still and vaguely ragged.

Great – a tramp.

That was all she needed.

Unless it was the guy she'd spotted earlier. But surely that was impossible. He couldn't have got ahead of her like this.

Either way, this was a sod of a situation.

Unavoidably, Shelley considered the recent murders, but then just as quickly reminded herself that the newspapers insisted those were not random but connected to local gangs fighting for control of the drugs trade. They were no threat to her at all.

Even so, this was a hell of time to have neglected to bring her chemical mace or her rape alarm. She'd assumed that in the town centre, surrounded by good-natured revellers and with her car parked virtually at the Town Hall's back door, she'd be completely safe. She glanced over her shoulder. Nothing stirred in the murk, but she knew that if she headed back there was only one route – through that gate, into that yard, back to the T-junction. And she was now absolutely certain that she'd seen someone hanging around there.

Assuming it wasn't the same person who was now here. But it couldn't be. Simply couldn't.

Deciding there was only one way to find out, she started forward, slow and steady, keeping well to the left. As she drew closer, the taller and thinner the figure looked. In fact, the more she advanced, the taller it looked than anyone. It was seven feet now, maybe eight feet.

At first Shelley wasn't just baffled but appalled. And then, very quickly, she relaxed again.

It wasn't a figure at all, but a piece of cloth hanging under a fire escape. Thanks to the gloom of these backstreets, it had briefly resembled a man. She stopped alongside it, amazed that she could ever have made such an error – only to hear a prolonged squeal of metal somewhere behind.

The gate to that small yard.

Shelley hurried on, passing the fire escape, coming to a crossroads. She had some vague notion that if she turned left it would take her towards Westgate Street, where most of the pubs and clubs were located. It wouldn't be heaving on a Thursday night, but there'd still be people around. But before she got there, the route led into a second covered area, a virtual subway passing through the guts of yet another of those unused buildings. Only the faintest light glimmered at its far end, showing that it was partially flooded. She took it anyway, struggling to keep her feet. Hanks of old cable hung down, there were cans and bits of paper scattered – chip or kebab wrappers. Surely that meant she was almost back to civilisation?

Something clanked behind her.

She spun around. Again there was no one. Shafts of moonlight cut through the planks above, dappling the spectral dimness.

Shelley pressed on. And now she could hear something. A low rumbling; an engine turning over? That had to be good news. She ran, emerging from the tunnel, turning another corner and there seeing a row of bollards, and beyond those a cobbled backstreet, and, merciful Heaven, streetlights all the way along. But not just streetlights, lights from windows too. She could even hear muffled music. She was at the rear of one of the Westgate Street pubs, she realised. Not only that, there was a taxi waiting there, its engine chugging, headlights spearing the gloom. Inside, a driver awaited his fare.

Heels clattering on the cobbles, Shelley scrambled up to

the car, a Fiat 500. The taxi driver was a young Asian guy with spiky black hair and a happy, likeable face. He was busy playing with a mobile phone, so he didn't notice her until she tapped on the passenger window. He had to power the window down and was halfway through telling her that he wasn't available before he got a proper look at the outfit beneath her coat. His eyes almost popped.

It would have been comical had she not been so frightened.

'I need to get home,' she said, trying to restrain her emotions. A panicking woman might put him off no matter how sexy she was. 'It's only a couple of miles away, so you can be back here quickly. But if it's a problem, I'll pay you double. I honestly don't mind.'

'Er . . . erm . . .' The taxi driver glanced at his watch, and then towards the pub. There was no sign of movement from its open back door.

'Come on, come on,' she chuntered.

'All right, yeah, get in.' He flipped the lock.

Shelley yanked the passenger door open.

'Where to?' he asked, ostensibly staring straight ahead, but in truth eyeing her sideways.

Everything was still on show, but Shelley didn't care as long as he got moving. 'Barnhill Crescent,' she said. 'You know that? It's in Tilton.'

'Yeah, I think so.' He put the Fiat in gear.

She finally allowed herself a sigh of relief, only to sense a flicker of movement beyond the window. She glanced around. The driver looked too, but not before there was an impact that shook the whole car. The sound of the window smashing inward was louder than Shelley could ever have imagined. Fragmented glass showered over them, and all they could do was shield their eyes. They didn't get a chance to shout or scream. Neither even saw the black-steel muzzle come jutting in at them, the thickly gloved finger depressing the trigger behind it, or the blinding glare as blazing fuel burst over them, filling the entire taxi with roaring, searing flame.

Chapter 14

A few years earlier, Heck's sister Dana had reached out to him in a determined effort to rekindle their relationship. Heck had initially responded doubtfully, feeling that as the bad blood between them could never be put right, why bother trying? But Dana had persevered, and gradually she'd broken down his resistance. It had particularly bothered him that otherwise he might never have had any participation in the life of his niece Sarah, Dana's sole child from her unsuccessful marriage. They'd slowly but surely reconstructed the bridge between them, though it was more by Dana's effort than Heck's. She now, at least as he saw it, overcompensated for what had happened by demanding that he visit them at every opportunity, that he stay with them every time he was up in the Northwest, and that he interact with them far more than he considered necessary.

'It's nice to get text messages from you on our birthdays,' she'd once said. 'And to get cards at Christmas. But talking to you on the phone at least once a week would be nicer.'

This was a warmth of spirit that Heck still found it difficult to return in full – and that wasn't just down to Dana. She was six years his senior, and when they were children she had bossed him and Tom around as mercilessly as only older sisters could. But she'd also been beautiful and vivacious and clever, which had made him proud of her among his mates, and of course, because she was a sibling rather than a parent, he'd also been able to confide in her, trust her and seek her advice on personal matters. Inevitably, he'd come to adore her – so much so that years later, when she'd sided with his father during that terrible fall-out, it had hurt him all the more. Even now, the sense of betrayal was raw in his memory. Ultimately, though, the reason he disliked coming back to 23 Cranby Street, which Dana had inherited after their mother's death, was less to do with his sister and more with that chapter of his life in which the Heckenburg family home was the epicentre.

As he regarded the house from his stationary car, it was an uninviting prospect, even without the historical baggage. Not that he had much choice at present. He climbed from the car, grab-bag in hand, and crossed the pavement. He'd half hoped the key his uncle had given him wouldn't work, but it fitted snugly and the lock turned. The door clicked open and he stepped inside.

As he'd expected, it was chilly in there, his breath vaguely visible as he walked around downstairs switching lights on. It was the archetypical terraced house: a small living room at the front, a kitchen/diner at the back, a narrow hall connecting them and a stairway in between. Upstairs, there were two bedrooms, a bathroom and a tiny boxroom. His parents had once occupied the main bedroom, while his and Tom's beds had been crammed into the second one and Dana had used the third. These days, Dana had the main room, Sarah had the second, and the boxroom was a spare. Heck had slept here once before since the big fall-out, and it had proved perfectly adequate, but he had no inclination to go upstairs and find himself a bed at present. The downstairs was spick and span, carpets vacuumed, corners dusted, everything put away or neatly in its place – Dana was almost obsessively house-proud – and despite Heck's lifelong antipathy to sleeping on couches, he only needed to enter the lounge, switch on the real-flame gas fire and feel the blast of warmth from it, to decide that he was camping out in there. The couch was large enough, a cushion would suffice for a pillow and he could get a fresh blanket from the airing cupboard at the top of the stairs. It would create minimum mess anyway, which only seemed fair to the house-owner who had no clue that he was here.

There was one possible drawback to lodging in the lounge: the photographs.

Several of these were arrayed on the mantel over the fire. The first that caught his eye was an updated image of Sarah, now well on her way to growing up, appearing smart and sensible in her school uniform, and, with her long dark hair, finally turning into the sort of looker her mother had been. Secondly, there was a more familiar shot of his parents; if he remembered rightly, it had been taken at a distant relative's wedding, and his father in particular had hated the whole event, as was evident from his unsmiling visage. In reality, they'd been an odd couple: George Heckenburg of burly, foursquare physique, with a tough look about him and slicked black hair, Mary Heckenburg small by comparison, almost petite, with refined, elfin features. Yet they had, on the whole – until *that* incident – been as good a mum and dad as anyone could reasonably hope for. The third photo depicted Heck and Tom as young children, Tom slightly bigger at that stage, both in pyjamas and grinning excitedly as they knelt amid a chaos of torn-up Christmas wrappings. Their father had always been a stern watcher of the family accounts, but they'd never lacked for anything. Christmas in particular had been a fun time back in those days. Briefly,

Heck wondered why his sister had opted to frame and display such an old picture – this one must date from 1980 at the latest – though, he realised, it was probably the only one she had showing her two younger brothers together.

He decided to turn that last one to face the wall – at least while Dana wasn't here.

But then, just as quickly, he relented.

These images were uncomfortable reminders of times past, but they weren't something Heck was unused to. Even now, he kept a scruffy old scrapbook, its charred cover mainly sticky-tape, in which he'd collected photographs of all those murder victims he'd ever got justice for during his career. They were mugshots mostly, from parties or holidays or family albums, the faces they portrayed invariably laughing or smiling, betraying no knowledge of the dreadful event creeping up on them. It never made for cosy reading. Having convicted their killers wouldn't bring them back from the dead, nor negate the pain they'd suffered – but Heck still found it instructive, a forceful reminder of why he did what he did. In comparison, all that these Heckenburg snapshots were good for was showing how great things had once been for him as opposed to how they were now. That also hit where it hurt, but alongside the scrapbook they were easily tolerable. If nothing else, Heck's photo-gallery of the doomed was a daily reminder that the past was done – no amount of tearful regret would change things there – so why stress about it?

But of course, that was a simple thing to *say*.

That night, he tossed and turned for hours underneath his single blanket. The walls of the small living room closed in on him, liquid red-gold patterns from the gas fire swarming up them and across the ceiling. The heat became intense, the air stuffy, and for a brief time the atmosphere in there was almost hellish. As he drifted in and out of tortured sleep, it was impossible to resist the flood of distorted memories with which this place was impregnated, let alone rationalise them.

And of course Tom was embroiled in all of them.

Tom – one of the most significant figures in Heck's life, and yet someone who'd only graced the stage for a very brief part of it, someone who'd been gone so long now that Heck only had the vaguest recollection of how he'd actually felt about him. He'd loved him, certainly – they were brothers after all – but he'd hated him too, at times, during those harrowing end-days when Tom was no longer the person he'd grown up with but someone completely unrecognisable.

There was no doubt that Tom himself was responsible for many of the problems that in due course tore the Heckenburg family apart. It wasn't entirely his fault that he'd become an addict. It was just that drugs were by that time everywhere, penetrating deep into the traditional working class whose domestic problems had previously owed more to alcohol abuse. Tom had initially smoked weed, but one thing led to another. By the time he was studying for his A-levels at Bradburn Tech, he was taking heroin. He dropped out without even sitting his exams, and settled down to a life of seeming inertia on what were then scanty benefits, most of which his angry father took from him anyway. They clashed relentlessly, George Heckenburg, who believed in punishment and discipline rather than rehab and counselling, resorting to ever more heavy-handed tactics, transforming the once happy home into a place of misery and conflict.

In many ways, George Heckenburg had been a good man and a stolid example to his children: a hard worker, a churchgoer, and a staunch opponent of anything anti-establishment, anything 'loutish'. But he wasn't good under pressure.

Heck would never forget the awfulness of that moment when the phone-call disturbed them just after two in the morning, everyone in the house knowing instinctively that it would involve Tom, who by then was long in the habit of staying out all night. At first it was a relief to learn that he'd merely been arrested. It could have been something much worse. But then a secondary piece of news was delivered that was infinitely more terrible: Tom wasn't just under arrest for burglary, he was also being held on suspicion of carrying out the Granny Basher crimes.

The anger and rage in the house that night, the shouting and bawling, the kicking of furniture – it had had to be heard to be believed, and it probably *had* been heard. By the neighbours at least. But losing their dignity in the eyes of those they'd known and been respected by all their lives was only the beginning of the Heckenburg's problems. Because after the anger had come the fear.

Tom's future had looked bleak before, but now suddenly it barely looked tenable.

These days, Heck knew from personal experience how much hard work and diligence it took to bring a successful prosecution against any suspect in a series of crimes as sensational as the Granny Basher attacks. And if the suspect was innocent it would be so much the harder. Back in those days, behavioural science hadn't been that big a deal. Motives were either obvious – he's a druggie who needs to score – or they were dismissed as irrelevant. Even so, it wouldn't have been easy to frame someone for a string of offences he hadn't committed. But from the start of this process Tom Heckenburg was at a big disadvantage.

He'd been out of the house on every occasion when one of those crimes had occurred, without once being able to adequately account for his movements. In most cases he hadn't been able to remember; in others there were no witnesses to corroborate his near-incoherent explanations. To make things worse, by this time he'd developed a reputation in

138

his neighbourhood for slyness and dishonesty, and of course it was known that he was an addict, which was another reason for people to take against him – nobody rushed forward to give him a character reference.

Of course, the family solicitor had been confident; Tom was innocent, so he'd be OK – it was only one year since the Birmingham Six had been exonerated on appeal, and the public had no taste for another colossal miscarriage of justice. Even then, after he was charged and remanded in custody, his distraught family were reasonably hopeful he'd be cleared. Aside from the confession, what evidence was there that wasn't circumstantial? And it was clear that his confession had only been given under duress. But, by the time they got to trial, the prosecution had remedied this shortfall. They made a very big deal of the fact that, since Tom Heckenburg had been arrested, the Granny Basher crimes had ceased. In addition, witnesses had now been found who'd seen Tom in the areas where the attacks had occurred, often in the correct timeframe. It was a sad fact that witnesses could always be found – for good or ill. Heck knew that from bitter experience. There were all kinds of reasons why people were willing to offer false testimony. But in this case they might have been telling the truth. Tom's endless nocturnal wandering in search of drugs, or the money to score drugs, was strange and worrying to those householders who happened to glance out of their bedroom window at three in the morning and see him tottering down their street. A well-used burglary kit was then produced which had been found in an allotment shed that Tom and some of his drug-addled mates had used as a shooting gallery.

After that, even Heck had briefly wondered if Tom was the real culprit, but in later years he came to realise that, even if the kit hadn't been planted by the investigation team, which he now suspected it had, there was a viable reason for it being there – Tom *was* a burglar by his own admission. But the court only had his word for it that he'd never raided actual houses, focusing instead on pubs, shops, cafeterias and the like. Who in that frenzied atmosphere, with the black and blue faces of little old ladies adorning newspaper covers for weeks on end, would believe such a preposterous defence?

And that was a big part of the problem.

The fevered press coverage, while not overtly prejudiced against Tom, had created a furore about oddballs wandering the streets at night, about creatures on the margins of society, creatures who were worthless, creatures who for whatever reason were a menace to civilisation. On that basis, the public had eagerly bought it that this thieving, druggie outcast was the guy they wanted. On reflection, Tom hadn't stood a chance.

With the fragile state he was in when he commenced his life sentence, he was never going to last very long in captivity. In fact he didn't last a month, let alone thirty years. The inquest jury was later told that Tom was raped 'about fifty times' during that short period, though in truth it was anyone's guess how much abuse he'd suffered. In reality, it was probably unquantifiable.

Little wonder he'd chosen to end it.

Even now, sweating and delirious with fatigue, Heck didn't cry. He had no tears left for this particular memory. But it was agonising to recall the arrival of that terrible news.

They'd received it here, in this very room.

The wails of anguish from his mother, his father ranting and railing at God, literally shaking his fist at the ceiling, Dana calling foul-mouthed curses on the police officers responsible, whom they were all increasingly certain had framed their loved one – a certainty that would *really* explode three weeks later on the arrest of Luke Gaskell . . .

Frustrated by the futility of this reminiscence, Heck strug-

140

gled to his feet and padded out of the room. He was only wearing shorts and was running with sweat, so the chill in the kitchen gripped him immediately. But he ignored it as he went to the sink to get a glass of water.

Why did you do it? he berated himself. *I mean, really – why would you go and do something so crass? And why did you do it the way you did . . . to announce on the occasion of your eighteenth birthday, only three years after Tom's death but in front of all your family and friends, that you'd applied to join the cops?*

It wasn't as if the law had covered itself in glory even after Tom had been posthumously acquitted. The family's disbelief knew no bounds when they were informed that the police internal enquiry was being wrapped up, having uncovered no culpability on the part of its own staff. Tom had been wrongly convicted but it was entirely accidental. It was tragic for sure, and everyone was heartily sorry about it, but circumstances had conspired against the lad, along with his own cravings and weaknesses, rather than corrupt police officers.

And once you'd done it, regret it as you might, there was no going back. Was there?

He suddenly wished Dana was here instead of overseas somewhere, enjoying a holiday. Even more so, he wished Gemma was here. He could do more than lay his head on a soft, understanding shoulder then. But after he'd washed his glass and stood it upside down on the draining board, he rubbed at his left eye with the heel of his palm, and realised that it was moist, wet even – and he was glad that neither of them was present.

Chapter 15

Bradburn Central Police Station, located on the town's Market Street, was an architectural throwback: red-brick Victorian Gothic, complete with tall, arched casements, narrow towers and steep gable roofs. It looked more like an old primary school than a police station. A horde of press vehicles, including several vans with TV aerials on top, were double-parked along the station's front. A tight access road led around the side of the building to a pound overflowing with rusting hulks, and a staff car park without an inch of space available on it.

Heck was forced to drive the adjacent streets for ten minutes, and when he got back to the station, hot under the collar and with a bright gleam of sweat on his brow, he was half an hour later than he'd wanted to be. He then had to wait a further fifteen minutes at the front counter before he was dealt with, sharing it with another bunch of unruly reporters jostling and shouting for attention. But it was while he was here that Heck heard about the double slaying the previous night.

'That's right, two more,' a female journalist was shouting into her mobile. 'A taxi driver and his fare were burned to

142

death inside his cab. Bold as you like, this flamethrower killer. Walked up and did for them both while they sat outside a town centre pub.'

Heck hadn't yet heard about this. He'd had too many other things on his mind the previous night to bother watching any news programmes. The desk clerk, a large-boned, blonde girl in the smart pale-blue uniform of the Greater Manchester Police civilian staff, finally turned to him. He straightened his tie, smiled, showed his warrant card and explained who he was.

She regarded him with something like deep scepticism before hitting a buzzer and drawling: 'First floor on the right, the old Comms Suite.'

Beyond the double-glazed personnel door, there was a forced atmosphere of business-as-usual. Phones were being answered as briskly and efficiently as ever. But now that he was actually in the heart of the building, Heck could detect a heaviness in the air. Almost certainly this was partly because of the army of pressmen outside, whose crammed-together vans and cars and noisy personnel could be glimpsed through every window, but mainly he suspected it was the nature of the crimes suddenly confronting this relatively small divisional police station. Every face he saw – officers and civvies alike – looked pale and stern.

He expected the atmosphere to be lighter in the Incident Room itself, or MIR as it was known, Operation Wandering Wolf having mostly been assembled from experienced detectives, including a number from SCU and GMP Serious, men and women from off-division who were less likely to be emotionally involved in the torment of Bradburn. He entered it through a pair of swing doors. It was a surprisingly small but compact office, lit by garish yellow strip-lights on the ceiling and smelling faintly of sweat. Though it couldn't have been in operation more than a week, it already had that stuffy, lived-in feel so typical of the average police workplace. Crime-scene photos and intelligence reports covered every wall and display board, while the desks and cabinets were laden with over-crammed baskets of files, phones, laptops and half-drunk mugs of coffee.

As Heck sidled in, a group of about twelve detectives were jammed inside, several of whom he immediately recognised as SCU officers, including Gary Quinnell and Charlie Finnegan. For the most part, they chewed on pens or wrote in their pocketbooks, while a trim young woman of about thirty stood in their midst, briefing them. She wore a black skirt-suit and black high-heeled boots, her black hair tied in a sharp knot at the back of her head, though Heck had the impression that, if untied, it would fall to extraordinary length. She was the first to glance around when he entered, turning a handsome but rather severe face towards him.

She indicated with a nod that she'd be with him shortly, so he stood awkwardly in a corner and placed his laptop on a shelf. The woman continued with the items on her agenda. Heck knew he ought to pay attention, but couldn't help glancing around, spotting two side-by-side sections at the far end of the room, which had been partitioned from the main area with glass doors and hanging blinds. Bronze Command offices, no doubt, the place from which all policies, protocols and procedures would be implemented, though where Gemma had pitched up he couldn't tell. As SIO and senior Silver Command, her pad might not even be physically connected to the MIR.

There was no sign of her either, though, given the events of the previous night, it would have been odd if she hadn't been out and about. That probably went for the rest of the taskforce too. The relative handful of officers Heck saw here probably represented only a segment of it. Quinnell and Finnegan nodded in response to Heck as his eyes roved across them. The rest ignored him.

'OK, that's it,' the dark-haired woman concluded. 'You all know where you are and what you're doing. Let's get to it.'

With scuffles of feet and a scraping of chair legs, the room came alive, bodies moving in all directions. The woman shuffled her paperwork as she approached Heck.

'So . . . DS Heckenburg?'

'Correct,' he replied.

'Katie Hayes.' She offered a slim white hand. 'DI.'

Heck shook with her. 'Pleased to meet you, ma'am.'

'Originally from GMP Serious,' she explained curtly. 'Currently deputy SIO on this bloody disaster.'

'I've heard of you, ma'am,' he said, though he'd always assumed she'd be more bullish; only last year, she had arrested and convicted a prolific kidnapper, and later secured him a full-life prison sentence.

For her own part, DI Hayes seemed equally bemused by Heck. She appraised him in detail as they stood there, eyeing him up and down unashamedly until it reached the point where he became self-conscious. He was smartly suited-up for the occasion, he'd shaved, he even had clean shoes on.

'Sorry,' she said, lips pursed. 'I'm not seeing it.'

'Ma'am?'

'I'm not seeing why your gaffer rates you so much.'

Heck couldn't help feeling vaguely abashed by that. 'I wasn't aware she did.'

'What – she goes round inventing cool-sounding jobs for all her personnel?'

'Sorry, ma'am, I don't –'

'Forget it.' She turned and headed towards the partitioned area on the left, clearly her personal office. 'It's just that I've never heard of an enquiry team having a "Minister without Portfolio" before.'

Heck ambled in awkward pursuit, only for Gary Quinnell to block his path.

'Forty-five years for Wheeler,' the big Welshman said, gripping Heck's hand in his ham-fist and pumping it. 'Good job, boyo.'

'How'd the wanker take it?' Charlie Finnegan wondered, sliding up in his usual vaguely untrustworthy fashion.

'Not like a man,' Heck said, distracted.

'Hah, tough shit,' Finnegan sneered. 'He's going to have to learn to, though, isn't he?'

Heck would normally have shared in such dark humour, but memories of Tom again invaded his head and he merely nodded as he diverted across the room to the open door of DI Hayes's office. Its interior was quite small but nevertheless crammed with much more office equipment than it had been designed to hold, not to mention stacks of files and other documentation, all of which overburdened its high shelves to the point where it looked as though an avalanche of paper would shortly engulf the room.

The DI herself stood by her desk, again skimming through files.

'Erm . . . Minister without Portfolio is a kind of SCU quirk, ma'am,' he said.

'Yeah?' She no longer seemed especially interested. 'What does it mean precisely?'

He shrugged. 'It means I have a watching brief on the whole enquiry, I pick up any slack, I fill in here and there . . . wherever I'm needed. It also gives me time to generate my own leads and, if necessary, chase them down. Really it just means that I'm a lead-investigator. That I have a roving commission. I work the streets, I work the snouts, the crims . . .'

She glanced around. 'So you're a thief-taker?'

'I get a few collars, yeah.'

'And apparently you're local?' She'd clearly been thoroughly briefed about the role Heck would be playing here,

146

but there was obviously a pecking order and she wanted to establish it from the off.

'I was born and raised in Bradburn, ma'am, yes.'

'And yet somehow you ended up in the Met.'

'Well, I joined GMP originally, but I transferred south when I was two years in.'

She filched a pen from her skirt pocket and inscribed notes on the latest document. 'Any particular reason?'

He hesitated. 'Personal stuff.'

'Nothing that's going to affect your ability to function on our behalf, I trust?'

'No.'

'Good.' She straightened up from her desk. 'Well, we can always use thief-takers. God knows, I wish I had one on every street corner. And you knowing your way around is a big plus.' She sounded friendly enough in context, but her tone remained curt, brusque. 'We've got liaison attachments from local plod and divisional CID, but, as you probably know, most of Operation Wandering Wolf comprises your lot – almost none of whom come from this part of the world at all – and our lot, GMP Serious. We get over here to Bradburn every so often. There's plenty heavy crime here, but only recently at the rate of one murder a week. So a lot of *us* are still feeling our way around too.'

'I must be honest, ma'am,' Heck said. 'It's a while since I've been to this neck of the woods. I need to have a proper mooch about, if you know what I mean.'

'Yeah, well . . . you won't like everything you find. They've knocked the place down and built it up again half a dozen times since you lived here . . . as opposed to the employment rate, of course, which they knocked down and haven't bothered rebuilding at all. That doesn't make things easier from a police perspective. Lots of drinking, lots of drug-taking. And now we've got two underworld factions who appear to be scrapping it out to the death.' She sniffed, suddenly thoughtful. 'I understand you're the detective who first uncovered this torturer-for-hire, Sagan?'

Heck nodded. 'I turned up the intel that led us to his door, yeah.'

'Bit of a clusterfuck, that, wasn't it?'

'Or words to that effect, ma'am, yes.'

'Never mind.' She finally put her paperwork down. 'At present, he's only *one* member of the merry little band we're trying to take down. You *are* onside with that, by the way?' She eyed him keenly again – quite a character test she was putting him through, he realised. 'John Sagan may have shot one of your colleagues – a close one, I gather – but it's not just him we're going for. We're after the whole lot of them.'

'I understand that, ma'am.'

'We've got seven murder victims already, and that figure's likely to increase.'

'That's fine, ma'am. Let's go get 'em.'

'Ready to pitch straight in, then?'

'Ready and willing.'

'DSU Piper said you would be.' DI Hayes leaned across her desk and picked up another pile of bulging buff folders, bound together with several elastic bands. 'She's currently at the crime scene off Westgate Street, by the way. You're aware there were two more flamethrower deaths last night?'

'Yep.'

'How much do you know?'

'Only what I overheard at the front of the nick,' Heck said. 'Presumably you guys can fill me in on the rest?'

'Best if you fill yourself in.' She handed him the armful of folders. 'From this lot. It's a potted history of the enquiry to date . . . obviously minus any leads or evidence that may have come in over the last hour or so.'

A cursory downward glance revealed that the folders were

packed with documentation; crime reports, photos and witness statements, not just relating to the homicides the previous night, but most likely to all those committed so far, possibly with additional notes and observations from crime-scene examiners and other specialists.

Perhaps pre-empting an objection, DI Hayes spoke again.

'The policy file's available for perusal too. Hard copy or online. Good luck, though – it's already the size of the Yellow Pages. The main thing is Miss Piper wants you to fully familiarise yourself with the case overall. That makes sense, doesn't it, DS Heckenburg?' She pinned him with a cool but satisfied stare. 'You being our Minister without Portfolio.'

'Ma'am –' he tried not to object too volubly '– this'll take me all day. I'd rather just get out there and –'

'Yeah, Miss Piper said you probably would. She also told me to ensure I didn't listen to any, quote, "flim-flam", and fully authorised me to pull rank in any way I see fit to ensure that you fully comply with her instructions. Not that I would need authorisation, would I, *Sergeant*, being as I'm your official line manager?'

'No, ma'am, you wouldn't.'

'Good.' She pointed out through the open door across the MIR to the far opposite corner, into which a desk had been shoehorned, though it was so small that there'd be just enough room on it for his laptop, with a beaker of tea on the shelf behind. 'That's your desk over there. Now, you won't need a slide-rule to know that from where I sit in here, if I keep the door open, which I will, I'll have a perfect line of vision . . . and will know the exact moment you stand up and try to go somewhere else.'

'With all respect, ma'am, what if I need a pee?'

'You can go for a pee anytime you like. It's just down the corridor.' She smiled. 'So long as you get through this lot first.'

'Can I at least get a brew?' he asked.

'Course you can. The tea-making kit's in the opposite corner to your desk. You can make me one while you're at it.' She pulled her chair out and sat down, booting up her desktop, their business seemingly done. 'Oh, milk and half a teaspoon of sugar.'

He moved stiffly to the door.

'And DS Heckenburg?'

He glanced back. She was watching him intently.

'That's *half* a teaspoon, not three quarters. Trust me. I'll know the difference.'

Chapter 16

Heck wasn't sure if DI Hayes's determination to put him in his place before they had any chance to get off on the wrong foot meant she suffered from some kind of inferiority complex – though he doubted this after her score the previous year – or if she was only doing Gemma's handiwork, the SIO having advised her that Heck could be very useful to a murder enquiry but only if they kept him on a tight leash.

If it was the latter, he didn't object to it per se. He knew he'd caused Gemma problems in the past. It wasn't that he was naturally insubordinate or disobedient, but he could never resist making his own running if he felt the official line was off-track – which was an increasing cause of concern to his gaffer, as she feared it implied to others that their former relationship as boyfriend and girlfriend was limiting her control over him. It had probably only been a matter of time before she'd decided to give him a babysitter. But he wasn't going to let it be an issue at present. One thing both Gemma and DI Hayes had been right about: he needed to familiarise himself with the case first, and so he got stuck into it.

However, as he dug through the new reams of paperwork

he'd been given, it rapidly became clear how complex this business was, and how distressing.

The previous killings he was already familiar with, though the extra documentation filled in the remaining blanks – in the most intricate and gruesome detail, several new aspects of it catching his eye in particular. The most recent incident, the double-header the night before, was no less horrific than the others. The two latest victims – Shelley Harper, who was 36, and Nawaz Gilani, 22 – had been attacked while seated in Gilani's taxi cab at the rear of the Stags n Hens bar on Westgate Street. They'd literally been engulfed in several gallons of burning petrol, which had been sprayed at them through a smashed window via a jet-stream system, which yet again was most likely to have been a military-style flame-thrower. The resulting fire had raged with such heat and fury that the car had been reduced to blistered wreckage long before the Fire Brigade arrived, even though they were called to the scene by people inside the pub relatively quickly. By then, the bodies had ceased to resemble anything human. The crime-scene photos displayed twisted, blackened manne-quins partially melted into the charred interior.

Gilani had been identified speedily because the car was still recognisable from its chassis number, while Harper was traced through the Renault Clio parked at the back of the Town Hall, for which the burned female corpse possessed a key. Forensic analysis of the female corpse had also revealed fragments of the 'Our Mavis' costume that Harper had been wearing that evening. There was a growing hypothesis that Nawaz Gilani had been the main target and that Shelley Harper had got involved by accident. This assumption appeared to stem from the none too fantastical belief that certain taxi drivers were known to make illegal late-night deliveries – drugs, prostitutes and the like.

But already Heck was unconvinced by that.

To start with, Gilani had no form. He came from a respectable family and was never known to have been in trouble in his life. Secondly, his taxi had been booked in advance, and by a customer in the pub – not by Shelley Harper. This meant she'd grabbed it opportunistically, even though her own car was just around the corner and apparently in full serviceable condition. Which was suspicious behaviour on her part, to say the least.

There'd been no post-mortem on either body yet, so there was no way to tell if the woman had been drinking – that might explain why she'd gone looking for a taxi – but several people who'd attended the drinks function after the unveiling ceremony had already been interviewed, and none had seen her take a drop of alcohol. So why had she ignored her own vehicle? It wasn't as if she might have forgotten where she'd left it, or had missed her way in the dark – reportedly, she'd left the Town Hall halfway through the party by one of its rear exits, which meant that she'd have walked right past the parked Clio.

The most obvious explanation was that someone had physically prevented Harper from getting into her car. Could the killer have followed her out of the Town Hall maybe? That seemed unlikely given the equipment he loaded himself down with – body armour, a petrol tank in a harness, a flamethrower no less. More likely he'd scoped out her vehicle and had been waiting there for her. At that late hour, there'd have been no one else around – she might have been about to climb into the car, had suddenly been confronted by this terrifying figure, and ran. That would also explain why she'd appeared at the rear of Stags n Hens rather than at the front; to do that, she'd have had to thread through a maze of unlit backstreets late at night, but if she'd been running from someone that would be more understandable.

Of course, on the face of it none of this made much sense.

153

As far as Heck could tell, Shelley Harper had been a local model, beauty queen and wannabe actress. She'd done one nude spread a long time in the past, but that had strictly been softcore. She hardly matched the victimology of the others. He spotted one notation appended to the crime report by DI Hayes, which wondered whether she might have had some connection to Vic Ship through her regular attendance on the Manchester club scene. Could she have worked for him as an escort girl maybe? Could she have been one of his many mistresses, or mistress to one of his cronies?

This was good thinking by Hayes; such a theory was far from implausible, but it was pure imagination at present.

Heck pondered Shelley Harper. As yet there was no portrait taken of her before she'd died. She was unmarried, had no children and her parents were both dead. She had one alternative other: a certain Jake Witherspoon, her on-off boyfriend. Apparently she'd had a stormy relationship with him, but it had never been known to result in violence – at least, none that had been reported to the police. In any case, Witherspoon had already been interviewed and had a rock-solid alibi for the previous night.

As Heck perused all this stuff and mulled over possibilities, the landline on his desk rang.

'Incident Room,' he said, still distracted. 'DS Heckenburg.'

'Ah,' Gemma's voice said. 'You've finally graced us with your presence?'

'I graced you with my presence about two hours ago, only to be told –'

'I'm in no mood for lip, by the way. I wanted you fully *au fait* with this case before you actually got started. Now is that all right with you?'

Heck straightened in his seat. 'Yes, ma'am, of course.'

'Good. How soon can you meet me at the Queen Alexandra Infirmary? I'm in the mortuary at present.'

He shuffled the paperwork. 'I think I'm ready to come now.'

'Good. Foot to the floor, if you don't mind.'

*

When Heck arrived at the Queen Alexandra Infirmary, or Bradburn Infirmary as it was known locally, it was almost noon. This was a lowering Edwardian structure, first opened in 1909, but it had been extensively redeveloped over the decades since and now comprised many departments. The entrance to the Infirmary mortuary proved elusive. Heck finally rang Gemma on her mobile and was directed around to the rear of the building. The mortuary attendant who showed him in, a towering, ox-like youngster with sloped shoulders and a huge jaw covered in fuzzy red stubble, was busy chomping on an immense bap, which looked to have been crammed with ham, lettuce and mustard, specks of which rained down onto his white scrubs. He led Heck to a cool, white-tiled chamber with walls of stainless-steel refrigerator cabinets to the right and left, and two porcelain slabs in the centre, both currently occupied by horizontal forms covered in opaque plastic sheets. The place was thickly scented with the usual combo of bleach and formaldehyde.

Without even bothering to put a glove on, and without any request from Heck, the attendant drew back the first sheet. 'These are last night's two fatalities,' he said, his mouth half full of ham and bread. 'This is the female.'

There wasn't much left that was even vaguely identifiable as human, or that wasn't black and crisp as an overdone steak. Heck had seen much in his many years of detective work, but this kind of thing never ceased to hit him in the pit of his stomach. The stench of burned, melted flesh didn't help much either. Voices now distracted him. He glanced over his shoulder as Gemma and another officer, both clad in disposable white smocks, came in through a side door.

'Nasty mess a flamethrower makes, eh?' the attendant said, still chewing.

'So long as it doesn't put you off your lunch.' Heck turned to Gemma. 'Ma'am?'

'Can you give us some space, Mel?' she told the attendant.

He dropped the sheet and stumped away. Heck now realised that he recognised the other officer; it was DI Ron Gibbshaw from the Organised Crime Division, which was a surprise.

'What do you think?' Gemma asked Heck.

'I think I'm glad I only had a cup of coffee for breakfast.'

'Well, it's not going to get any better, not in the short term.' She planted her hands on her hips. 'The rate these poor sods are coming in, the hospital's agreed to reserve this entire section of the mortuary for our use. So, we've got those APs believed to be victims of Vic Ship's faction on this wall –' she indicated the righthand cabinets, before turning to the left '– and those thought down to Shaughnessy's faction on this one.'

Heck indicated the twosome occupying the slabs. 'And this pair smack-bang in the middle.'

'That's partly because they haven't been fully examined yet. But also because we haven't completely confirmed they're connected to the case.'

He nodded. 'Well, looks like we've got it all organised.'

'What we've actually got here, DS Heckenburg,' Gibbshaw said, disgruntled, 'is a complete bloody nightmare. We're on a gangland battlefield that's going to keep us all occupied for a very long time.'

Heck eyed the guy warily. He supposed it was inevitable that Gemma would have given in to the pressure eventually. It wasn't just that OC had been stridently demanding some

156

involvement in the case, but it would have been preposterous not to attach them at least in some capacity, given that gangster-related homicides were their speciality. Thus far, though, Gemma appeared to have been true to her word. Ron Gibbshaw was the only OC officer Heck had seen since he'd arrived here. He held high rank, of course; possibly he was even joint-DSIO with Katie Hayes, but most likely that was the compromise that had been reached.

It was just about bearable, Heck decided.

He knew Gibbshaw reasonably well. He was a typical OC guy, big, burly, time-served and, despite haggard features – tired eyes, a scruffy beard and thin, greying hair – he was an adversarial character, argumentative and opinionated, but he'd know a thing or two about the underworld and would be keen to put Reg Cowling's murderer behind bars.

'It's certainly a tangled web,' Gemma said. 'At present, no one at all is talking.'

'Unsurprising if *this* is the outcome,' Heck replied.

'The assassins on both sides are being ultra-careful. We've no forensics thus far. The CCTV from the canal is the only physical evidence we've acquired and it tells us precisely squat.'

'Well, it tells us this flamethrower man's working alone,' Heck said. The other two glanced quizzically at him. 'I haven't seen it yet, admittedly, but according to the report, it depicts one assailant with no sign of a back-up team.'

'Professional hitmen often work alone,' Gibbshaw pointed out.

Heck mused. This wasn't entirely his own experience, not when those hitmen were targeting fellow mobsters.

'What are you saying?' Gemma asked. 'That you *don't* think these burnings are down to Lee Shaughnessy?'

'Shaughnessy's our best bet at present,' Heck had to admit. In truth, he couldn't think of anyone else it was more likely to be. Self-evidently there was a war being waged here, one ultra-violent act having kick-started a succession of retaliatory strikes. But it still didn't entirely add up. He glanced at the two shrouded forms on the nearby slabs, the blackened, twisted things that had once been human. If the flamethrower man was part of Shaughnessy's crew, they were going very overboard with this.

'Has anyone, you know –' he shrugged '– spoken to Shaughnessy?'

'Of course we've spoken to him,' Gibbshaw said. 'He doesn't know anything about it. And he's shocked and mortified that anyone could have been so cruel to his good mates Calum Price and Dean Lumley.'

Heck could just picture the snot-nosed little bastard looking po-faced and pious as he made this calm response to intense questioning.

'But it's a mess,' Gemma said. 'We don't even know where Harper and Gilani fit in.'

'Or even if they're connected to the case,' Gibbshaw added, reiterating a point the SIO had made earlier.

'You don't seriously think we've got two flamethrower killers in Bradburn?' Heck said.

'We don't know it was a flamethrower on this occasion,' Gemma replied. 'As I said before, we need confirmation. The CSIs are still examining the car – what's left of it. All we've really got until they report back is a standard case of arson with intent to endanger life. It could have been a Molotov cocktail that was used.'

Heck was unimpressed by that possibility, but he knew she had to cover all bases. 'Either way, ma'am . . . I've read the preliminary theses, and I wouldn't spend too much time looking into the taxi driver's past.'

'Why?'

'Let me rephrase,' he said. 'I'd allocate at least as much

time to looking at Shelley Harper. And I guess you think that too, because I rang Eric Fisher on the way up over here from the nick, asking him to do just that, and he told me you'd got onto him earlier, asking for the same.'

'And ground gained nil,' she replied. 'At least so far. Superficially at least, neither Harper or Gilani have got connections to the Manchester underworld.'

'More puzzling to me is that it isn't tit-for-tat,' Heck said. 'At least not so far.'

'How do you mean?' Gibbshaw asked.

'If the firebug is on Shaughnessy's side,' Heck said, 'which at present we assume he is, he just keeps on prodding, doesn't he? I mean, Shaughnessy appears to have provoked this whole thing with the sex-shop attack on March 7 – that in itself seems odd to me, given that he's the smaller fish. In return, he lost two of his own men a couple of weeks later. He's struck back since then, when that dealer was killed by the canal. But now he appears to have struck again. And this weapon, this flamethrower – it's more than vicious. They tried to outlaw flamethrowers even during World War Two, didn't they? What I'm saying is, it's like Shaughnessy's doing everything he can to goad a much bigger outfit. And he isn't even waiting his turn any more.'

Gibbshaw shrugged. 'It's a war. These goons don't follow codes of chivalry, like "first it was your turn, sir, and now it's mine".'

'It's not a matter of chivalry,' Heck argued, 'it's a matter of common sense. Shaughnessy's small-time compared to Ship. And Ship isn't just going to go away because it gets rough. He's already got Sagan on board, he's got the Russians . . .'

'You're assuming these people are as sane as the rest of us,' Gemma said.

'I don't know, ma'am. These low-level hoodlums, they

always have a kind of animal cunning, a survival instinct. They tend to steer away from anything that could really damage them, let alone destroy them outright.'

She considered this. 'We're starting to think that Shaughnessy's willingness to fight Ship is down to the Incinerator himself.'

'The Incinerator?' Heck said.

'Your firebug,' Gibbshaw replied. 'The press have already dubbed him "the Incinerator".'

Heck pondered this, fascinated. OK, it was only a moniker – yet another sensationalist nickname dreamed up by an enterprising journalist – but it reinforced the image in his mind that this flamethrower-wielding maniac might be a lone-wolf operator.

'Let's face it,' Gibbshaw added, 'they don't need some fancy torturer like Sagan on their books if they've got this guy. He's just as terrifying, just as effective.'

'Surely the flamethrower itself is some kind of lead?' Heck said. 'Have we ever heard of any other flamethrower attack anywhere else in the UK? Is it even possible that someone like Shaughnessy could have access to one, let alone someone who'd know how to use it?'

'The thesis is that he's somehow acquired this equipment and this knowledge, and that this in itself is what's emboldened him to attack Ship,' Gemma said.

'You mean he suddenly feels he has strength in his corner and he's just going for it?'

'Attacking again and again, hoping to do as much damage to the Manchester firm as possible.'

'You mean before they obliterate him once and for all?'

She looked frustrated. 'Like I said, it's a confusing mess, and at present we've barely penetrated it.'

'And just out of interest, where's Sagan while all this is happening?' Heck asked.

'We haven't got a lead on Sagan as yet.'

'Some of us aren't even one hundred per cent convinced he's here,' Gibbshaw grunted.

'Oh, he's here, sir . . . somewhere,' Heck countered. 'I can feel it.'

'You can *feel* it.' Gibbshaw snorted. 'Great, cool. To hell with all those time-consuming criminal investigation procedures.'

'It stands to reason, sir.'

'It doesn't stand to reason at all,' Gibbshaw retorted. 'Ship's the kingpin up here. Why would he hire a private contractor? He's not just got his own gun-hands, he's got the Ruskies too.'

Heck shrugged. 'Perhaps to distance himself from the actual murders. He's an obvious suspect, plus he's got GMP Serious on his case.'

'One thing you've always been great at, Heck, bending the facts to fit the theory.'

Gemma was about to intervene to prevent a sharp riposte when her mobile rang. She fished it from her pocket and signalled to the other two to wait, while she strode out of the room.

'What's up, Ronnie?' Heck asked Gibbshaw, when she was out of earshot. 'Outside your comfort zone? Northern accents a foreign language? Can't relax unless you're surrounded by diamond geezers?'

'Not at all,' Gibbshaw replied, looking coldly amused. 'I'm just wondering what kind of wild-goose chase you've brought us on this time. We're supposed to be looking for John Sagan, who killed one copper and put two others out of the job with critical injuries. And yet now we're sniffing around an underworld squabble in the arse-end of nowhere because you fancied popping home for a bit.'

It occurred to Heck that he'd underestimated Gibbshaw. The guy *was* keen to put Sagan in jail, but he was keener still to do it on the Organised Crime Division's terms.

'Sagan's here,' Heck assured him.

'There's not a shred of evidence to suggest he is.'

Heck thumbed at the wall of cabinets on the right. 'Those two jerks over there were chloroformed. All Sagan's other victims were chloroformed too.'

'You can get chloroform anywhere on the black market. It's hardly a smoking gun.'

'We had a tip-off.'

'Yeah . . .' The shadow of a smile crossed Gibbshaw's face. 'I'd love to know who from. Someone reliable this time, I hope, not some psycho bitch with an axe to grind.'

'Well, if you're not happy with this gig, Ronnie, why don't you just butt out? I'm sure Gemma won't mind. You're only here as a sop to your own bosses anyway, to stop them whingeing to Joe Wullerton.'

Joe Wullerton was official Director of the National Crime Group, not just the overall commander but a diplomatic mediating power when its various constituent parts – the Serial Crimes Unit, the Organised Crime Division and the Kidnap Squad – jockeyed with each other for resources or just about anything else they could think of. Thus far since his appointment, he'd proved sympathetic towards Gemma's investigations, but he was a politician too – he had to be to wield such power and influence – and his support was not always guaranteed.

'Yeah, you'd like that, wouldn't you?' Gibbshaw sneered. 'One less beady eye fixed on you. I mean, we can hardly rely on Piper to do that, can we? Everyone knows you've got her wrapped round your little finger. Or is it your middle finger – or is it your two middle fingers?'

'You fucking slimeball . . .'

'What's going on?' Gemma said, re-entering and finding them squared up to each other.

'Nothing, ma'am.' Heck stepped back.

162

'Nothing? Are we dick-measuring already, even with this carnage lying around us?'

Heck looked sheepish. 'Different viewpoints on how we should proceed, that's all.'

Gibbshaw nodded, as if this was exactly the truth of it.

She gazed at them both with severity, knowing they were lying, her worst fears perhaps confirmed that an Organised Crime Division officer, still hurting from the loss of his friend, was likely to cause friction with those SCU officers he might indirectly blame for it.

'Anything good, ma'am?' Heck asked.

'As a matter of fact, yes, there is – on two fronts. First of all, Eric Fisher has just emailed us a load of bumph concerning Shelley Harper. It seems she *is* connected to Vic Ship's firm. She was once a hostess at one of his clubs. Later on, she became his mistress. That relationship ended long ago, but it's a clear connection.'

'And it won't go down at all well that someone's just burned her alive,' Heck said.

'If we thought this fight was nasty before . . .' Gibbshaw concurred.

'What's the second bit of news, ma'am?'

'It seems we've acquired some CCTV footage from last night. It shows a car belonging to Marvin Langton leaving the area where the Harper and Gilani burnings occurred – and at roughly the right time.'

'Seeing as Langton once used fire during a Wild Bunch attack, he seems a very viable suspect in this case, ma'am,' Gibbshaw said, though he still sounded frustrated – as well he might, given that he was here primarily to catch Sagan, not the Incinerator.

'Langton's used fire before?' Heck asked.

'Once,' Gemma replied. 'Seems he firebombed a Manchester nightclub when there were people inside it.'

163

'Different MO,' Heck observed. 'But OK, I see the link.'

'He's the most big-time of all these Bradburn sewer rats,' Gibbshaw said. 'If anyone's going to take the fight to Vic Ship, it's likely to be him.'

Gemma didn't initially reply. She was thinking hard.

'So do we stick an obbo on him?' Gibbshaw asked. 'See what his next move is?'

'He may not be their only killer,' Heck said. 'We could be sitting for days watching Langton, and in the meantime another one of them could go off and burn someone else.'

'And even if it is Langton, close target surveillance won't stop Ship and Sagan retaliating,' Gemma said. 'We'll have corpses up to our navels. I want to hit them hard – get right into their guts and end this thing now.'

'So we lock Langton up,' Heck said. 'I know it feels like a kneejerk. But we've got more than enough to pull him in on suspicion, and he's a mercenary anyway, not a loyalist. Who knows, we get him in a quiet room somewhere, and his allegiance might shift. He talks enough, and this gang war's over by next weekend.'

Gemma eyed him carefully before switching her gaze to Gibbshaw, who shrugged.

'OK,' she said. 'We make an early arrest.'

Chapter 17

'First thing yesterday we started checking road camera footage shot around the town centre on Thursday night,' DI Hayes explained as she drove. 'To see if anyone appeared who we recognised.'

'And Marvin Langton did?' Heck said.

'Langton drives a blue Hyundai i40 saloon. One such, with matching reg, was spotted heading south along Romney Avenue – away from the town centre towards Gulwick Green, which is where he lives. That was just before eleven-thirty.'

'An hour and a half after the attack.'

'Correct.'

She circled a roundabout, barely braking despite the wet conditions.

It was early, the crack of dawn, and a Saturday, so there weren't too many other vehicles around. The bulk of the police convoy – a bunch of unmarked cars carrying a number of Wandering Wolf detectives, two Tactical Support Unit vans with a bunch of armoured PCs with riot gear riding inside them, and two divisional uniform units, the response car and a prisoner transport – had no problem staying in formation.

Heck and Hayes were just behind Gemma and DI Gibbshaw, who rode on point in the command car. All those present, CID as well as uniforms, wore body armour marked with POLICE logos, and hi-vis, chequer-banded baseball caps. While Hayes drove, Heck assessed a sheaf of paperwork. It primarily comprised intelligence reports from the Longsight Division in inner Manchester, many of which related to Marvin Langton during his days as a Wild Bunch soldier.

He read quickly, turning page after page. In 2007, Langton had commenced a five-year prison sentence (of which he eventually served three) for committing arson with intent to endanger human life. He'd petrol-bombed the entry hall to a nightclub popular with a criminal faction at odds with the Wild Bunch. The door staff had managed to extinguish the flames before anyone was injured, but eighty grand's worth of damage was still caused.

Knowing this already, Heck turned more pages.

Of all Lee Shaughnessy's current crew, Marvin Langton, whose curious metal-grey eyes peered amusedly out from this latest mugshot, seemed a reasonable candidate for the Incinerator crimes, but Heck still had reservations.

During his Wild Bunch days, Langton had been notoriously brutal, and was suspected to have been involved in several murders. He hadn't been convicted of anything for a few years now, not since his move to Bradburn, but it was inconceivable that so prolific a gun-hand would lay his weapons down overnight, especially now that he was involved with another underworld crew. And, flamethrower or not, firebombing a crowded nightclub revealed an excessive lack of regard for human life.

'He won't break easily,' Hayes said. 'Langton, I mean. In 2011, the Wild Bunch leadership went down for long jail terms, mainly for drugs and guns offences. Langton was an enforcer, but elbows-deep in the violence, as that nightclub

166

incident illustrates. Trouble is there was nothing else we could prove against him. He certainly wouldn't cough to anything, and he wouldn't take a deal either. Deadpan in the interviews, wouldn't name names . . . a good soldier to the end.'

'And presumably no one else would name *his* name.'

She shrugged. 'That's the advantage of having a rep like his, isn't it? Who's going to dob you in? They might end up in the same cell . . . wouldn't that be fun?'

Heck pondered. 'Seems odd – that he's involved in all that, manages to get away scot-free, only to willingly get himself involved in all this.'

'Won't know any other way, will he? This is his life, his career.'

'I mean the flamethrower thing. Five murders in as many weeks? That's pretty extreme.'

'It's clear that him and Shaughnessy fell out badly with Vic Ship. Revenge can be quite a motivator.'

Heck was still unconvinced. 'Langton's a professional. So . . . what's his endgame here? What does he expect the outcome's going to be?'

She glanced sidelong at him as she drove. 'You're now having second thoughts? I thought it was your idea to lock him up?'

'No second thoughts, ma'am.' Heck closed the paperwork and stuffed it into the glovebox. 'I've always been of the opinion that you can learn at least as much from suspects you don't charge as suspects you do.'

'Well . . . whatever the hell that means, now's your chance to put it to the test.'

They swung onto the rambling, run-down housing estate called Gulwick Green. This wasn't the worst of Bradburn's many sink estates, but it had plenty of social problems, and crowds of stone-throwing youths had been known to gather in response to a police presence, though it was hoped that the earliness of the hour and the on/off rain would put paid to that today. There was certainly no one about as, one by one, the police vehicles switched off their headlights and glided into the cul-de-sac where Langton's downstairs flat was located.

By prearrangement, all conversations were silenced, doors were opened quietly, boots landed on pavements with extreme stealth. Still nothing stirred. Within seconds, everyone was in position.

Heck waited on the other side of the road with Gibbshaw, while the arrest team, which consisted of Gemma herself, Hayes, Gary Quinnell and several other detectives, muscled their way up the front path to Langton's ground-floor flat, three burly bodies from the first TSU, all of whom were equipped with visored helmets, shortened riot shields and staves, marching in front. The most physically impressive of the lot – a TSU officer who had to be six-foot-eight minimum – wielded the so-called 'love hammer', the front door exploding inward on its first impact.

With much shouting, the team piled inside, reappearing less than three minutes later, marching Marvin Langton between them, his hands cuffed behind his back, Hayes providing him with the verbal caution. The prisoner was only wearing trainers, shorts and a T-shirt. Clearly he'd been tucked up in bed. A girl in her late teens, with tousled hair and smeared make-up, appeared in the ground-floor window, naked except for the quilt she'd wrapped around herself.

In the flesh, Marvin Langton looked every inch the bruiser he was supposed to be. He had that ex-boxer's build, his squat, heavily muscled form implying raw power. However, he was grinning as if this was all a big joke, his single gold tooth glinting.

Gemma emerged behind them, talking with some of her

underlings. She broke off to signal the search team, which comprised both uniforms and CID. They advanced across the road, now suited up in protective clothing. They would turn the flat and any associated outbuildings or garages upside down in their efforts to find incriminating evidence – the flamethrower itself would be an obvious prize, but also petrol or petrol canisters, other weapons, body armour, the modified motorbike helmet the Incinerator had been seen to wear during the canalside attack, and any clothing they could send to the lab to be checked for traces of petrol, smoke damage or blowback splinters from Nawaz Gilani's shattered window.

A prisoner transport reversed around the corner, its rear doors and the cage doors within swinging open. Langton was placed inside without fuss. Officers from the second TSU formed a watchful cordon around the vehicle and the front of Langton's flat, shields hefted, though, aside from a few curious faces now appearing at the windows of the tenements opposite, there was no sign of activity.

'Good clean pinch,' Heck said, as Hayes approached him.

'Too clean, if you want my opinion.'

The transport's rear doors slammed shut, and it pulled away quickly.

'How did he reply to caution?' he asked.

'Laughed,' she said.

'Standard bravado.'

'Yeah, I know.' She looked troubled.

'What's the matter?'

'He didn't seem surprised. It was like he'd been expecting us.'

'Well, he *would* be, presumably . . . at some point.'

'Which is what's *really* bugging me,' she said. 'It'd be weird enough provoking a war with a crew that's bigger than yours. But to do it in the open? Right under the noses of the cops? Make yourselves the prime suspects?'

169

Heck shrugged. 'Crims are not always the sharpest tools in the box.'

Hayes shook her head. 'That doesn't apply to Marvin Langton or Lee Shaughnessy. They're sharper than this. Usually.'

Heck realised that he couldn't fault her logic in that regard.

*

'What?' Langton chuckled. 'So it's illegal now to pay tribute to a great old comedian?'

'Terry Bayber fan, are you, Marvin?' Gemma wondered.

She and Gibbshaw faced the prisoner across the interview-room table. Langton, having had his hands swabbed for petrol, was in the mandatory custody suit. A duty solicitor sat alongside him, scribbling in a pad.

Heck, Hayes and several others watched from the VDU room, a small closet of a chamber attached to the MIR, with several video screens, one of them wired to receive live feeds from the interview rooms.

Langton laughed again. 'Me? I love all classic comedy.'

'So what's the name of the Terry Bayber character that town centre statue portrays?' Gemma said.

'I said I'm a fan, not an expert. Look, all I was doing was going and watching the unveiling . . . what's the big deal?'

'That's the only reason you were in town last night?' Gibbshaw said. 'To watch the grand unveiling?'

Langton shrugged. 'Sure.'

'Who was that girl in your flat this morning, Marvin?' Gemma asked.

'Ah . . . Sandy. She's pretty new, but she's hot stuff, if you know what I mean. And before you ask, she's well old enough – she's nineteen. Going on thirty-nine, actually.' He winked. 'What she doesn't know, I'll tell you.'

'Did you take her with you?' Gibbshaw asked. 'To watch the unveiling?'

'How do you mean?'

'It's a simple question, Marvin,' Gemma said. 'Did you take your girlfriend with you when you went to see the Terry Bayber statue last night?'

'Or did you go on your own?' Gibbshaw said. 'Which would seem even weirder to me than you going in the first place.'

Langton sat back. 'On my own last night. Sand doesn't live with me. Just see her now and then.'

'So what time did she roll up at your place?' Gemma asked. 'Middle of the night? Early hours of the morning?'

'Waiting for me when I got home. She's got her own key.'

Heck knew what the interviewers were driving at. If they could find a reason to pull Sandy in, it would be interesting to see if the two stories matched. No doubt Langton would have prepped her beforehand, but if she was only a teenager she might struggle under the pressure of a full interrogation. That said, Langton didn't seem concerned.

'Where did you park last night?' Gemma asked.

'Erm . . . Goose Lane.'

'What time did you arrive and what time did you leave?'

'Got there around seven-thirty. Left . . . I dunno, sometime after eleven.'

'You know Goose Lane car park is covered by security cameras? We can verify that.'

'Good . . . so I can go home, yeah?'

'The unveiling was done and dusted by nine o'clock,' Gibbshaw said. 'How come you only headed home two and a half hours later?'

'Had a couple of drinks in a couple of bars. No alcohol though. I was driving.' Langton grinned again, his tooth a gold chip among pearls. 'Gotta respect the law.'

The bastard had covered all bases, Heck realised. Even if Langton *was* the Incinerator, he was a pro; he'd have set up alibis to protect himself, probably involving local bar staff, local barflies.

'You'll need to give us the names of the bars you went in,' Gibbshaw said.

Langton began to reel these details off, at which point Heck decided he'd seen enough. They'd been at this two hours now, and patently were getting nowhere. Langton looked as if he was enjoying himself. They could detain him for the full 24, but on this basis it seemed a slam-dunk he'd hold out – even if he was guilty, which Heck increasingly suspected he wasn't.

He left the MIR, walked down the passage, through the station canteen and into the rec room. This was a large, messy area with windows overlooking the road outside. There was a coffee table in one corner and a flat-screen TV in the other. Armchairs were ranged all over the place, littered with that day's newspapers. As they were between refs breaks, there was nobody present. Heck grabbed himself a coffee from the vending machine in the corner, strode to the windows and looked down. Additional press activity was now taking place on the station forecourt as word had got out that someone was in custody, journalists milling around, vans with TV antennae and satellite dishes on the top double-parked along the road.

As Heck had expected, the drink was very hot and very tasteless, but for a moment or two he barely noticed as he ruminated on everything they knew so far.

On the face of it, it was a reasonable assumption that if anyone in Shaughnessy's crew was operating the flame-thrower, it would be Marvin Langton. His casual demeanour on arrest could easily be a double bluff – he wouldn't be the first to pretend he had nothing to worry about in an effort to con his captors. By the same token, he was experienced, a player, he'd definitely be organised enough to cover his tracks, at the very least ensuring there was nothing incriminating on his own premises. But if Langton had been responsible for the murders of Shelley Harper and Nawaz Gilani, would he really have driven into the middle of Bradburn, where he planned to launch the ambush, in his own car? And again, Heck was nagged by that issue of someone like Lee Shaughnessy deliberately picking a fight with someone like Vic Ship, whose crime family was much larger and better resourced, especially as that fight now seemingly involved the torching of Ship's former squeeze.

That wasn't a challenge to a scrap as much as an invitation to Armageddon.

And that was another thing. Langton might not have been expecting the police this morning, but he clearly hadn't been expecting anyone else either. There'd been no guns in his flat, no armed guards in the area, and yet surely if he'd burned Vic Ship's girlfriend only the previous evening, he might have anticipated that the Manchester mob would come looking for him directly. And then . . .

Speak of the bleeding devil, Heck thought, suddenly spotting a vehicle he recognised.

It sat separately from the chaos of press and TV vans, on the other side of the road from the police station. Heck initially noticed it because it was parked illegally, but quickly realised that it was a white Mazda CX-5, with a number of men inside.

According to the intel file, Lee Shaughnessy drove a white CX-5.

There'd even been an accompanying photograph of it – and this was the same vehicle.

Knowing this was an opportunity that likely wouldn't come again, he threw the foul coffee away, unstrapped his

Kevlar vest – the less attention he drew from the press outside the better – and hurried downstairs in his shirt and tie, leaving the nick by the side personnel door. The press pack were still too distracted to notice him. He sidled through their ranks, and crossed the road in nonchalant fashion. The occupants of the CX-5 didn't notice him either. They remained unaware until he toddled right up to them, hunkered down by the driver's door and tapped on the window.

A face spun to look at him. All conversation inside the car ceased.

Heck grinned. There was no mistaking who he was looking at. It was exactly the same face in the file, the same face he'd seen plastered on every display board in the MIR.

'If it isn't the living legend that is Lee Shaughnessy.' Heck planted his warrant card on the glass and indicated for Shaughnessy to wind the window down. Shaughnessy made no such move – not at first, which gave Heck a chance to look the rest of them over.

There were five in total, and though he didn't like admitting stuff like this, they spooked him. If there was one thing even hardened coppers hated to associate with violent crime, it was the very young – because though the faces packed inside the Mazda were not exactly juveniles, he doubted there was one among them, with the exception of Shaughnessy, who was over 25. The gear they wore was a giveaway: designer jeans and trainers, short anoraks zipped to the collar, baseball caps, tasteless bling. Facially, they were lean, scarred and feral.

Again, though, none of this applied to Shaughnessy himself.

As the underworld leadership caste so often seemed to be, he looked less battered and more refined than his crew. He was handsome even, with smooth cheeks, grey eyes and short, neat, white-blond hair. He wore neutral black clothing – black jeans, a black sweater, which fitted his youthful form snugly.

174

Very slowly, the window descended. Shaughnessy threw an amused glance at his followers. A couple smiled, but the rest speared Heck with icy hostility in their eyes.

'Don't wish to have you at a disadvantage, Lee,' Heck said, leaning in and offering a contact card. 'I'm Detective Sergeant Heckenburg. I've just joined the taskforce here at Bradburn.'

Shaughnessy gave the card brief consideration, but made no effort to take it. 'What happened?' he asked. 'Mickey Mouse not available?'

Sniggers sounded from the rest of the team.

'Guess you're parked up here because you're waiting to collect your mate after he's done inside, eh?' Heck said.

'Just passing the time of day, Detective Sergeant.'

'You're parked illegally, Lee.'

'No other way around here.'

'Well, you've got that right.'

'Suppose you'd better give us a ticket.'

'Nah.' Heck shook his head. 'I'll tell you what I will give you, though – a warning.'

'Oh no!' Shaughnessy exclaimed.

Further sniggers from his mates.

'A *friendly* warning,' Heck added.

'No such thing, my man. No such thing.' Shaughnessy spoke with a local accent, but it wasn't broad or loutish. At the same time his manner of speech, his construction of sentences and such indicated a measure of education. It wasn't uncommon in Heck's experience for some dangerous gutter-rat to weave an image of acceptability around himself by upgrading his style, taking elocution lessons – and this never made them any the less dangerous, in fact quite the opposite.

'Think about it,' Heck said. 'Five flamethrower deaths, maybe more to follow . . . and all the victims on Vic Ship's payroll.'

175

Shaughnessy looked to his front. 'Just goes to show, Sarge . . . shit happens to the worst of us.'

'Too true, Lee. Not many serious crims last long in the North. Especially not little fish trying to get into bigger ponds, openly challenging the big fish that are already swimming there.'

'Hey, you boring cunt! Ticket us or piss off!'

This came from a brawny-looking character in the front passenger seat. He wore a hooded tracksuit top under his anorak, and had pale, almost white features, a scarred top lip and a blue star tattooed under his left eye, with what looked like sprinkled blue dots underneath it. He curled his lip when Heck glanced at him, showing brown, lopsided teeth.

'The thing is, Lee,' Heck said. 'I'm a bit different from all the others on the team . . . because I happen to know this is something you aren't guilty of.'

Shaughnessy remained eyes-front. His expression of studied indifference never altered.

'I mean, you're a bad lad,' Heck added. 'But *you've* not been burning up Mr Ship's Bradburn connections. You wouldn't do something as stupid as that, would you?'

'Hey, pal . . .' the star-faced man interjected again.

'Wind your neck in, son!' Heck told him. 'I'm talking to the shagger, not his used johnny-bag!'

A stony silence filled the car.

'Like I say, Lee, I don't believe you're behind these flame-thrower attacks. But do you think Mr Ship will share that view? And if he doesn't, this thing's soon going to turn into an all-out war, isn't it? And when that happens, what's going to stop you and the rest of the snot-nosed kindergarten here saying goodnight to grandma?'

Shaughnessy smiled. As if he'd thought this through already and it still didn't worry him.

176

'You know Ship's got some Russian muscle on board?' Heck said.

Shaughnessy said nothing.

'*Russians*, Lee. People who aren't easily impressed, but who'll be very, very keen to impress Mr Ship. I'm sure you and the rest of the Brains Trust have worked this out already, but the way I see it, there's only one thing standing between you and the apocalypse – me.'

Heck offered his business card again. Shaughnessy glanced at it, but still didn't take it.

'And I'll tell you why that is, Lee. Because no one else in the cops gives a rat's arse about you. They don't want a gang war on the streets of this town, but they don't want *you* either. They can't very well shoot you, so why not leave it to someone who can and will? But, believe it or not, I don't know you well enough to want to see your name in the obit columns just yet. So I'm keen on catching the real Incinerator, and it's probably in your interest if you help me.'

Now, finally, Shaughnessy looked around. 'You want *our* help?'

'Well, you'll be helping yourself primarily. Anyway, don't take this if you don't want – I'll *serve* it on you instead.' Heck flicked the card in through the window; it landed in Shaughnessy's lap. 'There you go. Just like a summons. I'm sure you've had plenty of those in the past.' He stood up. 'You better get wise, Lee. You lads are being set up. I mean, you may court this rep for being the new kids on the block, but the crew that's coming down on you will land like a pile of Godzilla shit. So why don't you run along and think about that, and when you're ready, give me a call. Or alternatively stay here –' Heck shrugged '– watching the cop shop from your motor, being all scary and gangsta-like. Till a traffic warden comes along, of course. Then who knows, maybe you can bump her off . . . that'll put you somewhere Vic

Ship won't be able to get at you. For a few months at least. Till you wind up in the lifers' block, where I'm sure Mr Ship will have a lot more mates even than you.'

Heck didn't wait for a response, but circled the Mazda and crossed the road towards the nick. Behind him, an engine revved to life and tyres squealed as a vehicle spun quickly away. He glanced over his shoulder. The Mazda was gone, but more interesting was the lack of business card twirling in its wake. Shaughnessy hadn't thrown it out before driving off.

Chapter 18

The problem with throwing out a lure was that there was no way of knowing how long it would be before you could reel in the catch. However, Heck had several other things to occupy his mind with. After Shaughnessy had gone, he wandered back up to the MIR, which was empty except for one or two detectives on the phone, and slouched across to his desk in the corner. The previous afternoon, more out of gut instinct than any kind of thoughtful design, he'd laid out all the crime-scene photos relating to the sex-shop attack. He'd looked them over several times since, and now stood there with hands in pockets, perusing them again.

It was Heck's experience that quite often in cases of serial murder the offender would himself be on a learning curve and was much more likely to make mistakes early on. Often, during a spree, the initial crime scene was scattered with clues, though that wouldn't necessarily apply to the sex shop. First of all, once the Fire Brigade had extinguished the flames, all they'd really left was a blackened interior, inches deep in water and strewn with charred, unrecognisable debris. Secondly, the Incinerator was no traditional serial killer. OK, what they were seeing here was a clear quest for abnormal psychological gratification – he wouldn't be doing this if he didn't enjoy it – but what if he was a professional too, one of Shaughnessy's acolytes, or maybe a contract killer who'd been brought in from the outside (like Sagan)? If so, there'd be no guarantee this was his first sequence of murders. You couldn't read anything into the fact there was no record of other flamethrower crimes in the UK; he might still be a seasoned killer, with this his weapon-of-the-moment.

But for all these doubts, Heck reassessed the crime-scene glossies, scanning the scabrous shell of the boutique, knowing there was always something you'd missed the first time if you just kept looking. And almost immediately detecting a possible oddity. He lifted one of the glossies and took a magnifying glass from a shelf to examine it more closely – only to be distracted by DI Hayes slamming her way in through the swing doors, looking vexed and frustrated.

He guessed this was because Langton was almost certain to get bailed. They'd failed to break him in the interview, more or less as they'd expected, but it was never easy releasing a suspect without charge when you confidently believed he'd had a role in the crime you were investigating. They would put a covert tail on him, but Langton was a time-served pro. He'd anticipate that, and for the time being at least would behave accordingly.

Hayes sensed Heck's eyes on her, and glanced over at him.

'Bad day, ma'am?' he said.

'I think we've all had better,' she replied.

'Langton was always going to be a hardcase in the interview room.'

'Yeah, but now there's another problem.' Something in Hayes's voice had subtly changed. 'It seems Langton isn't the only guy who's been keeping his gob shut today. For instance, Langton isn't the guy who's apparently been holding unofficial and from what I can see thus far *unlogged* interviews with some of our chief suspects?'

Heck turned to face her.

'We knew Shaughnessy and some of his boys were in the area earlier on,' she said coolly. 'Ostensibly to collect their mate once we'd done with him, but also to see what was going on. We fully expected that.' She arched an eyebrow. 'What we didn't expect was to see you cross the road and have a natter with him like you were old mates.'

'And do you think we are old mates, ma'am? Me being an ex-Bradburn lad an' all?'

'Don't try and be clever with me, Sergeant Heckenburg.'

'Whoa, whoa.' Heck raised a placatory hand, conscious that other officers in the room were glancing curiously over. He lowered his voice to a suitably respectful level. 'Ma'am, I'd feel a lot better if you'd call me Heck.'

'And I'd feel better if you gave me a straight answer.' Her voice was still terse, but she'd lowered it a little. 'What was all that about?'

He indicated her office. Still looking peeved, she stumped over there, held the door open for him and closed it loudly when he'd entered.

'It's honestly nothing to worry about,' he explained. 'I just, well, I sort of made a deal with Shaughnessy.'

'*Excuse me?*' Hayes had just thrown herself into her chair, but now her eyes bulged like shuttlecocks. 'What kind of deal?'

'An open-ended thing really. I'm not sure he's even bought it yet.'

'For Christ's sake . . . *what kind of deal?*'

Heck gestured vaguely. 'I told him I'm not convinced he's the man.'

She leaned forward on the desk. 'You cannot be bloody serious!'

'I told him that was my personal view, but that it wasn't necessarily shared by anyone else in the investigation team.'

'Damn right it isn't, and with good reason! You told him *that* . . . Suppose he *is* behind the Incinerator crimes?'

Heck shrugged. 'If that's the case, he writes me off as an idiot – we've not really lost anything.'

'And if he isn't behind them, I mean just for the sake of argument – what have we actually gained?'

'How many ears have you got out there, ma'am? How many snouts, grasses – I mean reliable ones?'

She looked bewildered by the question. 'Enough.'

'Do you think you know as many people at street-level in Bradburn as Lee Shaughnessy does?'

'Are you saying you expect him to help us find the Incinerator?' Hayes's voice almost cracked. 'Because if you do you're away with the bleeding fairies!'

'Shaughnessy's in trouble, ma'am, and he knows it. Even if he's got nothing to do with these murders, he's gonna cop the blame. He has to start looking for this guy.'

'And supposing that's true, why would he give him to us? Why wouldn't he just kill him?'

'Maybe he will. It won't be ideal, but at least there'll be no more burnings.'

It all seemed perfectly reasonable and logical to Heck, but it took DI Hayes several seconds to process what he'd just told her.

'Is this the way you normally work?' she finally said. 'Doing deals with ultimate lowlifes? Getting psychopaths to carry out hits for you?'

'I believe in using every tool available,' Heck replied. 'And I feel that's a more proactive approach than focusing fifty per cent of my energy on one suspect who most likely is innocent.'

She sat back. Clearly, now that she'd considered it, the

idea wasn't completely anathema to her. 'I admire your boldness of thought, Heck, but you realise this is one hell of a long shot?'

'That's the name of my game, ma'am . . . generating my own leads and chasing them down.'

'Even those that are so unlikely as to be unimaginable?'

'Not just those, ma'am. I don't know if you noticed, but I've been looking through the early crime-scene pix.'

'So?'

'The sex shop on Buckeye Lane's an interesting site.'

'OK . . .?'

'I assume it's still in our possession.'

'For the time being.'

'Good.' Heck opened the door. 'If you've got a minute or two, there's something down there I'd like to show you.'

Chapter 19

'In case you were wondering, the search at Langton's house has turned up nothing,' Hayes said, as they drove.

'Doesn't totally surprise me,' Heck replied from behind the wheel. 'But just out of interest, does Langton have access to any other properties?'

'We're looking into that now, but we don't think so.'

'I'd say don't waste your time, but I suppose we've got to cover every possibility no matter how fanciful.'

She glanced at him irritably, but he drove on.

Their destination was the small, burned-out unit on the corner of Buckeye Lane. Most of the front of the shop was covered by a forensics tent, and access to this was only possible by passing under a fence of incident tape, behind which a uniformed bobby stood guard. The once neon-lit letters comprising the shop's name – SADIE'S DUNGEON – were blackened and cracked and hung at lopsided angles. Smoke stains trailed up the wall above, smudging the windows of the five levels of flats stacked over the top.

Heck parked and climbed out. 'Was there ever a real Sadie here?'

'Not as we've been able to discover,' Hayes said. 'But Vic

Ship owns this place – most of it, at least. He bankrolled it when it first opened in 2003. He's got a few like this in the Northwest. That was after hardcore porn had just got legalised. He'd supplied enough illegal porn before, so he already had the network set up. Suppose he didn't want to miss out on the chance of a legitimate earner.'

They flashed their warrant cards and were passed under the tape and into the tent. Here they donned the usual Tyvek coveralls, disposable gloves and boots, and entered the crime scene, which essentially was a concrete shell so thoroughly burned out that there was almost no visible evidence of what it once had been – only the odd scrap of girlie mag lying amid the ashes, and a collapsed display board on which the sole remaining fragment of merchandise was a partial bikini made from scorched leather. The fire had been extinguished seven days ago, but the stench was still eye-watering. It was also evident that SOCO had not yet finished with the scene, some areas doubly roped-off by reams of tape, camera tripods remaining in place, evidence labels everywhere.

'One of the reasons I have some doubt this hit was ordered by Lee Shaughnessy and/or carried out by Langton is because this entire block of flats could have gone up,' Heck said. 'God knows how many innocent people would have died. The same with the Shelley Harper and Nawaz Gilani murder. Whichever one of those two was the target, the other was collateral damage. That would be unusually careless for a professional hitman – I mean, even the stupidest gangland goon would expect a world of shit to fall on his head if that happened. But that's not the main reason I brought you here.' He set off down the length of the shop, feet crunching the charred debris. 'I want to show you something I spotted on the photos earlier.'

They turned a corner behind the point where the counter had once been, and entered a short passage. The fire had reached this too and surged down it, reducing its carpet and whatever lurid imagery had once adorned its walls to cinders, as it had the slightly unusual fixture at the far end: what looked as if it had been some kind of walk-in closet, only with a dividing wall between two separate compartments, the one on the right considerably narrower than the one on the left and still with the burned iron frame of a single chair placed inside.

'Uh-huh,' Heck said, nodding to himself. 'When I first saw this, I wasn't totally sure. It wasn't completely clear on a glossy, but now I'm up close to it, I'm certain.'

Hayes shrugged. 'OK . . . I'm waiting?'

'Well, what do you think this was, ma'am?'

She looked the closet-type structure over. 'I don't know . . . a storage cupboard.'

'Look closer. You enter the section on the right, the one with the chair, from this side – our side. In other words as a customer. But the door to the other's on the back.'

Hayes appraised it again. Heck pointed, indicating that the compartment on the left, whose floor was made from some black lacquered material and its walls apparently covered with what resembled glittery paint, had an entrance door on the other side, connecting with some kind of staff-only area, though this also had been reduced to a shell.

'It becomes more self-evident the more we examine it,' Heck said, fingering the shards of smoke-stained glass running along the footing of the dividing wall. 'Check out this two-way mirror in between. Not to mention the fancy lightshow.'

A row of different-coloured bulbs was visible on the left side of the mirror.

'Good grief,' she said slowly. 'This is a peepshow booth?'

'That's what I thought.'

The phone shrilled in Hayes's pocket. She fished it out and answered. 'Yes, ma'am . . . yeah, course. ETA ten.' She still looked distracted as she tucked the device away. 'Gemma wants us all back at the nick . . . debrief on today's arrest before this evening's video conference.'

Heck shrugged. 'Fine . . . but what about this?'

'The significance of which is what?' she asked.

'We only found *two* bodies in the ashes, ma'am. The blokes who worked here. Now all along we've been operating on the basis there was nobody else here – no customers, for example, because the shop was attacked after hours. But what if there was a woman here? Someone who was working in this booth when it happened?'

'We've uncovered nothing to indicate that.' But Hayes was clearly giving this possibility serious thought.

'According to the first responders' sit-rep, the shop's back door was wide open,' Heck said.

'Doesn't necessarily mean someone got away.'

'No, I agree . . . but it *could* do.'

She gazed at him wonderingly. 'You're saying we may have a surviving witness?'

'Time to set those *really* reliable grasses of yours a *really* challenging task, ma'am.'

*

'Let's face it, we expected him to stonewall us to death,' Gemma told Gibbshaw and several others as they walked along the corridor. 'It's frustrating as hell, especially the search teams turning up nothing. But we've got to play by the rules. We can't hold him . . . we might as well let him go.'

'Ma'am!' Hayes said, catching up with them from behind, she and Heck having just ascended the station stairs. The DI was bubbling with nervous energy. 'We may have a new lead on the Incinerator.'

Gemma stopped in her tracks, regarding them both curiously. 'Tell me.'

Hayes explained their new theory about the sex shop.

'Hmmm,' Gemma said. 'That's good. That's very good in fact. Because I'm about to break the habit of a lifetime, and divide our forces.'

Hayes looked puzzled. 'I'm not sure I follow, ma'am.'

'Everyone into the office if you please.' Gemma stood aside as Gibbshaw and the other taskforce members filed past.

Hayes and Heck hung behind until everyone else had gone.

'I think we're making insufficient progress here because we're spreading ourselves too thinly,' Gemma said. 'In trying to concentrate on both underworld factions at the same time, we're getting nowhere. As from today, and I'll formalise all this in the briefing, I'm forming two separate investigation teams. One to focus on the landfill murders –'

'You mean the crimes we're assuming are John Sagan's?' Heck interrupted, already suspecting that he knew where this was going.

'Correct. And the other to focus on the Incinerator.' Gemma headed away down the corridor towards a door marked LADIES. 'Katie, you're DSIO Incinerator,' she said over her shoulder. 'Heck, you're with her.'

'Ma'am!' Heck said, but the toilet door swung closed behind her.

He turned to Hayes but, clearly pleased with what she'd just heard, she strolled cheerfully into the MIR, leaving him alone in the corridor. Unable to help himself, he barged into the Ladies, without knocking.

Gemma was bent over a basin, dabbing her face with cold water. She glanced at him in the mirror, startled. 'And what the devil do you think you're doing now?'

'Ma'am, John Sagan is SCU's priority,' he said. 'Why not just give the Incinerator to GMP?'

She turned to face him, drying her hands on a paper towel. 'I'm dividing resources as best I can.' She spoke slowly but dangerously. 'The Incinerator has accounted for five lives already, and Sagan – if it *is* Sagan – only for two. Now you tell me which needs greater emphasis? Not that I need to explain myself to you.'

She screwed the towel up and threw it into a bin.

'Actually I think you *do* need to explain it to me.'

Again, she looked startled.

'If what you're saying is you need to focus more energy on the Incinerator killings, fine,' he said. 'I concur. But why does that need to include me? John Sagan is *my* case.'

'There is no mine, ours or yours in criminal investigation, Heck. How many times have I had to tell you that?'

'DI Hayes seems more than capable. She'll catch the Incinerator. Let me go after Sagan.'

'DI Hayes is from South Manchester. She's not a Bradburn girl. In fact, *you* are the only specialist investigator in the entire taskforce with local knowledge. That means the higher of the two priorities needs *you* working on it.'

Hoping she'd made things clear, she moved to the door.

'I bet Gibbshaw's still on Sagan, though, isn't he?' Heck said.

When she turned this time, her blue eyes smouldered. 'Did you not hear a word I just said?'

'I bet he's DSIO Sagan? Is that bloody right?'

She jabbed a furious finger into his face. 'You hit me one more time with that tone, Sergeant, and I swear – I'll kick you back to London so fast the g-force'll kill you.'

'Gemma, just promise me that this is not political,' he said. 'I mean, I accept that Gibbshaw has to be on this investigation because he's Organised Crime Division. I can even accept that he needs to be there for the Sagan takedown. But please don't tell me that the deal also involved me being pushed sideways.'

'Sideways?'

'I get it that because I was there when Reg Cowling died and didn't manage to save him, it's given OC a get-out clause, has allowed them to perform just enough mental acrobatics to convince themselves that part of the blame for this lies elsewhere . . . but please don't tell me you're giving that crap some respectability by paying lip-service to it.'

'Heck . . .' She made an effort to steady her voice. 'We came up here to catch a professional murderer, only to find that we are dealing with at least two, one of whom is significantly more active than the other. I don't know why Sagan's keeping a low profile or for how long he will, assuming it *is* Sagan –'

'You don't need to keep saying that.'

'I will keep saying it, Heck, until we know for an indisputable fact that Sagan is here. And that's something else you need to think about. If I hadn't taken this *whole* case on, we'd be up here now team-handed for no obvious reason. And how long do you think Joe Wullerton would have tolerated that? The main point is that this Incinerator character is running around Bradburn, *your* hometown, lighting people up like Roman candles. Now, bad guys or not, you tell me if that's not an SCU case . . . that it wouldn't normally have you salivating?'

He couldn't really respond to that, so she moved to the door.

'And if DI Hayes and I just happen to turn something up that leads us to Sagan instead of the Incinerator?' he wondered.

'Share it with me and Gibbshaw,' she said, exasperated. 'Or, if the situation allows, lock him up yourself. It's not a Goddamned competition.'

'Ma'am . . .'

She looked back at him again as she opened the door, but

her face was set, her expression fixed, her decision made –
she was beyond determined to go ahead with this plan.

He was about to say: *'This is a personal favour I'm asking
for, ma'am, and perhaps that's out of order. But I don't see
how it could really mess things up. You know I can help
you catch Sagan; I'm the one who first discovered his existence. It makes perfect sense to use me – does the politics of
the job override all that?'*

But he didn't. Because she surely ought to know that by
now.

She shrugged, waiting impatiently.

'Nothing,' he said. 'It doesn't matter.'

'Right. Well, come through to the briefing, please. We've
wasted enough time already.'

He followed her out onto the corridor, where Hayes had
reappeared from the MIR. Gemma pushed past her as she
went into the office. Hayes glanced quizzically at the door
to the Ladies, from which they'd both just emerged, and then
at Heck.

'You and her really *have* got something special, haven't
you?' she said.

'Not any more,' he replied.

Chapter 20

Hi Mark

I gave you my number a few days ago, but you never called. However, I'm not reading anything into that. I know you're likely to be pretty busy at the moment. To be honest, I shudder when I think of the work you must be engaged in at present. But let's not talk shop, eh?

I'm rather glad you weren't in when I called at Dana's house earlier today, because I'm not sure I'd have the guts to do this face to face. That's why I'd prepared this note in advance. Basically . . . when I saw you the other night, for the first time in I don't know how long, something leaped inside me. I know that sounds melodramatic, but it's completely true. We were close once – more than close actually, and when we stopped seeing each other, we remained friends, didn't we? Good friends. From my own point of view, Mark, I've always felt I had a kind of kinship with you. Something much stronger than the norm. And just seeing you walk into the pub the way you did, and to see that you'd changed so little, that you were still more or less the Mark I remembered – it was an absolute flashback to a much happier time in my life.

I know things have been rough for you, Mark. Father Pat's filled me in on all the details since we last spoke, and it's actually quite appalling the way you were treated. I'm not sure if this is an opportune time to mention it, but things have been pretty messy for me as well. It's astonishing the way you don't see horrible things creeping up on you, isn't it, and then the way they suddenly change your life in the most shocking and irreversible way?

What I'm trying to say with all this is that we were kindred spirits in the long ago past, Mark . . . and perhaps we could be kindred spirits again?

Please don't misunderstand me. I don't know what your current 'situation' is. So I'm not asking you out or proposing a date or anything so crass. But I wouldn't at all mind reviving our relationship if that's possible, just to see where we stand.

I'm sorry if this sounds terribly bold and forward of me, but I've learned in recent years that you can't hang around and wait for good things to happen. They invariably don't. Bad things happen instead. If you want the good stuff, you've got to go looking for it, and there's never any time like the present.

Feel free not to reply to this message. I didn't intend to embarrass you by writing it, and I assure you I will not be offended if that's what you choose. But if you fancy hooking up for a bit of a chinwag, some fond reminiscence about the good times, I'll be in 'Eight Till Late' (which is on King's Parade) tomorrow night, between seven-thirty and nine.

I'd love to see you there.

XXX
Kayla

Heck read the letter one more time before shoving it into his pocket and sauntering into the glitzy bar.

It had been waiting for him on the doormat when he'd returned to Dana's house the previous evening. His initial thought might once have been to avoid any such further contact like the plague. He was up here in Bradburn to work, not play; that day alone he'd officially been off duty, but had spent it voluntarily sitting in the MIR, ploughing through witness statements for anything they might have missed. Anything to get the case closed quickly and get the hell away. But then, of all his memories connected with this town, Kayla was one of the brightest. On top of that, Heck was as red-blooded as the next man, and it was quite some time since he'd had any meaningful female contact. His long-ago relationship with Gemma had left its mark on him, but his unspoken desire for her now was almost exclusively physical – he felt increasingly distanced from her in emotional terms, simply because their mutual commitment to the job constantly put barriers between them. It hardly felt disloyal to occasionally look elsewhere.

It could also be pretty rewarding.

Kayla looked amazing that evening in a green wrap dress and heels, a colour scheme that perfectly matched her violet eyes and raven locks. By comparison, Heck felt a little self-conscious in the same suit, shirt and tie that he'd been wearing on the job. Not having expected any social activity, he hadn't come up here with a full suitcase.

She was perched on a high stool next to the bar, and greeted him with a kiss on the cheek. She was drinking a champagne cocktail and offered him one, but he said he'd prefer a light ale.

The Eight Till Late had the lure of a jazz club, but without the actual jazz: all grainy hardwood surfaces, low-key lighting, low beams, low tables and low sofas exclusively of

194

the plush and crumpled variety. It was divided into numerous rooms, each with its own crackling fireplace, and, this being a Sunday night, it wasn't especially busy.

Once served, the twosome moved away from the bar and found themselves an alcove in a corner, a dimly lit recess, where they settled side by side on a springy couch.

'So I hear you started in the Greater Manchester Police, but somehow ended up transferring to London,' Kayla said.

'That's right,' Heck replied. 'I joined GMP in 1995, when I was eighteen. In that regard I'm probably the last of an ancient breed. No one so young could ever join the cops these days.'

'They must've seen something in you they liked.'

'I'm not so sure.' Heck sipped his beer. 'They knew about the miscarriage of justice involving Tom. That had only happened three years earlier. Even though the family had received a big compensation package, I think they felt honour-bound to take me. Would've looked bad if they'd rejected my application out of hand.'

'Not necessarily,' she said. 'They might have seen a young man driven to put the world right.'

'That's certainly the way I saw myself. A view that wasn't shared by Mum and Dad . . . as Uncle Pat's told you.'

'Well . . . yeah.' She sat back, lipstick glinting in the moody lighting.

'They made my life a total misery.'

He took another sip, not entirely sure why he was telling her all this, but feeling strangely comfortable about it; back in the day, Kayla had been more than just a bit of fun – the problem was that, at the time, he'd possibly been too immature to recognise it.

'I couldn't really explain to them why I'd joined up,' he said. 'They wouldn't have believed anything I said. Even though it was only a couple of bad-egg coppers who'd been involved in framing Tom, they blamed the entire institution. Folk do that when they're in despair, don't they? They strike out. Overnight I became *persona non grata*. Even Dana wouldn't talk to me . . . at first. She only came round after I'd moved down to London, and she thought she was going to lose me too.'

'And after you arrived in London it was all easy,' Kayla said. And chuckled.

He chuckled too. 'Yeah, sure.'

'Like I said, your uncle's already told me a lot about this. I'm sorry I pried. After I saw you the other night, I couldn't resist it.'

'I thought you'd have forgotten I existed by now.'

'I sort of had.' She signalled to the barmaid for a couple more drinks. 'Don't get me wrong, you were always there in the back of my mind. All my exes are there . . .'

'I don't know whether to be flattered or offended.'

'There're a couple I'd like to forget totally,' she said, sighing. 'You remember Rick Toovey?'

'Yeah,' Heck said. 'He was at school with us, wasn't he? Tall guy, studious, reckoned he was destined for great things.'

'Well, I married him.'

'You married *him*?' Heck didn't mean to sound so startled.

'I know.' She pulled a face. 'I thought he was destined for great things too.'

'And I'm guessing he ended up not being?'

'On the contrary. He's now a senior consultant at Preston Royal.'

The barmaid arrived with their next drinks.

'So why am I talking to Kayla *Green* this evening?' Heck asked, after she'd gone. 'Why am I talking to you at all?'

She sat back. 'Rick was a great doctor. All his patients loved him. Apparently his bedside manner was utterly charming . . . especially if the patient was female.' She frowned distantly, as though puzzling over something intangible. 'I maybe wasn't the best spouse myself. Perhaps I could have done more to win his affection.' She sighed. 'Whatever . . . whoever's fault it was, in the end it didn't work out.'

'Well, that happens.'

'He's married again now. With kids.' Her frown deepened, her brow creased. 'That part of it may have been *my* fault . . . that I wasn't able to give him little ones.'

'Come on,' Heck said. 'Hardly your *fault.*'

'Either way, it's water under the bridge.'

She made an effort to brighten, but her thoughts were still lost somewhere in the past.

'Sorry to hear all that,' Heck said, already having what he knew were selfish reservations about this meeting. He had plenty of baggage of his own without taking someone else's on too. 'Uncle Pat said you'd had a bad time recently.'

'Oh . . .' She tried to make light of it, to wave it away. 'None of this was a long-lasting problem, if I'm honest. It was ten years ago. I reverted to my maiden name and threw myself into the business with Dad . . . and then he died too.' As quickly as it had returned, her humour faded again; her eyes partially glazed. 'So many people die, don't they, Mark, just when you need them most.' She peered at him, unblinking. 'Jess died, you know.'

'Your younger sister Jess?'

'Who else?'

Heck was genuinely surprised. Jess Green had been seven years Kayla's junior. She wouldn't have been much past thirty.

'About two years ago,' Kayla said. 'There was no actual reason why it . . . *Oh, sod it!*' She shook herself, forcing a smile. 'Listen to the pair of us. How mawkish is this? We'll end up crying in each other's arms at this rate. Come on, change of subject, something cheerful! How's the police business? Must be going well if you finished up at Scotland Yard?'

'I've had a few good collars, I suppose.'

'I'll say. I may have forgotten you in the interim period, Mark, but when I saw all that stuff in the paper, it reminded me what a top bloke you are.'

He smiled awkwardly. 'I'm not sure about that. But, well, I've had some luck.'

'Gimme the details. Come on, leave nothing out.'

Heck actually spared Kayla many of the details, but he spoke a little about the more high-profile cases he'd been involved with in the last few years. Of course he only referred to aspects of these distressing enquiries that were already out in the public domain.

Not that Kayla seemed in any way distressed.

'Wow,' she said. 'That's what you call living.'

'Never quite feels that way at the time,' Heck replied.

'Yeah, but look at the good you're doing. Chasing these animals all over the country, and putting them in cages – where they belong.'

Her eyes flashed as she said this, even in the lurid half-light. Her voice was hard with feeling. For the first time, Heck wondered how her sister Jess might have died.

'There're more than a few animals in Bradburn who need caging, aren't there?' she asked him, though it wasn't really a question.

'Well, things are rougher round here than I remember. Has this high-level crime been going on in town for a while?'

She gave it some thought. 'Not so the average guy on the street would notice, but there've been more and more addicts around every year. I mean, the church has tried to pick up some of those pieces. Father Pat runs a couple of counselling and rehab groups for local folk who've fallen through the cracks: alkies, druggies, prozzies. Usually all three at the same time. But this new thing that's coming in, this fentanyl . . . that's pretty disgusting by any standards.'

Heck knew all about fentanyl. A synthetic high, about fifty times more potent than pure-grade heroin, vastly more addictive and responsible for many more fatalities, it had originally been used in hospitals and clinics as a strong anaesthetic, but was now in the hands of criminals – and it would make complete sense that it was causing problems here in Bradburn. Bulk orders for fentanyl were being met in Chinese laboratories and then being trafficked into Europe by the Russian mob. That could well be the trade-off that Vic Ship was getting for allowing the Tatarstan Brigade onto his turf: an inexhaustible supply of a very cheap-to-produce and hugely profitable new drug.

'Bit of a mess,' he said, thinking aloud.

'Yeah, but we've got you here now, haven't we?' She beamed at him as she finished her cocktail.

What exactly does she think I'm capable of? he wondered.

As if sensing what he was thinking, she winked and added: 'No pressure, Mark, eh?'

'Let's just say that Operation Wandering Wolf is a big one,' he said, 'and that we won't be going anywhere else until we've closed these people down.'

'To be honest, you'd be doing us more of a favour if you *gunned* them down.' She snapped her handbag closed and stood up. 'The whole lot of them.'

Heck was initially unsure how to respond. That had been a fleeting comment, a throwaway, but again she'd packed it with intense feeling.

'That's . . . that's not really the way we work these days,' he said.

'I know.' She circled around the table and headed away across the bar. 'Worse luck though, eh, Mark? Worse luck.'

It might have been an optical illusion created by the fire-light, but fleetingly he'd fancied there were tears sparkling in her lashes.

He watched her carefully as she sashayed towards the Ladies. The reservations he'd started feeling about this dalliance were now coming thick and fast. Kayla clearly had *lots* of baggage. It wouldn't be unusual for persons of a certain age. But from what he was seeing here, she was having trouble controlling it – and that didn't bode well.

On reflection, there'd been something vaguely forced and desperate in her attitude ever since they'd become reacquainted. It had been odd, almost eerie, the intensity with which she listened when he'd spoken about his recent cases; the way she'd hung onto his every word. What was she seeing here? he wondered – the Mark Heckenburg she'd known and dated or some ludicrous fantasy version of that, the errant knight finally returned to sweep all her troubles away?

She'd lost a succession of close ones, including Jess – a peaches-and-cream junior-school girl when Heck had last seen her, a sweet, innocent kid who'd adored her older sister. What story lay there he couldn't imagine, but it must have been a monumental blow to the recently divorced, recently orphaned Kayla. No wonder she'd found religion. Though maybe even religion hadn't been enough in this circumstance – and that could be the problem.

If what Kayla needed was a crutch, he wasn't the one to help her. He had his own issues, plus a job that had killed almost every relationship he'd ever had.

It wasn't the case that he was being selfish . . . Heck smiled broadly as she came prettily back across the room towards him. No, he definitely wasn't being selfish. It was simply that he could never be right for her. His uncle's thinly veiled warning outside The Coal Hole last Thursday night now made perfect sense.

When she sat down again, he ordered them another round of drinks, non-alcoholic this time as they were both of them driving, and from here on he kept his body language stiff and neutral. Their chatter remained affectionate and fond, but Heck maintained as much coolness and distance as was possible while still being polite, refusing to laugh too loudly at her jokes, failing to explore the more emotional depths of their memories. What was more, Kayla seemed to sense this and even reciprocate, slowly adjusting her position so that she was facing him rather than sitting alongside him, steering clear of any subject with a softer or more personal edge. When ten o'clock came, and Heck decided that he was ready to go, she apparently felt the same.

She allowed him to get her coat and put it on her. They walked outside arm in arm but in platonic fashion. Heck escorted her to a neat little Ford Fiesta parked in a nearby side-street. Here, she gave him a quick cuddle, pecked his cheek and produced her car key.

'We need to see each other again while you're up here,' she chided him. 'We've always been friends, and friends are a good thing – even old friends who you haven't seen for ages. You can't live a full and normal life without friends, no matter how much you think you can.'

'Who says I think I can?' he replied.

'You can't fool me, Mark Heckenburg. I know a lonely soul when I see one. Someone who's buried themselves in their job to hide from all the other bits of their life. I'm an expert on that.'

She kissed him again, lightly – another friendly peck. And then climbed into her car and closed the door. He stood back and watched as it rumbled to life, backed out of its parking space and drove away, wafts of exhaust billowing behind it.

It was only a five-minute walk to the spot where Heck had left his own car. He was still pondering the fentanyl business as he trekked around a corner and approached his Megane – it would definitely be worth a note in the policy file – when he spotted the shadowy outlines of several figures standing by the nearest wall to the vehicle. His advance slowed as more and more of them emerged, deliberately stepping out into the pavement.

At this late hour, the Sunday evening streets were all but deserted, but there were twelve of these guys at least, maybe more. One by one, they turned to face him – slowly fanning into a line that didn't just cover the pavement but most of the narrow side-road as well, and of course blocked all access to his car.

Heck halted ten yards short of them. The dim street-lighting was adequate to show him a bunch of faces he wouldn't have wanted to meet during the day let alone late at night: hard, angular faces; faces that were cut, scarred, grizzled; that were scuffed like shoe-leather; that had been hammered on anvils. Faces that could be aged anywhere between thirty and sixty, they were so graven by time and violence. If their faces didn't say enough, the weapons they now produced from under their hoodie tops or leather jackets or dark-khaki combat gear, did: pipes, bats, belts, chains, wrenches. Heck spotted one particularly ghastly implement – something that looked like a Rambo knife, a guarded hilt and nine or so inches of thick, shiny steel, its glinting razor-edge partly serrated. It was clamped in the hand of an outlandish-looking individual who strolled forward like some kind of unofficial foreman. He was of average-to-strong build and stood just under six feet, but bizarrely, given the distinct chill in the air, was bare-chested under a fleece-lined denim doublet, his naked arms long, apelike and muscular and covered with black cobweb tattoos which ran all the way down from his brawny shoulders to a pair of black leather gloves, and extended across the whole of his exposed torso. His hair was shaved into a skull-cap on top of his odd, bean-shaped head. His eyes were small and far apart, his nose broad and flat. When he smiled, a big wet mouth split him ear to ear, revealing the jumbled blades of shovel-like teeth.

'So . . . Detective Heckenburg comes out to play, uh?' he said in a strong Russian accent, which at first was tough to decipher. 'You been a bad boy, detective. Now we deal with you.'

Heck turned and ran, digging into his pocket for his phone. In a storm of stomping footfalls, the gang charged. He crossed King's Parade at full speed. It was lined with pubs, bars and clubs, but most of them were now empty, others in the process of closing; there was no guarantee he'd find safety in one of those anyway – he'd seen enough barroom beatings in his time.

A lone car had to swerve to avoid him, its horn yowling like a siren. Even then Heck's phone proved elusive. He ran on. Directly ahead stood the entrance to a black alleyway. He didn't break pace as he galloped down it.

Vic Ship's crew had finally arrived, and that posed two immediate questions.

First of all, what did they want with *him*? Secondly, just how *badly* did they want it?

That second question was answered in short order by the cacophonous echo of booted feet as they entered the passage in pursuit, bats raised, chains twirling. The fact they weren't shouting and bawling was not encouraging. It meant they didn't want anyone else to know they were here, and that, whether he stopped or not, his ass was most likely grass.

Some fifty yards along, the alley ended in two gates facing each other. The one on the left was wooden and about seven feet tall. It looked as if it was closed and locked. The other was a similar height, but made from metal bars. That might be locked too, but at least he could climb it.

Heck leapt, slamming his hands, knees and shins into the iron lattice – only for the gate, which was old and corroded, to swing open. He jumped off again, dashed through and kicked it closed behind him – just as the first of the hoodlums reached out for him. It wasn't the tattooed Russian, but a younger guy, nineteen at the most with a broad, athletic frame. The gate's upper horizontal bar smashed into the bridge of his nose. The crack of cartilage was like a gunshot. The kid howled, gloved hands clasping a bloody fountain as he tumbled back among the feet of his confederates, one after another of whom fell on top of him.

Heck shouldered the gate back into its frame, and yanked down on a stack of crated bottles standing to the left, which collapsed like a building, filling the gateway, glass exploding. Panting, he backed away. The gang drove their bodies forward like human battering-rams, slowly shoving the portal open again. Still, fleetingly, they were held back.

Heck spun around. He was in some kind of pub yard. In the darkness he could just about discern its dimensions: it was small and triangular in shape. Pulling his phone out, he hit the reading light: paving stones glimmered wetly; a door led into the pub, but this too was closed. If he banged on it and yammered, help might come, but probably not in time. The only avenue of escape was the rear wall. It was ten feet up at least, but more crates were stacked against it, forming steps. With a grinding of wreckage, the gate behind him was forced open further. Still not having phoned for help, Heck spun back to face them. One had now got into the yard. He saw a cap tugged down on a spiky red thatch, red sideburns, a beak-like hatchet nose – and a blag-handle flying through the air. He dodged; it missed him by millimetres.

They grappled, Heck driving a knee into the guy's groin, clasping both fists together and slamming them down hard onto the back of his neck. In the process, his phone flirted off somewhere, its light instantly deactivated.

'Shit!' he swore.

Another one came at him. Taller than the first, heavier set, with a walleye and horribly scarred cheeks. His weapon of choice was a chain, which he swept down from on high. Heck threw a defensive arm up. The chain wrapped around it. Heck used it to haul himself forward and head-butt the bastard in the teeth. But the chain-man barely wobbled, hitting Heck in the side of the neck with a forearm that felt like a sledgehammer. Heck replied with his right fist, bursting his opponent's nose wide open. Still the guy came on, his good eye glistening like a silver coin as he drew a long, curved blade from under his coat.

'Do it!' a Russian voice hissed from the bodies pressed behind the gate. 'Do him, kill him . . . gut him like a fish! A fucking fish, but leave some for the rest of us, *da*!'

The chain-man – minus chain but armed with his blade – lurched forward again. Heck backed away, grabbed another crate of bottles and hefted it. It connected full with the guy's blood-drenched visage, more glass breaking, wood exploding, dropping him in a heap. As the guy fell, Heck spun, clambered with speed up the teetering stacks and vaulted clean over the top of the high rear wall.

Chapter 21

The ten-foot distance between the top of the wall and the floor seemed further dropping down the other side than it had done climbing up.

Heck hit dank flagstones, landing hard and awkwardly, the force of it driving his knees up into his diaphragm, which smashed the air from his body as though from a bellows. All he could do was roll there groggily, nauseated. But the shouting and swearing on the other side of the wall, and a clatter of heavy feet on bottle-filled crates, brought him back to reality. Swaying upright, he found himself in another dismal alley. He staggered along it, passing more gates and yards, further piles of bottles and cans, skips filled with rancid wrappers and waste food. Occasional security bulbs flared to life as he passed beneath them, but most often he was in near-darkness. The pursuing pack had got themselves under control to a degree, clamping down on the shouting and swearing, though the rumble of their feet suggested they were close behind, their chains and bats jingling and clunking on the flags.

The thought encouraged him that if they'd wanted him dead, they'd have come with guns. But who said they hadn't?

And even if they didn't want him dead, that wasn't necessarily good news.

In the depths of the urban night, there were plenty things worse than death.

Ahead, he heard the rhythmic rattle and clank of a locomotive in motion, then the toot of a siren. He rounded a corner onto a cinder path, the left side of which was bounded by a high mesh fence. Beyond that lay railway lines.

Bradburn North station was about four hundred yards ahead. He could see the lights and the distant, squat outline of its trackside buildings. The dark form of a freight train trundled slowly out of sight. But this path didn't lead there. If Heck's memory served, it headed in roughly that direction, before swinging back towards clubland, passing through an arched entry and connecting with another street, which at this time of night would be deserted. If Ship's men were the professionals they reputedly were, they might already know about that and could have sent a posse to block that route. The most obvious way to throw them off was to cross the railway lines. Beyond those lay one or two additional nightclubs, but many of the plots over there were 'awaiting redevelopment', in other words empty industrial units whose former use was forgotten. There'd be trash-crammed alleys, broken-down doors, derelict rooms – hiding places galore. But getting over there wouldn't be easy.

Heck scaled the fence, the sound of multiple feet in the adjacent passage giving him added impetus. He swung his aching body over the top and all but dropped the full distance to the ground on the other side. But there his real problems began.

Bradburn North was on the West Coast Mainline, but it wasn't just a wayside stop. It functioned as a gateway station to the northern half of Britain. Various other railways converged on it. So there were eight sets of tracks between here and the other side. Crossing two high-speed rail links in the dark would be risky enough . . . but eight?

A voice hissed behind him.

Before he could turn, a gloved hand snatched his collar. Heck was yanked back against the mesh. Mustering all his strength, he lugged himself away, breaking the hold and turning. He saw crazy eyes in a gore-dabbled face; it was the kid whose nose he'd flattened earlier.

He flattened it again, driving his fist through a gap in the mesh, making full contact.

The kid was propelled backward. Meanwhile the rest of his friends rounded the corner, the cobweb-covered Russian leading the charge to the fence. Heck loped away across the tracks, looking neither left nor right. Behind him, the crew landed one by one from the fence-top and gave immediate chase, shouting again.

The first train appeared when Heck was halfway over – right in front of him. Almost simultaneously, another appeared directly behind, heading in the opposite direction.

Stunned by the cacophony of noise and light, the kaleidoscopic flicker of rushing windows, the glaring flash of sparking cables overhead, he flung himself down on the strip of oily gravel, a hot vortex of wind blasting over him and all along the perilously narrow passage. When both trains had gone, he rose dizzily to his feet, risking a backward glance as he stumbled on.

The pursuing horde was spread out as they crossed over – a row of black lupine shapes coming on at full speed.

The next train shot through as Heck approached the last of the railway lines, but again he barely saw it, just stopping short, his feet carving furrows in the grit. He threw himself down in a ball, more thunder and lightning filling his head, the roar of the siren fit to burst his eardrums. It hurtled past, carriage after carriage; the London to Glasgow Express maybe, or the Caledonian Sleeper, in which case it would take an age to clear, and all the time those bastards behind were getting closer. He turned and gazed across the strobe-lit tracks, to see that they too had been cut off by a train. It howled the other way at astonishing speed, its piercing cry filling the night.

Heck blinked hard. He'd so totally lost sight of his pursuers that for a hopeful second he fancied it had mowed them down, but then, through the blur of its wheels, he saw a forest of legs as the crew waited helpless on the other side.

But, if nothing else, it had bought him extra time.

He leaped up again, tottered on across the last line and blundered down an embankment choked with tangles of weed. At the bottom there was a brick wall – not especially high, about five feet, which after the previous obstacles was nothing whatsoever. He threw himself up and over it. There was more of a drop on the other side – about seven feet. Again he landed heavily; again he winded himself. But no pain no gain. He staggered down an alley beside another massive warehouse. It rose sheer into the darkness, yet Heck knew it from old. Formerly a siding depot for the old North West Railway company, it had been adapted into a nightclub in the 1980s, still functioned in that role and was known as the Uptown Emporium.

If Heck had his geography right, he was on the north side of it. The so-called Iron Bridge lay on the south. This was a footbridge made completely from iron, with slatted sides. It spanned a low-lying car park, but on the other side of that multiple passages led off among flats and houses. If he could make it that far, he'd be home and away.

He sidled around the vast structure, finally reaching its south side. A long, straight alley yawned in front of him, hemmed on the right by the club, but open to the elements on the left. He could follow this all the way – a distance of about a hundred yards – to the nightclub's front doors. But long before, if he turned sharp left, he'd be onto the Iron Bridge.

The problem was that access along here was again restricted: more sacks of beer cans, more crates filled with empty bottles. Lots of gateways on the right opened into service yards behind the club, many overflowing with rubbish. He stumbled past them all, still hearing voices behind. Yet now they sounded further away; the railway had hampered them significantly.

The Iron Bridge came up on his left. He turned thankfully onto it and slogged his way over. It was only eighty yards to the other side. He'd be across in no time. It barely mattered that his feet loudly clomped the riveted steel.

Until he realised there was someone ahead.

Heck slid to a halt, sodden hair prickling as he realised that what he'd first thought were echoes was the sound of another crew advancing onto the bridge from the far side. Then he spotted them: a pack of figures emerging along the footway through the gloom, though clearly they hadn't yet seen him. He backed slowly away, dumbfounded as to how this was possible. He'd assumed they'd lack local knowledge. They were a Manchester crew with a contingent of Russians. Though, on reflection, that wouldn't have stopped them scoping out the district while he was sharing drinks and a joke with Kayla. It wouldn't have been difficult for them to acquire a street-map of Bradburn – every newsstand sold one.

Sweat spraying off him, Heck clambered the bridge's iron-slatted side and peered down over its parapet onto the car park below. There were only one or two vehicles down there, the main spread of the bare tarmac lying empty. But it was a seventy-foot drop at least.

He clambered down onto the footway and leaned against

the slats, chest heaving. The mob were still approaching, heavy feet tramping the metal. He had no option but to hurry back the way he'd come, which he duly did. He reached the passage behind the Uptown and headed left. They might have put a guard at the front of the club to prevent him circling round, but then again they might not – there was no guarantee either way. But no more than five or six yards along, he found that this option was closed too – there were more voices ahead.

They had completely boxed him in.

No other avenues of escape remained – apart, possibly, from one.

A crazy idea wormed through his panic-stricken skull. Circa 1991, when he and his rugby mates had first been lads around town but still weren't old enough to legally enter nightclubs, they'd found a way to access the Uptown Emporium by an exterior dumbwaiter.

Heart racing, Heck ran into the nearest service yard.

It was small and wallowing in trash. But he groped his way forward. He didn't know if the ancient, creaking mechanism was still here, but now a tall, squared-off structure built against the nightclub wall, a brick chimney-like annexe to the main building, emerged from the blackness.

It *was* here. The next question was: did it still work?

The dumbwaiter had been operated manually by a rope-and-pulley system. Nightclub staff had used it to lower empty bottles and cans down the shaft to a car park-level yard, where most of the bins and dumpsters were kept. All those years ago, Heck and his mates had been able to climb inside this thing, one by one, and lower themselves down the shaft to a midway point where there was an aperture connecting with a flue, which led down to the Gents toilets on the Uptown's basement floor. Once there, they would climb through into the main club, merging with the regular clientele while none of the door staff were any the wiser.

The club was closed at present, but he'd still be safer inside it than out here.

His desperate, sweaty hands roved over the bricks – and yes, there were still two wooden, cupboard-like doors. Slimy and rotten, but with handles attached. He pulled them apart. The hinges squealed, but it hardly mattered as there was now so much noise from the passage behind: feet drumming on the bridge's metal footway, guttural voices shouting.

Foul air exhaled into Heck's face as he leaned into the void.

First he had to check that the platform was intact. The last thing he wanted was to plunge seventy feet down a brick shaft. He prodded around with his fingers. It was still there, albeit damp. He leaned on it. It wasn't just damp; it was sodden – the whole thing had rotted through. Behind him, voices filled the night. Heck glanced back, and saw slashing beams of torchlight beyond the yard.

With torches, they'd find the dumbwaiter. So he couldn't just hide inside it, he would have to go down.

He clambered through, shuffling on his knees onto mildewed woodwork. It groaned; there was a dull creaking of ropes. He ignored this as he closed the doors behind, enfolding himself in rank blackness. He felt around. If memory served, the rope passed up and down again through corresponding holes somewhere on the right side of the shaft, looping around a pulley high overhead. It had never been a completely straightforward process descending by this method. First, you needed to kick at a braking-peg somewhere on the left, levering it out of the shaft-side groove underneath. The dumbwaiter would then descend under its own weight. You could control its speed by manipulating the ropes and, when you wanted to stop, you kicked the brake back into place. It sounded easier than it was, especially in the dark.

He found the ropes first – they were stiff and greasy with disuse, but still intact, still taut.

But now a vertical line of light split the blackness in front of him.

Heck froze, ice sprouting on his sweat-drenched form.

They had caught the doors to the dumbwaiter in the glare of their torchlight.

That didn't mean they'd noticed it, or even would figure out what it was. But he couldn't afford to make a sound. He heard them talking, a weird polyglot of Russian and Mancunian.

'Nayka!' a Manc voice said. 'What the fuck're you playing at? You said you'd chased him round here!'

'Goddamn it, we did!' a Russian voice replied. Heck recognised it as the spider web guy.

'He wasn't on the bridge. We'd have met him. You lost him somewhere . . . fucking idiot!'

There were more grunts, more foul-mouthed curses.

'Fuck it . . . Kemp, you English fuck!' Nayka replied. 'He's here. All of you . . . the bastard finds him fucking lives!'

'Whoa . . . what's that?' a different Manc voice blurted. 'Meter cupboard or something?'

Heart pounding, Heck kicked into the blackness on his left. The sole of his shoe jarred against brickwork, sending an agonising jolt into his hip.

'Fuck was that?'

Heck kicked out again, wildly.

With a crunch of wood, an aged peg broke – and the platform dropped, taking Heck down with it. At first slowly; ancient cogs and wheels groaned through layers of rust and debris. But then faster and faster, soot and filth showering on top of him as reams of clag were torn from the encircling walls. The double doors above burst open, light flooded in.

'Fuck is this?' Nayka's voice boomed.

The rate of descent accelerated until Heck was in freefall. And of course the brake-peg had broken. He grabbed for the ropes, catching hold and reopening the burns already stinging his palms, and even then only slowed his descent slightly, the aged hemp sliding in sweat and blood.

'Fucking rope's moving!' the Manc called Kemp bellowed.

Heck clamped the rope to his body. It still slithered upwards; he still descended, albeit more slowly.

'Fucker's climbing down! Here, grab it, boys, grab it! Pull him back up!'

Black shadows roiled in the torchlight overhead as they grappled with the rope, bringing the dumbwaiter to a standstill. Again, Heck clawed around the inside of the shaft, fingers finding flat, wet bricks – until on the nightclub side they detected a jagged-edged cavity.

It was the same as it always had been – that old aperture was still there.

Heck was larger now than in his teenage days. It wouldn't be easy forcing his body down that black, airless rabbit-hole. The alternative might be worse, but it was still horrendous, snaking backwards into a steel tube that enclosed him to the contours.

'Up!' he heard Kemp shouting. 'Pull the fucking thing up!'

'*Het!*' Nayka replied. 'Fuck that – this goes on too long!' A metallic *snap* and *slick*. A firearm being cocked. 'Enough *derr'mo*!'

Three thudding reports followed, all aimed down the shaft. With careening impacts, the slugs hit the sides and made explosive contact with the dumbwaiter platform, reducing it to a mass of falling scraps.

Silence ensued in that tall, dark chamber, amid twists of smoke and dust.

If anyone alive had been looking up it, they'd have seen

214

the silhouetted head and shoulders of a figure against the torchlight as it leaned over and looked down.

'*Vic will shit!*' Kemp croaked.

'Let him fuck his shit!' Nayka retorted. 'How much this fucking son-bitch cop know, uh? Maybe everything, maybe nothing. Now he say nothing. Where this fucking thing lead?'

'Car park, I suppose.'

'Go. All you – get your fucking asses down! Find his fucking body. If nothing else, we take back to Vic . . . show we do our fucking job!'

Heck had been so busy sliding down the flue that he hadn't heard the first two shots, though he couldn't avoid the third – it had ricocheted from the edge of the aperture, the slug caroming inward, punching a fist-sized hole through the metal skin only a couple of feet in front of him.

He lay in the tube, heart thumping, sweat pumping. Only when the voices had fallen silent, the gang presumably making their way down to the car park, did he allow himself to breathe. He now had only one real option: make his way through the nightclub and force an exit somewhere at its front. If he didn't activate an alarm while crossing the interior, he certainly would when he started kicking and throwing his shoulder at doors. That would send these bastards running.

He slithered on down, catching his knees and elbows on riveted edges – just as he had all those years ago when he was a teen chasing skirt and beer. However, it was ancient and corroded now, snags of it plucking not just at his clothes but at his flesh. He'd be a mess by the time he got out of this place, but he couldn't afford to dally. When Ship's mob reached the bottom of the dumbwaiter shaft, they'd wonder why his body wasn't there. They'd think that he was clinging on somewhere. They might fire a few more shots, but worse still they might climb up themselves, at which point they'd discover the aperture. Of course, it all depended on how much time they were prepared to give themselves; they were on foreign soil here, so they wouldn't want to hang around indefinitely, especially if there was a chance their target had evaded them. He was a cop, after all. If he'd got away, how long before he came back with reinforcements?

At the bottom of the flue, Heck kicked an aged iron grid, which in the past he and his mates had to manually shift out of the way, though now it fell apart like melted chocolate. He inched his way out through another tiny gap, before dropping several feet into the dank black chamber that had once been the Gents toilets. The air in there was stale, malodorous, and it dripped with damp.

The door leading out into the access passage was again stiff with disuse. Heck had to batter it with his shoulder, loosening it in its frame, before he could grate it open. On the other side, the passage was filled with builders' rubble. It was still too dark to see anything, but he knew piled bricks, shattered masonry and an overturned cement-mixer when he tripped and stumbled over them. He blundered to his right for several yards – this had been the route into the main body of the nightclub – only to discover a brand-new wall barring further access.

He stepped away, panting in the blackness. The Uptown Emporium was still open for business; he'd seen that for himself when driving past the other day. But clearly not this lower section. This part was now derelict and closed off – which meant that he was trapped again.

He backtracked, passing the toilet door and heading in the other direction. There was progressively less rubble along here. Soon it was just a bare passage; paved floor, decayed plaster on the walls. If he remembered rightly, there was a flight of steps just ahead, descending to a fire-escape door. He slowed, located it with his toe and made his way down cautiously. It was so dark that his eyes still hadn't attuned. There was no light at all – until a few yards beyond the foot of the stair, when a faint yellow radiance appeared on the left. This would be the old fire-door, the light seeping in around its edges from the sodium lamps covering the car park. As Heck approached it, he heard multiple screeches of car brakes behind it.

He threw himself to the side of the passage, listening intently.

Several doors thudded open and closed, and then came the rattle and crash of boots impacting on what sounded like rusty metal. Heck remembered there'd been a wrought-iron fence along the boundary of the car park separating it from the Uptown.

He sucked in a breath so tight it was almost painful as several of those feet came clumping up to the fire-door – only to divert sideways towards the foot of the dumbwaiter. Again he heard voices, though they were too muffled for him to make sense of what they were saying. He slid forward along the wall, ears pricked. Moans of anger and bewilderment were followed by swearing and shouting. Heck pressed his ear to the door.

'Where – where the fuck is that bastard?' This was Nayka.

'You must've only winged him,' Kemp said.

'What – and he survive this fall? You fucking kid me?'

'I don't see any blood, Nayk,' a different voice replied. 'Look . . . there's a bit of the dumbwaiter tray here, but I don't see nothing else.'

'This cannot be. I skin that cop bastard alive when I catch him.'

Trails of sweat snaked down Heck's body as he listened.

'Look, now . . . search. He can't be far! I skin him and salt his wounds.'

Heck glanced back towards the passage stair. He supposed

he could retreat up there, and try to insinuate himself into the builders' rubble. Yeah, like they wouldn't find him there. He wondered if he could scramble back into the flue and make his way up to the shaft. But how was he going to get up it – by using the rope?

Yeah, course, he thought. *It's not so old and slippery that you won't fall straight down it, break your legs, your hips. And then have that Russian headcase to deal with.*

However, the tone of the conversation on the other side of the door had now changed.

Cooler heads were having their say.

'Nayka, we've got to go, mate.' This wasn't Kemp, but another Manc.

Kemp agreed. 'Yeah . . . if you wounded him, or missed him, and he got away – or even if he wasn't in that shaft to start with – he's still on his toes. And he's a copper, remember. That means the first phone he gets to, he'll call a fucking army. We've got to shift.'

'*Chush' sobach'ya! Pizdayob!*'

'Nayka, I can square this with Vic. I've known him all my life. He's not going to post my body-parts to my wife and kids like your fucking nutters would.'

'Son of a bitch!' the Russian spat. 'For this, I rip his fucking guts while he breathes! Make us look like *dolboeb*!'

There was another clatter of metal as they moved back to the car park. Still Heck listened. From outside, the fire-escape door would be a solid rectangle of black-painted wood, with no handles or bells. If they'd noticed it, they'd presumed no one could have got in that way.

'Nayka, you and me, we go and see Vic personal,' Kemp said. 'The rest of you – kick it!'

Engines growled to life, tyres screeching as vehicles rocketed away into the night. Soon there was only a single voice. It sounded like Kemp, and seemed as if he was on a phone.

'Yeah . . . yeah,' he said. 'We're coming in now. No worries, Vic . . .'

Heck leaned on the escape-bar. It depressed easily, and the door clicked open. He'd gambled there'd be no alarm connected to a section of the club that was now abandoned. It was a serious gamble – there was no guarantee the rest of the gangsters had gone yet – but he knew he had to do more than skulk in the darkness when an opportunity like this had presented itself. If absolutely nothing else, he had to figure out who he was dealing with.

He opened the door an inch or so, exposing deep weeds and thorns, and a flattened section of fencing. On the other side of that, a car roared past, heading off the car park at speed. About fifty yards away, he saw the cobweb-tattooed form of Nayka climbing into a BMW. In the immediate foreground, only one other vehicle remained, an Audi A3 soft-top. A stunted, rat-like figure stood alongside its open driver's door, a mop of tar-black hair hanging shoulder-length over a tan leather jacket. He was busy inserting a phone into his back pocket. Beyond him, Nayka's BMW blazed away, aiming for the far end of the car park, where there was a turning circle.

It was now or never.

Heck scampered across the trampled vegetation and broken fence, snatching up a length of rusted pipe as he did. The rat guy, Kemp, spun around, his ugly, nobbled face stretched lengthways in disbelief – but he was too late to prevent the pipe crashing down on his cranium. He slumped to the ground, senseless.

Heck rifled the guy's pockets, finding his phone and keys, and felt under his jacket, where a Makarov pistol was slotted into a shoulder-holster. Keeping as low as he could – that Russian lunatic was only at the far end of the car park, swinging his BMW around 360 degrees – Heck shoved all of these into his own pockets, took out his cuffs and fastened the guy's hands behind his back, before dragging him up and bundling him into the soft-top's rear footwell. Heck leaped behind the wheel himself, just as the BMW came growling back. It slowed, but Heck flashed his headlights, and Nayka, apparently suspecting nothing, drove on.

Sweating anew, Heck pulled out behind him.

As he did, he grabbed Kemp's phone and tapped in a number. It went straight to voicemail.

'This is Detective Superintendent Piper. I can't take your call right now, but please leave a message and I'll get back to you ASAP.'

'Ma'am, it's Heck,' he said. 'Just thought I'd let you know . . . looks like I'm on my way to Manchester for a meeting with Vic Ship. Seems he's been looking for me. The only difference now is we're doing it on *my* terms. I'll try and keep you clued in. But if something happens to me tonight . . . say, if I disappear without trace, at least you'll know who's responsible.'

Chapter 22

They had just joined the M61 motorway, Heck following closely behind Nayka in the stolen soft-top, when Kemp came round in the footwell. Initially, he groaned and cursed incoherently.

'You just – just –' he stammered in a thick, blathering voice, 'you just made the biggest mistake of your life, pal.'

Heck half-rotated in his seat, and dug the pipe lengthways into Kemp's ribs.

'Owww . . . you bastard!'

'If I need to hear from you, Mr Kemp, I'll ask. In the meantime, shut it!'

They drove on, the prisoner groaning. It was now late, well past midnight, and the traffic at this hour was sparse, which made it relatively easy to stay in touch with Nayka, even though he had a tendency to put his foot down. At Walkden, they swung south onto the M60, and then around the Winton interchange, heading east on the M602. The stark, Spartan architecture of Salford flitted past: the soulless tower blocks, the bare concrete undersides of flyovers.

Heck increasingly wondered what he was doing. It would

be easier and much safer to go after Vic Ship and his crew tomorrow, with the full knowledge and support of Operation Wandering Wolf, at which point he could lock them all up legitimately. The problem with doing it that way was that these were serious criminals who would clam up. They wouldn't be sweated, they wouldn't be conned, and no one would grass on anyone else unless the game was absolutely up for him. Ship would almost certainly claim ignorance of the incident, and there'd be no physical evidence to connect him to it. At best, a few of his lesser underlings would go down for assault and attempted abduction, and Heck would still be no nearer to catching John Sagan the Incinerator.

'Hey, dickhead!' Kemp grunted. 'You realise you're fucked ... you haven't cautioned me, you twatted my head ... that's police brutality for sure. Keeping me on the floor like this is mistreatment. Fucking nonce, none of this is legal.'

They left the motorway, circling the roundabout onto Regent Road.

'Hey, fuckface, d'you hear me? My brief'll have your underkeks on his trophy wall.'

'Don't waste your time trying to hide behind the law,' Heck said. 'There's no law here tonight.'

'You fucking dope,' the prisoner snorted. 'Do you actually know who I am? Do you know what's going to happen to you for this?'

They slowed down as a red light approached. Heck pulled up behind Nayka, and took advantage of the interlude to turn around again. But instead of sticking the piece of pipe into Kemp's ribs, he jammed the muzzle of the Makarov there, and cocked it.

The prisoner went rigid. He glowered up, eyes blazing malignantly between streaks of clotted blood. But he said nothing else.

'You still think you're under arrest?' Heck asked him. 'You

perhaps haven't got some street-thug instinct to tell you differently? You and your boys came to Bradburn to kill me, Mr Kemp. That means all bets are off. We aren't going to a police station, and you don't have any rights. So any more gob-shit from you, and it won't be Vic mailing your body-parts to your family, it'll be me mailing your body-parts to Vic!'

Heck struck him again, this time with the pistol but in the same part of the ribs as before.

Kemp cringed and choked with pain.

The lights changed to green, and Heck hit the gas. There were no further interruptions from the dim space behind as he followed the BMW along Regent Road, onto the Mancunian Way and finally south along Stockport Road, at which point they veered off into a maze of dingy backstreets where only one in every two or three lamps seemed to work.

After turning half a dozen corners, they trundled over cobbles up to an open pair of tall, rusty wrought-iron gates, which gave onto the forecourt of some vast, dark industrial building. There were several other vehicles parked in there already, and Nayka's BMW was funnelling slowly through the entrance to join them. Heck declined the option, and parked on the left side of the cobbled road, some thirty yards in front of the gates. He climbed out, Makarov in hand, and hunkered down on the car's offside. A couple of seconds later, the glow of the BMW's headlights, which he could still see through the rusty bars, was extinguished. There was a *thud* and *clump* as a car door was opened and closed. Another few seconds passed, and the tattooed form of Nayka appeared. He regarded the soft-top curiously. When a furious kicking and shouting commenced inside, he advanced towards it, faster and faster until he was running.

But Heck only sprang over the bonnet as the Russian reached the rear nearside door.

Nayka was stunned to find the cold muzzle of a pistol pressed into the base of his skull.

223

'Keep your hands where I can see them,' Heck said.

'This you, detective?' the Russian asked. He sounded amused. Warily, he stuck his arms out to either side. 'This you? You do our job for us, uh?'

'Turn around . . . slowly! So bloody slowly you might die of old age first.'

Heck backed away a couple of inches as the Russian swivelled around to face him, his weird oblong features split by that loopy, toothy grin.

Heck lunged, clobbering Nayka's left temple with the Makarov. The *smack* of steel on bone echoed down the cobbled street. 'That's for being dumb enough to think you could fox me in my own town!' Then Heck smacked him across the right temple. 'That's for being dumb enough to think you could fox me in any case!'

Nayka went down heavily and lay moaning on the cobbles. Heck searched him, finding first the Rambo knife, which he lobbed away into the blackness, then another handgun – a Serdyukov self-loader, or SPS – a short, blocky pistol, but slightly larger than the Makarov – and finally a mobile phone, which he smashed with the SPS's hilt. He opened the rear door to the soft-top and threw the SPS into the front passenger seat before dragging Kemp out by the legs. The guy landed on his nose, grunting with pain, swearing.

'On your fucking feet,' Heck said, backing away, so that both remained in his field of fire.

With his hands still cuffed behind his back, Kemp struggled – so much that Nayka, now streaming blood down both sides of his face, was able to stagger upright first. He assisted his Mancunian friend, hauling him to his feet by the collar of his tan jacket.

'Very good,' Heck said, as they stood dazedly in front of him. 'Now, we're going to see Mr Ship. You lead the way.' They turned and stumbled towards the wrought-iron gates, where Heck halted them again. 'But we're not going in together. Turn and face me.' They did so, battered faces etched with hatred. 'Nayka –' Heck dug a keyring from his pocket and tossed it over '– unfasten Mr Kemp's left handcuff.'

The Russian sneered. 'If you know my name, cop, you know what I can do.'

'I know you bleed like the rest of us, pal, I know you can die . . . and that'll do me at present.'

'So shoot me, uh. See if I care.'

'Yeah, sure . . . you're ready to pop your clogs now,' Heck scoffed. 'Without a chance to get even? And all over a pair of handcuffs. Can't see it somehow. Now do as I say, or I cave your head in again. You may survive tonight, but at this rate you'll need someone else to feed you.'

Nayka hawked up a wad of phlegm, spat it out and, very reluctantly, did as Heck instructed. The left handcuff was opened.

'You – Kemp,' Heck said. 'Turn, face the gate. Hook your left arm through the bars.'

'What're you up to?' Kemp asked. 'Are you that stupid? What the fuck you doing this for?'

'Let's not get into another conversation, Kempy. You always end up with broken ribs when me and you chat.' Kemp sneered as he hooked his left arm around two of the bars. 'Very good,' Heck said. 'Put 'em together again.' Kemp crossed his wrists, now enfolding the two bars. 'Excellent . . . you, Nayka, snap 'em back into place. That's it – recuff him, so he's fastened to the gate and can't run off anywhere.' Nayka did so, re-attaching the cuffs, locking his mate into stasis. 'There you go. Easy, wasn't it?'

'Your death won't be,' Kemp said.

Heck ignored that. 'Nayka – throw me the key.'

It landed near Heck's feet. He reached down and recovered it, the gun trained squarely on his Russian captive.

'Step away from the gate,' Heck said. 'A couple of yards – no more.'

Nayka stepped away, now grinning again, spookily. Heck approached Kemp to check the cuffs were secure, which they were. He also tested the bars; they were solid.

'Look on the bright side, Mr Kemp,' he said. 'At least I'm sparing you Vic's wrath. Nayka here is gonna get the full brunt of it.'

'He'll kill you for this, copper,' Kemp sneered. 'Telling you, pal – this is going to end really badly for you.'

'Maybe.' Heck glanced around. 'Just out of interest, what is this place?'

'Seeing as you'll never be leaving it alive, it's the old soapworks in Longsight. It's been up for sale a long time, and it's likely to stay that way. Certain people we know ensure that prospective buyers *never* come here. No one does.'

'Very scary,' Heck said, taking the mobile phone from his pocket. He tapped in Gemma's number again. As before, he got the pre-recorded message. 'Ma'am . . . Heck here with a quick update. My meeting with Mr Ship will take place in the old soapworks somewhere in Longsight. Can't give you an exact address but it isn't far off the A6. Don't send anyone yet, if you don't mind. I feel sure I'm about to learn something good, here. Course, if I don't check in again after two hours, well, you'll know where to make tomorrow's first fingertip search.' He cut the call, stuck the phone in his pocket again and turned back to Kemp. 'Not really adapted to the mobile phone age yet, have we?'

'Fucking smartarse, that's not going to help you. None of this is going to help you.'

'We'll see.' Heck looked at Nayka. 'All right, my friend – walk. Let's go and have this meeting we're all so looking forward to.'

226

Nayka turned, almost nonchalantly, and strolled in through the open gate: a long, confident stride, hunched back, sloped shoulders. 'You give us good runaround, man,' he said.

Ahead of them, the building loomed closer. It clearly had been a factory at one time, but was long out of use. Heck saw scabrous walls, exposed beams, a clutter of bricks and broken tiles on the ground.

'You smash Mental Mickey's nose.'

'Keep your voice down, Nayka.'

A doorway yawned directly in front. Beyond it lay a straight corridor; what looked like dull red firelight was glimmering at the far end.

'He owe you big time for that. And he collect . . . you know these guys . . .'

Heck thwacked the Makarov against the back of Nayka's head. It was a *thunking* impact, the Russian twisting where he stood, before sagging down to his knees.

'I said keep the noise down!' Heck hissed. 'I don't need you warning people we're coming!'

Nayka knelt there, dark blood welling through the shorn bristles on his scalp. Heck grabbed the collar of his fleece-lined doublet and yanked him back to his feet.

'*Mu'dak!*' Nayka whispered.

'You asking for another?' Heck said, propelling him along the first corridor.

'You no ordinary British cop,' the Russian snarled.

'You fucking got that right, pal.'

Some five yards from the open door at the end, Heck heard voices: mutters of conversation, idle, casual; a bunch of guys who weren't expecting anything, let alone the worst.

'All right!' he shouted, as he shoved his captive through the gap. Nayka almost stumbled, but Heck grabbed his collar again to keep him upright. 'You wanted me, gents . . . *I'm here!*'

Chapter 23

What had once been the main shop-floor in the old soap-making plant danced with reddish firelight exuding from a number of braziers. The factory was long disused, its bare asphalted floor running off for maybe a hundred yards, only broken here and there by cement pillars.

At least thirty men were present, most grouped in the central area. They were a variety of types: different ages, colours, sizes. Some wore crumpled jackets and ties, as if they'd been called here from the office or a function. A couple were in overalls, others in tracksuits, jeans and hoodie tops. Several of them were armed with punk weapons like bats, blag-handles and pipes.

All gazed open-mouthed at the main door.

Even the five dogs they had with them stood silent, ears pricked up. These were two full-grown Rottweilers and three pit bull terriers. All were on chain leads and had spiked collars, and were viciously scarred around the heads and faces. The presence of these brutes explained the dried bloodstains and gnawed bones all over the factory floor – and maybe the bundle of concrete posts and wreaths of wire-mesh propped against the nearest pillar, which looked as if it could all quickly be assembled into a temporary corral.

'Well, well,' Heck said, keeping a tight grip on Nayka's collar and making sure the Makarov was visible on his shoulder, its muzzle pressed under his ear. 'If there's no crime anywhere in Manchester tonight, we'll know why . . . the main causes of it are all here. I see you've even brought your pets with you. I've never felt as wanted.'

One of the dogs issued a low, rumbling snarl.

'What the fuck . . .?' one of the men stammered, stumping forward.

'Easy!' Heck raised the pistol.

A couple of the others had lurched forward too, but now halted.

They still looked communally stunned, mouths gawping, eyes popping in the firelight.

A few dozen yards away on the right, a row of offices was partitioned from the main workshop by a partially glazed wall. One of the office doors slammed open and two figures now emerged. Heck recognised the first as Vic Ship. The Manchester kingpin was dressed in a dark green suit and slightly paler green shirt. As in his police mugshot, he had heavy, brutal features, a tattooed gorgon on his neck, and greasy grey hair bound in a short pony-tail. His hands were gnarled and thickly knuckled, and covered in chunky rings. The guy with him was maybe the more public face of the firm. He was young and good looking, with wavy light brown hair. He wore a tie with his sharply cut Norton & Townsend suit, and didn't sport a single tat, nor a scrap of cheap or tawdry jewellery.

'Fucking bastard!' one of the others snapped, focusing on Nayka's bloodied face. The dogs pulled on their leads, jowls wrinkling back on hideous, sword-like fangs.

'Everyone stay calm,' Ship said in a gravelly voice. He and

his deputy had advanced and were now mingling with the rankers.

'You tell 'em, Mr Ship,' Heck advised him.

'You've made a big mistake,' the deputy said quietly.

'Maybe,' Heck replied. 'But this could turn sour for *all* of us. The main question is how valuable is your St Petersburg connection?' He twisted the Makarov muzzle into Nayka's ear. 'Is this guy just a soldier who no one'll miss? Or is he the clown-prince, and will his family feel it badly if he gets popped while he's over here?'

'Put the gun down, son,' Ship said slowly. 'You're well out of your depth here.'

'*Hey!*' Heck shouted, spotting that one of them was sidling into the shadows. '*Back where I can see you! And you, hiding behind that pillar . . . out, now!*'

The two mobsters slid back into view, hands raised.

'Fucking cop bastard!' the younger one of the twosome said. 'You fucking dead-arsed pig –'

'Trevor!' Ship interjected. 'Shut . . . your . . . sodding . . . trap!'

'Yeah, zip it, Trev,' Heck said. 'There's no room for hotheads in negotiations like these.'

'You realise you're in a situation that's completely out of your control?' Ship said. His accent bespoke the tough back-streets of inner Manchester; when he spoke, it was from the side of his mouth, through clenched teeth – but his tone was calm, controlled. 'Whatever happens, there's no way you'll emerge from this in one piece.'

'You'd better hope I do, Vic. Because my gaffer knows exactly where I am, and if I don't check in with her in a couple of hours, she'll be coming right to this door . . . and guess what, she'll have an awful lot of mates with her.'

'You expect me to believe that when you're here on your tod?'

'Maybe you'll believe this idiot.' Heck poked Nayka's cheek with the Makarov. 'Tell him.'

'Is true,' the hostage said sullenly. 'He called in. They know.'

'If they know, boss, they'll be on the way now,' one of the others warned. 'We should –'

'It's not my style to bring the cavalry when all I want to do is talk,' Heck cut across him.

This was greeted by a short, bemused silence.

'So . . .' Ship shrugged. 'Talk.'

'First of all, I'm sure you lot didn't come here with toys either. So let's see the hardware. And by that I mean the *real* stuff. All of it, now – on the floor.'

Ship gave a wintry smile. 'And meanwhile what do you do?'

'I keep wielding the upper hand, Mr Ship. Which is perfectly reasonable given you've got a thirty-to-one advantage.'

There was another brief silence, but the gang boss seemed genuinely interested to see what would happen next. He glanced at his cronies and nodded.

'Boss!' someone protested.

'*Do it!*' he barked.

Gradually, a succession of weapons clattered onto the asphalt: not just the bats and pickaxe handles Heck had already seen, but pistols, knives, machetes.

'Smart move,' Heck said. He now noticed a hanging leather harness attached to long straps that were looped over a steel beam in the ceiling. 'You fellas pick the strangest places for your weird sex games.'

'You're fucking dead, you piece of filth!' one of them growled.

'We'll break you in half, pig!' the young one called Trevor shouted. 'We'll see you in the fucking Pain Box!'

Ship threw a swift, freezing glance in his direction.

Though fleetingly elated to hear those crucial words 'Pain Box', Heck immediately realised that it was even more crucial *not* to react, not to show that it meant anything to him.

'I'll treat those threats with the contempt they deserve,' he said, 'given that some lone operator with a flamethrower is doing a total number on your Bradburn operation . . .'

Ship's eyes narrowed.

'Or is that what the pooches are for?' Heck asked. 'You thought I'd have something to tell you about the Incinerator, eh?'

The encircling bodies were now taut with tension. Lips quivered; there were low, profane curses. The dogs whimpered and snarled.

Heck dug the Makarov deeper into the side of Nayka's head.

'*You!*' he shouted.

A burly guy with a shaven dome and a face as nicked and mauled as any of the dogs' was hanging onto the harness straps. He held them with one hand, though no doubt it would require two when he was raising and lowering someone in the midst of those snarling, slashing snouts.

'Let it go, bud,' Heck said.

The chrome-dome hesitated.

'Let it go . . . or Nayka gets the first and you get the second, right in the middle of your fat froggy face.'

'Do it,' Ship said tightly.

Grudgingly, the chrome-dome obeyed, and the harness fell to the floor, the straps whipping up and over the beam and fluttering down on top of it.

'Good,' Heck said. 'In the meantime, Mr Ship, here's a tip you won't need to rip out of my flesh. Brutalising coppers is a bad idea. Long term, it's likely to backfire on you.'

'You're supposed to be a copper?' Ship replied scornfully.

'Aren't coppers meant to be upstanding citizens? Aren't they supposed to be clean as whistles? Yet not so long ago you were in conflab with a right bunch of tearaways.'

Heck didn't reply straight away. He ought to have realised that Ship's firm would have spotters in Bradburn, probably sitting on Shaughnessy and his crew, during the course of which they'd noted the gang leader in close conversation with Heck outside the police station. They'd put two and two together and come up with five, but it was an easy mistake to make.

'That's right,' Heck confirmed. 'Just like I'm in conflab with you now . . . and I'm gonna tell you exactly the same thing I told him. Someone is stirring it. Some privately employed mad-dog, who's either got an axe to grind with you, or Shaughnessy, or both of you. I don't know who he is, but he'd clearly like nothing better than for you two to tear each other a new one.'

'So that's it?' Ship's deputy said. 'Shaughnessy's not behind these burnings . . . and we have to take *your* word for it?'

'What do *you* think, Vic?' Heck asked Ship. 'Are these attacks Shaughnessy's style? Are they even within his capability?'

Ship smirked. 'He doesn't have any fucking style . . . or any fucking dignity. Soft little twat even rang me up the other day to reassure me it wasn't him.' Ship shook his head, tutting with disdain. 'And as for his capability, well . . . we live and learn, it seems.'

'You're fighting a war for no reason, Vic – and you know you are. You also know it's a war you can't win because you don't even know for sure who your opponent is.'

'This the best he can do, the little shit?' Ship's deputy scoffed. 'Send a bent copper round to plead his case for him?'

'This is all great talk, Vic,' Heck said. 'But you're fooling no one. The truth is, Shaughnessy would have to be off his

233

rocker to pick a fight with a firm like yours. And you know he would.'

Ship looked thoughtful. 'Just for the sake of argument, Detective Heckenburg, let's say you're *not* on young Lee's payroll. How well do you think you know him?'

'I'm learning more about him all the time.'

'Well, learn this: he'd rape and strangle his own mother and sell her carcass for meat if he thought there was a quid in it. He's a lowlife of the worst order.'

'I understand that he's pissed you off.'

'Pissed me off?' Ship laughed. 'That'd be the understatement of all time.'

'Yeah, but you haven't hit him as hard as you could,' Heck said. 'You haven't wiped him off the face of the map yet. Instead you grabbed two of his boys on March 24 and tried to torture some intel out of them –'

'I have no fucking clue what you're talking about,' Ship said.

'But they didn't give him up, did they . . . the Incinerator? You know why, Vic? Because my guess is they didn't know who he is any more than you do. So you got uneasy about it, didn't you? And your next move was to try and drag me here – a so-called Shaughnessy insider, and a copper to boot. If I couldn't give you the inside track, no one could, eh?'

'You done?' Ship asked simply.

'He'll be done like a fucking kipper!' one of them said.

Heck could sense their agitation growing, becoming over-whelming.

'Scared yet?' Nayka chuckled. 'You should be.'

Heck backed up a couple of yards, increasingly unhappy about the black entranceway behind him. He shuffled side-ways so that it stood to his right, dragging Nayka with him.

'You really think I'd come all the way here to plead Shaughnessy's innocence if I knew he was guilty?' Heck said.

234

'How much would he need to pay me to take a chance like this? And how do you think my real boss would react if she knew I was on someone else's roster tonight? You've already had it confirmed that she knows what I'm doing.'

Ship gave Heck another long, probing gaze.

'The Incinerator's real enough, Vic,' Heck said. 'No one's denying it. And whether he works for Lee Shaughnessy or not, he's quite clearly targeting your Bradburn connections and doing a damn good job of it. And again . . . you know that already without needing to hear it from me.'

Ship remained blank-faced. There was stone silence from the rest of his firm.

'You've got a deadly enemy out there,' Heck added. 'Even if it *is* Shaughnessy, it won't be an easy fight, and how open it leaves you to GMP Serious will be anyone's guess. Ever since this thing kicked off, they've been watching you, old pal. They can't wait to bang you away. You saw the sentences the Wild Bunch got. How'd you like a bit of that action?'

Still Ship said nothing.

'And what if it's not Shaughnessy?' Heck asked him, 'and you've put all your efforts into the wrong crew? Won't be your finest hour, will it?'

Now all the hoodlums stood in silence. They might not like what they were hearing, but they had no option but to listen. Heck's eyes roved across them and focused on their leader again.

'No more torture murders, Mr Ship. Those two bodies in the landfill – that was nasty. I mean *really* nasty. Any more like that and all deals are off the table.'

Ship half-smirked. 'Deals?'

'Anything you get on who's doing this to you . . . you give it to me. Especially the Incinerator. I'd *really* be interested in meeting him.'

There were disbelieving sniggers at the sheer audacity of this.

'And we just walk away, is that it?' Ship still smirked, but it was noticeably lacking in humour.

'That'd be your most painless option.'

'Yeah . . . there are no such options facing *you*!' someone else retorted.

'Your call, Vic,' Heck said. 'Call off your torturers, walk away from this war with your firm largely intact. Leave us to deal with the human fireball.'

It would have been a hopeless plea even if Heck had possessed the authority to make such a deal. He knew the gang boss would reject the offer outright, if for no other reason than to save face. At least four of his people had been wiped out, and he would sit back and let the cops do the running? No chance. His reign of power would be over in an instant. But it was worth doing this to plant the germ of an idea in Ship's mind that maybe – just maybe – he was fighting the wrong enemy. It had also been useful to Heck as a probing exercise. Without him even trying hard, they'd confirmed that Sagan was on their team. That info alone was worth the risk of this confrontation. The main problem now was how to get out of here alive, and deliver it to the taskforce.

'Anyway,' he said. 'I'm off. With or without a promise from you that you're going to leave this to us. I'll consider it's been worth the trip from Bradburn if you at least think about it . . . and when I say *it*, I mean your business, your cash-flow, your liberty . . .'

'You're a ballsy bastard, I'll give you that,' Ship said.

'You invited me here. And in return I'm doing you a big favour.'

'You reckon?'

'I could've come to this shithole team-handed, I could have locked you and every one of these goons up for attempting to abduct a police officer. But instead I came alone. Like I say, to talk.'

'So I owe you one, do I?'

'Maybe.'

Ship pursed his lips and nodded. 'All right, that's fair. You've got a count of three.'

Heck held the pistol up. 'This is loaded. And I'm not relinquishing it.'

'One,' Ship said.

Heck planted his foot in Nayka's backside, shoving him violently forward. Then ran.

'Two!' the voice echoed behind him. 'Three . . . *fuck him up!*'

Heck hit the night air outside at what felt like a hundred miles per hour, but already his ears were ringing with the yowling and snarling of the five dogs. He didn't know what kind of start he had, and it was only forty-odd yards from the factory entrance to the factory gate, but already he could sense them gaining, could hear the accelerating skitter of paws. As he ran, the gangster Kemp, still chained to the open gate, craned his neck around to face him.

'Whoa!' Kemp shouted. 'What's going on?'

Heck dipped into his pocket as he ran, to try and find the key, but he already knew that he wouldn't have time to unlock the guy's cuffs.

'Genuine apologies, pal!' He ran on past the struggling captive.

Kemp shrieked as the first of the beasts tore into him. A few yards down the street, Heck spun around, Makarov in hand. Despite the darkness, he could see the dogs were all over Kemp, savaging him, though one, the fifth, had ignored this easy target and was venturing forward. More distantly, triumphant shouts sounded from their keepers. But they had only just emerged from the building and weren't yet clear about who was being attacked. Heck pegged off three quick shots in their basic direction, but in all cases aimed high, seeking only to drive them to cover. He turned and ran on. The fifth dog bounded in pursuit.

Heck thumbed the electronic fob. Just ahead, the soft-top's lights flickered. Ten yards and he was home and dry. But then he tripped, and though he didn't fall, he went staggering forward, losing impetus and coordination. Slaver-filled snarls sounded at his heels.

Even though the car was unlocked, he wouldn't have enough time to get inside. He turned again, taking aim, but it was too late for that – the dog, a frothy-jawed, pop-eyed monstrosity of a Rottweiler – reared up, snapping at his hand. Heck yanked it out of the way, turned frontward again, and caromed headlong into the soft-top's front grille – it slammed his midriff, smashing his upper body down on its bonnet.

The Rott also crashed into the stationary object, stunning itself.

For several stupefied seconds, they lay on the cobblestones together. But as Heck dragged himself to his feet, the dog jumped up too, rearing again, jaws snapping savagely. Heck hammered down with his pistol, cracking it on the skull once, twice, three times. Yelping and whining, the dog ducked and rolled. He couldn't shoot clean as it squirmed crazily away from him. Still winded, Heck felt his way around the vehicle – only for the dog to barrel into his legs from behind. He clubbed it again, raining blows on its back and head.

It cowered, squealing. But now another of the brutes approached, a squat, brutal shape galloping down the street from the factory gates.

Heck kicked the dazed Rott away from him, scrambled to the driver's door, lugged it open, threw himself inside and slammed it closed. As he threw the Makarov onto the passenger seat and jammed the key into the ignition, the second dog, an American pit bull, sprang onto the bonnet,

238

its muscular body ramming the windscreen, which spider-webbed with cracks.

Heck knocked the car into reverse and tromped the gas. The soft-top roared backward down the alley, but still failed to dislodge the dog, which initially was only visible as a mass of fur and gnashing teeth. Heck swung the car round a tight corner, mounting the kerb and smacking the base of a cylindrical steel post with a road-sign at the top. He jolted against the back of his seat, but the dog was flung upward onto the roof. He felt the weight as it landed on the soft leather overhead, and heard the scraping and scratching of its claws as it tried to gain a purchase. Frantically, he switched gears, dragged the wheel left and floored the pedal, accelerating away down the next alley. Framed in his rear-view mirror, the damaged street-sign teetered and toppled, crashing slantwise across the passage, blocking the procession of headlights now spilling out through the factory gates.

Heck got his foot down all the harder, pushing the needle up past thirty towards forty. But somehow the pit bull was clinging on, rending the fabric of the roof. Trained to assail its quarry until death, it ripped and tore, burrowing its way through directly above Heck's head. He braked hard, trying to unsaddle it, but also to avoid a wheelie bin – in which he failed. The soft-top struck the bin side-on but explosively, the car screeching to a halt. The dog was hurled sideways, spinning through the air, and yet such was the clasp of its jaws on the shredded leather that it didn't fly loose but swung around to the front. It bounced onto the bonnet on its back, righted itself and scampered back up the windshield as Heck changed gears. When he hit the pedal again, it was already back above him. The hole it had ripped was large enough for it to force its snout through, its hot drool spattering down Heck's face.

He clawed at the passenger seat, but both the Makarov and the SPS had been thrown into the footwell by the collision, and were out of reach.

With no other choice, he jammed his foot to the floor.

Snarling like a wolf, the dog worked its way down, feral bloodlust gurgling from its throat. But directly in front now, the alley ended at what looked like a proper road. Heck saw real streetlights, cars passing. He sped towards it, banging over potholes and bits of rubbish. This time the bastard thing had surely had it; even a pit bull's jaw muscles couldn't resist an emergency stop at this speed. But then it touched the top of his head, nudging him with its nose, grizzling his scalp with its teeth.

Heck ducked. Its entire head was now through the gap as it slashed and bit. He threw an arm up to fend it off, and half-forgot about the road, only hitting the brake when it was too late.

Tyres smoking, the soft-top careered into the middle of a junction. Despite the hour, there were other road users around. They veered past, horns blaring, as he skidded 360 degrees through the intersection. The dog, its head trapped in the roof fabric, was flung violently forward, and then back, and then from side to side, battering the car with its body.

At what point its spinal cord shattered, Heck couldn't say, but when he came to a halt in a park gateway over a hundred yards from the alley, its lifeless corpse hung limply down the outside of the driver's door. He shoved upward, slamming his hands again and again into the mangled muzzle, until he'd pushed the grotesque thing out through the hole.

It dropped heavily out of sight.

Heck wanted to sit there for several minutes, shaking, teeth chattering. But how long would it take so many guys to move a fallen street-sign? He threw the car back into gear, pulled a three-point turn in the park entrance, and swung out onto the road. Fleetingly, he didn't know where he was or which way he needed to go, but none of that mattered so long as he went somewhere.

Chapter 24

Vic Ship was in the old soap-making plant, behind the bare desk in his makeshift office, when his minions finally reported back that the cop had got away. It didn't trouble him – he'd half expected that; in some ways it suited him. Otherwise, he'd never have given the guy a head-start.

This wasn't a real office, not any more – just a slightly private place in which to insulate himself from the common herd whenever they assembled here, and to reinforce the impression that he was the man, the one you needed permission to actually speak to. But there was no decent equipment or furniture in here, just scraps and relics left over from the days when this gutted structure had been in normal use. Rubbish cluttered the corners; dust-laden blinds covered its outer windows, which were uniformly dingy and cracked. Ship and his number one fixer, Alan Cornish – the young presentable guy who'd accompanied him during Heck's brief interrogation – now sat one at either side of the litter-strewn desk.

While they waited, Cornish flicked through pages on his iPad.

Slowly, the rest of the crew reconvened on the old factory's shop-floor, dogs yipping and whining, men arguing. The first one to come to the office was Nayka. He didn't bother to knock, but noticeably – further lessening his 'iron man' image, along with the blood and bruises he still sported – he now wore a hoodie top under his fleece-lined doublet, even though it concealed his notorious cobweb insignia. It amused Ship to see the Russian in this reduced state. Ever since arriving in Manchester, this semi-official spokesman for the St Petersburg syndicate had adopted a leadership role, treating his British colleagues as newcomers to the urban crime scene.

At present, he was fuming.

'You gotta kill this Goddam cop!' the Russian stated flatly. In the fashion of most of the psychopaths Ship knew, Nayka's humiliation had enraged him but it hadn't humbled him. 'You gotta kill his family, his friends, everyone who knows him.'

'Says who?' Ship asked. 'You? Just coz you got your itsy bitsy face mucked up.'

'Is the code.'

'Not round here.'

Nayka's angry face twisted further. 'You let him speak you like that . . . some pigshit cop? You let him shame you in front your *bratva*?'

Ship sat back. 'Far as I could see, Nayk, he was tipping us some kind of wink.'

'*Chto za hoy!* One of your dogs died.'

'Our dogs die all the time, usually in the ring. Am I supposed to cry?'

'Tony Kemp get hurt.'

Ship eyed him, amused. 'Tony Kemp fucked up. As did you. You were supposed to bring Heckenburg back here. Not the other way round.'

'Vic! This son-bitch cop one of Shaughnessy's rats?'

Ship glanced at Cornish. 'What do *you* think?'

The fixer shrugged. 'If he is part of their crew, why didn't

243

the rest of them come with him? Start shooting, turn their flamethrower on the whole lot of us?'

Nayka glanced from one to the other, as if he couldn't believe what he was hearing. 'You say Shaughnessy not behind this . . . just because he not come here?'

Cornish stood up. 'Whoever's doing this is fucking nuts. Shaughnessy's crew are a bunch of psychotic kids. They might fit the bill, but . . . I dunno, shouldn't tonight have given them an opportunity they couldn't miss?' He shrugged again. 'Their pet cop follows our team here . . . he finds a lot of us all in the same place. He's got a phone, guns. Why are we still alive?'

'That copper really strike you as the sort who'd hang out with a bunch of nutty kids?' Ship wondered.

'Hard to tell,' Cornish said. 'He's got balls, I'll say that for him.'

'We send them to his family in fucking parcel post,' Nayka snapped.

'What exactly do we know about him?' Ship asked.

Cornish consulted his iPad again. 'Thus far, name and rank. I can look him up though.'

Ship shook his head. 'Save that for later.'

'Later?' Nayka said. 'Nothing? No payback?'

Ship stood up. 'You need to understand something, Nayk . . . in Britain we don't kill coppers. Not unless the situation's very extreme.'

'And what this – fight in schoolyard?'

'We need to consider what Heckenburg told us. As you know, I was already halfway there myself. Those two goons of Shaughnessy's should've talked under that much torture . . . we have to assume there was nothing they could tell us. That's why I'm not engaging in World War Three. At least not yet. This Incinerator bastard may have nothing to do with Lee Shaughnessy.'

Nayka shook his head. Fresh blood trickled down his cheek. 'Vic – you no ignore this!'

'You need to relax more,' Ship said. 'Al, we can't use this place any more. Put the word out.'

Cornish nodded.

'How this make you look in St Petersburg?' Nayka asked them. 'You really kind of guy we do business with?'

Ship had been about to leave – Cornish was holding the office door open for him – but now he turned slowly around.

'Putin lean on my people,' Nayka said. 'Russia not so good for men like us. We need new place. We come here, we could make your life very good . . . or very bad.'

Ship half-smiled. 'Are you actually threatening me?'

'*Njet*. But is fact, my friend.' Nayka gave that now familiar but never less than unnerving toothy grin of his. 'I here to watch you work, how you say – assess. See if you be good friend or easy foe. What you want me to tell, uh?'

Ship's smile faded. 'The beast from the east shows his claws at last . . . and very nasty they are too.'

Cornish closed the door again.

Nayka's grin broadened. 'You think to send *me* home in box. But not cop. How that look?'

Ship regarded him. They weren't over a barrel with these Russians. They had options, but the crime scene in the UK was changing rapidly. Even the oldest and most deeply rooted firms had to change too, had to evolve if they wanted to survive.

'I don't deny that what that bastard Heckenburg did tonight was a right liberty,' Ship said. 'Whether he helped us out or not, you're right, Nayka – he cheeked me. But this isn't Russia, and we play a bit nicer than you lot do. And if you boys are going to move over here, you're going to have to play it nicer too. You know why? Because if you think Vladimir Putin's a rough customer, you haven't met the Greater Manchester Police. However, yeah . . . Heckenburg got in my face tonight. And never once did I intend that he was just going to walk away from that. But this is a cop, not some smackhead who owes us a few bob. So we're not going to cowboy this fucking thing, and I'm not getting involved personally. Nor is anyone else on my network.'

Nayka groaned. 'Not this fucking freelancer again.'

'He's good,' Ship retorted.

Nayka threw his arms out. 'Me, *I* good too. I do it! Say word!'

'Are you serious?' Ship asked him. 'After tonight, they'll have an all points from here to Land's End on a dickhead with a Russian accent whose collection of tats stands out even in this age of rebels without causes. No, the job will get done – on *my* orders, at some point, when the time is right. Not just Heckenburg, but Shaughnessy too. He's the one who's *really* got it coming, because even if he's not behind these murders, he's taken what's ours, and that can never be. So rest assured, it'll be nasty and messy and horrible enough even for you and the rest of your bloodthirsty rabble over there in the land that time forgot. But as far as the world's concerned – *we'll* be squeaky clean from start to finish.'

Chapter 25

It was almost two in the morning when Heck finally got back to Bradburn.

He'd initially had no clue where he was headed, but gradually his frazzled nerves calmed and his stomach settled. He'd noticed that he was progressing south through Levenshulme and into Heaton Chapel. From here, it was a simple matter of continuing towards the M60, and then following it north again in a clockwise direction.

His first port of call on returning was the town centre side-street where he'd left his Megane. He parked behind it, reclaimed the two firearms from the footwell, tucked them under his jacket and climbed out. The Audi soft-top, which might have cost thirty grand new, was in pretty poor condition, particularly at the rear where it had lost its bumper bar and the bodywork was crumpled. In addition, the bonnet was scored by claw-marks and it would need a new roof. Big deal. Someone would eventually report it as a knocker, the official owner – Ship, or one of his crew – would be informed, and they'd have to arrange for collection and repair. But that was their problem now.

Heck trudged across Westgate Street. There was no one

else around. Every bar and club was closed, not so much as a winking on-and-off neon sign to light his way back to the mouth of the alley he'd run along previously. When he walked down there again, the rusted gate still hung open. He entered the pitch-black yard. He slipped Kemp's phone from his pocket, tapped in his own number and was rewarded by a flashing blue/green pattern in the farthest corner. A sharp electronic buzzing followed.

Heck retrieved his phone, switched Kemp's off and traipsed tiredly back to his Megane. He climbed in, turned Kemp's phone off and threw it into his glovebox, and then waited while the interior of the car warmed up. His breath formed a cloud on the inside of the windscreen. He scrubbed it away with the elbow of his jacket, and glanced down at himself. Given the state of his torn and dirty suit, it looked as if he'd be in casuals from tomorrow. Only now, hours later, was he feeling the extent of his physical efforts, his limbs leaden, his joints aching and stiff. He likely had bruises where he didn't even know he had body-parts.

Wearily, he stripped his tie off and speed-dialled Eric Fisher. It switched immediately to voicemail – hardly surprising at this hour of the morning.

'Eric, it's me,' Heck said. 'Sorry for calling this late, but glad I've not woken you. Here's a job for first thing tomorrow morning. I need you to get onto Interpol. Find out anything you can about a Russian mobster called Nayka. That's all I've got on him, I'm afraid, apart from the fact he's covered all over in spider-web tattoos . . . get me chapter and verse, if you can, yeah?'

He cut the call, slid his keys into the ignition and brought his vehicle to life.

The drive across town was less complex than usual owing to the absence of traffic – it was now the early hours of Monday morning, so Heck reached his destination swiftly. As he pulled up and parked, his phone began buzzing. Assuming it would be Eric Fisher, who possibly had been woken after all, he put it to his ear, another apology forming on his lips.

'Heck – what the hell's going on?' Gemma asked. She sounded as tired as he felt.

'Oh, ma'am . . .' he said, surprised. 'Everything all right?'

'No, it bloody well isn't! Of course it bloody isn't! I've been trying to get you for the last five minutes. First you don't answer your own phone, and there's no answer on that last one you called me from –'

'Ah, yeah . . . no one on that line now. Sorry, ma'am, didn't expect you to call at this hour.'

'What's this crap about you going off to Manchester for a meeting with Vic Ship?'

'I tried to give you a call at the time, to explain,' he said.

'Yeah, well, I've been busy. MIRWeb video conference with Joe Wullerton. All bloody night. So I've literally only just got your messages.'

'It's OK. If you were about to send the cavalry to look for me, there's no need.'

'Well, that's good news, I suppose.' She sounded genuinely relieved, if still a little cross. 'That would've been my next call. So what's actually been going on? And just the facts if you don't mind, not the usual embroidery.'

'It was a bit naughty of me, I admit –'

'No kidding!'

'– but an opportunity came my way and I had to take it.'

Her brief silence implied her usual disapproval of such recklessness. 'So you *did* go to see Ship?'

'Kind of.'

'For Christ's sake, Heck . . . did you or didn't you?'

'I met him, yeah.'

The silence lingered for so long that Heck thought she'd cut the call.

'And you're still in one piece?' she finally asked.

'Nearly got turned into dog-chow. That wouldn't have been much fun.'

'What happened?'

'I can forward you the details later, but that address I gave you, that soap-making place – I suspect it gets used for dog-fighting, at the very least. We could do with tipping off GMP Longsight, even if we do it anonymously.'

'Are you in a secure position now?'

'Suppose so. I'm in the car park outside your B&B.'

'*What?*' She sounded genuinely startled.

'You're in The Blackwood Arms, yeah?'

'Yeah. What're you doing here?'

Heck glanced up, and saw a curtain twitch back in one of the pub's first-floor windows.

'I'm not totally sure.' It was as honest an answer as he could give at that moment. He wasn't exactly agog with tiredness, but he was bone-weary. Even as he tried to ponder the situation, his thinking became steadily fuzzier – probably as much through shock as fatigue. 'Erm . . . but I know I didn't want to do this over the phone.'

She said nothing.

'Can I come up? Oh – unless you're not alone, of course.'

'Wait there.' She sounded even more irritable than usual. 'I'll come down and let you in.'

The Blackwood Arms was a typical town centre Bradburn pub: tall and narrow, built from basic red brick, in every sense an industrial-age structure. The door connecting to its upper rooms was located at the back, facing the cinder car park where Heck was waiting. It opened and Gemma stood there, blonde hair fetchingly tousled, wearing a short, front-tied dressing gown covered in Japanese dragons.

'Hurry up, it's cold,' she said testily.

He walked in, and she shooed him up a steep, narrow, unlit stairway.

'Before you start shouting, you might as well know the whole story,' he said, on entering her room, which, unlike the pub's functional exterior, was rather cosy: a plush carpet, an armchair at the writing desk, a double-sized bed with a plump eiderdown on it. 'It's not just Ship. I've had a meeting with Lee Shaughnessy too.'

Gemma gazed at him askance as she closed the bedroom door behind them, though this was mainly because only now, in the rosy glow of the bedside light, had she noticed his dirt-encrusted hands and ripped and oily clothing, not to mention the spatters of blood down the front of his shirt. It was several seconds before she actually realised what he'd just said.

'Sorry . . . you spoke to Shaughnessy as well?'

'Yeah.' He picked up the kettle. 'On Saturday.'

'Saturday!' she exclaimed. 'That was the day before yesterday. When were you planning to log it? Except, wait – don't answer that question. It would have been when you'd got round to it, wouldn't it . . . when you'd stopped sulking about me taking you off Sagan?'

Heck shrugged. 'It's only one day late, ma'am – and we've all been busy. Can I have a brew, by the way?'

'What?'

'I'm running on empty here.' He took the kettle through to the en suite bathroom and filled it and, on returning, sorted himself out a mug and a teabag. 'Do you want one?'

'*Heck!*'

'Thing is . . . I think there's more going on here than a straightforward underworld war. No one else does, so it fell to me to chuck some bread on the water. If we get nothing out of it, fine . . . it's no big deal, surely?'

She watched him, flabbergasted, perhaps wondering if he

wasn't all here. Heck wondered that himself. He brushed a hand through his damp, tangled hair. Very close calls sometimes had that effect on you: shook you up, blunted your inhibitions, left you feeling a little bit crazy.

'So you spoke to both Ship and Shaughnessy,' she said patiently. 'And let me guess – they've denied killing each other's men? Well, there's a switch.'

'No . . . it *is* a war.' He poured the boiling water. 'But there are question-marks. Ship regards Shaughnessy as the shit on his shoes, and Shaughnessy hates him right back . . . but both seem, I don't know, surprised that all this has happened. To Ship, Shaughnessy's a pipsqueak who would never dare start something like this. He even sent a crew over to nab me, so they could find out exactly what the score is. Meanwhile, Shaughnessy's trying to be cool about it, like, you know, he doesn't care, he's not scared, he'll fight anyone. But I'm not so sure about that. He's a player but he's young, and his lieutenants are even younger. I've looked some of them up on the system, and two years ago they were selling weed on the backstreets. Strictly small-time. Not the sort you'd expect to be challenging empires with flamethrower in hand.'

'So what are you saying – someone else is stirring the pot?'

'Well, they've stirred it now, haven't they?' He slumped into the armchair, tea in hand, and slurped some. 'Got a life of its own now. It's going to run and run . . . but basically, yeah. Someone – whoever the Incinerator is, I suspect – has engineered this gangster war.' He slurped again, desperate to replenish lost reserves of fluid and sugar. 'I considered the possibility of a vigilante – but seriously, how many private citizens in Bradburn know enough about the underworld to take this kind of direct action, let alone would have the wherewithal? I mean, a flamethrower! That's heavy. And how would a vigilante feel about collateral damage? Because the Incinerator's caused an awful lot of that so far. Most likely it's some kind of underworld malcontent. You know, someone deliberately trying to create discord –'

'Heck!' she said sharply, cutting through the meandering ramble. 'What exactly did you talk to them about, Ship and Shaughnessy?'

He glanced at her, confused. 'Erm . . . *this*.'

'This?'

'Yeah – what I've just said. I told them that both their operations are being stalked by a third party, and that it would be in both their interests to find out who.'

Gemma looked aghast. 'So you've basically given them a licence to break some legs?'

'They're going to do that anyway, aren't they? They're going to take a hard look at everyone they've ever pissed off, and that'll be a pretty long list on both sides of the divide. But if we can actually stop them engaging in open war, we must. Otherwise, we'll have more and more murders to investigate, more and more suspects, and that'll cloud any waters that John Sagan happens to be swimming in. Oh, by the way . . . he's definitely here.' Heck finished his tea in a gulp and put the mug down. 'One of Ship's goons confirmed it over at Longsight.'

Gemma found herself having to sit down on the bed.

He eyed her, briefly distracted by her bare, toned legs, her red-painted toenails.

'Sorry,' he said. 'Quite a bit to drop in your lap at this hour in the morning.'

She visibly shuddered, and then stood up again and walked to the tea-making table. Instead of getting herself a cuppa, however, she took a small bottle of scotch from the top drawer, and tipped at least three fingers into a glass.

'Ship's as verminous as they come,' Heck said. 'His normal

team are tough enough. But he's got some very nasty Russians on board too. I know, I met them tonight. I'm thinking they've bribed their way in by offering him a shedload of cheap fentanyl –'

'Heck, just stop!' She rounded on him, glass in hand. 'One thing at a time, for God's sake.'

'I can't prove that by the way – about the fentanyl. It's just a theory –'

'Yes, all right!' She knocked at least one finger back and stalked across the room.

'Probably a good theory, though,' he said.

'Of course it is. Why not? Fentanyl! Hooray, that'll be the next scourge to hit the streets! But we can't solve all the world's problems in one night, can we!' She turned to face him, looking badly flustered as she reappraised his damaged clothing, the dirt, the blood. 'Just tell me – did you yourself do anything during this trip to Manchester that I need to be worried about?'

He thought it through. 'Nothing that's going to get reported to the police, if that's what's concerning you.' He nodded at the glass of spirit. 'Any chance I can have one of those?'

'Shut up.' She made a visible effort to calm down. 'You're telling me you went and fronted Vic Ship's crew? Just like that . . . on your own?'

'It wasn't by choice. They came for me first.'

'Why go after *you*? There are fifty-odd detectives working on this case.'

'They saw me gassing with Shaughnessy outside the nick, and assumed I was one of his.'

'Jesus wept!' She swilled down the rest of her whisky. 'How am I going to write all this up? Does that ever cross your mind when you go off on these madcap adventures?'

He shrugged. 'I'll give you a statement. A full one if you

254

like . . . a special Health and Safety conscious version if you prefer . . .'

'Damn it, Heck, this is not a joke!' Again, Gemma made an effort to keep her voice down, clearly aware there were folk in other bedrooms. 'You're seriously telling me you tailed them all the way to Manchester? A bunch of suspected killers? Without telling anyone, without asking for any kind of support?'

'I tried to get you. Didn't think it would be a good idea to put it on the airwaves generally. If the world and his brother had turned up in Longsight, what would be the most we could throw at them? That they'd been planning to abduct a police officer. Ship wouldn't have coughed to it for one – he wasn't even in Bradburn.'

'You shouldn't have gone!' she snapped. 'You should have reported straight to the MIR.'

She banged her glass on the writing desk and kneaded her forehead. Fleetingly, she didn't even seem angry with him . . . just tired, worn to the bone.

'One of these days, your shift's going to end, Mark, and –' she made a helpless gesture '– and you're just not going to be there to sign off. And then I'll have to write that up too, won't I? But we've had this conversation before. Maybe a hundred thousand times.'

'Gemma . . .' He stood up, frustrated himself. 'We've made progress tonight. We now *know* that Sagan's on the plot. We've got a stronger-than-strong suspicion that the Incinerator is an agent provocateur –'

'That's your imagination.'

'Vic Ship thinks it too. Even Shaughnessy didn't dismiss the idea.'

'Damn it, Heck – I just can't believe you think it's acceptable to do your job this way!'

'I saw an opportunity to gather some intelligence, so I took it.'

'At extreme risk to your own life.'

'Is this like –' He shrugged. 'Is this a *personal* thing?'

She glanced slowly round at him. 'What do you mean?'

'Is your main issue here concern for *me*?' He tried not to smile at the thought of this.

She eyed him incredulously. 'Are you suggesting what I think you are?'

'Well . . . *you* let me in here.' He grinned. 'You're virtually naked, it's three o'clock in the morning. Do you care about me again, Gemma? I mean more than you normally would for a colleague in danger?'

She shook her head. 'You cheeky bloody ape.'

'Listen.' He yanked at his shirt-collar to loosen it. 'I've had a pretty rough night, and, like I say, it's late. So can I stay here?'

'Don't be so bloody ridiculous.'

He moved to the armchair. 'I mean on *here*. I can sleep sitting upright, me.'

Her voice hardened. 'I said don't be so bloody ridiculous.'

'It's just that . . .' He looked her in the eye. 'If you feel about me the way I feel about you –'

'We've had *this* conversation before too. There's the door, Heck. Use it.'

Disgruntled, he opened the bedroom door, but hesitated to leave. 'You know, I went out with an ex-girlfriend tonight. That's how these fun and games actually started. Those bastards were lying in wait for me when the date was over. Nothing happened between us, by the way, so no worries there –'

'I couldn't care less,' Gemma said.

'Her name's Kayla Green and she's a real looker. What's more, she's keen. But during the course of the evening, I decided she wasn't the girl for me. There hasn't been one since you and me broke up.'

'That's a pity. You've tried enough of them out.'

He eyed her curiously. 'That something else that's bugging you?'

'Don't flatter yourself, Mark . . . and stop wasting my time.' She pointed along the corridor towards the top of the stairs. 'I'll see you in the office in the morning. We'll try and formalise these events on paper, and see if we can get something out of them that actually resembles a lead.'

'Deep down, I don't think you want me to leave.'

It wouldn't have been true to say that the sudden turn in the conversation had left Gemma blushing, but there was a rare pinkish tinge to her cheek. Even so, she pointed again, very firmly.

'I will see you in the morning.'

He held his ground. 'Do you ever stop to wonder, Gemma, why it is you can't get a bloke – a woman who looks like you? Or if you can get one, why you can't keep him?'

'You are so out of order here, Sergeant, that I only need to whisper about this and you'll be straight out of a job.'

'I'll tell you,' he said. 'It's the same reason I can't keep a girl. Because what we do, day by day, is so bloody extraordinary – and I choose that word carefully – that nothing we come home to at night can live up to it. In comparison, other people with their little problems . . . they seem pointless.'

'I can see you've had a hard night, Mark,' Gemma said slowly. 'I can see that you're very strung out. That's the only reason I'm giving you the opportunity to leave this room right now.'

He turned into the corridor, but swung around again when he was halfway down it. She watched him from the doorway. Still looking flushed. And still listening.

'What I'm trying to say, Gemma, is . . . I can understand that I get under your skin, that I'm lackadaisical when it comes to procedure, that I sometimes behave like I've nothing to lose. And your career-minded, straight-down-the-line, "dot every i and cross every t" approach drives me up the bloody wall too. I get it that you don't like the thought we're destined to be together. So try looking at it this way – we're *doomed* to be together. How does that sound? And like it or not, time's running out. We're fighting two crime syndicates from Hell here. We could both be dead by the weekend. So what do you say . . . *ma'am?*'

'I say: any more of this, Mark, and I'll write you off sick with a recommendation for mandatory psychological evaluation.'

'Promise me you'll at least consider it. Because I can't stand this farcical pissing around and pretending that we don't care for each other.'

'Go back to your sister's house. I will see you in the morning.'

And to ensure he did just that, this time she slammed the door.

Chapter 26

Heck felt as if he'd only been asleep a few minutes when his phone buzzed.

He sat upright, fuddled, assuming this would be the office. But when he looked, the call had come from a number he didn't recognise. He also noticed, to his surprise, that it was almost half past six in the morning. He'd been out cold for the last three hours.

He put the phone to his ear. 'DS Heckenburg.'

'Yeah, I know,' came an odd croaky voice, which Heck immediately realised was being faked.

'Who is this?'

'Don't talk, just listen.' The voice might be a put-on, but it possessed a clear Bradburn accent. 'You're looking for a lass called Mindy-May. You'll find her hiding in that brothel on Blaymire Close.'

The caller hung up.

Heck tried a call-back only to be told the number was not available. He made a note of it anyway, though almost certainly it would refer to a throwaway mobile, something that could no longer be traced. He also wrote down the name, Mindy-May.

If the caller had been who he thought and hoped, this was potentially a big step forward. Of course, with no idea about the informant, there had to be a question-mark about how reliable this intel was. But if nothing else, it was another lead.

It was earlier than even he'd normally be up and about. After last night's shenanigans he could probably do with an extra hour, but the phone-call had woken him as abruptly and completely as a bucket of iced water. Grabbing another forty winks now would be elusive and pointless.

Plus, there was simply no time for sleep.

He rummaged through the soiled rags of the clothing he'd worn the previous night, which now lay strewn across Dana's lounge carpet, extricated the few important bits and pieces he needed, and screwed it all up into a tight ball. He walked through into the kitchen, deposited it in the bin, laid some bacon strips on the grill, filled the kettle and hurried upstairs to have a shave and a quick shower. He came back down to eat dressed casually in jeans, trainers and a plaid shirt, and carrying a zip-up brown suede jacket.

By 7.15 he was back on the road.

It was another dismal grey morning, raining steadily, the heavy rush-hour traffic honking and growling noisily as it fought its way through the crack-of-dawn dimness. But as usual on a Monday morning, Bradburn Central police station was already a hive of activity . . .

*

'You think this message was kosher?' Gemma asked.

She was seated behind her desk in her private office, which was about three doors along the corridor from the MIR. As always when she was running an enquiry, its door was permanently wedged open, junior staff free to come and go as necessary, but only Heck and Hayes were present now. Gemma continued to examine the grubby piece of notepaper on which he'd scribbled the details he'd been tipped off about earlier on.

Heck shrugged. 'Don't know, ma'am. It could be a hoax, but we still need to act on it. Whoever it was, they clearly know we're looking for a possible witness to the sex-shop attack – a woman who may have been working in the peep-show at the time.'

'They didn't actually say that, though?' Gemma pointed out.

'No, ma'am.'

'So it could be something else?'

'Could be,' Heck conceded.

'Who do you *think* it came from?' Hayes asked. She watched him coolly, having, on first checking in this morning, listened in stunned silence to the events of the previous night, and immediately afterwards turning truculent towards him (mainly, he suspected, because he hadn't taken her to Longsight with him).

Heck pondered before answering. 'I wouldn't be surprised if Lee Shaughnessy had something to do with it. Quite a coincidence that I get the call on my personal phone only two days after giving him the number.'

Gemma, who, as was her wont, was doing a remarkable job of not even looking ruffled by her messy confrontation with her shellshocked sergeant the previous night, seemed thoughtful. 'Shaughnessy, eh?'

'Or one of his crew,' Heck said. 'I can't be certain, but whoever it is, they know we're looking for a missing woman. No one outside Operation Wandering Wolf should know about that.'

'Unless they're involved in the crimes themselves,' Hayes said.

'In which case why inform *us*?' Heck replied. 'Surely it's more likely that Shaughnessy picked this up on the underworld grapevine because he's extra well connected?'

'Could it be Vic Ship?' Hayes wondered. 'Did you leave him a calling-card too?'

'No, I didn't. But why would it be Ship? He's already been shown up in front of his team last night. Do you think, if he had a lead on the Incinerator, he'd share it with the police?'

'So far we've no evidence anyone survived the sex-shop attack,' Gemma reminded him.

'There's no record of a woman even working there,' Hayes said.

'Would there be?' Heck asked. 'If you were doing it for pocket money? It's not exactly something you'd want tracing back to you. On top of that, you might not like paying tax . . . there're all sorts of reasons why you'd be happy to take your wages in brown paper bags for doing a job like gyrating nude in a smeary glass booth.'

Gemma glanced at Hayes. 'Do GMP have any record of a brothel on Blaymire Close?'

'Not to my knowledge, boss.'

'Nothing your local snouts have come up with?' Heck asked her.

'I haven't had a chance to speak with them yet, but that's where I'm going next.'

'Blaymire Close is a residential district, isn't it?' Heck said. It was just north of the centre, and he seemed to recall that though it was in a very working-class part of town – lots of red-brick semis, but yards rather than gardens and very little greenery – it also had an aura of respectability. 'We obviously can't just raid properties at random around there.'

'Like I say, I'm getting onto it,' Hayes said.

'What about the name, Mindy-May?' Gemma wondered.

'Nothing in the system, ma'am,' Heck said. 'But that may be something else DI Hayes can speak to her grasses about.'

Gemma looked at the DI. 'Take care of that *now*, will you, Katie . . . let's get this ball rolling.'

'Yes, ma'am.' Hayes threw another brief, irritated glance at Heck, and departed the office.

Gemma mused. 'No name or proper address, no employment record. Assuming this lass exists, she likes to fly under the radar.'

'She obviously doesn't want any legal involvement,' Heck said. 'Given that she witnessed two men being murdered with a flamethrower, you'd have thought she'd come to us voluntarily. Presumably she's too scared for that. Whatever the reason, we obviously need to speak to her.'

'I agree. In the meantime, how are *you* this morning?'

Now they were alone, she treated him to a flat, even stare, but still looked unhurt by the way he'd spoken to her the night before, scarcely even fazed by it – which, conversely, made him feel slightly guiltier about it – not that he ever felt especially guilty about having cross words with the former love of his life. The situation between them was, in some ways, untenable. They worked so closely together that they were almost joined at the hip, and yet there was precious little chance of their ever being an item again. Innumerable factors – personality differences, attitudes to the job, rank itself – put an immense gulf between them. Not that this prevented Heck, in moments of extreme stress (or when he was drunk), thinking he could span that gulf with a single bound. Gemma, the more level-headed of the two, always resisted, of course, but was that because she wanted to or because she had to? She would never say, and though Heck knew it was completely outrageous of him to keep pushing his luck in this way, he increasingly resented her unwillingness to even discuss the matter.

'Look,' he said awkwardly. 'I'm sorry about last night.'

'We're not talking about that,' she replied. 'Not yet. I asked if you're fit for duty today?'

He shrugged. 'I'd rather be working than not. But I suppose that's not what you're really asking . . .' Before he could elaborate, the phone began buzzing in his pocket. He fished it out and saw that the call was from Eric Fisher. 'Mind if I take this?'

With an exasperated waggle of the fingers, she waved him from her office.

He put the phone to his ear as he walked out into the corridor. 'How we doing, Eric?'

'Nayka . . .?' Fisher began.

'Yeah.'

'As in the Russian toerag you were enquiring about last night?'

'That's the one.'

'Do you mind me asking what this is actually about?'

Heck left the building by its rear personnel door, seizing the unlooked-for opportunity to get away from the station before Gemma's concerned enquiry turned into the inevitable roasting.

'Well . . . he may be connected to this gangland dust-up in Bradburn.'

Fisher briefly contemplated this. 'He's bad news, I'll tell you that. Assuming we're talking about the same person.'

Heck climbed into his Megane. 'Just let me know what you've got.'

'Well . . . it's not a great deal at the end of the day. The St Petersburg Criminal Investigations Directorate are not especially forthcoming with intel at the present time, international relations being what they are . . . but Interpol have managed to get some details from them.'

Heck cradled the phone between his jaw and his shoulder

as he drove out of the car park and joined the morning traffic. 'Shoot. I'm all ears.'

'They've only really got one Nayka listed. You said something about your suspect being covered in cobweb tattoos? You're certain about that?'

'Certainly am.' Realising this was going to be more than a quick natter, Heck put the phone down and hit the speaker-phone switch. 'They're all over him. Arms, torso – maybe his whole body, for all I know?'

'Yeah, that's the man,' Fisher confirmed. 'OK, sounds like we're talking about Grigori Kalylyn. He's a hoodlum well known to the St Petersburg cops as a *brodyaga*.'

'A what?'

'A *brodyaga* is a specialised warrior. Someone who's more than just muscle. Back home, Nayka's role was extreme enforcement. A soldier who was fully authorised by his bosses to use any amount of violence and terror to achieve their goals.'

'Well, that would fit.'

'Nayka's also a hardline Tatarstan loyalist. And before you ask, the Tatarstan Brigade started out in Kazan, which is about a thousand miles south of St Petersburg, and are regarded as one of the most dangerous crime syndicates in Russia. Back in the early 2000s, they literally terrorised their way into the St Petersburg crime scene, and that takes some doing, I'll tell you.'

'I figured he was the real deal,' Heck said. 'What else have we got?'

'That's about it. Like I say, it's bare details only.'

'Did the Russian cops offer any opinions as to why he might be over here in the UK?'

'No, but apparently they weren't surprised. And let's face it, mate, he's not going to be over here for a holiday, is he?'

'I suppose that depends what he does for R&R. At present nothing would surprise me.' Heck swung through a busy

265

intersection into Budworth. 'All right, Eric . . . can you email this over?'

'Will do. Take care, Heck . . . oh, *Heck!*'

'What?'

'I mean it, take care. This character, Nayka . . . you don't get to be a *brodyaga* for nothing. This guy's likely to be as loopy as they come.'

'Yeah, I've already got that.'

'But he won't be stupid either. To reach the rank of *brodyaga* you've got to be trusted implicitly by your gaffers. He may be a maniac – in fact he *will* be a maniac, but he won't be an idiot.'

'Thanks for that, mate.' Heck turned into Blaymire Close. 'Speak to you later.'

As streets in this district went, it wasn't especially shabby, but it wasn't smart either. Most of its properties were semi-detached or rows of townhouses, in some cases adapted into bedsit flats. All boasted tiny strips serving as walled-off front gardens.

Heck cruised slowly along, not entirely sure what he was looking for. Contrary to the popular image, brothels did not look like brothels. There'd be no tawdry neon signs, no red lights showing. Brothels that actually made money did so because they were discreet. It could be any one of the everyday houses he now passed, and most folk who lived here would never know about it. He assessed the various buildings as he passed. Some curtains were drawn, others open. A few houses were in good condition, others less so – but there were no obvious giveaways. The one or two pedestrians he saw looked like ordinary citizens trudging to work. But among them he recognised one of the lads from the taskforce, a DC Dave Klebworth. Heck hadn't got to know Klebworth yet, but apparently he was a local officer on liaison from Bradburn CID. That would make him useful to this situation.

A balding, podgy, toad-like figure in his mid-forties, Klebworth was currently dressed in army-surplus pants, a ragged sweater and a donkey jacket, and was slouching along the road in the forlorn fashion of the middle-aged unemployed. He was probably here on DI Hayes's behalf, sniffing out anything he could. And as a guy whose beat was this very patch, he'd doubtless be more effective at this than Heck would.

Deciding that he'd already cramped DI Hayes's style enough that day, Heck turned off Blaymire Close at the first opportunity and drove back towards the nick.

In truth, he quite liked what he'd seen of Hayes so far. She was young but had been promoted early, which meant she was both efficient and ambitious. All that was good, as it implied that she liked to get results and didn't fanny around with politics. The previous Saturday, when she'd learned about his unofficial conflab with Lee Shaughnessy, she'd rightly hit the roof but hadn't taken it any farther than that because she recognised the usefulness of the contact. The same thing applied when she'd found out this morning about his trip over to Longsight. If anything, she'd looked jealous that she hadn't been involved in that. She was no shrinking violet, DI Hayes, and she clearly didn't mind the unorthodox approach, so long as it worked.

A girl after Heck's own heart then . . . in which case it was all the more important not to vex her too much. She was better placed than he was to locate this brothel on Blaymire Close, assuming it existed, so why attempt to steal that thunder?

He returned to the station and the MIR, where, having heard that Gemma had now been summoned to a meeting with Gold Command (several of GMP's local top brass, including the ACC – so that wouldn't be over any time soon), he spent the next two hours trying to make himself useful in the VDU room.

A bunch of officers were scanning videos of the town centre during the hours leading up to and after the attack on Shelley Harper and Nawaz Gilani. As always, the enormous mass of CCTV footage that had been sequestered for inspection was a mixed blessing. Though on the surface it might appear as if the streets surrounding the Stags n Hens bar were thoroughly covered, with barely a minute unaccounted for in the relevant timeframe, the quality of the visuals was poor: grainy, dark, constantly pixelating. As it was highly unlikely the Incinerator would openly be walking around in his flameproof gear and carrying his weapon in hand, it seemed a tall order to get anything from this. The only visual reference point they had on the Incinerator thus far was the short piece of video caught by accident on an exterior camera at the Waterside nightclub next to the Leeds–Liverpool Canal on the evening of April 3. That film had been shot from a high angle, and again was dark and grainy, though it appeared to depict the murder of the drugs dealer Danny Hollister. Heck had viewed this footage several times now, but didn't see that it could hurt to watch it again.

It was just as horrific as it had been before.

The camera, which looked lengthways down the canal from the towpath alongside the nightclub, revealed little – until in the near distance a staggering white flare appeared from the black mouth of an alleyway. It was a human being, engulfed head to foot in flames. The blazing form tottered across the towpath and fell into the canal. Despite the dreadful quality of the film, a cloud of steam visibly plumed up.

Once again, the hairs at the nape of Heck's neck stiffened as a second figure emerged from the alley, a humped, featureless shape in its bulky body armour, armed with a firearm-type weapon, obviously the flamethrower, wearing a helmet, and with some heavy appliance strapped to its back. The helmet looked as if it had a faceplate attached, while the appliance was almost certainly a petrol tank. This second figure strode along the towpath for about thirty yards before crossing over the canal via a metal footbridge. As it did, the first figure, visibly blackened and twisted, had clawed its way up onto the opposite bank, where it lay shuddering. Briefly, nothing was distinguishable until the second figure strode up to the first and, with another searing flash, more flame was jettisoned, immersing the prone shape, which writhed and squirmed in the blast.

The victim didn't last long this time. He rolled around frantically, once again a human fireball, but eventually lay still. By now, the killer – a monstrous, featureless outline – was stumping his way back to the canal bridge, which he crossed almost nonchalantly before vanishing up the alley.

Detective Sergeant Sally Gorton, a hefty but good-looking girl with a loud voice and infectious laugh, was coordinating the footage scan, and was busy at a screen of her own.

'What do we know about this guy Danny Hollister?' Heck asked her.

'A dealer from way back,' Gorton replied. 'Mainly on behalf of Vic Ship. But a user too. Never did an honest day's work in his life, benefits scrounger, all the usual.'

'What about his background?'

'Familiar enough pattern. Not a particularly bad family. But his older brothers and sisters were a rotten influence. He basically came of age in the late 70s, surrounded by these hippy radicals who brainwashed him into believing that all coppers were corrupt agents of the state, while drugs-suppliers represented the voice of the people. How that happens, I don't know. You need a brain like a sponge to start with, if you ask me. Either way, it helped him find his route in life early – and qualified him to do precisely nothing else.'

'Except burn like an Olympic torch.' Heck replayed the grim video.

There were some, no doubt, who'd think this a just outcome for a man who'd spent his entire adulthood poisoning others. Heck didn't concur. From his paperwork, Hollister had been a typical underworld fall guy. He might have thought he was connected, but in reality he was never more than a fringe player, probably less than that. He couldn't even be classified as a 'soldier'. 'Camp follower' would be a better phrase, one of those who thought they were rebels but in fact were always destined to die first.

A bit like Tom, eh? Heck thought. *In fact, very like Tom.*

His phone began buzzing. He glanced at it, again seeing a number he didn't recognise, though not the same one as earlier. He stepped out into the corridor, but rather to his surprise the caller was his Uncle Pat.

'Mark, I wonder if you'd like to call for lunch at the presbytery today?'

'Erm . . .' Heck hadn't made plans for lunch. Usually it was no more than a quick sandwich on the fly.

'Unless you're busy, of course,' the priest added. 'But try and make it if you can. I think we should have a bit of a chat while you're up here. It'd be bloody awful if the next thing I knew you'd gone back to London and we'd barely even spoken. On top of that, Dana would never forgive me.'

Heck was about to dig some excuse up – he didn't have time for family stuff at present, when he remembered something Kayla had said about his uncle running a kind of outreach programme – *for local folk who've fallen through the cracks: alkies, druggies, prozzies. Usually all three at the same time . . .*

He wasn't sure how feasible this was, but might his uncle, or someone his uncle could put them onto, know anything about the brothel on Blaymire Close?

'Lunch is fine,' Heck said. 'What time?'

'I've got the noon Mass, but straight after that would be good.'

Heck glanced at his watch. It was half past eleven already. 'I'll be there at half-twelve.'

'Good man. See you then.'

Chapter 27

Heck parked on the church car park, but, hearing the warbling tone of a hymn inside the venerable old structure, opted to wander around the churchyard until Mass had finished. Perhaps inevitably, he drifted to its far west corner, where, though he'd never seen it, Dana had once informed him in a letter the family plot was located.

From this side of the church, much more of the refurbishment was in evidence. What would normally have been a striking window of blue and red glass bearing a vivid portrait of Christ beseeching Heaven, trickles of blood streaming down his face from a crown of rose-thorns, was obscured by an immense climbing-frame of scaffolding and plastic sheeting. A workman plodded along its upper tier in overalls and a woolly hat.

Inside the church, the congregation had moved on to the next verse. It sounded like 'Lord of All Hopefulness', which, if Heck's distant memories of dutiful attendances at church as a good Catholic boy were accurate, he'd always thought one of the most moving of hymns. He seemed to recall that it was often sung at funerals to commemorate a life well spent and after that the reward of Heaven. Almost unavoidably, he felt another brief pang of loss – childhood, innocence, a less complicated era when good things came thick and fast and there was an alluring certainty that even better was to come if you stayed on track – before turning his back on St Nathaniel's and surveying the grave, which lay alone beneath an elm tree.

It was neatly kept, two borders of mown grass enclosing a bed of white gravel.

The simple headstone was engraved:

GEORGE DEREK HECKENBURG
1939 – 1999

MARY WILMA HECKENBURG
1944 – 2003

THOMAS PETER HECKENBURG
1974 – 1992

'Don't worry,' came a cheery voice. 'They're pretty well looked after here.'

Heck turned, and saw Kayla Green coming down the path towards him. She wore a heavy puffer-jacket and a bob-cap, from under which her raven hair protruded in fetching bangs. A long-handled, stiff-bristled brush lay across her shoulder. She smiled at him.

'Kayla, I . . .?'

'Surprised to see me again?'

'At this time of day, I suppose, yeah. Isn't Monday a workday?'

Not that it looked as if she hadn't been working. She was pink-cheeked and watery-eyed; her front fringe hung damp with perspiration. She leaned on the brush, as if wearied from using it.

'In all honesty, Mark, things aren't great with the business. We haven't got very much of it, to be blunt. Still . . . gives me a chance to help Father Pat out.'

'Thought you were Eucharistic minister, not a gardener?'

'Doing a bit of everything at present. Father Pat's getting on, as you may have noticed . . . can't sweep last year's leaves away all by himself.'

'Doesn't he have a caretaker for this?'

'Not full-time, no.'

'No altar servers?'

She frowned. 'Mark, the servers get time off school to help him say Mass, not maintain the grounds. And before you ask, he doesn't have a deacon either. In fact –' she sighed '– we're short of priests across the board these day. There aren't even many lay-people come here who are under the age of fifty . . . unless they're up to no good. Country's going to Hell in a handcart, I'll tell you.'

Heck always prided himself on being difficult to surprise, but he was genuinely taken aback by this. He'd found it hard buying into the concept of Kayla Green the Eucharistic minister, even though he supposed that religious conversions did sometimes happen. But to find her doing odd jobs around the church as well – that really astonished him.

'Why are *you* here anyway?' she asked.

'Uncle Pat's invited me for lunch.'

'Oooh . . .' She looked impressed. 'That's more of a treat than I've ever had.'

'I think he wants to thrash some stuff out.'

'Ah . . . things that never got said, eh?'

He nodded. 'I kind of hoped we could just gloss over all that, to be honest . . . pick things up as they were.'

She chuckled, although it was a strange sound, lacking in humour. 'No one can do that, Mark. No one can just carry on the way things were.'

Heck didn't understand what she meant by that, but he wasn't in much of a mood to discuss it. 'To be honest –' he headed along the path towards the church '– I haven't got time for family stuff at present.'

'So *make* some time.' She fell into step alongside him. 'I should scold you for that – tell you that you won't know how much you'll miss your loved ones until they're not there any more, but you already know that, don't you?'

'Yeah, I suppose so.'

'But you should still make time, Mark. No man's an island, and all that.'

She stared straight ahead as they walked.

She was certainly full of surprises, he thought, this new-look Kayla.

'What did you mean?' he asked as they followed the gravel path at the side of the church. Inside, the hymns had finished, and ahead of them a handful of congregants, mostly old ladies and one or two old men, trailed out from the church's main door. 'When you said no one comes here under fifty unless they're up to no good?'

'Well . . . what do you think the problem is?' she said. 'I wouldn't say I have to clear syringes out of the graveyard every day, but it happens from time to time.'

'Addicts come here to the church?'

'Sure. Along with the alcoholics and various other hoboes.'

'You mean as part of this counselling service Uncle Pat runs?'

'Good God, no. He holds those sessions down in the Mission Hall in town. No . . . sometimes they come here asking for charity. Usually, if someone sees them and asks what they're up to, they say that. Other times it's been to steal the collection boxes. At least four have gone in the last two months. One was even broken off the wall where it had been fixed with screws. Another time, Father Pat

275

caught a couple of them washing their needles in the holy water font. A new baby was due to be baptised in it later that afternoon.'

Despite his experience at the sharp end of criminal investigation, Heck shuddered. 'I hope he's reported all this.'

'Oh, sure. Your guys come round whenever we call, but you're busy, aren't you? You've got real crimes to solve. And I'm not being flippant when I say that. Old ladies getting burgled, young mums getting mugged . . . a girlfriend of mine was stopped in Candlewood Park last year, while she was pushing her two-year-old in a pram. Broad daylight, but the bastard held a knife to her kiddie's throat till she coughed up some cash. Can you imagine that?'

Heck didn't need to imagine it. The official stats would have the average man on the street believe that crime in the UK was falling, but in fact violence was on the rise. And it wasn't just restricted to inner-city areas. Increasingly, every part of the country, be it urban, suburban or rural, now played host to a low-key but rather vicious crime-wave, which was fuelled not just by drugs but by hopelessness, wretchedness and, of course, that strange new twenty-first-century form of immorality wherein almost everyone apparently felt entitled to anything they wanted.

But Kayla seemed to be taking it harder than most.

'You shouldn't let this get to you, love,' he said. 'These things are always going to be with us. I mean, we do what we can in terms of damage limitation, but don't let them rip your life apart. Really – don't. That's no solution for anyone.'

Ahead of them, the tall, angular shape of his uncle had now appeared among the last of his parishioners, still in his purple Lenten vestments. The priest now turned, spotted them and walked down the path in their direction.

'Afternoon, Father,' Kayla said.

'Kayla.' The priest nodded to her.

'I've done the graveyard paths and steps. I'm going round to the car park now, and then I'll do the memorial garden.'

'Thanks, Kayla, that's very kind of you indeed. The presbytery kitchen's open. Make sure you go in there and get yourself as many cuppas as you need. Don't mind us.'

'I won't, thanks. See you later, Mark.' And she strode away, booted feet crunching the gravel.

'So,' Father Pat said to his nephew. 'Been to see the family?'

'I have. Thanks for tending the grave so well.'

'Good grief, don't thank *me* . . . Dana won't let anyone else go near.'

Heck glanced back at the headstone, just visible under the distant elm. It was difficult not to picture the passing seasons and the lone figure of his older sister, a melancholy shape constantly there, tirelessly ordering and reordering the last resting-place of her all but extinct family.

'You hungry?' the priest wondered, interrupting his thoughts.

'Yeah . . . as you mention it. Had a very early brekky.'

'Excellent. It'll only be fish and chips . . . I've sent Mrs O'Malley out to get it for us.'

*

With all the renovations going on, it came as a surprise to find that the presbytery interior had hardly changed since Heck's youth. It was basically a labyrinth, all narrow rooms and draughty corridors, everything drab and functional. About as far from the traditional image of the cosy village vicarage as you could get, and with minimal décor aside from the usual plethora of Catholic memorabilia: crucifixes on mantels, plaques depicting Christ as the Good Shepherd or Holy Child, plus those ubiquitous statuettes of saints.

As promised, lunch consisted of a slab of battered cod

each, two portions of mushy peas and two piles of heavily salt- and vinegar-covered chips. Mrs O'Malley, who'd returned to the presbytery ahead of them, had set it all out on two dishes on the dining-room table, along with cutlery, two mugs, a pot of freshly made tea and a plate of buttered bread, before vanishing to the kitchen, where she busied herself noisily.

'You know, Mark,' Father Pat said, stripped to his black shirt and clerical collar, and tucking in heartily, 'everything happens for a reason. I'm sure you've heard this before.'

'Tenet of Christian belief, isn't it?' Heck ate too.

'That's part of it, I suppose,' the priest agreed. 'What I'm saying is . . . if what happened to you hadn't happened, you'd never have become a police officer, let alone the successful police officer you are now.'

'I'm a success, am I?'

Father Pat looked surprised. 'Absolutely you are. I've seen your name in the papers.'

'Shouldn't believe everything you read in the press, Uncle Pat.'

'Well . . . you've still done OK. That's plain. So in some ways it's all come right.'

Heck smiled to himself. 'You sound like Mum. She used to say stuff like that when Dana complained to her about the state of the world. "It's all part of God's plan. God will fix it. God knows all. God is love." I mean, where's the evidence for any of that? I'm sorry if that's an irreverent question to ask, but in my line of work it gets difficult believing in God.'

The priest studied him as he ate. 'And what about the Devil?'

'Oh, the Devil . . . well, that's something else. It's a lot easier to believe in him.'

'"Easier" . . . of course. That's the key word.'

Heck smiled again, remembering well how his uncle's strong faith had girded him for even casual arguments about

278

religion. But he didn't smile broadly; there were still serious things to be said here. 'I'll be honest with you, Uncle Pat – I don't remember the last time I felt any inclination to step inside a church.'

'You're an atheist now, are you?'

'I wouldn't say that.'

'So . . . what? You're too damn lazy to go to Mass?'

'I've been called a lot of things in my time, but lazy isn't one of them.'

'Let me guess – it was the Church's fault that Bradburn showed you the door?'

Heck regarded him coolly. 'It was the Church's fault . . . or rather it was *your* fault that I wasn't even informed Mum and Dad had died. That I was effectively barred from their funerals.'

The priest frowned. 'I didn't like doing that. But I had to respect their final wishes. You surely understand?'

Heck helped himself to more bread. 'If I'm honest, I'd already given up on you guys. And that's nothing personal, by the way. All this, you, my family, Bradburn . . . I put it behind me. Closed the door. And by the looks of it, there weren't too many who were sorry about that.'

'Not at first, no. But a feeling of betrayal can do that to people.'

Heck knew who they were talking about here. 'How *was* Dad in his final days?'

'Bitter, brooding. When he wasn't coughing his lungs up.'

'I don't suppose he ever mentioned –'

'You? No. Not once.'

Heck nodded. He'd expected nothing less; so much so that he was almost numb to the pain it tried to cause him. Almost.

'Your mother spoke about you though . . . after George died. Asked me if I knew how you were getting on.'

Heck recollected his mother: small of stature, very gentle; spirited enough and firm of hand when they were mischievous youngsters, and devoutly loyal to their father.

'Why didn't you tell her to ring me?' Heck said. 'Dana got my phone number from somewhere eventually. Mum could have too.'

Father Pat shook his head. 'Don't underestimate the influence George had on her, Mark. As far as she was concerned, your dad hadn't really gone anywhere.'

'She still could've rung me . . .'

'Or *you* could've rung *her*!' The priest sat back. '*You* were the one at fault in their eyes.'

'I was sinned against too, you know,' Heck retorted. 'I mean, first she lets Dad drive me away. Then she bars me from his funeral. She wasn't my favourite person around that time.'

'And it never occurred to you that she might die too? I mean, she was getting on, she was ill.'

Heck hung his head. 'It should have, I know. But when you're that angry, that frustrated . . .'

'At least tell me things are OK with you and Dana? I mean, she made a real effort to find you after your mother died . . .'

'Oh, things are fine there. She's never off the phone or the email.'

'Now she's got you back, she's going to hang onto you. Least, that's what she says.'

'Well . . .' Heck placed the cutlery on his empty plate. 'I may see her while I'm up here. Though that depends on factors beyond all our reach, I'm afraid.'

'On which subject –' Father Pat looked thoughtful as he wiped his hands on a napkin '– you're aware that Kayla Green's sister died?'

'Yeah. She told me.' Heck pondered that. 'I get the impression it made quite an impact on her.'

'Did you know Jess Green?'

'Yeah, course . . . back in the day. Looked a lot like Kayla. Younger version obviously, but very sweet, very bubbly, always eager to please. Not quite as wild or as tough as her big sister.'

'Perhaps if she *had* been, she'd have lasted longer.'

Heck shrugged. 'So . . . you going to tell me what happened?'

Father Pat poured them both another cup of tea. 'Their father was the last surviving parent, you may recall, and after he died, the girls were left on their own. Kayla was trying to run the family business . . . not that she was particularly adept at it, but it was the only thing they had. Jess, meanwhile, went off the rails a little bit.'

'I see.' Heck felt a vague discomfort; already he could sense where this was heading.

'She was twenty-two by then. It had all happened at just the wrong time. No guiding hand when she needed one, I suppose. She finished up staying out all night, dropping out of college.'

'This is going to be a familiar story, isn't it?'

'I'm afraid so, Mark, yes.'

'Drugs?'

'Routine stuff at first . . . but later on something called China White.'

'Yeah . . . that's fentanyl. Or a heroin/fentanyl combo. Either way, a couple of hits of that and you're hooked for life.'

Even now, with everything he'd seen during his long years of ministry in an economically depressed town like this, Father Pat looked shocked by what he'd witnessed. 'It turned her into a facsimile of a person. It's like she wasn't really alive.'

Heck nodded. He didn't need to have seen it for himself

in his own family to know just how much damage a hard-drug dependency could wreak on ordinary, everyday people.

'Kayla was struggling to make ends meet at the time,' the priest added. 'Couldn't be dealing with Jess's daft behaviour. Tried to ignore the whole thing . . . Jess got into worse and worse company.' He sighed. 'She ended up becoming a prostitute without anyone really noticing how or why. Around that time the drugs got heavier, this fentanyl business . . . Anyway, it really upset Kayla, obviously. So she finally took charge of the situation. Did everything she could . . . but Jess was too far gone by this time. She kept running back to this hideous life she'd fallen into. The years rolled by, but it was too much for her. She wasn't just on drugs by then, she was ill, getting beaten up and used for the price of a cigarette. In the end, about two days short of her thirtieth birthday, some council workers found her body blocking a storm-drain.'

'Good Lord,' Heck breathed.

Mark, I've always felt I had a kind of kinship with you. Something much stronger than the norm.

Now he understood what Kayla had meant by that. It was less to do with that hot, sexy night they'd spent in that tent in their mid-teens, and more to do with the years since.

'That's why Kayla's always here at the church?' he asked.

The priest shrugged. 'To be honest, I'd only previously known them as kids, when they were school-age. But I got a lot more involved when Kayla brought Jess down to one of the support groups I'd set up in town. We did everything we could. Kayla really threw herself into it – trying to make up for lost time, I suppose. But some people are hell-bent on self-destruction. Or so it seems.' He shook his head. 'After it was all over, Kayla came back here. Said she'd been amazed by the work I was doing and was eternally grateful for how hard I'd tried to save her sister. Said she'd rediscovered the meaning of life during that whole ordeal. No doubt, to your ears that sounds naïve and silly?'

'Well . . .' Heck wasn't entirely sure why his uncle would think this.

'It *was* naïve and silly. The real reason she's here, Mark, is because she's hiding from the world. St Nathaniel's has become a refuge for her. She feels isolated, lost . . . she let the family business go to rack and ruin anyway, so there's nothing for her on the outside any more.'

Heck nodded his understanding.

'That's why I mentioned the other night that you should go easy with her. I mean, she hides all that stuff well . . . she's still a fine-looking girl.'

'I get it, Uncle Pat, I get it.'

As though she'd been listening in and had taken the lull in the conversation as her cue, Mrs O'Malley came bustling from the kitchen and started removing their crockery.

When she'd gone again, Father Pat arched an apologetic eyebrow. 'I'm sorry you've come back to a world that must seem upside-down compared to the one you left, son.'

Heck snorted. 'I'm no stranger to it, don't worry. That's why I'm here, after all.'

'Yes . . . I suppose it is.' Briefly, Father Pat looked despondent at that thought.

'There's actually something I'd like to ask you about all that,' Heck said. 'These help groups and counselling sessions you've been running – for addicts, street-girls and the like. Anyone attending ever mention who they might work for . . . *where* they might work?'

'Oh, goodness, no.' The priest looked shocked he should ask. 'We never touch on anything like that. Their lives wouldn't be worth living if they started giving that kind of information out.'

Heck eyed him carefully, almost through force of habit

283

assessing his body-language, searching for signs of deception. Father Pat noticed this, and reddened slightly.

'None of them have ever mentioned a place on Blaymire Close, for instance?'

'Blaymire Close . . . in St Martin's parish?'

'Yeah, Budworth.'

'Well . . .' The priest shrugged. 'They've never mentioned anywhere, like I said. Even if they weren't too frightened to talk to us about stuff like that, we'd never pass it on to the police. We'd lose their trust if we did. Surely you realise this, Mark?'

'That's usually the way, I suppose.' Heck smiled ruefully. 'But it's always worth a try.'

'It's a horrific situation, I admit. Must be a daily battle for you chaps . . . a real struggle.'

'Sometimes, yeah.'

'I wish I could offer you twelve legions of angels, son, but my influence with the Almighty seems to be limited these days.' The priest sighed. 'Best I can do is provide a good lunch every few days you're up here and a couple of decent whiskies if you ever fancy popping into The Coal Hole.'

'Hey, we fortify ourselves any way we can.'

Before Father Pat could reply, a bleep from Heck's phone indicated the arrival of a text. He glanced at it. Katie Hayes was the sender.

Blaymire Close brothel located. ETA to nick?

He quickly keyed in a response:

En route.

'Sorry.' He stood up. 'Gotta go.'

'A breakthrough in the case maybe?'

'Could be.' Heck moved to the door.

'Take care, son.'

'Always do . . . Listen, your influence may be waning, Uncle Pat, but perhaps put in a good word for us with the Big Guy anyway, eh? Can't ever hurt.'

The priest nodded and smiled as Heck headed out, closing the outer door behind him. At which point Mrs O'Malley returned to clear what remained of their dishes.

'He's become a heathen,' she said pointedly.

'Didn't you just hear him ask for God's help?' the priest said tersely. 'You clearly heard everything else.'

'All I heard was an effort to get private information out of you.'

'He asked for our prayers, and he'll get mine at least.'

'He's not the boy you remember, Patrick. The moment he put on the King's uniform, he changed.'

'"The King's uniform"!' the priest scoffed. 'He's a police officer, not a member of the Black and Tans.'

'He's become a darkman. He said that himself. It's where he's been, it's what he's been doing . . . he's got it all over him.'

'In case you hadn't noticed, Margaret, he's actually here to fight the darkness.'

'He'll bring it to your door, Father.' She shook her head portentously. 'You mark my words . . . he'll bring it right to your door.'

Chapter 28

'Mindy-May's real name is Sonja Turner,' Hayes said over the phone as Heck drove back towards the station. 'She's a local girl, twenty-seven years old. Past form for possession, soliciting and disorderly behaviour. But she's kept clean for the last few years . . . at least, she hasn't been arrested for anything. Currently embroiled in a custody battle with her ex-boyfriend over their two young kids.'

'Which explains why she doesn't want anyone to know she was moonlighting as a stripper,' Heck said. 'And why she didn't come to us voluntarily.'

'*If* she saw what happened. We don't know for sure it's the same girl.'

'Have you checked the boyfriend out?'

'He's a military contractor. Been out in the Falklands for the last three months.'

'OK . . . what about this brothel?'

'Supposedly it's located at 27, Blaymire Close. I drove past earlier. Looks as ordinary as they come, but I think the intel's sound.'

'We'll soon know. Listen, ma'am, I'll be back at the nick in ten. In the meantime, can you speak to Gemma?

We need authorisation to go undercover. We also need a wire.'

*

Blaymire Close lay silent and deserted. It was late-afternoon and would soon be turning to dusk.

Heck, Hayes and Gary Quinnell, all dressed down in jeans, trainers and sweatshirts, drew up in Hayes's beige Ford Contour thirty yards down the road. Hayes was wearing a bomber jacket, and had tucked her long black hair into a scruffy baseball cap. A silver-grey Saab 9-3 pulled up a few dozen yards behind them, carrying Charlie Finnegan and Dave Klebworth.

Hayes cut the engine, while Heck checked the microphone taped to the shaved patch on his chest. He tapped it. Two loud bangs sounded from the speaker on the dashboard.

'You sure you're OK with this?' Hayes asked, as he unfastened his seatbelt.

'No problem. I don't anticipate trouble, but you never know.'

'Just keep your eye on the job,' Quinnell chirped from the back seat. 'Don't let them saucy women lead you into temptation.'

'Hey, I was in church a couple of hours ago,' Heck retorted.

'Yeah?' Quinnell sounded amazed. 'Didn't hear the earth crack or see the sky catch fire.'

'I'll take that as a sign the Almighty's on our side today.'

'He's always on my side, boyo . . . not so sure about yours.'

'If we can put a sock into the banter!' Hayes said impatiently. She turned to Heck. 'You sure you know the entry codes?' From her sober expression, she seemed more than a little unsure about this operation. Gemma had signed off on it without needing much convincing – she had regularly authorised the use of undercover operatives – but the DI was under no illusion: if it went belly up, it was her arse in the sling.

'So long as your grass was on the ball, we'll have no problems,' Heck said.

'OK . . . well, we're only outside if you need us.'

'Just stay sharp, boss.' He climbed out and closed the car door behind him, before traipsing to the other side of the road, thumbs hooked into his jeans, face etched in the happy-go-lucky grin of a guy with a pay-packet in his pocket and lots of ideas about how to spend it.

'He'd better not screw this up,' Hayes said quietly.

'Don't worry about Heck, ma'am,' Quinnell replied. 'He's pretty good at this sort of thing.'

'What's that, knocking on prozzies' doors?'

'No – making like he's a bad fella.'

'Gee, I wonder why.'

On the other side of the road, Heck sauntered up to number 27. It was yet another ordinary-looking red-brick townhouse. All its downstairs windows were curtained, but a wooden sign on the front door read:

Tradesmen to the rear

An entry stood on the left, arched and rather dim, apparently leading to the back. Heck walked down it. Halfway along, there was a door without a handle. A sliding slat was fitted in an aperture at head-height. This too was closed.

He gave the coded knock, which was three rapid taps, followed by a brief delay and then a fourth. What sounded like a pair of high heels clicked across a tiled floor on the other side. The slat was drawn back, and a woman looked out. She was in her mid-forties and attractive, but heavily made-up, with a short tangle of jet-black hair.

'How can I help you, love?' she asked pleasantly.

'Hi . . . erm, Kaplain sent me.'

'And what's your pleasure?'

'Toad in the hole.'

She closed the slat, there was a rattle and bang as at least two bolts were drawn back, and the door opened. She stepped aside, admitting him into an everyday suburban kitchen. There was even a pan bubbling on the stove.

'I'm Sookie,' the woman said, closing and bolting the door behind him and offering a bejewelled hand. She had a curvaceous figure showcased to perfection in a filmy white negligee, and beneath that white lingerie and stockings. 'Come this way.'

She walked from the kitchen, prettily and yet businesslike on her red velvet heels, through a short hall and into a tastefully furnished lounge. A real-flame gas fire burned in the grate, warming everything nicely. She turned to face him again. Briefly, the alluring smile slipped.

'It's fifty for a massage, seventy-five for a toss, a hundred for a blow, two hundred for the full works – straight. I don't do anals, golden showers, CP, sub-dom or anything like that. But I can give you addresses where they do. For a fee, of course. We don't practise unsafe sex, you use our rubbers and you pay for them afterwards.'

'Do I get a choice of women?' Heck asked.

Sookie regarded him carefully. 'Will I not do?'

'Hey, no . . . I fancy you something chronic. But I was led to believe there was more than one of you working here.'

'Were you indeed.'

Another door in the room creaked open. A man of about thirty entered, casually – *too* casually – folding a daily paper. He was short but thickset, with sloping, apelike shoulders and a shaved bullet-head. The sleeves of his T-shirt had been torn off, exposing heavily muscled and tattooed arms. With his sunbed tan and diamonds glinting in either ear-lobe, everything about him said 'pimp'.

'Who told you that?' the man asked, rolling the newspaper tightly.

Heck shrugged innocently. 'Don't you always have more than one? I mean, what if I wanted two at the same time . . . so to speak?'

'Could be arranged,' Sookie said. 'Not at this short notice though. And not today.'

'Ahh – right.'

'Still with us?' she asked.

Heck shrugged again, and nodded.

'Fancy a drink first?'

'Yeah, great. Scotch, if you've got it.'

Sookie moved to a drinks cabinet and tipped two fingers from a bottle of Bells into a cut crystal tumbler. Heck smiled and nodded, but was acutely aware of the man watching from behind.

'It's just –' Heck said '– well, it's just that I heard you had a girl called Mindy-May working here? I heard she was pretty good.'

Sookie managed to splash whisky all across the top of the drinks cabinet.

'Ice?' she asked in a voice suddenly as brittle as the glass in her hand.

'Nah. I'll take it as it comes.'

She turned, smiling again, and exchanged a quick, covert look with her burly guardian, before he withdrew from the room. Heck accepted the drink and nodded his thanks. He sipped at it and grinned, the daft lad again with more money than sense.

'So – is she in today? Mindy?'

'Yes, she is,' Sookie said.

'And is she available?'

'Why don't you finish your drink, and I'll take you up.'

'Great, smashing.'

He sank the scotch and handed the empty over. It seemed more than suspicious that he hadn't been asked to pay at least half the fee in advance. That was the usual form. Sookie opened the door and stepped into the hall, beckoning him.

'It isn't very often we get requested by name,' she said.

'I just heard she was really good,' he replied, following.

'You're obviously a bloke who knows what he wants.'

There was no sign of the pimp when they arrived at the foot of the staircase. It was dark at the top. The next door along, presumably the front door, was heavily curtained.

'Up there,' Sookie said, still smiling. 'First door on the left.'

Heck started ascending. Below him, Sookie headed off towards the lounge. He watched the dimness above, warily – but then, with a sharp rustle of cloth, the curtain over the front door whipped aside, and the pimp, no longer armed with a newspaper but with an aluminium baseball bat, leaped out. In two strides he'd mounted the stairs behind Heck and swept the bat downward at his head. Heck, who'd been expecting this, ducked and barrelled backward into him.

They fell together, limbs tangled, to the bottom of the staircase.

'Get in here!' Heck shouted in a strangled voice. 'Officer under attack!'

It wasn't initially clear whether Hayes and Quinnell had heard this, but his assailant certainly hadn't. A rough, brawny customer, he was all over Heck as they wrestled on the hall floor. Heck's first priority was to ensure the bastard couldn't get into another position from where he could swing the bat, and so clamped himself to the guy like a limpet. The pimp struggled gamely, but though he was physically strong, he didn't have much technique. Heck finally twisted the bat from his grasp, mashing his head into the pimp's face twice in rapid succession. As the pimp sagged backward, bloody-mouthed, Heck threw a hard right, slamming it on the side of his jaw, flinging him against the newel post, from which his head rebounded like a football. Sookie now hurtled in from the kitchen, screeching, carving knife in hand.

Briefly, she looked wild-eyed, capable of anything, but suddenly there was a furious hammering at the front door. Muffled voices clamoured: 'Police officers! Open up or we'll break the fucking door down!'

'They're not kidding,' Heck said, swaying to his feet. 'I'd do as they say.'

Sookie's jaw sagged. 'You're a copper? All this bloody fuss, and you're a sodding copper!' She looked furious, but at the same time relieved.

Heck pulled out his wallet and flipped it open, revealing his warrant card. 'DS Heckenburg.'

She dropped her knife to the carpet.

'*Police officers!*' There was a massive blow on the other side of the door.

'All right! For Christ's sake, I'm coming!' Sookie shouted.

She studied Heck's ID in passing as she stepped over the groaning pimp, drew the curtain aside and yanked back bolts. The door crashed open, and Hayes, Quinnell, Finnegan and Klebworth forced their way inside, the three DCs armed with ASPs. Meanwhile, Heck dragged the pimp over onto his front and cuffed his hands behind his back.

'You, my friend,' he said, 'are a dickhead of the first order.'

Hayes grabbed Sookie, twisting her arm behind her back too. 'This one coming?'

'Let's speak to them first,' Heck said. 'Off the record.'

He hauled the pimp to his feet and frog-marched him

through to the lounge. Hayes did the same with Sookie, who wildly protested her innocence. Behind them, Quinnell grinned ear to ear as he closed the front door.

In the lounge, the captives were thrown side by side on the couch. The pimp, who'd come round properly now, glowered as the three cops stood assessing them.

'What's your name?' Heck asked him.

'Cowley . . . Scott Cowley.'

'Well, Scott, I suggest you save that mean look for the clink. Bloke like you, all muscle and no bite, they're going to love you in there.'

'You should've told us who you were,' Sookie said, almost crying.

'Why should I?' Heck replied. 'I didn't know who *you* were. Anyway, cut the crap. Where's Mindy-May?'

'Upstairs, in the back room. But she won't come out. She's petrified.'

'She tell you about the sex-shop attack?'

Sookie nodded dumbly.

Heck glanced at Hayes, whose cheeks coloured – this was the first real confirmation they'd had that they were on the right trail.

'What do you think *we're* here for?' the DI asked Sookie. 'We'd have given her protection.'

'But only on your terms, yeah?' Cowley sneered. '*And* if she's willing to go to court . . . which'll be near enough a death sentence for her.'

'Go upstairs if you want,' Sookie said. 'But that door locks from the inside and she won't even open it for me –'

'She won't open it for anyone,' Cowley cut in.

'And what role do you play in this, Scott?' Heck asked. 'Apart from getting the old riding crop out if the girls don't deliver?'

'I look after them. That's all.'

'I'm sure you're worth every penny,' Finnegan said with a snigger.

'Why'd you come at me with the bat?' Heck asked.

'Why'd you think?' Cowley snorted. 'No punters are supposed to know Mindy-May's here.'

'Gimme a break, Scott. Do you seriously think anyone on your network of lowlifes can keep their gobs shut?'

Cowley shook his head. 'You still *might've* been him . . . the Incinerator.'

'We were trying to do you a favour, coming here covertly,' Hayes said. 'If we hadn't been concerned to keep things quiet and keep you people safe, we could have got a warrant and kicked the bleeding door down. Drawn the attention of the entire street. Now we've almost had to do that anyway, thanks to you.'

Cowley averted his eyes. 'I always knew this'd be a fucking disaster.' He turned and, without warning, head-butted Sookie on the cheek; there was a smack of meat on bone. 'Stupid fucking bitch!'

Heck yanked him up to his feet by his T-shirt and tripped him, pitching him down face-first onto the carpet, before dropping on him from behind with his knees, eliciting a combination of shocked gasp and agonised yelp.

'You're a less impressive guy by the minute, Scott,' Heck said. 'Now, as things are, I'll shortly be arresting you for attempting to cause grievous bodily harm. I'm pretty sure we've got enough to do you for managing a brothel as well. Do we add battery too? It's all piling up, pal.'

'Do your fucking worst,' Cowley muttered. 'We were dead as soon as that stupid tart's mate turned up here.'

'If you don't fancy a trip to Bradburn nick via Bradburn A&E, I suggest you stay here on the floor and don't sodding move.' Heck stood up again, turning to Sookie and leaning down to check the side of her face, which was blotched a nasty shade of red. 'You all right?'

'It's nothing I haven't had before,' she said, probing it, grimacing with the pain.

'You'd better take us upstairs. The sooner we get this over, the better.'

She nodded, and climbed tiredly to her feet.

Hayes turned to Quinnell, Klebworth and Finnegan. 'Have a look around . . . make sure there's no one else here. And one of you keep a close eye on this sunbed wank-stain.' She kicked at Cowley's foot. 'I'd hate him to give us a reason to really beat his brains in.'

Chapter 29

'Go back a bit, you and Mindy-May?' Heck asked Sookie, as she led him and Hayes up the stairway.

'I was on the game when she was a toddler,' Sookie said over her shoulder. 'We've known each other a while though. Did a mum-and-daughter thing for the *Inside-Out* website.'

'Nice,' Hayes commented.

They arrived at the top and took a passage to the rear of the property, where a locked door stood to the left. Sookie tapped on it gently, as if it was a sickroom. 'Can I come in, love? It's me.'

'What was all that racket?' came a muffled enquiry from the other side.

'Scott chucking someone out.'

'Who?'

'Just some drunk.'

There was a brief pause. 'You sure?'

'Would I lie to you, pet?'

There was another pause, longer than before. And then a key turned in a lock and bolts were withdrawn. Heck went hard at the door, Hayes close behind. It swung open, the girl on the other side staggering backward, wailing with fright.

She was pale-faced and spotty, with red eyes, mascara-stained cheeks and long, fair hair, though at present it was straggly and sweaty. Her baggy shorts and vest did little to accentuate a bony, semi-emaciated figure; both her arms were striated with needle tracks. To be fair to her, the stink probably owed as much to the room as its occupant. It was small and dingy, and littered with crumpled clothing and bedsheets; all its windows were closed, and a portable electric fire blazed in the corner.

The girl's eyes flitted from one intruder to the next, but finally locked on Sookie.

'You bitch . . . what have you done?'

'It's for the best, love,' Sookie said in a voice that begged for understanding.

'Oh, Jesus . . .' Mindy-May reached behind her as she backed off, producing a switchblade, which she snapped open to a length of five inches.

'For God's sake, girl, we're police officers,' Hayes said. 'Put the knife down.'

'Does everyone in this house carry weapons?' Heck asked Sookie.

'At times like this, what do you think?'

'Just drop the blade, OK?' Hayes said again. 'We don't want to have to arrest you too.'

'No chance!' Mindy-May backed to the far side of the room. 'I'm not going with you scum!'

'Come on, Sonja,' Heck coaxed her in a softer tone. 'I can call you Sonja, can I?'

She looked bewildered that he knew this was her real name.

'Come on,' he urged her. 'Just put the knife down, eh?'

'I don't know you . . . I don't know any of you.'

'We've already identified ourselves,' Hayes said. 'We're police officers. You're safe.'

'Yeah, right! You got your fireproof overalls with you? Because I haven't. How about a shield to protect you against a flamethrower? I must have left mine at home too.'

'I understand why you're frightened,' Heck said. 'Believe me, I do. But there's no need. You come with us, and this maniac won't get anywhere near you.'

'You can't stay here, love,' Sookie added. 'You wouldn't be safe here, would you?'

'Yeah, well, you've proved that, haven't you – *you cow!*'

'Mindy . . . come on,' Sookie pleaded, looking genuinely hurt.

'You can't blame Sookie,' Heck said. 'She did her best for you. She's got that meathead downstairs, but he's no bloody good. And she has to let people in . . . she has to make a living, doesn't she?'

'You can't stay here for ever, love,' Sookie advised her. 'I told you to go to the coppers. Said you'll have to eventually. Scott said it too.'

'Put the blade down at least,' Hayes urged her. 'You can clearly see you don't need it.'

Slowly, warily, Mindy-May lowered the knife. In a belated nervous reaction, her fingers uncurled and it dropped to the rug.

'Kick it into the corner, eh?' Heck said. 'Where it can't do any harm.'

Mindy-May didn't kick it. She only had socks on her feet, and the switchblade was still open. Instead, she bent down, picked it up again and tossed it onto the rumpled bed.

'That's better.' Heck relaxed his posture, trying to put her at ease. 'At least we don't now think we're gonna get gutted alive for asking the wrong question, eh?'

'You say that as if this is some kind of joke,' Mindy-May said. Her voice turned shrill again. 'I bet you don't know what it's like to live in fear, do you, *for fuck's sake!*'

298

'I wouldn't say that,' he replied. 'Every time I pursue a killer I live in fear. That he's going to kill again before I nail him, and maybe again after that, and maybe again. You're correct, Sonja, this isn't a joke. Right now, everyone in this room has a very serious job to do. You included.'

She shook her head quickly. Too quickly, Heck realised. Way too quickly.

'I can't help you!' she asserted. 'All right? You need to understand that. I can't!'

'I haven't even asked you a question yet,' he replied.

Her face reddened. 'It doesn't matter what you ask me . . .'

'Oh, I think it does, Sonja. You know why? Because I think deep down you're a decent person. I think you saw something terrible happen and you want to make it right, but you don't quite know how.' He gave her his most earnest stare. 'Is that correct?'

'But I don't know anything . . .'

'You know what you saw, Sonja. That's all we want to talk to you about. Nothing else.'

'I . . . erm . . .' she stuttered helplessly.

'Let's start with an easy one,' he said. 'What happened at Sadie's Dungeon?'

'You don't already know?'

'Like I said, I want to know what *you* saw.'

'It was . . .' She struggled to find the words, her hollow cheeks tinging even brighter red. 'It was knocking-off time. I was getting changed, and then I heard this . . . shouting, and these screams.' Fresh tears bubbled from her eyes; she clamped a hand to her mouth. 'Jesus, those screams . . . you've never heard anything like it. It was Les and Barrie. I . . . couldn't help myself. I ran out of the dressing room . . . and soon as I got into the corridor, I felt the heat . . . and saw the fire at the far end. I had to go down there. That was the only way out. I was in a kind of daze, I suppose. Anyway . . . that's it.' She shook her head wildly, eyes turned glassy. 'That's all I saw. Fire . . . everywhere. And those two poor lads blazing . . . I mean really *blazing*, like logs on a bonfire. I just legged it out the back way. Obviously I legged it. I wasn't going to hang around inside a burning building, was I? *For fuck's sake, why the fuck would anyone do that?*'

Heck nodded. 'I agree, Sonja. Absolutely I agree. Trouble is . . . that's a pack of lies, isn't it?'

She looked perplexed. 'What the hell are you talking about? *You weren't sodding there!*'

'One minute ago you mentioned the word "flamethrower", which indicates to me that you actually saw a lot more than you've just admitted to.'

Again, she shook her head. 'I know about the flamethrower because I saw it in the news.'

'If you're worried that giving us a full statement will endanger your position with regard to the custody of your kids,' Hayes said, 'we've spoken to one of the duty solicitors at Bradburn Central. And they don't think it necessarily will. Pole-dancing, lap-dancing . . . they're legitimate lines of work these days. Lots of women who do it have kids, families.'

'Bet those other women haven't got my dodgy background though, have they?'

'Cooperating with a police investigation into a series of murders will be to your credit,' Heck said. 'How would that suggest you're anything other than an upstanding citizen?'

'And if I don't cooperate I suppose it'll be exactly the opposite? *I fucking knew it!*'

'I didn't say that, Sonja.' He made calming gestures with his hands. 'I'd rather you helped us because you *want* to help us.'

'And who's going to help *me*?' she demanded in a near-shriek. 'What happens if you lock this nutcase up but his

300

mates come after me? What happens if I'm put on some kind of kill-list? What'll the chances be of getting my babies back then?'

Heck had to admit that this situation was complicated. There was only so much he could do to reassure her. Whatever action they took, the road facing her was rocky.

'As things stand, if you give us something we can use, you'll go into Witness Protection,' he said. 'There's no reason I can think of why you won't be able to take your kids with you.'

'*But there's nothing I can fucking give you!*' she insisted, shrieking again. She was amazingly quick to irrational fury, which was often indicative of a disturbed mind.

'Sonja, have you taken anything today?' Hayes asked. 'I mean, it's obvious you've had dependencies in the past.'

'I'm clean now, I swear it! I'm completely clean!'

'Well, calm down then, because you're not helping your-self or us.'

'That's what I'm saying!' the girl blurted, more tears spilling down her cheeks. 'I'm no good to you in this. All right, yeah – I saw his face. But it was covered with oil and soot, and I only got a glimpse –'

'Hang on!' Heck interrupted. 'You saw his *face*?'

'Course I did.'

Heck glanced at Hayes, who looked equally surprised.

'Isn't that why you're here?' Mindy-May asked.

'Well, yeah . . . but wasn't he wearing a helmet?'

'He had something like that on – at first,' she said. 'When I ran into the shop, the whole place was burning, floor to ceiling. But there were big gaps in the flames. And I saw him standing in the middle. He had this flamethrower-type thing. He'd just finished using it, squirting fire out like it was from a hosepipe. And then he just stopped, and he lifted the front part of his helmet up.' She slumped onto a stool by the dressing-table, weak, almost lifeless. 'I think it was only then when I really cottoned on to what was happening. I saw Les and Barrie on the floor, burning . . . And him, that monster . . . he was looking down at them, and all around . . . and there was this smile . . . the Devil's smile, I tell you. . . It was the most evil thing I've ever seen. It was like it made him so happy, you know . . . what he'd done. And those lads were still screaming. And he was so fucking happy about it . . .'

'He'd lifted his visor up so he could look properly, you mean?' Heck said. 'So he could admire his own handiwork?'

'More than admire. Jesus, he was getting *off* on it. And then he saw me, of course.' Her voice cracked; fresh tears streamed from her eyes. 'At first, it was like he was . . . totally shocked. Like he hadn't known there was someone else in there. Anyway, I turned and ran like the clappers. There was a fire-door at the back of the shop. It was hanging open, the whole door-frame was burning. But I had to go through. I knew he'd burn me too if I stayed. I got through it like a whippet, I'll tell you. I was only half dressed, but I just ran and ran and ran. Oh, Christ . . .' She broke down into shoulder-heaving sobs.

Sookie hurried over, and wrapped her arms around her.

'It's OK,' Heck said. 'Take a sec. Can we get you a brew, or something?'

'I'm all right,' she sniffled, making a visible effort to get herself together. 'Thought – I thought he'd come after me, you see. That's why I just kept running, I was that frightened.' She shuddered violently.

'How much of a look at his face did you actually get?' Hayes asked.

'Like I say, it wasn't that good – it was black with soot. Too much glare from the fire . . . my eyes were blurred with sweat, tears.'

'When you say he was black with soot – could that have

been an optical illusion caused by the glare?' Hayes asked. 'I mean – could he actually have been a black guy?'

The girl hung her head. 'I don't know.'

'If he was grinning, did you see his teeth?' Heck wondered. 'Anything odd about them . . . like maybe one was a different colour from the others?'

'I didn't notice that . . . maybe I wasn't close enough.'

'Okay,' Heck said. 'How big was he?' I mean across the shoulders?'

'He had all this heavy gear on –'

'Yeah, but you stood face to face with him, Sonja. Was he a big guy, was he brawny – I mean, like a boxer?'

'I don't think so . . . but I didn't hang round to check.'

Heck glanced at Hayes again. Thus far, it was a no-go on ruling Marvin Langton either out or in.

'Do you remember much else about him, Sonja?' Hayes asked. 'For example, could you help a police artist make an e-fit?'

Mindy-May dabbed at her eyes with a tissue Sookie had extricated from her cleavage. 'I'll – I'll do my best. But I don't think I saw enough for that.'

'You can look at some photos too, yeah?' Heck said. 'See if anything strikes you?'

She nodded tiredly, but suddenly became alarmed again. 'What happens to me if you get him? If I give you a statement, I'll have to give evidence, won't I?' Again, her voice rose. '*For fuck's sake, I'll have to face him across a court! And then there are his bleeding mates!*'

'You seem very sure he's got mates, love,' Hayes said.

Mindy-May looked bewildered the DI could ask such a question. 'Isn't that what this guy is? Some kind of gangster, like a hitman? That's what they've been saying on the telly.'

'We don't watch the telly, Sonja,' Heck told her. 'We want facts, not speculation.'

'Unless you're telling us you actually *recognised* him as part of a crew?' Hayes said.

'She doesn't know any crews,' Sookie put in. 'She never has contact with any of that stuff.'

'Whether he's part of a crew, or not . . . even if he doesn't have any mates, I can't face him in court!' The girl shook her head frantically. 'Not some bloke who thinks it's funny to set fire to you!'

'Listen, whoa.' Heck palmed the air again. 'Video-link testimony is sometimes admissible. Maybe you could speak from behind a curtain. There're lots of ways we can protect your identity these days.'

'Whatever happens, you can't stay here, love,' Sookie said gently. 'You know that.'

'I just . . . *no!*' With new energy, Mindy-May tore loose from the older woman. She stumbled across the room, crying again. '*I can't do it . . .*'

'Sonja, there are loads of reasons why you must,' Hayes said firmly. 'Not least because he knows you saw him. That means he may have been looking for you all the time we have. Suppose he'd got here first? What if you refuse to cooperate with us now, and we leave you be, and he comes to see you later on tonight? When you're all in bed?'

'Come with us, Sonja, and help us put this madman away,' Heck said, 'and trust me, the world will seem like a much safer place.'

It didn't take a lot more than that.

The girl wailed some more, and wept on her friend's shoulder, but increasingly she listened to their coaxing and cajoling. When the decision finally came, it came suddenly and without warning. Mindy-May had clearly felt the walls closing in. The mere fact she was in hiding would have prevented her participating further in the custody battle for her children, so that was a losing strategy in the long run, and it was anyone's guess how close the police were to apprehending the Incinerator anyway. At least this way she'd be on the inside. Everything would be above board. And, as they'd said, she'd be safe. Or safer.

'If I'm going I have to go *now* . . . to the nick, I mean,' she sniffled. 'Like you said, he could be on his way here already.'

They were eager to comply. She dragged a dress and a coat on, pulled the hood up, worked her feet into some flat shoes, and allowed them to escort her downstairs. There they waited in the hall, while Heck opened the front door and checked that the coast was clear. Another damp, chilly evening greeted him, but there was no movement on the street.

'OK,' he said quietly.

Hayes slipped across the road, fishing out the keys to her Ford. She jumped in, switched its engine on and eased it over to the other kerb, pulling up in front of the house.

'Go,' Heck said, patting Quinnell's shoulder.

'G'bye, pet,' Sookie said from the stair, tearfully, but Mindy-May had already left, Quinnell hustling her across the pavement and into the back of the Ford.

Heck didn't immediately follow. He told Klebworth and Finnegan to wait for him outside, and headed back into the brothel's lounge, where Scott Cowley, his cheek bruised and nose and lips crusty with dried blood, sat on the couch, hands still cuffed behind his back.

He watched sullenly as Heck dug something from his jeans pocket. Then, to his surprise, was yanked to his feet and turned roughly around.

'Who do *you* think the Incinerator is, Scott?' Heck asked.

Cowley shrugged. 'Obvious, isn't it? One of Lee Shaughnessy's. Right bunch of psychos he runs with up on the Lawkholme. The Britannia Boys . . . Jesus wept.'

'That's why you're so frightened, is it?'

Though Cowley looked more irritated than frightened.

'We never had anything to worry about before,' he said disgustedly. 'We're an independent outfit. We had nothing to do with Vic Ship and his Manchester mob. He's never even offered to buy us out. But the moment Shaughnessy finds out we sheltered Mindy, it's over for us.'

'You know for a fact it's Shaughnessy, then?'

Cowley eyed Heck contemptuously. 'I'm not grassing him up, if that's what you're asking.'

'But you *know* it for a fact?'

'You don't need to know it, it's obvious. Every fucker's saying it.'

'So you *don't* know it?'

'What's your game, eh?'

They locked gazes, Heck wondering if he was seeing anything in the pimp's eyes aside from brute animal ignorance and suspicion, and deciding that he wasn't.

'You and Sookie keep your gobs shut,' Heck said, 'and I see no reason why any of this needs to get out.'

He wasn't entirely sure about that, of course. Someone somewhere had tipped him off – and it remained to be seen who, which wasn't a comforting thought, but whoever that person was and for whatever reason, they'd wanted the girl safely in police custody. It was thus a safe bet they wouldn't also seek to send the Incinerator here. Cowley didn't look convinced, however.

'You telling me your firm isn't as leaky as a bucket full of bullet holes?' he said.

'Yeah, that's what I'm telling you,' Heck replied. 'And I'm telling you something else too.' He inserted the handcuffs key. 'I'm cutting you loose.'

The pimp looked even more suspicious. 'Why?'

'Coz you're obviously a decent bloke and I'm all broken up about hitting you.' The bracelets came free and Heck shoved them back into his jacket. 'Christ's sake, Scott . . . I'm sure you can't be *all* brawn and no brain at all. Think about it.'

Cowley rubbed at the weals on his fat wrists. 'Uh . . . I . . .'

'OK, well, there's clearly no time for that ponderous process. So here's the deal . . . which is non-negotiable, by the way. You say you're not a grass, and that's fine – keep saying it. If anyone's actually listening. But the reality is, from now on, you work for me.'

Cowley's brow furrowed. 'I don't get you.'

'I have snouts all over the country, Scott. And I consult them every so often, usually with very specific requests for intel. I don't do gossip, I don't do chat – it's strictly the business end of things. And guess who's going to be my main man in Bradburn?'

'No fucking way. I said I don't grass, didn't I!'

'The alternative's simple. I get the local vice team onto you. The Blaymire Close operation then disappears up its own fundament, and you with it.'

'If this is about Shaughnessy, I don't actually know anything. I'm guessing.'

'I'm aware of that, and it isn't. It's for future reference.'

'Look, I've never grassed before. I'd be useless.'

'You're useless anyway, mate. But you won't need to do it often. Like I say, my enquiries will be occasional and specific, and never traceable back to you, unless –'

'Unless what?'

'Unless you piss me off.'

'I don't want to go on no list,' Cowley said adamantly. 'That's what you lot do, these days, isn't it? It's all official like. There's a book with all the snitches' names and addresses in.'

'We don't have to do it that way. Be a lot cheaper if we

don't. My way, all you'll be is an ear. You won't need to call me, I'll call you. But I'm telling you, I want something good . . . or this gig's up. By the way, the same applies if I find you've laid another finger on Sookie – and I *will*. It's not her fault you screwed up today.'

He moved out into the hall, where Sookie watched silently from the staircase. Cowley followed him, still rubbing his wrists. Heck stopped by the entrance.

'There's one other option, of course,' he said.

'What's that?' Cowley grunted.

'You can give up the pimp business. Go straight. Get a proper job. Be a constructive member of society.' Heck opened the front door. 'Then I won't be able to touch you . . . will I?'

Chapter 30

By the time Mindy-May reached Bradburn Central, it was quite clear to her that it was as much in her interest to identify the flamethrower guy as it was in the police's. But this didn't prevent her voice turning whiny and peevish again, and it didn't restrain her foul-mouthed outbursts, or the frequent scrubbing of hands through hair and frenzied wiping away of snot and tears. Partly to calm her down, she was taken to one of the station's soft interview rooms, where she was able to provide Katie Hayes and Sally Gorton with a long and very detailed witness statement. When this was complete, an artist showed up with electronic sketchpad in hand, and began to construct an e-fit.

Heck watched from the VDU room. At length, Gemma came and joined him. With the underworld war in Bradburn now deemed an official 'critical incident', she'd been ensconced for most of the day in an upstairs office with Gold Command to devise a community impact assessment. To Heck, this kind of thing, which was basically a glorified and extensive admin procedure, had always felt like a distraction from the senior detective's real role, which ought to be the pursuit and appre-hension of murderers. It was a particular irritant on this occasion, because if Heck himself couldn't work on the Sagan case, he'd have felt better if Gemma at least was keeping a close eye on Gibbshaw and making sure he was getting things right, rather than spending half her time tangled in red tape. That said, there was no doubt that Bradburn was a town in crisis at present; tensions were high and people were frightened – and looking after the ordinary folk was not something a conscientious SIO like Gemma would ever willingly neglect. And it wasn't as if she'd been out of touch all day; she'd heard them out regarding the undercover op on Blaymire Close and had sanctioned it straight away.

'Everything go all right up there?' she asked, watching the screen.

'Swimmingly,' Heck replied.

'What have we got from her so far?'

'An outfit and a crazy smile.'

'We already had the outfit from the CCTV footage at the canal.'

'She's corroborated it then. She's also confirmed that we're only after one guy.'

Gemma didn't look impressed by that. 'Let me guess . . . because she only saw one guy.'

'It's a persuasive argument, ma'am.'

'His support team could have stayed outside the sex shop – in a parked vehicle, perhaps.'

Heck couldn't deny this possibility, though it felt like a slim one – what use would the Incinerator's assistants have been parked up outside if the flamethrower had malfunctioned and the shop proprietors had gone at him with coshes?

'What about the crazy smile?' Gemma wondered.

'If I'm honest, ma'am, it doesn't promise much – not from what the girl's said so far. But perhaps we should see what the artist comes up with before writing this lead off completely.'

310

On the screen, Mindy-May was now demanding a break, aggressively complaining that she was tired and wanted to sleep. When DI Hayes suggested they get another half-hour in, the girl swore and called her a 'fucking heartless bitch'.

'She been like this all evening?' Gemma asked.

'Yeah,' Heck said. 'She's a headcase.'

'So even if she does give us something, can she stand up to cross-examination in court?'

He shrugged. 'As hostile witnesses go, this one would be a nine out of ten. But at present she's all we've got.'

'I hear Katie Hayes has sorted out a safehouse for her?'

'Yeah. For a few days at least. Till we can get Witness Protection onside.'

Hayes, who'd departed the interview room half a minute earlier, now appeared alongside them. She looked haggard and bleary-eyed.

'Well?' Gemma asked.

'She's hard work, ma'am,' Hayes replied. 'Which is a bit frustrating. I mean, she had a scare, obviously. So I suppose it's understandable she's a nervous wreck. I've asked her to give us another half-hour. Then we'll pack in and start again in the morning. Once the e-fit's completed we can get her to look at some photos.'

Gemma pondered this. 'Any thoughts yet where the original tip-off might have come from?'

'Not yet,' Heck said, increasingly discomforted by the thought that someone else out there knew that Mindy-May was a potential witness to the sex shop. OK, whoever they were, they obviously had no vested interest in preventing her talking to the cops, but if they knew about Mindy-May, others might know about her too.

Hayes, meanwhile, had her own reasons to be concerned about this.

'That's something else that's worrying me about this

311

testimony,' she said. 'As long as we don't know everything there is about this lass and how we got to her, that makes her unreliable all-round. I mean, who's to say she's not in league with the Incinerator? What if all this evidence she's supplying us with is a diversion?'

'If she's *pretending* to be frightened,' Heck said, 'she's a damn good actress.'

'Maybe, but too many of these histrionics in court, and it won't take long for the jury to side against her.'

They were talking in circles, Heck realised, frustrated. They needed more to work with.

'You off somewhere?' Gemma asked as he pulled on his jacket.

'I am, ma'am. Blaymire Close.'

'Why?'

'Because everything's suddenly looking like it may hinge on who tipped us off.'

'Thought you were of the opinion that was Shaughnessy's mob?' Hayes said.

'It may have been,' he replied. 'I said all along they could cooperate – that they'd so want this guy wrapped up they'd be happy to leave it to us. But if they found out Mindy-May was hiding in that brothel it means the word had already hit the street. It means that someone else, who we haven't yet met, knows more about this than we do.'

'OK,' Hayes replied. 'But I'm coming with you.'

'No, I'll go with him,' Gemma said.

'Ma'am?' Hayes sounded disappointed. 'Surely, as DSIO Incinerator, I should be –'

'Not in my opinion,' Gemma replied coolly. 'You've got a significant witness here, Katie, whom we need to be a little more cooperative. That's your priority.'

'With respect, ma'am, I disagree. I'm a senior investigator on this case, and –'

'And I'm *the* senior investigator, DI Hayes, and my decision will stand. You don't just have to get something useful out of this girl, you also need to supervise her transfer to the safehouse. So you've actually got two priorities before you chase other leads. I'm sure DS Heckenburg won't have a problem with *my* company.'

Heck shrugged. 'Not at all, ma'am.'

Gemma glanced at Hayes again. 'Don't worry . . . we'll not be going at it like rabbits the moment we get some privacy.'

The DI turned a distinct shade of red and strode stiffly back towards the interview room. Gemma pulled her own coat on, and she and Heck walked out to the personnel car park.

'She's not made any comments to that effect,' Heck finally felt brave enough to say.

That was a lie, of course, though he'd now decided that he liked Katie Hayes. He wasn't going to drop her in it for no reason. Even so, Gemma made no reply until they were on the road together in his Megane.

'Who?' she asked, somewhat unnecessarily.

'DI Hayes . . . about me and you, I mean.'

Gemma gazed directly ahead. 'Apparently she's very efficient.'

'She seems to be. I mean, she's a bit of a bull at a gate . . .'

'Oh . . . I wondered why you had an affinity with her.'

Heck drove on. 'She's been good to work with so far. Enthusiastic, gets things done . . .'

'The sort of young career policewoman I might at one time have been able to inspire, eh?'

'Ma'am, I don't know where you've got the idea that she thinks me and you are an item.'

'She doesn't need to think we're an item to think less of me, does she?'

Here it finally comes, he now realised. *The inevitable bollocking.*

'Ma'am, she hasn't said any –'

'I've got ears, Heck, and I'm not stupid, so don't treat me as if I am.' For once, though, Gemma didn't raise her voice. 'She doesn't have to go around gobbing off crudely like that bloody political appointment Ron Gibbshaw to display a certain level of disrespect.'

'I don't think she disrespects you at all. Look, she cheeked you back there because she doesn't like being left out of the action, which is kind of to her credit. If you don't mind me saying, I think you're being a bit paranoid about this. I've said I'm sorry about that thing at your B&B, and I meant it. It won't happen again.'

Gemma glanced round at him, her expression unreadable in the liquid shadows.

'I don't actually mind you making moves on me, Mark. It's happened all my career – from various quarters and all ranks. And I'll respond to you the way I do to the rest of them – I'll belittle you till you're half an inch high, or I'll slap you down with casual ease. But I've said this before, and I'll now say it one last time: what I don't like is you exploiting our former status by bending the rules of this game to breaking point. Because I'll tell you now, I'm tired of fighting a daily rearguard against the idea that you and me share some kind of secret bond, that you are my favourite and that you enjoy special privileges. So I'm going to make a final plea that you try to understand my position. Just once in your life. And if that's not possible, perhaps try to understand your own. For example, do you enjoy being a detective in the Serial Crimes Unit?'

Heck was trying to concentrate on the road, but this seriously unnerved him. 'You know full well . . . it's the only thing I've got.'

'On a scale of your usual glib responses, that's a new low. There are lots of posts for experienced detective sergeants in all the police forces of England and Wales –'

'Yes, but I like SCU, ma'am. I'm at home here, it's my comfort zone.'

'OK. So, if you and I were to get it together again – I don't just mean officially, I mean in *any* shape or form – you understand, don't you, Mark, that we couldn't keep working in the same department?'

'We did when we were younger.'

'And it didn't pan out, did it? We rowed. A lot. In fact, you ended up dumping me. Now just consider that – *I* got dumped. Talk about an experience I'd never had before.'

'I soon knew I'd made a mistake.'

'You *didn't*. That's the whole point.' Gemma still didn't raise her voice, although it remained sharp, penetrating; this was a message she was clearly determined to ram home. 'We can have each other . . . or we can have the job. We can't have both. That's not me being mean. That's a simple fact of life. And if it's something you haven't thought about before, Mark, you need to start thinking about it now. And not just now, may I say, but every time you decide to treat me like your ex-girlfriend instead of your boss. Am I clear on that?'

'Yes,' he said gloomily.

'Yes what?'

'Yes, ma'am.'

'And now, still on the subject of facts – perhaps you'd like to explain to me why we're going back to this brothel on Blaymire Close?'

'What? Oh, yeah. Sorry . . . bit distracted.' Struggling to get his scrambled thoughts in order, Heck swung the Megane in among the parallel rows of terraced houses dividing up the Budworth district. 'It's occurred to me, and it's an ugly possibility, but Katie Hayes got me thinking. Could Mindy be playing us? Suppose these fire-attacks have been carried out by Shaughnessy's crew all along. I mean, I still don't fancy them for this – but if they *are* responsible, she could be part of it.'

'You mean she could be a plant?'

'Yeah. You know, ma'am, I might really have screwed up on Saturday when I told Shaughnessy that I thought we were looking for a lone operator.'

'As in you could have given him a really good idea?'

'Well . . . given him an opportunity to put himself and his crew in the clear by sending his undercover agent, Mindy-May, to *prove* my theory.'

Gemma pondered this. 'So who are we going to see now?'

'There's a pimp works at the brothel called Cowley, and another hooker called Sookie. She's older than Mindy-May, and more than a little wiser. On reflection, I'm not sure we've got every scrap of information out of those two that we can.'

However, a couple of minutes later, when they pulled up across the road from the brothel, an odd reddish light flickered behind its downstairs windows. Heck all but jumped out of the car, Gemma following quickly.

'You smell that, ma'am?' he said in a tight voice.

She wrinkled her nose. 'Something's burning.'

'Or it's already burned. *Shit!*' He charged madly across the road and down the entry. Gemma hurried after him.

Halfway down, the full smoke and stench engulfed them. They gagged and wafted their way through. The side-door had been smashed wide open, the jamb showing extensive splintering at the point of the central lock, as though from a Halligan bar. In addition, there was massive scorching around the peephole. Even before he entered, Heck could picture what had happened:

The coded knock at the door.

Sookie, for whom it was always business as usual, tip-tapping across the kitchen in her sexy undies and pretty heels.

As per the rules, drawing back the slat.

But instead of seeing some eager customer's face, being greeted by the char-black muzzle of a flamethrower, which blasted her backward across the kitchen.

A different tool then employed to force open the door.

He clamped a handkerchief to his mouth as he fought his way inside. Even so, he could taste roasted human meat at the back of his throat. Gemma retched and coughed.

Extensive pockets of fire burned on all sides. The kitchen cupboards, the worktops, the floor itself were blackened and smouldering. But the first thing they were properly able to distinguish in the smoke-smothered room was a twisted corpse, crisped and featureless, with greasy flames dancing up and down it as it lay against the row of far cabinets. It was from this where most of the choking smog issued. The only part of the corpse that hadn't been torched, its feet, were still neatly slotted into a pair of red velvet shoes.

'You said there were two people here?' Gemma gasped, eyes streaming.

Heck kicked open a connecting door. They glanced through it into the hall, which had also been gutted by flame, and in many sections was still burning. This area was denser with smoke, having contained more fabric. Yet in the middle of it, halfway along, a contorted shape knelt in a pool of fire. This figure had been flambéd to the point where it resembled an *objet d'art* rather than a living being. No human features remained, but the baseball bat was clearly visible, hanging limp from the extended scabrous claw that had once been Cowley's left hand.

'This has only just happened,' Heck said, retreating. 'The bastard's only just been here.'

Unable to tolerate the choking stink any longer, Gemma staggered outside after him. She was already fiddling with her radio.

'DSU Piper to –' she coughed, only for Heck to violently shush her.

'Christ's sake!' she snapped. 'We need the Fire Brigade!'

'Ma'am . . . listen!'

'Heck, this house is still burning, what the hell am I supposed to be –'

'Shhhh!'

Reluctantly, she fell silent. And from a neighbouring street, heard the dull thud of what sounded like a car boot being closed.

'Bastard's just packed his gear away,' Heck hissed.

'Heck, this is no –'

Another thud sounded. A car door closing. A motor revved, and an engine growled to life.

Heck starting running.

'*Heck!*'

'I'm in pursuit!' he shouted over his shoulder. 'If you can secure the scene, ma'am . . .'

He slid to a halt beside his Megane, and yanked the door open. Then waited again, sweat prickling his face. He could still hear that engine. It was difficult to know the direction on a quiet night like this when sound travelled every which way, but he took a gamble that it was somewhere ahead and to the left. He leaped in, gunned the car to life and drove quickly down Blaymire Close to its far end, which was a cul-de-sac, though progress was still possible from here: a ginnel, no more than a foot passage, led off northeast, while a slightly wider alley, a backstreet between two more rows of terraced houses, ran northwest.

It was at the far end of this latter route where Heck spotted the suspect vehicle – a saloon car of some sort, a

318

Peugeot estate possibly, wallowing slowly away. However, the instant Heck turned into the alley himself, the Peugeot's driver, who had obviously spotted him in his rear-view mirror, got his foot down, his motor rocketing forward, rubbish and wastepaper spinning from under his wheels. At the next corner the Peugeot swung left.

Heck followed at speed, jack-knifing his car round in pursuit.

Chapter 31

Initially Heck chased the fugitive down a B road with residential properties on either side. He didn't want to risk racing along here, but that wasn't stopping the driver in front, who sped recklessly to the first junction. On the next turn, potholes in the road had filled with rainwater. Both cars skated across, Heck sliding sideways as his wheels locked. The Peugeot driver got his foot down again. Now they were on a main road, heading towards the town centre.

'DS Heckenburg . . . Operation Wandering Wolf, chasing a suspect in the Incinerator murders,' Heck shouted into his radio. 'Oldenshaw Way, heading into town . . . suspect driving a grey Peugeot estate, index: Papa-Quebec-two-three-Whiskey-X-Ray-Victor.'

Directly ahead, the traffic lights had changed to red. A Citroën Picasso was sitting there, exhaust chugging. The Peugeot swerved around it, cutting through the intersection. Heck swore, having to copy the manoeuvre. Very fortunately, nothing was coming from the other directions.

'Bridge Street, heading north,' he shouted, though already a mass of static-filled messages were scrunching back and forth.

Two pedestrians scuttled out of the way as the Peugeot made a sharp left, swerving around to the rear of Marsden House, a bleak, functional building which had served as Bradburn's main social security offices for so long that it was known simply as the 'Dole Shop'. Beyond this, they swung into another backstreet, though it had been narrowed by a line of vehicles parked on the left. The Peugeot ploughed recklessly past, shearing bodywork, snapping off wing-mirrors. The next junction was a crossroads, narrow avenues leading in all directions, but mostly into the realms of dereliction. The fugitive hit the gas as he cleared the parked cars, spinning left. Heck screeched around the bend in pursuit, skidding through an acre of mashed cardboard. Now they were on aged cobblestones, bouncing and jolting. But Heck had gained ground. At the next turn, he struck the Peugeot a glancing blow with his front bumper, shattering its nearside light cluster. He'd have come up alongside it had they not suddenly run into an alley so tight that its walls were almost flush to either side of their cars.

Heck thought the chase was over. This had to be a cul-de-sac.

But fifty yards in front, the Peugeot's headlights reflected back – not from the flat brickwork of a dead-end, but from an immense set of double doors with a single plank nailed across them.

The fleeing driver accelerated.

'Can't be bloody serious!' Heck shouted.

The doors crashed open on impact, the Peugeot vanishing from view. Heck followed, with no clue where he was headed.

'Still in pursuit, still mobile!' he barked into his radio. 'But inside a building somewhere to the rear of the Dole Shop. Some kind of derelict mill or factory. Could use support, over!'

For hair-raising moments, they careered side by side through a vast, dark space, weaving amid endless concrete pillars. The Peugeot veered left, as though attempting to circle back. In an effort to pre-empt him, Heck swerved left too, tromping the gas, seeking to overtake him on the inside if he could – only for an old, heavy desk to loom into his path. He braked and swung right, falling back into the Peugeot's wake, having lost fifty yards, in fact now only glimpsing the fugitive vehicle as its tail-light vanished through an internal door. Heck burned through the doorway after it, slamming his pedal to the floor. This next passage ran seventy yards, and was cluttered with cardboard and plastic bags, which flew up behind the Peugeot like fluttering, dust-shrouded ghosts. Ahead, meanwhile, there was another set of doors. The fleeing driver caromed through them, splinters of wood and metal flying back over his roof, hailing into Heck's windscreen.

Outside, they hit a paved yard, its mossy, misaligned flag-stones so greasy they were more like an ice rink. The Peugeot slewed across, fishtailing through an open gateway, its rear offside banging on a brick post but insufficiently to impede it. Heck lost traction while attempting the same, fighting the wheel as he spun in a complete circle, but righting the Megane in time to thrust it through the same gap.

Another alley lay ahead. Fifty yards along, the Peugeot's tail-light receded and receded – and vanished, simply winked out.

Heck wondered if the bastard had turned his lights off. But then realised the truth.

A steep flight of stone steps dropped to a lower level.

The Peugeot descended them with a violent crashing and jolting, but still made it to the bottom, where it roared away along an entry that connected at its far end with another main road. Heck was half-minded to jam his anchors on, but just touching the brake sent him into another skid. Instead, he tromped the gas, and he too went down the steps, buffeted between his seat and the car's ceiling. He struck the bottom with such force that he thought his airbag might deploy.

Thirty yards on, meanwhile, the battered Peugeot veered left, disappearing again.

'Still in the town centre!' Heck shouted. 'Think we're on Bradburn Low Road, heading south.'

Bradburn Low Road was not the best route from Heck's perspective, as it led away from the central conurbation into the residential districts, where there were lots of backstreets, garages and carports to serve as hiding places, and of course plenty of potential collaterals should there be civvies about. But they never made it that far.

The Peugeot breached the next set of lights. Other road users veered away, horns yowling. The Peugeot hurtled through, but Heck had to negotiate the chaos more carefully, only one eye fixed on his target. Even though an open road now lay ahead, it again went left. Heck followed, jolting down a dirt ramp and then running along the cinder towpath to the Leeds–Liverpool Canal, which was at times so tight that a line of wrought-iron fencing on the left gashed his bodywork, while on the right his wheels trundled the heavy stone slabs edging the waterway.

Again, he relayed this info through the radio.

When the fence fell behind them, the Peugeot swerved left again. Now they were on Anderson Brow, all that remained of Anderson Pit: a virtual desert, a rubble and clinker-littered spoil-land. It was stippled with flashes, ochre-yellow mini-lakes formed where worked-out coal seams had collapsed. As a child, Heck had believed these were bottomless; as an adult, he knew they might as well be – they were deep enough to swallow a car whole.

The Peugeot surged ahead, but erratically, zigzagging – possibly because it had taken so much damage, or because the driver was tired or maybe even injured.

Only when it was nearly too late did Heck realise the true reason.

Bits of old mining equipment, hunks of corroded machinery, were strewn across the ravaged ground. He had to spin the wheel, as though in a dodgem car, to evade them.

'Anderson Brow,' he shouted at his radio. 'Headed east.'

Beyond these hazards, the ground sloped downhill. A vista opened up, black as night, though across its centre lay a thin, ribbon-like road, the yellow blobs of streetlights arrayed above it.

'Anderson Brow, approaching Hinks Lane, fifty plus!' Heck yelled. 'Will some of you bastards please get your arses here!'

What lay between here and Hinks Lane was anyone's guess, but the Peugeot was prepared to chance it, almost taking flight as it clattered over another obstruction. Heck swerved in pursuit. The road drew rapidly closer, but now, just as Heck was gaining again, the rutted track transformed into wet grass; suddenly it was like the Cresta Run.

One second Hinks Lane looked a long way away, the next it was right upon them.

There was no traffic in sight, but Heck couldn't imagine there wouldn't at least be a fence. He braked hard, his Megane shrieking into a tailspin, the world cavorting past his windscreen, before, with a howl of blistering rubber, he ground to a halt beside a low wall, about four feet tall, made from heavy green stone. The Peugeot slammed into the wall side-on, and yet somehow, though it was a shuddering impact, its driver got his foot down again.

The Peugeot lurched forward, this time following the wall.

Heck tried to do the same, but for several crucial seconds got nowhere, his back wheels churning mud before catching and jerking him onwards.

The Peugeot had gained eighty yards. It cut left through an open gateway onto Hinks Lane. Heck managed to do the same – only to find that about fifty yards ahead the Peugeot had skidded to a halt on the left side of the road. Even as Heck watched, a hooded figure jumped out of it, ran around the car and hared away on foot across the next stretch of wasteland. Heck pulled up behind it, leaped out and gave chase. He dragged the torch from his pocket, aiming it ahead as he jabbered into his radio, catching sight of a grey-clad shape at the extreme end of his visibility, but also scanning the ground in front of him – something about this felt wrong.

Abruptly, the running figure changed direction, veering back towards the road. Heck was bewildered – something was *badly* wrong.

A small building hove into view on the left. Little more than a brick outhouse, with a black doorway in the side. Heck's heart thundered as the running figure made a beeline for this and vanished into its interior. Did he have another weapon in there? Could that be his base? It seemed unlikely; it didn't look as if there'd be room to swing a cat.

Heck came to the doorway himself, and peered in, breathing hard – seeing only the metal handrail to a dank concrete stair, which spiralled down underground.

The air-raid shelters, he realised, heart sinking.

Most of the derelict mills and factories in Bradburn dated to the prewar years. Nearly all had constructed their own air-raid shelters, many of which were still intact and in fact interconnected, meaning there were masses of maze-like tunnels and chambers underground: an incredible playground for adventurous kiddies, but a parental nightmare given they were also a hangout for tramps, druggies and the like.

It felt rash – because clearly at no stage tonight had his opponent been on anything less than familiar terrain – but Heck followed him down there.

He halted at the bottom, having descended about twenty feet, sweat dripping amid a fog of breath. The stagnant reek of abandoned tunnels assailed him. His torchlight roved over walls of brickwork scored by time and damp, spray-painted with slogans so old as to be almost indecipherable. There were two further routes from here, arched black entrances that bade no one enter. A distinct but dwindling echo of footfalls sounded from the right.

Heck lurched along that way. The torch speared maybe thirty yards ahead, yet still he stumbled over heaped masonry and spiked himself on the wreck of a broken school chair. Just beyond that, the passage turned a sharp corner, bringing him around by ninety degrees, so that when it ran straight again, he felt as if they were doubling back. He progressed another hundred yards before hearing a sound ahead – a sluggish grating of metal.

'No . . . *NO!*'

He galloped forward, but no sooner had the steel gate emerged into his torchlight than he heard the echoing *clunk* of a bolt being thrown.

It must have taken a strenuous physical effort to close that gate; its hinges had to be ancient, but it was massive and ungainly and it completely filled the passage. Its lower half was of riveted steel, thick with rust though still very solid. Its upper half consisted of a square steel frame fitted with thick bars. Heck threw his shoulder against it, but though it gave slightly at the top, it wouldn't budge at the bottom, which was almost certainly where the bolt had been rammed home, probably driven into a socket bored in the concrete floor.

He shone his torch through, and saw that the fugitive had turned to face him. He was no longer running, but slowly – very slowly – retreating into the darkness. He stood just a little shorter than Heck, his bodily dimensions hidden by a dusty grey boiler suit, beneath which he wore a grey sweat-top with the hood pulled up. Underneath that hood it was so dark that only a partial face was visible, the vague outline of a jaw. Clouds of hanging breath spilled out.

'You out of your mind?' Heck gasped. 'You really think you can rampage around this town, burning people alive?' He pointed through the bars. 'Listen . . . I don't care who you are or why you think you're doing this, but I'm telling you, pal, I'm bringing you in . . . alive or dead, it'll be your call. But it's going to happen. You'll make a mistake, nutters like you always do, and I'll be there at just the right time.'

The figure halted, as if contemplating this threat. More thick breath wafted from under his hood. Then he turned and bolted into the darkness. And Heck knew why. He'd been correct when he'd thought they were doubling back on themselves. They were now almost back at Hinks Lane. There'd be an exit to it nearby – but one which, thanks to the bolted gate, he himself couldn't reach. He'd have to go the long way around.

He ran back, as fast as he could, making it to the stair in what felt like record time, though in reality the minutes had flown by. He ascended breathlessly, panting so hard that it hurt his chest. Then he had to negotiate the rough ground again, tripping and stumbling until he reached the road. By now, a quarter of an hour had passed. The night was silent.

The only vehicle sitting under the row of streetlights was his own dirty and dented Megane.

Chapter 32

Having summoned the Fire Brigade, who managed to make the brothel safe and also searched the premises for further victims, finding none, Gemma was left with a devastated crime scene. By the time Heck returned there, uniforms were in the process of taping the building off, along with the access-ways at the side and rear, and doing their best to hold back a horde of curious onlookers. Gemma had already despatched a small number of bobbies to start calling on the neighbours to establish whether there were any witnesses. She herself was outside the tape, smoky-faced and wearing her disposable gloves, relaying her detailed initial assessment to Comms by phone.

She cut the call as Heck approached.

He shrugged. 'I lost him.'

'So I heard.' Her blank expression gave nothing away.

'It didn't help that I didn't get much support.'

'It didn't help that you gave misleading directions.'

Heck sighed. When support units had finally located him, he'd only then discovered that he wasn't actually on Hinks Lane, but Culraven Road, a parallel route across the same colliery spoil-land, but a mile and a half further west.

'What can I say, ma'am? My memory for local geography's a bit rusty –'

'Save it for when you get back to the nick.' She pulled her gloves off. 'In fact go there now. Write it all up while it's still fresh in your memory. You can give me a ride back too.'

They walked down the street, which swam with shifting patterns of blue light thanks to the beacons of the patrol cars blocking off its far end.

'I'm sorry, ma'am.' Heck pinched thin air. 'I was *that* close to him. Literally. Bloody barred gate was all that separated us.'

'I'm sorry too,' she said. 'An enquiry like this, you only get so many chances.'

'We'll get more. I mean, we came up here to catch John Sagan, but this Incinerator guy . . . he's a special case in his own right. He loves it, and he's going to keep on doing it.'

Gemma didn't reply. They'd reached a section of road now taped off as a special RVP for Wandering Wolf personnel, whose vehicles were still arriving. Gibbshaw climbed out of the first, pulling his coat on. He was DSIO Sagan, so this was officially nothing to do with him, but at times like this it was all hands to the pumps.

'Something good?' he asked.

'Nothing good,' Gemma replied. 'But it's the Incinerator again. Two blasts of intense flame. Two vics.'

Gibbshaw glanced at Heck. 'I hear you got close?'

'Not close enough. But the VRM . . .'

'Stolen plates,' Gibbshaw said. 'Lifted last year on the outskirts of London.'

'I see.'

'We've circulated them anyway. But if he's got one set of iffy numbers, it's highly possible he'll have more. All he needs is a quiet place in which to swap 'em around, and he's gone.'

'Yeah,' Heck replied. 'Damn.'

*

Gemma made another couple of calls while they drove back to the station, and once Heck had parked went straight indoors without speaking to him. Heck meanwhile circled his Megane to check how smashed up it was after the chase – finding that it was every bit as bad as he'd expected. As he stood there gloomily, wondering if there was any chance at all he could pass this bill on to the taskforce, another vehicle came roaring into the car park and screeched up alongside him. It was Katie Hayes's beige Ford Contour, and by the pungent, oily reek from under its bonnet, it had been going at some pace. The lady herself leaped out, pulling off her baseball cap, releasing an untidy mass of long, black, sweaty hair.

'Heck!' she all but shouted. 'You know we have rules up here about police pursuits?'

'I have a rule too. I pursue the bastards till I catch them.'

'Except it didn't work out that way, did it?' Her eyes flashed and there was a real catch in her voice; she was hopping mad.

Deciding he didn't need this hassle now, he turned and walked towards the personnel door.

She followed him. 'It would also have helped if you'd given us proper directions.'

He turned back tiredly. 'Ma'am, after so many years away, I'm not totally *au fait* with the road layout in this town. But I know what's really pissing you off – you wanted to be there for the takedown tonight, and you weren't. By the smell of your engine, you've been screwing it all over Bradburn. You really wanted to get in on it, didn't you?'

'You cheeky chauvinist sod!' she said slowly.

'What?'

'So I'm driven by the same enthusiasm for the job you are, but I get slagged off for it?'

'I'm not slagging you off, ma'am.' He held up a placating hand. 'I'm truly not. What I *am* saying is that you've got to take it on the chin sometimes. We don't always get our man. Believe me, I'm as cheesed off about it as you are. And I'm sorry about the misdirection. Genuine mistake, OK? I'm not really the Lone Ranger. I do believe in teamwork, I just need a team who can keep up with me.'

Perhaps because she understood that sentiment well, she chose not to rise to it.

'I hear you got some face-time with him?' she said.

'Nearly. No distinguishing features, if that's what you were going to ask. I'll tell you what, though, he knows his way around. Ran through those backstreets like a rat in its own tunnel, knew about the air-raid shelters, lured me right into them . . .'

'So he's local. Puts him firmly back in Shaughnessy's court, wouldn't you say?'

'Or he's a private citizen who also happens to be local – and who has a big beef with the mob.'

'Heck, come on . . .'

'Or he's neither of those things. He's just done his homework very well indeed.'

'So basically we've gained no ground whatsoever?' Hayes said.

A few yards away, the personnel door opened. DS Sally Gorton and a couple of other female officers in plain clothes emerged, escorting Sonja Turner, aka Mindy-May. Clearly they were en route to the safehouse.

'Not necessarily,' Heck said.

Gorton's team were headed towards a parked-up Qashqai,

but now he hurried to catch up with them. 'Sonja, wait!'

The girl pulled a weary face. 'Aww, no . . . I need sleep.'

She seemed as bolshy and irascible as earlier; it hadn't been moderated by one iota of grief – which meant she hadn't yet been told about the deaths at Blaymire Close. That was a good thing; Heck hoped she wouldn't be told until they'd finished with her, as it might shock her into silence, and that would help no one.

'There're a couple more questions I need to ask,' he said.

'Listen, mate, *I'm fucking exhausted, all right?*'

'*HEY!*' he shouted back with such force that it stopped the party in their tracks. '*There's a madman out there burning people alive, and you're complaining that you're tired!*'

'DS Heckenburg –' Gorton tried to intervene.

'This is important,' he told her.

Gorton turned to Hayes, walking up from behind. 'Ma'am?'

'Leave it, Sally!' Hayes said curtly.

'I want to ask you a very important question, Sonja,' Heck said. 'Are you for actual real?'

Her cheeks paled a little. 'I don't know what you mean.'

'Have you been totally straight with us?'

'I've – I've told you everything there is.'

He tilted his head. 'I wonder if you have?'

Her voice became wheedling, tired again. 'Look, I don't understand . . .'

'Who else apart from Sookie and Scott Cowley knew you were hiding in that knocking shop?'

'No one.'

'You told no one else at all that you were there?'

'I said "no one", didn't I!'

'You were in that minging bedroom, what . . . twelve days? How did you survive?'

Now the girl looked frightened as well as bewildered.

From her evasive body-language, Heck could tell that she was struggling. She wasn't happy answering these questions. It might just mean that she was genuinely exhausted, but it could also mean that she was being deceptive.

'Sookie looked after me,' she stuttered. 'Brought me food, cups of tea, all that stuff.'

'You're sure that Sookie told no one?' he said. 'What about Cowley?'

'Why would they do that? They knew I was frightened, that I needed to hide.'

'How many other girls work in that brothel?'

'Couple. But Sook sent them home the night I turned up. Said they'd have to work the streets for a couple of weeks.'

'And you're sure none of them saw you?'

'Yeah. She took me straight upstairs and put me in that room.'

'What about when Sookie had her own customers in? Could any of *them* have noticed you?'

She shook her head. 'I always kept quiet, and that room was locked.'

'What about going to the bathroom? Could one of the johns have spotted you then?'

'I never did . . . there was an en suite bog and shower attached. Surely you saw that?'

Heck recalled the stuffiness and stench in that locked upper room. Even the window had been firmly closed. It really had felt as if the girl had sealed herself in hermetically, as if she'd truly been scared. But there was something about Sonja Turner that Heck no longer trusted. She'd lied to him before, only telling him as much as she was happy for him to know.

'I'm going to tell you something, Sonja – whatever kind of normal life you think you can have, *we're* the only chance it'll happen. Do you understand? But even we have limitations if we don't have all the facts.'

'Duh! What do you think I'm trying to hide from you?'

'Don't respond to my question with a question of your own,' he said; that was another classic evasion tactic.

'Do you think I'm dumb or something?' she snapped. 'Do you think I want to die as young as this . . . like so many of my mates have? And you don't need to give me that big bad copper stuff either. You lot are nothing compared to some blokes I could name. And there was no bleeding sign of you when Jess copped it, was there?'

'Whoa, what did you say?' Heck was briefly stumped. '*Jess?*'

Instantly, she became guarded, perhaps wondering why that interested him. 'She's no one. Just another girl who didn't make it.'

'Jess who?'

'I said she's no one –'

'*Don't give me that bullshit!*'

'Heck, easy,' Hayes warned him.

'Everyone's someone, Sonja,' he said. 'Jess who?'

'Jess Green,' the girl replied. 'It's not important. She's got nothing to do with this.'

'You knew Jess Green?'

She shrugged. 'I was her friend, yeah. Sort of.'

'What the hell does "sort of" mean?'

'She was just a girl I met on the streets . . .'

'Rubbish, Sonja! Bloody rubbish! Hers was the first name that popped into your head. She must've been more to you than that.'

'All right.' She shrugged. 'We got quite close, but I don't see what that's got to do with –'

'I'll decide what it's got to do with it. What happened to her?'

'She OD'd. You've probably got a record of it somewhere.'

'And that's all it was – an overdose?'

'You say, "That's all it was" like it wasn't fucking horrible.'

'There are degrees of fucking horrible, Sonja . . . at least she wasn't burned alive, eh?'

The girl grimaced, a combination of misery and horror.

'Just out of interest, was it suicide?' Heck asked. 'Had Jess endured just about all she could?'

'Does it matter?' came the mumbled response. 'There's only ever one way out of that life.' She glanced up. 'But Jess had nothing to do with any of this. It was two years ago.'

'Did you and Jess work together? I mean when you were out on the street.'

'Sometimes.'

'Down at Sadie's Dungeon, by any chance?'

'We were kids. We needed money to score.'

'That's not what I asked you.'

'Yes, all right! We both got recruited to work there about the same time –'

'Down at the Dungeon?'

'Not at first . . . first it was parties and such, you know?'

Heck did know. So-called 'hooker parties' were a time-honoured way to bring new girls into the profession.

'After that it was other places,' she said.

'What about the Dungeon?' Heck persisted. 'Did you both work down at the Dungeon?'

'Yeah. Sometimes. Sometimes Barrie and Les organised other gigs for us.'

'So Barrie Briggs and Les Harris were basically your pimps?'

She hesitated to reply – yet another demonstration of these wretched creatures' slavish instinct to protect those who used and abused them.

'They're both dead, Sonja,' Heck reminded her. 'So they're not going to object to you talking. I'm guessing the answer's "yes", and I'm guessing they were Jess Green's pimps too?'

'It was only semi-official.'

'Uh-huh. So, equally semi-officially, you were both working for Vic Ship, weren't you?'

'We never saw *him*,' she said. 'He was just a name we heard mentioned.'

'Well, of course he was. Ship's got eighteen layers of fall-guys before the shit hits his fan.'

She shrugged again. 'Some people can't be touched.'

'I'm sure that's what he'd like you to think, love. But someone out there with a flamethrower has a different take on it, don't they?'

There was a brief silence, during which Sonja hung her head with what Heck suspected was exaggerated weariness. She tried to lean against Sally Gorton for support. The burly detective sergeant was clearly tempted to put an arm around her thin shoulders, but resisted.

'We're done here,' Heck said. 'She can go.'

Gorton and the other two plain clothes officers steered her towards the waiting Qashqai.

'Sonja!' Heck called after her.

She glanced back.

'You're going to be in Witness Protection for quite a while . . . longer than you might have anticipated. If anything else occurs to you, you know, which might be vaguely important, which might actually save your life, make sure you give us a call, eh?'

When the protection detail had gone, Hayes came up and stood at Heck's side.

'She's still holding something back,' she said. 'You realise that, don't you?'

'Oh, yes.'

'In the meantime, who's Jess Green?'

'I don't know for sure. Local lass – street-girl. She *did* die from an OD. All that's true. But I had no idea she was part of Briggs and Harris's stable, such as it was.'

'Is that relevant to this case? I mean, if she died two years ago?'

'Again, I don't really know, ma'am . . . I suppose it depends how long the wound it caused has festered for, doesn't it?'

'Heck, if you've got something in mind, you'd better share it with me.'

'As soon as I get something that isn't nonsensical, ma'am, you'll be the first person I call.'

She stared at him for a long time, before turning and walking in through the personnel door. Heck went the other way, climbed into his Megane and closed the door behind him.

Basically, it had to be impossible.

It was – how had he put it? 'Nonsensical.'

But the circumstantial evidence was slowly stacking up.

Jess Green had whored for Vic Ship associates Barrie Briggs and Les Harris. He wondered if she might have got her regular fix from Danny Hollister – not that it especially mattered; Hollister was still one of Ship's main suppliers in Bradburn, so it was all one and the same. Heck wondered how Kayla might have discovered all this . . . and he concluded that it wouldn't have been difficult. She'd personally taken her sister to outreach programmes, to rehab sessions, support groups and so forth, which would all have been full of drug-dependent prostitutes just like Jess. If Jess herself hadn't talked, others would have.

Kayla . . .

Who he'd seen for himself was badly damaged by her sister's death.

Who his uncle had warned him about, saying that she'd retreated from reality.

She had a motive to attack Ship's operation. There was no question about that. She had a better motive than Lee Shaughnessy did.

But still, it had to be nonsensical.

Heck tried to put obstacles in the way of his thesis.

The Incinerator was strong, robust. He launched his attacks wearing heavy, flame-retardant armour. That could only be a man, not a woman. That said, Kayla had been a superb athlete as a youngster, and from what he'd seen she was still in good shape now; only the other day he'd caught her energetically sweeping months of leaves off the church-yard steps and all it had raised on her was a light sweat.

OK, well . . . he'd confronted the Incinerator face to face, and there'd been nothing there of the lovely, voluptuous girl that was Kayla. But then that bulky fireproof suit had completely de-sexed whoever he was facing; no way could he have said for certain that it was a man.

All right, in terms of pure logistics, what about the flame-thrower? How could someone like Kayla, who was completely unconnected to the criminal world, have conceivably got her hands on a weapon like that? And then he remembered that her dad had trained her as a mechanic – and that she'd inherited a well-equipped workshop from him. It wouldn't be easy for some lay-person to construct a flamethrower, but it wouldn't be impossible either.

On top of all this, something else now struck him, and his blood ran cold.

It was a line that Kayla herself had given him, a throwaway comment that she'd made only a few minutes after he'd first been reintroduced to her in the pub.

'I'm a dab hand with a panel-beater, me . . . and an absolute killer with a blowtorch.'

Chapter 33

It rained again that night, intensely, starting at about one in the morning and continuing well past first light. Heavy, bullet-sized drops machine-gunned down in a relentless cascade, drowning the whole town, leaving many of its lower roads and backstreets completely under water.

It was still raining when Heck woke up that morning, though not with the same ferocity as during the night, but creating a joyless scene outdoors all the same.

'So much for sweet little April showers,' he said, grabbing a black coffee before dressing. He donned his scruffs, substituted walking boots for his trainers and pulled on his jacket. But less than a mile from his sister's he gave up on rush-hour, which was as chaotic and slow-moving as ever, a scenario not assisted by the closure of several routes due to flooding.

Instead, he parked by a greasy spoon on the edge of a lorry park, wandered inside and ordered himself a Full English.

As he wolfed it down, he speed-dialled Eric Fisher.

'Heck . . . it's not seven yet.'

'I know, get up. I need you to make some further enquiries about Shelley Harper.'

'I gave Wandering Wolf everything I had last Friday.'

'I know. But I need you to probe a bit deeper.'

'There is no deeper, mate. She's got no police record.'

'Use your noggin, Eric.' Heck pushed his empty plate away. 'We – as in the whole police service of England and Wales – must have some access to former Vic Ship associates. Either blokes who've turned or cons who are still inside and may need a favour. Here's a starting-point – you remember Cameron Boyd?'

Fisher mused, fuddled with sleep. 'Erm . . . currently doing fifteen for aggravated burglary?'

'Correct. I was the arresting officer, you may recall. Boyd was a Longsight crim. Not officially connected to Ship, but he could have an inside track on their activities.'

'And why would Boyd talk?'

'Now and then I've used him as a snitch . . . against his will.'

'Got something good on him, have you?'

'Couple of years old now. Its shelf-life's just about up, but tell him if he can give us anything useful on Shelley Harper, even if it's only gossip, he's free and clear.'

'I'll try.'

'Advise him that it's not a big deal. We already know that, for a brief time at least, Shelley was Vic Ship's girlfriend – probably one of many. I just want to know if she was ever anything more to him than that.'

'I'm guessing this is Priority One?'

'No, but I need to know soon.'

'OK, leave it with me. And fuck off, by the way . . . I was enjoying that dream.'

The line went dead.

Heck gazed through the bleary café window. Beyond it, the traffic was a sludge of glaring headlights, the dark, moth-like forms of pedestrians flitting back and forth.

He still had doubts that Kayla Green could be a genuine suspect, but increasingly these flamethrower murders were hanging by a single thread – Shelley Harper.

The more he pondered it, the more probable it seemed that Kayla had learned from her drug-addled sister that Vic Ship's crew were the source of all their woe. It was equally likely that Jess had named Barrie Briggs and Les Harris as Ship's men in Bradburn, along with Danny Hollister. But Heck did not see how Kayla could ever have learned about Ship's fleeting dalliance with Shelley Harper. A gold-plated scrote like Ship probably waded through a sea of prostrate girls, all pretty no doubt, all with more ambition than sense. Shelley Harper would have been one of many, and anyway, this had happened years ago and seventeen miles away in Manchester. No, Jess Green could not have known about Harper. This was now the fly in Heck's ointment, the issue he had to resolve before he could make this suspicion a thing.

His phone began buzzing on the table-top. The call was from Gemma.

'Ma'am?' he said.

'Are you having trouble getting in?' she enquired.

He saw that it was now nearly eight o'clock.

'It's problematic, yeah, but actually I'm following a new lead.'

'What new lead?'

'A prozzy died in Bradburn about two years ago, from a drugs overdose. Her name was Jess Green. I'm researching the background a little.'

'You think it's relevant?'

'Well . . . only if you're prepared to consider that the Incinerator might have nothing to do with Lee Shaughnessy.'

There was a long pause.

'I *am* prepared to consider it, Heck,' she said. 'But only if you bring me something persuasive.'

'That's what I'm looking for this morning.'

'All right. But I need you to be done by lunchtime.'

'That's unlikely.'

'I think you misheard me, Heck. I *need* you to be done by lunchtime.'

'Ma'am –'

'Let me explain, which as you may know, I rarely bother to do. We've finished with Sonja Turner. The e-fit's done and Katie Hayes and I are holding a press conference at noon, where we're going to publicise it.'

'OK.' Heck scraped his unshaved jaw with his fingernails. 'Does it look like anyone who might exist on this planet?'

'It's as bland as bland can be, but you know how these things work.'

He did, of course. E-fits, like the photo-fits that preceded them, rarely resembled the suspect they were supposed to portray. But they were not for the consumption of the general public as much as for people who might actually know the suspect. Perhaps, if they already had concerns about this person, the e-fit might present a face that was similar enough in some vague way to prompt a telephone call to the police.

'It could be male or female for all I can tell,' Gemma added.

'Male . . . *or female*?' Heck said.

'Like I say, it's bland. Let's just keep our fingers crossed that we get *something*.'

He didn't respond. His thoughts were racing.

'Heck?'

'Yeah. I understand, ma'am. Sorry.'

'Follow your lead. But listen, I don't want you spending all day chasing shadows.'

'Course, ma'am. No problem.'

He cut the call, and stared again through the window.

Male . . . or female?

342

Gemma had just been talking. She wasn't actually proposing that the Incinerator was a woman. And however you cut it, Kayla was still a long shot. The longest of long shots.

More interesting now was the revelation that they were going live with the e-fit. Suddenly, sniffing around Jess and Kayla Green felt as if it could wait. Heck had one other line of enquiry that urgently needed attention, and maybe this was an opportunity to give it exactly that.

*

Heck knew that Lee Shaughnessy's centre of operations could be found on the Lawkholme because Scott Cowley had implied that it was. It wouldn't have surprised Heck anyway, as the Lawkholme – one of the most economically depressed corners of Bradburn – was everything that modern sink estates aspired to. Located on the windswept outskirts of town, it was an unremitting tale of deteriorated housing blocks, rubbish-filled back alleyways and desolate streets lined with rickety old cars and strewn with litter. At least the rain had now stopped, but as Heck drove up there his mind boggled that anyone had ever thought places like this could provide a decent home for ordinary people. Substandard housing from the outset, an absence of basic amenities, poor transport links – only one or two buses had ever included it on their routes, and none did now – and, more important than anything, a significant and deliberate distance placed between itself and the town centre had ensured that in due course it would become a dustbin for the borough's problem families . . . which had hardly helped to improve things up there.

Cowley had referred to Shaughnessy's crew as the 'Britannia Boys'. That wasn't an official moniker, otherwise Heck would have encountered it in the intelligence files. Most likely it referred to the Empress Britannia pub, and implied that this was Shaughnessy's main hangout.

It wasn't difficult to find the place. The Lawkholme, like so many residential areas in the UK, had once boasted a boozer on every corner, but most of them had now vanished. The Empress was the only one left here. It wasn't much to look at: a single-storey structure with minimal decoration. It stood on the edge of waste-ground, and resembled a prefabricated bunker rather than a hostelry, one side red brick, one side pebble-dashed. It had a single-level roof, canted slightly to one side and covered in bitumen. Its windows were frosted, while daubings of graffiti were visible here and there on the exterior.

Heck made his first drive-past, along Lawkholme Avenue, the estate's main drag, just after ten o'clock that morning. He could have gone earlier, but he doubted there'd have been any activity around the pub at that hour. And he was correct. Even at ten, though there were several rubbishy cars and vans on its car park, most had the air of having been there all night; some, from their corroded state, had been present for considerably longer.

There was certainly no sign of Lee Shaughnessy's distinctive white Mazda CX-5.

He thus headed back into the town centre, parked in a side-street and literally window-shopped for twenty minutes, before returning to his Megane, and just to ensure that he wasn't completely wasting his morning, drew a clipboard from under his seat and dealt with a couple of bits of pending paperwork. It was just before eleven when he set off back to the Lawkholme. This time, he was pleased to see that other vehicles had assembled on the pub car park, including a dingy green-and-white van and, yes, that familiar white Mazda.

It was now ten past eleven, still too early for Heck's purposes. So again, he parked up on a side-street, this time on the estate itself, and scribbled his way through what more paperwork he could. At twenty to twelve, he shoved everything back under his seat, drove back to the Empress Britannia, and slid to a halt among the other vehicles on its car park.

Checking his watch again, he saw that it was now ten to twelve.

Perfect timing. He hoped.

He climbed out, locked his car and strolled to the pub's main door.

Inside, there was a cement-floored corridor with a single fruit machine in it and at the far end two toilet doors covered in peeling paint and chunks of dry chewing gum. A couple of disreputable-looking characters were hanging around in here. They were about twenty years old and wearing tracksuits, anoraks zipped to the throat, and baseball caps pulled down over spotty weasel faces. They leaned against the wall smoking joints, watching Heck curiously as he sauntered past into the main taproom. This was another drab affair: bare walls save for strings of glittery stuff dangling down at the back of a low stage in one corner, a linoleum floor, and strip-lighting overhead. Heck hadn't expected many customers, but various figures were dotted among the tables and chairs. They were exclusively male, most of indeterminate age and yet all with the disconsolate look of the long-term unemployed. Some read newspapers and sipped from pints; two faced each other in silence as they focused on a game of dominoes.

However, in the farthest corner, beyond the pool tables, there was a noisier crowd.

Eight or nine figures clustered, laughing and swearing amid a sea of empty bottles. There were no financial constraints

345

on view here. They were playing cards, slapping down wads of serious cash: tenners, twenties, fifties. Heck even saw jewellery on offer: rings, necklaces, watches.

The heroin trade clearly paid.

Lee Shaughnessy held court in the middle. The guy with the tattooed star and trickling stardust on his cheek was seated left of him. A rather slatternly-looking girl with a fake tan, brassy bottle-blonde hair and big earrings sat on his right, looking bored as she leaned on her fist. Shaughnessy had dressed down a little: his blond hair was brushed crisply back, but now he wore a red short-sleeved shirt hanging open on a string-vest. He glanced up as Heck wove through the tables. They made eye contact, but Shaughnessy merely smiled to himself and went back to his game.

The barman was an obese slob, flabby and lantern-jawed, with long, ratty hair, his sagging, porcine shape stuffed messily into scruffy jeans and a beer-stained shirt. His podgy hands, the fingers crammed with cheap rings and bearing the tattooed lettering 'Love' and 'Hate', clutched a well-thumbed copy of the *Daily Star*, though his attention was divided between this and the occasional lumps of grot that he dug from his nostril as he slumped on a stool. He remained preoccupied with this even when Heck arrived at the bar. One other customer was waiting there, though he already had a bottle of lager in his hand. He wore trainers, tracksuit bottoms and nothing else but neck-chains. His bare torso was blotted with homemade tats. He had a short thatch of spiky hair, odd, simian-like features, bulging brows and a sloped forehead. He turned and peered unblinkingly at Heck with lustreless, mud-brown eyes.

Though that was more interest than the barman showed; he remained seated, reading his paper and picking his nose.

'Hey,' Heck said. 'You working today, or what?'

The barman gave him an indifferent look. 'Are you?'

'That obvious, is it?'

'Always.'

'Pint of Best'll do it.'

Grudgingly, as if he really had lots of better things to do, the barman slid from his stool, fished around under the counter for an empty pint glass and began to draw the beer.

'The word is there're lots of drugs being sold in here,' Heck said.

The barman's gaze flitted up to him. 'That's a fucking lie. Anyone I catch dealing in here, they're out on their arses.'

Heck indicated the crowd gathered around Shaughnessy. 'How about these fellas? They wouldn't be the ones responsible, would they?'

The barman's expression changed. He looked at Heck askance. 'You really shouldn't do this.'

'Shouldn't I?' Heck considered that. 'So if I was to shake all these lads down, I wouldn't find anything naughty?'

'Seriously, if you want your palm greasing, this is not the way to go about it.'

'If I wanted that, I'd pat you on the head.'

The barman stopped drawing the beer. 'Best if you leave, I reckon . . . *officer*.'

'Yeah?' Heck said. 'You think you're chucking me out?'

'I don't want any trouble in here.'

'Christ's sake, Lennie, give him his drink!' Shaughnessy called from the corner. 'He may be stupid as fuck but at least he's got balls.'

Heck glanced at Shaughnessy, who was still laying down money. He turned back to the barman, who sullenly pulled the rest of the pint and slid it over. Heck paid and received his change, a transaction completed in absolute silence, the only sound coming from the television on the high shelf, on which a morning talk show was just finishing.

Heck noticed that the ape-faced guy with the bare top was still watching him.

Heck winked at him before heading to the corner, sidling past the first of the pool tables and standing alongside the card game. Most of the participants, Shaughnessy included, ignored him, though the guy with the star and stardust on his face was visibly agitated.

'You gonna go all Steven Seagal on us now?' Shaughnessy wondered. 'Kick the shit out of us in our own place?'

'I'd like to see him fucking try,' Stardust muttered.

'Just want to talk,' Heck said.

Shaughnessy raised his foot and shoved a spare chair part-way from under the table. Heck sat down. With the exception of Stardust, the rest of the card-players continued to ignore him. The ape-faced guy slumped into another empty seat opposite, from where he continued to watch Heck with unflinching intensity.

'This is Eyeball,' Shaughnessy said conversationally. 'We call him that because his hobby used to be going into pubs around town and staring people out he didn't like. Had more scraps than Floyd fucking Mayweather, usually without a single fucking insult exchanged.'

'One way to get on in life,' Heck commented.

'Trouble is – think he wants a piece of *you*.'

'In which case,' Heck said, 'it's probably better if he isn't party to this conversation.'

'I see.' Shaughnessy laid down a card. 'These are the ground rules, are they?'

'This is super-important stuff, Lee, and as before, it's likely to be beneficial to you and your crew. But I'm not wasting my time if some back-of-the-class loser who'd rather get a slap from the teacher than be ignored keeps trying to distract us.'

'That's tough talk when the exit's on the other side of the room.' The message was clear, but Shaughnessy spoke in an idle, unconcerned tone, his attention focused on his cards.

Heck turned to Eyeball. 'Hey, pal – take a fucking hike. Before your boss ends up knowing less by the end of today than he did when he got up.'

Eyeball bored into Heck with his weird, mud-coloured peepers.

'Play some pool,' Shaughnessy said quietly.

Still staring, Eyeball pushed his chair back, stood up and retreated three steps, before abruptly turning away to the pool tables.

'The rest of you can stay as long as you leave the chat to the big boys,' Heck said.

One by one, they glanced round at him, brows furrowed, mouths twitching.

Shaughnessy gave a distinctive rasping titter, almost a cackle. 'OK . . . suppose I should say it. *This had better be good!*'

Heck checked the TV screen over the bar. Adverts were playing. It was a little before noon, and the commencement of the lunchtime news bulletin. The main thing now was to keep them talking.

'The Incinerator struck again last night, Lee,' he said.

'You don't fucking say.' Shaughnessy sounded bored.

'Killed a girl in a house on Blaymire Close.'

'That's just nasty.'

'The *wrong* girl,' Heck said.

He watched them carefully, but detected neither a flinch nor a twitch from any one of them as they continued to play. Only after several seconds did Shaughnessy's eyes swivel up.

'You're waiting for some kind of response to that, I take it?'

'You're not interested to know more?' Heck asked.

'I'm sure if I *was*, I wouldn't have to play cryptic games with you, detective. Her name will be released to the public

349

in due course. Then we'll all know more, won't we?'

Cool bastards, these men, Heck told himself. *They've either carried out this hit themselves and have already realised it was the wrong girl, in which case they've had enough time to relax about it. Or they haven't done this hit at all.*

He glanced at the TV. The news was now starting.

'In actual fact, *two* people died last night,' he said. 'Both were what we'd call collateral damage. Bystanders – completely innocent.'

'Certainly a bad lad, this fella,' Shaughnessy replied.

'Yeah. Not much of a night's work, though. Two people dead, and the main target scarpered.'

Shaughnessy smiled again. 'You must admonish him when you catch him. Assuming you ever do.' He grinned at his crew, who snickered. 'Good word, eh . . . "admonish".' He glanced at Heck. 'I read *Wikipedia*.'

'Have you looked up the meaning of "smartarse"?' Heck wondered.

Shaughnessy mock-frowned. 'That's not very polite.'

'Because in trying to maintain your street-cool at all costs, Lee, I think you're missing something crucial. As long as innocent people are dying, it's going to make my colleagues more and more determined to nail the bastard responsible to the nearest barn door by his gonads.'

Shaughnessy played more cards. 'That'd be called insensitive policing.'

'You don't know the meaning of insensitive policing, son. But you will.'

Stardust finally jumped to his feet. He glared at Heck with livid hatred, saliva clumped in his mouth.

But Shaughnessy remained calm. 'And there's me thinking you didn't fancy us for this one.'

'It doesn't matter what *I* say,' Heck said. 'I'm a voice in the wilderness.'

Shaughnessy thought about that. 'Well, your support's appreciated. Even if your colleagues think you're basically showing your arse at the top of Bradburn Market Street –'

Another voice now intruded. It was the newscaster on the TV.

'Greater Manchester Police today confirmed that the house-fire at Blaymire Close in Bradburn last night, which claimed two lives, is believed to be connected to the underworld feud currently raging in the town.'

Heck looked up. Gemma appeared on screen. She was standing outside Bradburn Central with her usual air, whenever being interviewed, of glamorous efficiency.

'We can't say it for certain yet,' she admitted, 'but all the evidence we've managed to gather suggests suspicious activity.'

'So the fire was started deliberately?' a reporter asked.

'We believe so, yes.'

'And was a flamethrower used?'

'We think it probably was.'

The newscaster's voice intruded again. 'In a further development, Operation Wandering Wolf, which is the special taskforce set up to investigate the underworld violence in Bradburn, have released this e-fit of a man they'd like to speak to in connection with the crimes.'

Now Shaughnessy looked up at the screen – just as the e-fit appeared there.

As Heck had expected, it depicted a none too distinguishable face, clearly white Caucasian and yet smudged all over with soot. The jawline, the nose, the eyes, the brows were all strong and well-defined, but so standard in terms of shape and size that they could have belonged to anyone.

'The suspect is somewhere in his mid to late thirties,' the newscaster added, 'of medium build and approximately five foot eight inches tall –'

'*Fucking joking!*' came an angry howl.

Heck spun in his chair.

But the shout had come from Eyeball, and it related to an altercation he was having with a couple of the guys he was playing pool with. They weren't even looking at the TV, though others in the room were. Heck glanced at Shaughnessy, whose attention had reverted to the cards. He glanced at Stardust, who still watched him with undisguised malice, though even he seemed to have cooled a little. In fact, all across the taproom, the gang members were indulging in whatever it was they'd been doing previously.

None who'd seen the news bulletin had responded in any obvious way.

They couldn't care less, Heck realised. They'd surely have reacted in some shape or form to the sight of that face, because, nondescript though it was, if they knew the perp personally, they'd fear that it might be enough to render him recognisable to police informants.

He turned back to Shaughnessy. 'Did you tip me off about Blaymire Close, Lee?'

'You still here?' Shaughnessy asked. 'Thought now you'd delivered your good news, you'd have fluttered off.'

'I asked for some help the other day, and I got it,' Heck said. 'Presumably from you?'

'I'd be glad to help if I knew anything. Can't have bad men like that running around.'

'Course, if you were to confirm my suspicion that it was you or someone on your team who tipped me off, that would *really* put you in the clear. I mean, there'd be no sense you marking my cards about a possible Incinerator target up on Blaymire Close, and then going and whacking her yourself, would there?'

'Put some pasties on, Len,' Shaughnessy called to the barman. 'We're starving over here.'

352

The barman slid from his stool and disappeared into a back room. Shaughnessy returned to his game. Even Stardust was now ignoring Heck.

'Last chance, Lee,' Heck said. 'I'd like to dismiss you from this enquiry. You know why? Not, it may surprise you, because I think you're the sort of upstanding guy who should be next in line for a knighthood, but because you're the kind of vermin that makes a good suspect in any case . . . and in that regard you're complicating things for us. You know . . . getting in the way. But if you don't mind that, if you'd prefer GMP on top of you as well as Vic Ship, that's fine . . . we'll do it your way.'

'Yeah, no worries,' Shaughnessy said, distracted. 'See you.'

Heck pushed his chair back, stood and strolled away across the taproom with muted comments and snide chuckles ringing in his ears. Outside, he trekked across the car park to his Megane and climbed in. With a crunch of gears he drove to the exit, where he pulled out onto the main drag and hit the gas. In appearance, he was a beaten man; red-faced, helpless in his frustration, now heading out of Lee Shaughnessy's heartland at high speed.

But that was all for show. Because in reality he didn't go very far at all.

353

Chapter 34

Lee Shaughnessy and Benny Robson (he with the star and stardust tats on his cheek) left the Empress Britannia at just after four that afternoon. They'd both been drinking and had done a few lines of coke, but this was their usual status, so they didn't consider that it would affect their performance. They had meetings to attend, deals to make, wheels to turn. Like so many of his breed, Shaughnessy had several levels of soldiers around his inner sanctum of trusted loyalists. But he was a hands-on bloke too. His name carried weight in this town; his actual presence could change situations. Of course, this didn't mean there weren't problems at present. Things were more than a little tense than they had been for quite some time, and that was never good for business.

They sauntered across the car park and round to the front of the Mazda – at which point Shaughnessy stopped in his tracks. A pistol, a nine-millimetre semi-automatic, was sitting on the roof of his car just above the driver's door.

Shaughnessy rarely lost his cool. It didn't happen because he saw no value in it. The bull's innate weakness was the red rag. But the bull, like most of human society, was dumb. Shaughnessy wasn't. Until now . . . until, in the midst of a crisis he was putting a brave face on, he was presented with something else he'd never anticipated.

'What the fuck!' He snatched the gun down and hefted it in his right hand, firstly to see if it was loaded, which it wasn't, and then to see if he could identify whether it was one of their own.

Neither he nor Robson spotted the silent form come swiftly up behind. The first they knew was a brutal *smack* of fist on jawbone. Robson's knees buckled, the black flash of a second blow clubbing him in the nape of the neck, ensuring that when his face hit the ground, he was already unconscious. It happened so quickly that Shaughnessy didn't have time to react before his arm was grabbed and twisted behind his back, the gun wrestled from his grasp as he was slammed face-first against the Mazda.

'You're under arrest for possession of a prohibited firearm, you pimply-faced wanker!' Heck clamped handcuffs on his wrists, and raised the Makarov into view, looped by its trigger guard over his gloved finger. 'Dearie me, look at that. How fortunate I came along when I did and saw you. And how unfortunate for Stardust here that he tried to impede me in the execution of my duty.'

Shaughnessy was choked with rage. 'You won't get away with this . . . you fucking . . .'

'Get away with what?' Heck frisked him to ensure he wasn't carrying for real. 'Making a legal arrest? I'm only sorry there are no cameras outside this shithole you call a pub, so the world could see a very bad man get banged to rights completely fucking lawfully. In fact, it might be better even than that. Who knows how many murders this gun's been used in? This isn't just a very good day for law and order, Lee, it's a very, very bad day for you.'

At their feet, Robson groaned and tried to lever himself up.

Heck smashed a kick into his face, knocking him cold again.

'If Marvin Langton was here, you wouldn't be so quick with that caper,' Shaughnessy spat.

'Yeah, well, that's one of the disadvantages of being chief suspect in a murder case. You get a police tail. Kind of restricts what you can do, where you can go, who you can see.'

'You'll never make that gun charge stick.'

'You wanna bet?' Heck chuckled. 'You think Operation Wandering Wolf won't be more than willing to back me up on this? Any idea how much they hate you, son? They'll be all over you like a rash. They'll bury you so deep, your mates'll need to pipe the sunlight down to you.'

'And you'd let them would you, you bastard, when you've already admitted you know we're not responsible for these crimes?'

'Fucking right I'd let them. Firstly, because you're responsible for an awful lot of other crimes, which somehow or other your bad-boy reputation keeps you safe from. But mainly because so far you've done nothing but foul up my investigation. I'm trying to catch a couple of killers here – a real nasty pair – and yet you keep getting in the way, diverting attention, distracting resources. I gave you two or three chances to come clean and prove you're not involved in these crimes, but instead you had to give it the big "I am" for that fucking kindergarten you call a firm.'

'I can do it now,' Shaughnessy gasped as Heck applied extra pressure to his wrists.

'Too late, pal. Now we do it tough.'

He twisted all the harder, dragging a suppressed scream through Shaughnessy's clenched teeth. This was more than mere rule-bending, but Heck felt secure. He doubted anyone in this neighbourhood would call the cops on behalf of Lee Shaughnessy, plus the green-and-white van was conveniently parked nearby, blocking the Mazda off from the nearest line of houses.

'OK, OK!' Shaughnessy gibbered. '*I sent you that tip-off, that phone-call!* Who else was it gonna be? You gave me your number, for Christ's sake! Anyone else round here gonna have that?'

Heck paused. 'You made that phone-call yourself?'

'Yeah!'

Heck dug his mobile out, thumbing the keypad to check his records. 'Date and time?'

'I don't know what time it was . . .'

'Date and time, dog-breath!'

'It was yesterday, I know that. First thing in the morning.'

'Gimme a time specifically!'

'I don't know . . . between six and seven. I wanted to make sure you were at least half asleep, catch you off your guard, make it harder for you to trace me.'

'Yeah, how did that work out for you?' Heck examined the data. This part of the story checked out, at least. 'What did you tell me?'

'You don't fucking remember?'

'I want to hear it again! Word for word!'

'Erm . . .' Shaughnessy struggled to recall exactly. 'That there was this lass, Mindy-May. Part-time stripper and prozzie. That she was hanging out in a brothel on Blaymire Close. That she probably knew something about the sex-shop murders.'

That was close enough, Heck decided. He pocketed his phone. 'OK, next question . . .'

'Come on, man! I've confirmed it, haven't I? Gimme something back!'

'Hey! This isn't a negotiation, you know. You're under arrest! So next question . . . how did you know she was there? How did you know what she saw at Sadie's Dungeon?'

Shaughnessy struggled to breathe, he was in so much pain. 'One of our dealers . . . look, copper, you've not cautioned me, so nothing I say here can be used to drop me in the shi–'

'Don't tell me my job. Just tell me what I want to know.'

'She told one of our dealers.'

'Keep talking.'

'For Christ's sake, Mindy's a smackhead.'

'I thought she was clean.'

'Do me a fucking favour. They always say that.'

Heck clamped down on the irritation this caused him. Sonja Turner was going to make a cracking witness. 'And?' he said.

'Mindy worked for Barrie Briggs, who was on Vic Ship's payroll, but she wasn't joined to him at the hip. If she desperately needed gear, she'd happily buy it from us.'

'So let me guess. She called the candyman, and he went round to see her at her new address . . . on Blaymire Close?'

'Correct,' Shaughnessy said. 'He reckoned she looked a bit more strung out than usual. Asked her what the problem was, and it all came pouring out. She'd seen these two blokes get torched by some nutjob with a flamethrower. Once he'd heard this, he reported it straight back to me.'

Heck contemplated this. If nothing else, it explained Mindy-May's overall caginess. Being known as a stripper *and* a junkie would hardly help in her fight for her kids.

'This dealer?' Heck asked. 'Did he tell anyone else?'

'No chance. I made sure he knew not to.'

'*You* made sure?' Heck sneered. 'You know what, Lee? I reckon you couldn't organise a wank in a warm bath.'

'He's one of my best lads,' Shaughnessy insisted. 'I told him to keep it zipped. I trust him.'

'One of your best, eh? That'll be a euphemism for some walking sack of shit who can just about be trusted not to sell his own kids for pin-money. You tell him to keep it shut, so he only tells his pillhead girlfriend . . . who tells another pillhead, and suddenly it's travelling every which way.'

'Look!' Shaughnessy pleaded. 'We don't want this fucking Incinerator any more than you do. Obviously we don't. That's why I tried to give him to you. Any war's bad for business.'

'Especially a war with Vic Ship, eh? You scared of him, Lee? Come on, you can admit to it – now you're not show-boating in front of your mates. Because if you aren't, you ought to be. You're sauntering around up here like the cock of the walk, but in truth you're a set of street-corner tosspots. I'm only surprised he hasn't killed you all already.'

'We're safe up here.'

'Well, yeah . . . I'm the living proof of that, aren't I?'

'You're a copper. It's different. Vic won't send any of his goons up here, not even that psycho with his torture wagon –'

'*What's that?*' Heck said sharply.

'We're team-handed up here and Vic knows we're packing. I tried to make a truce with him, and he didn't want to know, but I'm gonna try again because –'

'*What psycho with his torture wagon?*'

'The one who did Cal and Dean.'

'What do you know about him?' Heck demanded.

Shaughnessy shrugged. 'Not much. Only that he's got a raft of kit in this caravan, and he uses it on anyone he's told to. Vic brought him in from outside so he can keep his own hands clean.'

'Where'd you learn all this?'

'We got an anonymous tip too.'

Heck rammed the gun into his ribs with a gut-thunking impact. Shaughnessy cringed in pain.

'Bastard!' he gasped. 'We got a tip – *for real!* Anonymous phone-call, just like you got. Whoever it was, they said this bastard was parked up at the Woodfold storage depot –'

'East side of Blackhall?'

'Yeah.' Shaughnessy still winced in pain. 'There's an empty parking space next to the units. We went up there, see if we could get hold of him. But he'd already gone. If he'd ever been there . . . if he even exists.'

'When was this?'

'Last Friday.'

'What time?'

'We got there early evening. Sixish. Like I say, he'd already skipped.'

Heck spun the gang leader round and pushed him backward against the car. 'I'll tell you what, Lee: from this point on, you've only got two jobs to do. First, you go and have a word with this dealer of yours. Give him a damn good talking to – and I mean *damn* good! – and you find out exactly who he opened his yap to, and where the information travelled to from there.'

'If that happened and it hit the streets, it could've gone anywhere.'

'You'd better hope it hasn't. Second, you use all the influence you've got, and by that I mean knock any heads together you need to, to discover who was behind that anonymous tip. If I can find out where mine came from this easily, you can find out where yours came from.'

Shaughnessy looked bewildered. 'You're not locking me up?'

'I don't need to.' Heck held the Makarov up again, now sheathed in a plastic evidence sack.

'You reckon you can keep pulling that stunt?'

'This stunt could be the end of your life as you know it, Lee. I've already told you, this gun isn't a toy – it's been used more than once. And now it's got your fingerprints all over it. And while I might not log it into evidence today, it can appear at any time in the future, at any place of my choosing. You understand what that means?'

'You think that makes me your bitch?'

'I know it does, son. And if you don't, you're finally believing your own publicity . . . which wasn't even a good idea for Al Capone, let alone a maggoty little dipshit like you.' Heck slid the key into the handcuffs. 'I'm letting you go for now – and the first thing you're going to do is get yourself back into that piss-stained shed, or wherever else the rest of your rodent-like cronies are hanging out, and start asking those hard questions I told you about. And as soon as you get some answers I want to hear, you get on the blower to me. You've done it once before, so I'm sure it'll be no hardship to do it again, especially as this time it'll be saving your arse.'

Shaughnessy dripped sweat. 'How do I know you won't stitch me up with that shooter anyway?'

'Well, thing is . . .' Heck had unfastened the cuffs, but now clamped the back of Shaughnessy's neck with his left hand, and tripped him over his extended left foot. *'You don't!'*

Shaughnessy landed face-first alongside Robson. The impact drove the wind from him, knocking him dizzy. He finally managed to glance up. But Heck had vanished.

Chapter 35

As a rule, Heck disliked strong-arming people. But there were times of *extremis* when for the good of mankind you simply had to get a result, and if that required ruthlessness, so be it. In any case, he couldn't imagine there were many who'd weep for Lee Shaughnessy. That said, he'd taken a risk, bushwhacking the guy out in the open. It seemed unlikely that Shaughnessy would press charges – he was the sort who'd prefer to resolve these issues on his own. But it had still been a risk.

As Heck threaded back through the winding alleyways of the Lawkholme, it started raining again. When he reached his Megane, which was parked in a deserted lot at the rear of a block of boarded-up flats, it was hammering down. Jumping inside, he mopped his sodden hair back and made a quick call to Gemma.

'Heck?' she said.

'Ma'am . . . I've got a possible fix on Sagan.'

'On . . . *Sagan*?' She sounded bewildered.

'Yeah, and listen – before you lose it with me, I wasn't looking for him. I've liaised with Lee Shaughnessy again today –'

'*Liaised* with him? . . . I see.'

'Sort of liaised with him. Last Friday he got an anonymous tip-off that the guy who tortured Calum Price and Dean Lumley to death had pitched up in his caravan in a parking bay near a bunch of lock-ups at Woodfold. That's on the east side of the Blackhall ward. Shaughnessy and his crew went straight up there, looking for payback, but he'd gone.'

'Lee Shaughnessy actually told you this?'

'Yeah. I know that means it doesn't sound kosher, but him and his crew know a lot about Sagan, ma'am – way more than I'd expect them to in normal circs.'

'And they got this intel from an anonymous source?'

'You're right to sound sceptical, ma'am. I was sceptical too. But it's worth checking, isn't it?'

'If you think there's any possibility Shaughnessy was being truthful with you.'

Heck glanced at the front passenger seat, where alongside his discarded gloves the Makarov lay in its plastic evidence sack.

'I think *he* was being truthful. Whether the tipster was being truthful with him is another matter. We don't know who this person is or what their motivation's supposed to be, and of course there was no caravan at the lock-ups when Shaughnessy got there. The advantage *we've* got though, is CCTV. There'll definitely be security cameras covering those lock-ups, and as we've even got the date and time – Friday, April 6, 6 p.m.-ish – it shouldn't take long to work our way back through the footage. If we do catch a glimpse of Sagan leaving, we can utilise footage from the surrounding streets too. Could give us an electronic paper-trail – help us follow him to wherever he pitches up next.'

Gemma gave a long, low sigh. It might just have been that she was tired, but there were times when Heck thought she found the leads he often gave her infuriating because

363

they reminded her that he was still her best investigator despite his inability to follow procedure, not to mention the nefarious methods she suspected he employed.

'I'll get someone onto it,' she said. 'Where are you now?'

'Behind the wheel of my car.' He gazed through the windscreen at the intensifying downpour. 'Though I'd probably be better off in a submarine.'

'You coming back to the station?'

'I've got one more lead to check out first, ma'am . . . and I promise that's connected to the Incinerator.'

'I believe you,' she said wryly. 'Why crack one murder case in a day, if you can crack two?'

'These leads may be nothing, you know.'

'I understand that. But good work anyway.' She cut the call.

'Not *good* work exactly,' he muttered as he hit the ignition and put the Megane in gear. 'But if it gets us somewhere . . .'

Heck steered out onto the nearest road, which already lay under a glistening sheet of water. The rain was now coming down furiously, restricting his vision to a few yards. But he couldn't afford to get marooned on the Lawkholme. There were things he urgently needed to do, so he pressed on across the vast sprawl of the estate as swiftly as he dared, wipers thudding. Thanks to the weather, he didn't meet much traffic while negotiating the dreary backstreets, so his initial progress was steady. But once he reached the main road on the edge of the Lawkholme, he found that rush-hour was commencing, its sluggish rivers of headlights pulsing blurrily through torrents of rain. As he ploughed frustratingly slowly towards the town centre area, his phone buzzed several times. On the first two occasions he let it shift to voicemail because he needed to keep both hands on the wheel. The third time he managed to glance at the device and saw that the call was from DI Hayes – so he ignored it then too. He'd decided that he liked Hayes and trusted her, but the last thing he needed now was a supervisor on his shoulder. However, when the phone buzzed a fourth time, the call was from Eric Fisher.

Now close to the town centre, Heck slid his car into the mouth of an entry, braked hard and put his phone to his ear.

'What've you got for me, Eric?'

'You were on the money with Cameron Boyd,' Fisher replied.

'I was?'

'I've just got off the phone with him. He's currently in Strangeways, where he's rubbing shoulders with some very unpleasant people.'

'He's no shrinking violet himself.'

'Yeah, but he's scared shitless because you're apparently blackmailing him with a fake attempted murder charge – murder of a police officer no less.' Fisher sounded unimpressed. 'Which, if it's true, is a bit naughtier than you simply having an unregistered CI.'

'To date, Eric, he's given us leads on a kidnapping, at least three blags and a whole bunch of murders. Trust me, it's been worth it.'

'Heck, if this clown ever gets himself a decent solicitor –'

'It'll be his word against mine. Anyway, like I say . . . if his new intel's good, I'll cut him loose.'

'Well, I think you'll find it reasonably interesting. Shelley Harper – Vic Ship's ex-girlfriend as was.'

'Yeah?'

'Seems her duties didn't just include servicing the boss between the sheets. She also had a recruitment job with his firm.'

'Recruitment?' Heck remembered Mindy-May saying something about herself and Jess Green getting 'recruited at the same time'.

'She first came to his notice hostessing at one of his clubs, but ended up being one of several . . . well, "scouts", I suppose you'd call them. Experienced girls who brought other less experienced girls on board to strip for him, perform in his porn vids and . . . well, whore for him.'

'Cameron Boyd gave you all this?' Heck was fascinated by that fact alone.

'Sounds like Boyd had some peripheral involvement with Ship's firm in his early days. Small-time pimp, minder for some of the girls . . . that kind of thing.'

'And Ship had a few of these recruitment officers, did he?'

'Several.'

'How did this thing work exactly?'

'Sounds like they were real glamour-pusses themselves,' Fisher said. 'They worked the various clubs, checking out the talent. Suppose it'd be the usual thing – they'd spot a couple of party girls they liked the look of, offer them work, modelling, dancing . . . you know the rest.'

'And this all happened in central Manchester, on Ship's own patch?'

'Not quite. According to Boyd, every one of these recruitment girls had her own area of responsibility.'

'You mean *geographic* area?'

'Correct. And get this, Shelley Harper's was her home-town – Bradburn.'

There was a long silence, during which Heck could barely say anything.

'This help in any way?' Fisher asked.

'Yeah, mate, it does,' Heck replied. 'Thanks a bundle.'

'Can I assume you'll pass this on to the rest of the team, seeing as Gemma was the first person at Wandering Wolf to enquire about Shelley Harper?'

'That you can, mate,' Heck said, but he was still lost in his own thoughts.

366

'Good. See you later, pal.'

'Yeah, mate.'

Heck sat there for several minutes.

How quickly and easily the fly had been extricated from the ointment.

Shelley Harper had been the sole reason he'd hesitated to call it in that Kayla Green should be regarded as a suspect in the Incinerator murders. Kayla and her doomed sister had been local lasses, Bradburners through and through. They were never likely to have encountered Shelley Harper in their normal lives, at least not Shelley Harper in her capacity as Vic Ship's girlfriend. But in her capacity as Vic Ship's talent scout – that was a different matter.

Shelley Harper recruited Jess Green, Heck thought, the final pieces falling into place. *A lively and attractive young girl . . . a bit wild after the recent loss of her father, a bit wayward, a bit reckless, clubbing eight till late in the town's nightspots, hitting the party circuit afterwards, taking all sorts just to keep going, sleeping around maybe – targets didn't get much easier.*

Heck shoved the Makarov into the glovebox, then climbed from the car, closed and locked it, and walked slowly down the rain-drenched backstreet.

'Jess finally told you about Shelley Harper too, didn't she, Kayla?' he mumbled to himself. 'Probably spotted her in the newspaper. She'll have said, "That's *her*, sis . . . that's the one who first got me into it." And so Shelley's name got added to the list as well, didn't it?'

The backstreet became an alley, which wound away between tall buildings, most now silent and empty. Perhaps 150 yards away, down at the alley's far end, it terminated at a high-wall, but first passed underneath the canopy of the old Lyceum, formerly Bradburn's only cinema but now, like so much else here, abandoned – a lowering, decrepit structure, the neon-bulb letters that had once adorned its frontage either broken or missing.

But Heck didn't walk down that far. Closer, on his left, a nine-foot brick wall marked the outer perimeter of the yard attached to what had once been Kayla's father's body-shop and now was hers. A few yards further down, Heck came to the entrance, which comprised two seven-foot-tall gates made from corrugated metal. Fastened closed by a single chain on the inside, they provided flimsy security, the two sections of corrugated metal hanging lopsided and covered in rust. Over the top, the wooden sign that had once read *Greenways Autofix* was now indecipherable with damp and rot.

Heck glanced over his shoulder. No one appeared to be headed in this direction. He pushed against the lefthand gate with his shoulder. It yielded inward, creating a gap of about twelve inches, before the chain pulled taut. He crouched and tried to slide through. Thankfully there was plenty of give in the old metal and, with a groan of corroded hinges, he forced his way to the other side.

It was difficult to work out exactly what now lay in the yard beyond; it was only early evening, but, thanks to the storm, the sky overhead was almost black. A few crates and barrels occupied distant corners, with tarpaulins draped over them, but it mostly appeared to contain rubbish – bits of car parts: wheels, bumper bars, exhaust pipes, broken-off doors, even an entire vehicle shell sitting on breezeblocks and either burned or stripped down to its bare metal – it was difficult to tell in the violent downpour.

In no way did this place resemble functioning business premises.

It almost looked abandoned.

In the centre stood the main workshop: a single-storey brick garage with a flexible, fold-down steel door at the front. Alongside that, a cluster of boxy prefabricated offices.

All the doors and windows were closed, and no light shone out. Heck started walking, circling the ramshackle building – but warily, guiltily. He'd entered these premises unlawfully; there weren't even grounds for a warrant at this stage, his suspicions based entirely on circumstantial evidence and, most likely, imagination. When he actually stopped and tried to think it through, it still seemed ridiculous. Kayla had clearly gone through some kind of breakdown. By the looks of this place, her entire life had turned to crap. But he'd known her so well at one time, and there hadn't been a murderous bone in her body. OK . . . she'd trained as a mechanic. She had tools and equipment to hand. But it took more than the physical capability to make a murderer.

'I'm an absolute killer with a blowtorch.'

Again, those words echoed through his head.

Rain swept over Heck in sheets as he prowled.

That comment could easily have been a coincidence. She might have meant nothing by it. If she actually was the Incinerator, would she have risked saying anything along those lines? It seemed ever more unlikely that Kayla could be involved, and yet it would explain so much.

Whoever the Incinerator was, he was almost solely responsible for kicking off this gangland war. And he was clearly not part of Lee Shaughnessy's outfit. Heck's initial theory that this had been a deliberate attempt by a third party to stir things up now looked a real possibility. But Kayla wouldn't have known how to do that. She might, at a push, have been able to build herself a flamethrower, but she wouldn't have possessed the knowhow to engineer an underworld conflict on this scale. She didn't know enough of the main players.

At least, she hadn't known them before her sister started working for them, and no doubt had picked up various names and gossip from other wretched souls trapped in the same hellish life.

No, it wasn't *too* fantastical, he decided, continuing to circle the structure. Kayla had plenty of reasons to seek revenge.

He'd now reached the back of the premises. There was a narrow gap here, perhaps no more than five feet across, running between the rear wall of the garage and the rearmost boundary wall of the compound. It was jammed with rubbish, a vast jumble of large, shapeless, jagged-edged items. But he was still able to see an egress point about halfway along it: some six feet from the ground, a row of three letterbox-shaped windows, each about one foot by three. Even with his vision obscured by the dying light, he saw that the middle window was open, if only by a couple of inches.

He made his way down there, clambering through tangles of dripping wet steel, broken frames, springs, rotted rubber tyres. But he reached the window without difficulty, fitted his fingers underneath it and lifted. It wasn't on a catch, and rose all the way, easily affording him entry, though he paused again to think.

He'd hammered Shaughnessy and his henchman earlier, but that was pretty routine stuff when it came to cop and gangster relations. In comparison, this was a lot more serious – if he entered this building now it would be a clear-cut illegal entry.

But there was patently no one here. It was now – he checked his watch – just after half-five. If for any reason Kayla was engaged in actual work on this semi-derelict site, which didn't look to be the case at all, she was unlikely to turn up at this hour and in these conditions.

But still he hesitated. It wasn't so much his conscience that bothered him – he wasn't going to damage anything when he got in there, he wasn't going to steal or assault someone; this would not be a burglary. But if he got caught, even Gemma would struggle to keep him in the job. And on top of that, a very good suspect would be lost to them.

I'm having a mooch about, he told himself. That was all; he was just being a good copper. He had a gut feeling and he had to follow it. Whatever he found in here, he couldn't even use it as grounds to secure a search warrant, let alone seize it as evidence, but at least he would know what he was dealing with.

He braced his elbow on the sill and swung his body up, slid in through the gap and fell full-length down into the dim interior, landing heavily on a work-bench, which clattered as tools spilled onto a concrete floor.

He jumped to his feet, listening intently. No sound of movement came back to him. He squinted around, trying to work out exactly where he was, though it was so gloomy in there and so filled with indefinable shadows that he couldn't at first distinguish anything. That said, it felt like a typical workshop environment, the air reeking of dampness and oil; as he walked, his feet kicked through drifts of rustling paperwork. When he took his phone out and activated the light, its hard, cold glow showed clutter everywhere, on worktops, on shelves, on the floor: old and rusted tools, loose wiring, tatty boxes with yet more desiccated paperwork overflowing out of them. A nearby bench was thick with dust; when Heck ran his finger along the surface, its tip came away black as coal. A few more neglected documents were scattered on top. He picked a couple up. They were final demands for unpaid bills. The most recent was dated almost a year ago.

Light in hand, he rotated, scanning every other corner of the junk-filled room, finally coming about-face – at which point he realised that someone had walked stealthily up and now was standing directly behind him. Heck choked in surprise, dropping quickly to his knees – as a huge, two-handed spanner swept sideways at his head.

Chapter 36

'So there's nothing you can give me at all?' Gemma said in a tone of deep exasperation.

At the other end of the phone, Dr Anna Sarkovsy, GMP's senior CSI, remained infuriatingly calm and matter-of-fact. 'Not from that underground passage, Ms Piper, no. We've got the threads from the old iron gate, probably originating from a pair of gloves . . . but unless someone provides a pair of gloves for us to cross-compare them with, we're no further on.'

'There are no boot-prints or anything?'

'The air-raid shelter ceiling has partially collapsed, so the floor of that tunnel was mainly compacted rubble. We're still looking. There's nothing so far, but the best we were ever going to get was a *fragment* of a boot-print.'

Gemma leaned back. 'How about tyre-marks from the car? For Christ's sake, Anna – my officer chased the suspect clear across Anderson Brow.'

'All of which has now been washed repeatedly by heavy rain, I might remind you.'

'It wasn't raining this hard when you and your team first went out there.'

'Ms Piper, Anderson Brow comprises about six square miles of open spoil-land, most of which is made of compacted slag, which is pretty resistant to even shallow impressions. In the short time available, we discovered nothing we could use. I'm sorry, but there it is.'

'Right . . . OK. Thanks for that, Anna. Obviously let me know when something does arise.' Gemma cut the call and sat back, thumbing at her aching brow. As she did, Gary Quinnell barged in without knocking. She glanced up at him. 'I sincerely hope this is good news, Gary.'

'Depends how you look at it, ma'am.' He grinned broadly. 'It's Sagan. I think we've got him.'

*

Heck ducked all the lower, dropping his phone in the process. It hit the concrete floor with such an impact that its light was extinguished, plunging them back into murk. There was a *swish* of air, as the spanner narrowly missed him. Even so, the towering shape standing over him, whose face he hadn't yet seen, would know exactly where he was, and even now would be aiming a second bone-crushing blow at his head. Heck sprang forward from his knees, catching his assailant in the waist with his shoulder. It was a full-on, battering-ram blow, and a female yelp split the air.

The figure doubled over and staggered sideways, before rebounding from the dusty workbench. Normally, Heck would have caught him with an uppercut as he tottered back into range, but now he knew that it wasn't a 'him'. Instead, he went for the spanner, which again loomed towards him, caught it with his left hand, twisted it from his injured opponent's grasp and hurled it away into a corner. After that, he grabbed the figure by the belt and flung her forcefully away from him. There was an echoing thud as she slammed into a wall of shelves, debris cascading around her as the entire structure collapsed.

Back on his feet, Heck blundered to the nearest corner. In those brief moments when his phone-light had worked, he'd seen a switch over here. He fumbled and caught it with his thumb.

With a dull hum, a faltering yellow strip-light activated overhead.

Heck spun around, resuming the combat position.

As he'd expected, the figure rising painfully to her feet on the other side of the room was female. She wore a jumper and jeans and held her left hand clamped to the side of her back. Though her dark hair hung messily over her face, it was quite plain who he was dealing with: Kayla Green.

He walked forward warily. As far as he could see, she had no other weapon.

'You all right?' he asked.

She looked startled rather than angry, straightening up and brushing her locks out of the way.

'Mark? What the hell do you think you're doing?'

'I could ask you the same thing. You almost brained me with that bloody thing.'

'I thought someone had broken in . . .' Her words tailed off as she eyed him curiously, and then glanced at the still open window. 'You *did* break in, didn't you?'

Heck could have made up some off-the-cuff lie like 'I just happened to be passing and thought I heard someone sneaking around', but in terms of childishness that would have been off the scale. If you wanted to avoid severe embarrassment, there was rarely a better option than coming clean.

'I forced entry, yes,' he admitted. 'As part of my investigation into the Incinerator murders.'

She regarded him with bemusement. 'And . . . why would you do that?'

'Why do you think, Kayla?'

Her confused features slowly lengthened. Her mouth slackened open. 'You . . . Mark, you think *I've* been committing these crimes?'

'I don't know, Kayla. Have you?'

'Why on earth would I?' She half-laughed. 'Mark . . . why would I be murdering people?'

'I think you already know the answer to that.'

'*No, I don't.* Mark . . . I'm trying to be a better person now. I go to church every day.'

'That doesn't mean very much, I'm afraid.'

'But I've never hurt anyone in my life. I've not even got a reason to.'

'And that bit definitely isn't true, is it?'

She still seemed perplexed by the accusation.

'What about Jess?' he prompted.

Slowly, her expression changed from one of bewilderment to one of near-complete disbelief. 'You mean . . . you're saying I'm murdering the gangsters who poisoned my sister? Is that it?'

'You're not exactly a bundle of forgiveness when it comes to the drugs problem in this town, Kayla.'

She grew progressively more irate as the truth of the situation dawned on her. 'And that's a crime? Whereas the maniacs supplying the stuff walk around scot-free!'

'Did you know a woman called Shelley Harper?' he asked.

Kayla didn't so much as flinch. 'Wasn't she murdered by this flamethrower man?'

'Yes, but did you know who she was? I mean, what she did for a living?'

'She was some kind of Page Three girl, wasn't she?'

'But you don't know anything else about her?'

'Excuse me, Mark!' Kayla shook her head. 'I seem to remember we were having a conversation about why you've broken into my home.'

'Your *home*?'

'Yes, I live here. Is that a crime too?'

Heck now noticed the open door through which she'd slid unnoticed into his presence. The room beyond it was dark, its walls made of bare brick, but now that his eyes were adjusting he could make out an iron-framed bunkbed, a side-table with books and a bottle of water on it, a portable electric fire.

'Kayla . . . you live *here*?'

She shrugged. 'I haven't got anywhere else. And while we're on the subject, I haven't got a flamethrower either. Why don't you look around . . . this time *with* my permission?'

Heck knew there'd be no point in that. Even if he turned this dump upside down, there'd be nothing here – otherwise she'd never have allowed him to look.

'Last Sunday night,' she said, her tone altering, turning contemptuous, 'when you lowered yourself to go on that date with me . . . you know, the one which unsurprisingly led nowhere . . . were you feeling sorry for me, Mark? Is that why you agreed to it? Or did you already have me down as a suspect? Were you there purely in a professional capacity?'

'Kayla, don't tell me you've never wanted to fix those bastards who did that thing to Jess?'

'Of course I damn well did.' She looked amazed he could even ask the question. 'But we all have different ways of dealing with crises, don't we?'

'And what was yours? Start a war? Make them kill each other?'

'Well, I'll tell you what it wasn't – it wasn't going and

376

joining the enemy. It wasn't betraying my family, becoming a part of the very organisation that destroyed their lives.'

Heck felt his cheeks colouring.

'I told you, Mark.' She lowered her voice again. 'I got involved with the Church after Jess's death because I wanted to change my life.'

'And you do that by sweeping footpaths?'

She shook her head. 'I thought *I'd* drifted a long way from what I once was. But *you* take the biscuit. I want to find myself again, I want something spiritual . . .'

'Kayla . . .'

'I *was* a wild child once. A drinker, a slut – you know that, Mark, you took full advantage of it.'

That stung him. 'You were up for it as much as I was!'

'Yes, but it was all a bit naughty, wasn't it? A bit sordid? A tent in the park, and all that. But it doesn't end there with me. Later on, I got a husband I never paid any attention to –'

'I thought he was a pillock who chased other women?'

'Takes two to tango, Mark. He wouldn't have gone there if he'd got what he'd wanted at home.'

'Kayla, that's ridicu–'

'Then I let my business ambitions get in the way of my relationship with Jess . . . until it was too late for her.' She shook her head again. 'I'm not a very good person, Mark. But when you say I've got no forgiveness in me, I beg to differ. Because that's exactly the way I'm trying to cope with this situation. By forgiving those animals. And believe me, it hasn't been easy . . . when I see the human wreckage they leave behind them.'

He watched her carefully, trying to read her stance.

'You look as if you disapprove,' she said with an unamused snicker. 'Or is it just that you wanted an easy arrest and an immediate confession? On which subject, aren't you supposed to have read me my rights by now? Is that what they call it over here?'

'You're not under arrest.'

'I'm not?' She looked genuinely surprised.

'Like you said, I've no authority to even be in here. But you have to understand why I've formed suspicions about you.'

She shrugged. 'If you've still got suspicions, Mark, we need to sort them out. Because life's hard enough as it is.' She bustled through into the room she was using as her sleeping quarters, returning with her tasselled leather jacket folded over her arm. 'I'll help you with your enquiries – interview me if you need to. I've nothing to hide, you see. And don't worry . . . I won't say a word about the unlawful entry you made to my premises.' She pulled her jacket on. 'Wouldn't want to cause any more problems for the blokes looking after the scumbags of this town, would I? Shucks, there I go again, saying things that might implicate me in the murders.'

'Look Kayla . . . I sympathise about Jess.'

'Course you do.' She grabbed a bunch of keys from a hook. 'You all do. I heard exactly the same tosh from the coppers who pulled her corpse out of that drain. But they didn't sympathise enough to catch the bastards who gave her the drugs that put her there, did they?'

'Look, are you saying you're willing to come down to the station and be questioned under caution?' he asked her. 'If so, we might be able to get this sorted out quickly.'

'I'm presuming it could still result in me being arrested as a suspect?'

Bloody right it could, he told himself. But in truth, she would have to admit to something pretty damning for that to happen now. There was plainly nothing suspicious on these premises, illegal though his search of them had been,

378

and Kayla was either completely innocent or the best actress he'd come across in the job thus far.

'It'll be a formal interview,' he explained. 'But you'll be free to leave at any time, and from your point of view it's an opportunity to put yourself well beyond suspicion.'

'Good enough.'

Her tone was now short and businesslike. She wasn't angry any more, but neither was she Heck's friend.

They left the building together, Kayla locking it up behind them, and plodded across the yard in sombre silence. Almost as quickly as it had begun, the deluge had diminished to a drizzle, and even that was now easing off, water trickling copiously away down every gutter. Kayla unfastened the padlock on the gates and they sidled through. Once on the other side, she reached through the gap and clicked the lock back into place.

'You want to follow me down to the nick?' Heck said. 'Like I say, you're not under arrest. So you can take your own wheels.'

She smiled. 'That'd be nice. If I had any.'

That comment puzzled him. He halted. 'I thought you drove a Ford Fiesta?'

'Oh, that. I hired it. Just for the night we went out. Appearances are everything, aren't they?'

She sounded disgusted with herself, but Heck was hardly listening. Instead, he stared down to the far end of the alley, where what previously had been a vague outline in the heavy rain was now visible as a car parked opposite the front of the cinema. And it quite clearly wasn't a Ford Fiesta.

'So that's not your motor either?' he said.

Kayla glanced towards it. 'I just told you – I don't own one.'

He took note of the parked vehicle's grey bodywork as he walked slowly towards it – and felt a slow creep up his spine.

'You've got to be kidding,' he said. 'You've got to be . . .'

'What?' Kayla wondered, following.

He didn't answer directly, but strode down what was left of the cul-de-sac, faster and faster until suddenly he was running, finally sliding to a halt when he was right alongside the vehicle.

It sat by the alley wall facing the cinema frontage. It was a grey Peugeot estate, and not only that – it had suffered extensive damage. Incredulous, he circled round to the rear bumper, which nestled alongside a shattered nearside light cluster (courtesy of his good self, of course) and kicked at it, at which point the number plate, which had also been damaged, fell off.

The VRM read: PQ23 WXV.

Heck's spine positively tingled.

He was long enough in the tooth to know that coincidences sometimes happened. But rarely on this scale. In truth, there was only one possible explanation. He turned to look at Kayla, who was peering at the half-wrecked Peugeot in bewilderment. Another impressive performance, he thought, reaching for his handcuffs – at which point they were distracted by a figure rising from a place of concealment between the Peugeot and the alley wall.

The first impression was that this figure was massively built. Though that might have been because of the heavy-duty dark-silver fatigues it was wearing, not to mention the leather harness holding the long steel canister slung down over its back, or its motorcycle crash-helmet which was specially augmented with an opaque, gold-tinted faceplate. In its thickly gloved hands it gripped what looked like an elongated oxyacetylene torch: a handled, triggered device with a fire-blackened jet-nozzle attachment. This device was connected to the fuel tank by a lengthy rubber tube.

Heck grabbed Kayla's arm and dragged her backwards,

but already the terrifying shape was clumping around the front of the Peugeot, hemming them into the cul-de-sac. Before they could even shout, it pumped its trigger and liquid fire ballooned towards them.

Chapter 37

Gemma followed Quinnell into the VDU room, where Ron Gibbshaw stood with his hands in his pockets and Sally Gorton sat in front of an array of screens.

'Looks like Heck's intel was good, ma'am,' Gibbshaw said grudgingly. 'We've managed to put an electronic vapour trail together.'

Gemma glanced at the central screen, on which a grainy black and white image, currently on freeze-frame, portrayed a row of closed garage doors with what looked like an empty parking bay alongside them.

'This is CCTV of that so-called storage depot at Woodfold, ma'am,' Gorton said. 'Isn't really worthy of the name, is it? That's the only parking space, by the way.'

'OK . . .' Gemma said. 'So what's so exciting?'

Gorton hit a button. The image flickered to life as half a dozen gloved and ski-masked figures swarmed into view, some leaping lithely down over the brick wall on the far side of the parking bay, others running into shot as though from an open gateway. A couple of them were sporting handguns, two or three others wielding pickaxe handles.

'This, I'm guessing, is Shaughnessy and his crew,' Gorton

said. 'As you can see from the timer –' she indicated a digital read-out in the screen's bottom right corner '– it's 6.09 p.m. on Friday, April 6. So all that marries up, and like Shaughnessy told Heck, they're too late. There's no one there.'

'All right . . .'

'So, we rolled it back in time a bit . . .' Gorton hit a rewind switch, the images rapidly flowing backwards, the masked figures disappearing again, and nothing happening at all until suddenly, at around three o'clock that afternoon, a vehicle with a black caravan attached reversed into view and parked alongside the row of garages.

Gorton hit 'freeze' and sat back, tapping her teeth with a pen. The car was a light-coloured Land Rover Discovery.

'That's not a dark-blue Jeep Cherokee,' Gemma observed.

'No, but he's almost certainly changed his motor since the incident down in Peckham,' Gibbshaw said. 'And that *is* a caravan.'

'Different colour.'

He shrugged. 'New paint-job. And anyway, for the avoidance of doubt . . . roll it back a little bit more, Sally.'

Gorton did as instructed, and a couple of seconds after the Discovery had reversed into view, the driver's door opened and a coated, bespectacled figure carrying a heavy haversack climbed out and backtracked away from it. Gorton hit 'freeze' again.

'That's John Sagan, isn't it, ma'am?' Gibbshaw asked.

Gemma's hair prickled as she regarded the figure on the screen. Some things had changed: the close-cropped fair hair was now jet-black and styled differently, greased backward. The round-lensed, gold-rimmed glasses had been replaced by a pair with horn rims and square lenses. But there was no mistaking him. The basic shape, the way he carried himself, the gait. And the face, of course. That everyman face had branded itself into her memory.

'That's him,' she said quietly. 'God almighty, that's Sagan. OK, where does he go next?'

'Well . . .' Gorton ran the video forward. The figure of Sagan threw his bag into the back seat of the Discovery, and clambered in behind the wheel. It quickly pulled away, drawing the caravan behind it. 'We obviously lose sight of him here, ma'am, but we don't lose it for long . . . we pick him up again on Salvation Lane, which is a pretty busy thoroughfare in that part of Bradburn. Means there's lots of cameras in both directions . . .'

'Let's see it,' Gemma urged her.

Gorton turned to the screen on her left and hit a few more buttons.

A fog of static cleared and a busy roundabout emerged, well lit by streetlamps.

'This is the Summerton roundabout,' Gorton said. 'And here –' as the Discovery and its caravan came into view '– is our boy.'

'OK,' Gemma said.

'You see the timer . . . it's only a few minutes later, so we're bang-on.'

'Yeah, go on, go on . . .'

The target vehicle proceeded across the roundabout and cut left along a dual carriageway.

'This is Summerton Way,' Gorton said. 'At this stage he was headed northeast, away from the town centre.'

'Don't tell me he's leaving the borough.'

'We considered that possibility,' Gibbshaw said. 'But just hang about . . .'

Gorton turned to the screen on her right and her fingers danced on the keys. This time the focus fell on a busy T-junction, the timer again indicating that only a couple of minutes had passed.

'This is where the slip-road comes off Summerton Way and joins Pendlebury Road,' Gorton said. 'You can see he's going left. Now, on the map . . .' She turned and indicated a large and detailed roadmap of Bradburn on the wall behind them. Quinnell had helpfully placed himself alongside it and indicated the route with his finger. 'You can actually see that, instead of heading out of town, he's skirting east, so he's staying inside the borough.'

'I see that,' Gemma said.

Onscreen, the Discovery had pulled up at a set of traffic lights.

'We're a couple of minutes and a mile and a half further on here,' Gorton added. 'This area's called Bowland Bridge. There are a few housing estates this far out, but not many. It's mainly disused industrial land.'

On the screen, Sagan swung right and again vanished from view.

'This is where we lose him,' Gorton said.

Gemma turned a pained expression on her. 'We lose him?'

'Yeah, but only from the cameras,' Gibbshaw interjected. 'We're pretty optimistic we know where he's gone. Sally!'

Gorton got to her feet and joined Quinnell by the map.

'This road he's on, ma'am, Hunger Hill, is pretty isolated and basically leads to one of two places: Bradburn Municipal Cemetery and Crematorium, which I can't see would hold much interest for him. And French & Sons Auto Traders.'

Gemma arched an eyebrow. 'He's gone visiting an auto trader?'

'Not quite,' Quinnell said. 'We've done some digging and Sam French specialises in estate cars, caravans, motor homes and the like.'

'I see . . .' Suddenly Gemma felt she knew where this was going.

'He's got a compound up there on Hunger Hill,' Gibbshaw said. 'A big one. It's crammed with about nine hundred vehicles, all in various stages of disrepair.'

Gemma nodded. 'And you think that's where he may have gone to ground?'

'It's locked, but most of the time unmanned.' Gibbshaw shrugged. 'Someone like Sagan could get in there easily. And, well . . . a vehicle pound already overflowing with caravans and motor homes would be as good a hideout as any. If not better than most. Natural camouflage, you could say. That's the downside of it. The upside is that Sagan's someone who rarely stays anywhere for long. But if this is as good a berth as we think, he might be tempted to camp out there permanently . . . or at least as long as he's needed up here in the North.'

Gemma nodded again. 'Well done, everyone. That's a hell of a job. We need to get up there as soon as we can. There shouldn't be any problem getting a warrant, at least.'

'No, the problem will be the other caravans,' Gibbshaw said. 'There are lots and lots of them, most of which were already covered by canvas and the like . . . as will Sagan's by now, I'd suggest.'

Gemma paused, pondering the problem.

'He'll not be there himself, of course,' Gorton added. 'But he can't be far away. Probably found a bed and brekky on one of the nearby housing estates. The main thing is, if we start a pattern search up there, ripping canvases off and what not – basically making a racket and causing a scene – we'll give him just the heads-up he needs.'

'We still need to get up there,' Gemma said. 'If nothing else, we need to sit on that place. How many exits and entrances are there?'

'I've sent Charlie Finnegan to scope it out properly,' Gibbshaw said. 'No situation report from him yet.'

'OK . . .' Gemma pondered briefly. 'Get everyone else up there who's free. I want that vehicle pound completely encircled.'

'Ma'am!' Gorton objected.

'We do it covertly,' Gemma said. 'I want observation points on every exit and entrance, but tell everyone to stay low. I want a twenty-four watch on that site. At some point, Sagan'll break cover again, and that's when we nab him.'

Gibbshaw followed her back through into her own office, where she kicked off her heels.

'Shall we go public on the new-look Sagan?' he asked.

'Not yet.'

'Like Sally Gorton said, he's got to be lodging somewhere close. We hit the evening news, we could have a phone-tip within the hour.'

'At the same time we could tip Sagan off that we've sussed his whereabouts. At the end of the day, if his life and liberty's on the line, I don't suppose he'll think he really needs his Pain Box, or whatever he calls it . . . or his latest dodgy motor. He could easily leave those behind for us to find. Probably in about a week's time, while he catches the next train out. Sit on that video-grab, Ron . . . at least for the time being.'

'Fair enough.' Gibbshaw waited in the doorway while she pulled a pair of wellingtons on. 'You must be pleased that your trust in Heck was rewarded.'

She glanced at him as she took her anorak from a locker. 'Try not to sound too resentful, if you can manage it. Heck's on our side, you know.'

'I know he is. I also know he's a good detective. But he's a wild card too. I don't even want to ask how he got the skinny on Sagan . . . when he's not even supposed to be working that part of the case. But the CPS are going to ask. They'll *need* to.'

'Let's not get ahead of ourselves, eh? We don't even know if that maniac Sagan's up there yet.'

'On the subject of maniacs, where *is* Heck?'

'Chasing a lead.'

'Off on his own again?' Try though he clearly did, Gibbshaw couldn't keep the disapproval from his voice. 'That doesn't help him when he has to account for his actions, you know, Gemma.'

'That's why I've told Katie Hayes to hook up with him as soon as she's free.' She shrugged her anorak on. 'In the meantime, DI Gibbshaw, you and I have a date on Hunger Hill.'

Chapter 38

Heck and Kayla staggered backward, their feet skidding as they retreated across the mossy, rain-slippery cobbles. The Incinerator faced the same problem. Instead of catching them full-on in a blast of bone-bleaching flame, he too slid half off-balance, driving his first jet leftward. Even so, he'd closed off their escape route. On all sides stood high walls and then the cinema frontage. It was to this that Heck ran, dragging Kayla with him. Beneath the canopy stood a row of recessed double doors, each covered with boards. Heck threw himself shoulder-first at the nearest. The wood was old and rotten; it cracked, sagging inward.

'Mark!' Kayla screamed as the helmeted nightmare approached from behind.

Heck slammed into the boarding again, this time smashing it through, exposing a grimy glazed door beyond. A single stout kick and its central glass panel shattered. Heck slid through, hauling Kayla after him, and once they were in, ducking sideways – just as a gout of flame pierced the gap behind them, throwing hot, writing colours to all corners of the cinema's derelict lobby. Gilded handrails led up a low flight of steps to a long-abandoned ticket booth. Mildewed film posters advertised *Jurassic Park*, *Sleepless in Seattle*, *The Fugitive* . . .

Heck and Kayla saw none of this as they clattered up the steps, veered sideways and crashed through a pair of swing doors into the auditorium. The Incinerator followed, his heavy-booted feet thumping the mouldering carpet. More flame speared in their wake, setting the doors alight. Red phantasms scampered ahead of the duo, who were only vaguely aware of the vast, cavernous space around them. Two aisles ran down to the front, both strewn with decayed detritus left over from the last film-show: cartons, lolly sticks, gum wrappers. They paused, gasping, before taking the aisle on the right. Heck glanced back. The hulking form of the Incinerator was silhouetted on a curtain of fire. He'd halted, presumably so that his visor-covered eyes could attune to the darkness. He took aim again, this time putting his flame-thrower to his shoulder. Another jet of flame spurted high and wide, arcing across the auditorium towards them. Heck grabbed Kayla's hand again and ducked sideways, blundering between rows of dirty, dust-laden seats.

'Mark . . . what's he doing here?' she stammered. 'Why's he –?'

'Just run! *Run!*'

The madman also cut across the auditorium, scrambling between rows of seats, intent on heading them off. Again, he unleashed hell, blood-red flame blooming towards them.

They dropped, taking refuge on the litter-strewn carpet. A wedge of fire surged overhead, after which they risked glancing up. Large portions of the room were now burning. The carpets, the upholstery, the seats and even the aged wall-hangings had ignited. The air was rank with smoke, raging with heat. But, untroubled by this, their assailant vaulted clumsily over the seats as he advanced. Flames licked at him, but with no effect. Heck and Kayla dashed on. They

390

came to the next aisle, and were tempted to divert back along it towards the entrance, but, pre-empting this, the Incinerator switched the angle of his attack and drove a wall of flame across their path, driving them back again, shepherding them down the aisle towards the front of the cinema, where what remained of the age-browned movie screen dangled in strips. To either side hung vast, swag-like drapes of formerly ornate brocade.

Heck yanked the phone from his pocket, but of course it was broken.

'You got your mobile?' he shouted.

'No, I didn't have time, I –'

'Shit!'

The Incinerator let rip another searing jet. They ran on, and this time were almost too late. Agonising heat flared up their backs. To either side, filth-impregnated seats exploded in flames. They spun around, choking, clothes smouldering, faces sodden and blackened by smoke. The Incinerator was less than twenty yards away. He again had them in his sights.

The next jet would envelop them.

On pure instinct, Heck flung his useless phone at the figure's head. It might have worked. The iPhone was a heavy device; had it smashed the plate at the front of the Incinerator's helmet, it would have exposed him to the fire as well, and maybe forced him to withdraw. However, the maniac merely dropped to one knee and it sailed past.

It bought them a couple of seconds, but now only one route lay open; the pathway along the front of the screen, which led to an exit-door in the far corner. They lurched down towards this, and found themselves in a fire-lit cement passage. Thirty yards ahead, the exterior exit-door loomed. They ran up to it and rammed down on the escape-bar. But the door didn't budge. Heck put his shoulder to it, though all he managed to do was wind himself. It was secured on the other side, probably by chains. There was no escape this way.

They turned frantically – just as the interior exit-door crashed open, and the Incinerator stood there. His silvery, flame-resistant armour had turned charcoal black. He was moving more slowly, almost sluggishly, which suggested that, shielded or not, he was finally feeling the kiln-like heat. Of course, he wouldn't be feeling it as they would.

They were trapped, with nowhere to hide.

Except for one faint possibility.

Ten yards in front, part way between the fugitives and their assailant, stood a side-door. Heck remembered it as another exit, this one connecting to the cinema's upper circle. The thought of ascending to the upper floors with the ground level ablaze was terrifying. But what choice did they have? He pushed Kayla forward.

The Incinerator halted, nonplussed by their apparently suicidal action. Then realised what they were doing. He raised his weapon, determined to turn them to hunks of shrivelled, sizzling meat. But they made it to the door first. Heck threw himself at it head-on. From the corner of his eye, he saw a bright yellow glare as the passage was filled with flame. The door swung open. They barged through it together, though the fiery barrage pursued them, blossoming up a black, narrow stairway behind them.

'Heck, this whole theatre is going up!' Kayla jabbered. 'We'll be killed.'

'It's our only chance. We'll get to a window or something.'

The first floor, when they reached it, was already filled with smoke. It was also intensely hot. They stumbled down the first passage, wafting at fumes just so they could breathe. Doors to the empty shells of offices stood on all sides, but none would provide a refuge. Like some medieval dragon, the Incinerator burst into view at their rear, repeated jets of liquid flame spurting ahead of him. The walls and ceiling of the passage were already vividly alight, but he advanced anyway. They fled on, rounding a corner, and finding the doorway to the upper circle. Through it, they saw the seating in the balcony, now lit a lurid crimson. Thanks to the ageing swags of material decking the cinema's walls, flames had spread to the ceiling and were consuming the once ornate plasterwork and exposed skeletal beams.

Heck turned back. The Incinerator was even closer, though, half-blinded himself by the smoke and the strobe-like glare, he hadn't spotted them yet. With each doorway he came to, he squirted a jet of flame through it. Heck scanned frantically for the main stair down. It ought to lie somewhere on their right, but the roiling smog hid everything. When Kayla grabbed his arm and lunged for the door to the upper circle, it occurred to him that maybe they could descend to the front of the balcony, and perhaps climb over it and drop down.

They hurried down between the seats. It would be a calculated risk, but when they got there it was like glancing down into Dante's Inferno. The entire downstairs was on fire. The auditorium's carpets, the rows of seats with their thick, decayed upholstery, and the tide of dried litter had proved combustible in the extreme. Driven back by heat, they found themselves in the access passage again – but flames were racing through this part of the building too. And amid them, framed against this seething orange/red backdrop, came the Incinerator: his massive, bulky outline, his barrel torso, his solid limbs, the heavy folds of his armour-like suit, which they now noticed was cinched around the waist with some kind of utility belt, numerous hand-tools tucked into it. The flamethrower, however, hung by his side.

He was featureless behind his blackened faceplate, but he

scrutinised them carefully – as though with sudden interest rather than homicidal fury.

They backed off, faces singed, eyes tearful.

He advanced a couple of ponderous steps, and turning first to the left, then to the right, sprayed arcs of liquid fire over those few parts of the upstairs not yet burning. Heck and Kayla found themselves hemmed into a tiny corner. Their clothes were smoky and wringing with sweat, their hair hung in sopping strands. They were so disoriented that only now did they notice the single functional door directly behind them.

Heck kicked at it, expecting it to be locked, yet it broke open on first impact. He yanked Kayla through into the darkness beyond. They hammered up a tall, steep stairway, brick walls sheer on either side. At the top, they kicked and punched at another flimsy door, which again was smashed open, and found themselves facing a dank, bare room that was knee-deep in rubbish, much of it ancient movie posters turned green and black with mould. Fading evening light spilled through a single narrow window only partly blocked by slanted planks.

Despite the horror behind, something about this dismal garret caused them to hesitate.

They sensed movement in there. A faint scratching sound, possibly; it was hard to tell.

Louder, though, came a clumping of boots as the Incinerator entered the stairwell.

Instinctively, they lunged towards the light, only half noticing how foul the smell was in this part of the building; it was like an old toilet or an untended zoo cage. When they reached the window, Kayla ripped at the planks, working them loose one after another. As more light spilled in, Heck glanced up – and saw rib-like ceiling joists a couple of feet above their heads. They were clustered with hundreds of

394

small, furry bodies hanging together like clumps of putrid fruit.

Bats, he realised – which explained the animal smell, though basically they were harmless.

That said, they'd be waking up very soon. He just hoped that Kayla – in her desperate, panic-stricken state – wouldn't respond to the sight with a scream. As more light infiltrated the room, she too spotted the creatures; she instantly froze, only for Heck to clap a hand over her mouth, and at the same time clutch her hand tightly to reassure her.

She nodded to indicate that she was OK and that she understood she had to be quiet. Even so, shivers of movement passed through the sleeping colony overhead, probably caused by the rising heat and the smell of smoke. And then, with echoing reverberations, the Incinerator's ascending footfalls sounded from the stair.

'Move it!' Heck hissed. 'Quickly!'

Visibly frantic, Kayla clambered up into the window-frame, where she halted, teetering, almost hyperventilating with fright.

'Oh . . . oh, my God, Mark!'

Heck stuck his head past her and peered down an eighty-foot drop into a rubbish-filled alley. At first it looked impossible; there was no other way from here. But then, a couple of feet below the window, he spied a narrow ledge. It was no more than seven inches wide, and still wet from the earlier rainfall. It ran away along the side of the building, turning at a right angle some ten yards to their left, where the cinema adjoined a different derelict building. From there, the ledge ran on past several more broken windows before continuing out of sight along the next alley.

Safety was only ten yards away.

But it would be ten yards of sheer terror.

Kayla resisted as Heck tried to ease her out. 'You can't . . . you can't be serious!'

'It's this or we burn,' he replied.

She glanced around, and saw the look on his face, and maybe because the alternative truly was even more awful, she stepped down onto that perilous ledge, switching her face to the wall, and whimpering loudly, began edging her way along it. Heck followed, though the sense of vertigo was already dizzying. It didn't help that the ledge was not level, and they had to hug the wall with their spread-eagled bodies simply to keep their balance. The wall consisted of flat, smoothly fitted bricks, with barely a finger-hold between them, but even without the terror behind, once they'd commenced shuffling along, moving slowly but determinedly because they had no other choice, it felt impossible to go back. They were intensely aware of the chasm yawning behind, and didn't dare glance downwards, not even at their feet, which was hardly ideal when to trip or stumble could be a disaster. Heck was particularly in danger, because he brought up the rear. He pressed his body and his left cheek hard into the bricks as he slid along, arms outspread, but the breath heaved through his chest. Each time, it felt as if the expansion of his ribcage would push him backward and overbalance him. Already the muscles in his calves and ankles had tightened to the point where they ached. When he suddenly felt cold, heavy droplets drumming the top of his head, he halted, wondering at first if he'd stepped underneath a leaky overhead gutter, but then realising that it had started raining again. In the brief interval while he pondered this, his right foot lost its grip on the moist ledge and skated sideways, clouting Kayla's left foot. She yelped out loud as she tried to steady herself, which they both knew would be heard inside the room if the Incinerator had entered it.

Fleetingly, the shock of slipping almost overbalanced Heck. He rocked on the balls of his feet, frantically digging his fingers into the tiniest cracks. He was still only halfway along, but Kayla was much closer to the safety of the open windows on the next building. The promise of this egged her on; once she was stable, she lurched on almost recklessly fast.

'Mark . . . I'm almost there,' she stammered.

He managed to stabilise himself, again pushing the side of his face against the bricks, and focusing on the section of ledge just ahead. Kayla had now almost made it to the corner beyond which stood the first of the windows. She was so close that she could probably step across the triangular gap and grab the window's sill. She glanced back towards him, only to fix on something just behind him – at which point her expression changed, all hope visibly draining out of it.

Though Heck felt that readjusting his position even slightly, just enough that he could lean back sufficiently to turn his head, would be a desperate undertaking, he had no option. He *had* to look round – and found himself gazing back several yards at the garret window, from which the blackened form of the Incinerator leaned outward, his featureless, gold-painted faceplate blank and impenetrable, his weapon trained squarely on the pair of them.

He raised the weapon to chest height, taking careful aim. From this range, he couldn't miss. His finger crooked on the trigger. Mesmerised, they gazed into the black hole at the end of the muzzle, where a dot of flame threatened a volcanic outpouring.

And then Heck shouted – as loudly as he could.

It was a bass, meaningless, incoherent roar, delivered with every scrap of air in his lungs, at the very top of his voice.

And it worked.

In the room behind the Incinerator, the bats exploded from their roosts.

The next thing, the madman was enmeshed in a blizzard of leathery wings and claws as the creatures poured out from the confined space in a living tornado. With wild grunts, he dropped the flamethrower's pistol section, which clattered down against the outer bricks, hanging by its rubber tubing, and beat around his head as the entire colony engulfed him.

Heck watched, fleetingly spellbound. But then a gust of wind blasted the rain full into his face. He blinked, again almost overbalancing, having to flatten himself hard against the wall, while the Incinerator struggled. A low sobbing drew his attention back towards Kayla, who he realised was crying with relief as she climbed through the aperture into the safety of the next building.

Heck still had several yards to go, but, without the pressure from behind, it was easier than it had been. Soon he'd made it to the corner. From here he reached out, took Kayla's outstretched hand and was able to step over the angled gap, plant one knee on the next window's sill and scramble through into the room beyond.

Chapter 39

The Fire Brigade reached the Lyceum long before any additional police units did. Heck watched their teams work amid the chaos of smoke and teeming rain. He himself was nearly 150 yards away, in the front passenger seat of his Megane, the wipers thudding back and forth to keep the windscreen clear. Kayla sat alongside him, wrapped in a foil blanket, still sipping the beaker of coffee the firemen had provided her with even though it had long gone cold. Her hair looked damp and ratty, and beneath the sooty smears her face was ash-grey, almost immobile. She was going into shock and needed to be seen by a medic, but no ambulances had made it over here just yet.

Meanwhile, Gemma's voice sounded again in Heck's ear. He'd lost his own phone, but had been able to call her on the phone he'd taken from the gangster Kemp, which was sitting in his glovebox when he'd stumbled back to his car.

'But you two are definitely all right?' she asked.

'We seem to be, ma'am,' he replied.

'And you're sure there was no one else trapped inside?'

He shrugged wearily. 'I dunno. Unless there were some hoboes dossing down in there who we didn't see, the only other person on the premises was the Incinerator.'

'Could he have been caught in it?'

'Well . . . the whole place was going up when we got out, and he was still on the top floor. He's wearing fireproof armour, of course . . . he might have been able to walk out, but I don't know. That was quite a blaze. The problem at the moment is that I can't get anywhere near the building to have a look.'

Halfway down the backstreet, the Fire Brigade had blocked further access by deploying their own incident tape, both an inner cordon and an outer cordon stretching across the alley. For their own safety, no one else was being allowed anywhere nearer than that.

'Have you liaised with DI Hayes yet?' Gemma asked.

'Not yet.'

'She's on her way. So stay put, OK?'

'Will do. Did you have any joy at Woodfold?'

'We did, as a matter of fact. We got Sagan on camera.'

Heck straightened up. 'It was him for sure?'

'One hundred per cent. We've managed to track him across town to a compound for disused vehicles at a place called Hunger Hill. You know it?'

'Sam French Motors or something. That's still there?'

'It certainly is. And at present we've got it surrounded.'

'Let me guess . . . he's gone to ground among all the wrecks?'

'Correct, and we can't afford to make a hoohah by going rummaging through a sea of canvas to look for him. He'll spot us from way off, and we'll never see him again. So we're sitting tight. Now listen, Mark.' Her tone altered from the usual clipped efficiency to one of subdued but intense emotion. 'Leave Sagan to us. Your priority is still the Incinerator. If he's not lying in the ashes of that cinema, make sure you at least get hold of his Peugeot. It's likely to be chocka with evidence. In fact, even if he *is* lying in there, he might be bloody unrecognisable . . . so we still need that car secured and cordoned off. Are we clear?'

'Affirmative.'

'As I say, DI Hayes can give you a hand. She's trying to get over there as we speak. Anything else new, get on the blower.'

'Will do.' Heck cut the call and sat back. At the end of the alley, the towering black edifice of the Lyceum was wreathed in smoke, but at least the searing glare of flames was receding. Around its feet, firemen still moved, semi-invisible amid clouds of billowing steam.

'You actually thought that monster was me, Mark?' Kayla asked in a feeble voice. She gave a chesty cough. 'For real?'

'I know . . . I'm sorry.' Heck didn't look at her. He could have kicked himself. What they'd faced inside the Lyceum had indeed been a monster. There was no arguing with the assertion. And that ought to have been the giveaway from the start. Because Heck *had* met guys like this before, and it was only then, when you were nose to nose with them, that you realised how much more than human they actually were. Whereas Kayla Green was . . . what? A miserable, lonely, disturbed girl.

'Listen, Kayla – I'm sorry, but I've got to get back to work in a few minutes.'

'You certainly have!' she said with unexpected passion. When she turned to look at him, her smoke-reddened eyes sparkled with tears. 'You've got to catch that *thing*! You understand me, Mark? If it didn't get burned up in there, you've got to catch it before it hurts anyone else!'

He nodded dumbly. As he did, a muffled voice hailed him.

'Detective!'

The Fire Brigade station officer had removed his breathing mask and was advancing up the road. Heck climbed out and walked down towards him. They met on the outer cordon.

'How we doing?' Heck said.

'All the fires are extinguished, but the place has been gutted.' The officer, an older man with chubby, lined features, raised the dripping brim of his helmet and brushed sweat from his forehead.

He lifted the tape so that Heck could climb underneath it. They walked back down the backstreet together, trying not to slip in deep pools of water. The grey Peugeot still sat outside the front of the cinema, which, ironically, remained untouched by the flames, though all its boarded doors had been jemmied open and were still belching smoke and steam, creating an otherworldly fog, in the midst of which the spectral forms of firefighters coiled their hoses and repacked equipment.

They halted there.

'The structure looks pretty solid,' the station officer added. 'Its bones are mainly concrete and steel. Can't be sure how stable it is, though – at least until we get an engineer's report. So no one can go inside it yet.'

'Any trace of a body?' Heck asked.

'Not yet, but there's something you may want to look at. Oh, what do you want us to do about this vehicle?'

Heck eyed the Peugeot. With its gashed and crumpled bodywork, it wasn't going anywhere.

'It's now a crime scene,' he said. 'If you can get some kind of tent over it, that'd be excellent. And perhaps draw up a list of all your lads who've had physical contact with it.'

The station officer nodded and signalled a fireman nearby to take care of it. Then he plodded on around the exterior of the burned-out cinema, Heck following. They took a narrow passage and, at the rear, entered what looked as if it had once been a loading yard, though it was now covered in a jungle of desiccated weeds. More smoke and steam surged across this from an aperture at the back of the main

402

building, where a fire-door hung open on mangled hinges. Bits of shattered plank and chain lay scattered around it.

'This was smashed open from the inside,' the station officer said. He indicated the shiny edges of exposed metal. 'Relatively recently.' Again, the phantom forms of firefighters shuffled around inside. 'Course, that doesn't mean it didn't happen a few days ago.'

'It didn't,' Heck said, recognising this as the cement-floored exit passage where he and Kayla had briefly been trapped. 'I was in there earlier. It was closed and locked. You're sure none of your lads broke this open?'

'They're the ones who reported it.'

'What would it take to do this?'

'Tools, I'd say. Someone's gone at these hinges with a hammer and chisel.'

'He had a hammer and chisel,' Heck confirmed, remembering the Incinerator's utility belt.

It seemed as if the target had escaped after all.

As Heck had pictured in his mind's eye, the armour-clad maniac had simply walked back down through the blazing structure, trekking right across the white-hot heart of the giant furnace he had created, and calmly hacked his way out into the open air.

It defied belief. It defied belief even more that Heck had ever considered Kayla Green a viable candidate for this role. As he pondered his error, he scoured the edges of the loading yard. The guy's vehicle was out of bounds, which meant that he was now on foot. Not only that, he was still kitted out in his flameproof armour; he surely wouldn't have wasted time hanging around here in order to strip it all off and bag it, so as he tried to flee the scene he'd have made a very clumsy and conspicuous figure. As Heck told himself this, his eyes fell on a lone set of tracks ploughing off through a mass of dripping bracken. He stooped down to it, immediately noting freshly snapped stalks and, underneath these, new green shoots that had been squashed into the mud.

Some cumbersome person had passed this way very recently.

'There's a Detective Inspector Hayes en route here,' he told the station officer as he straightened up again. 'Other coppers too. But DI Hayes is the one I'd like you to liaise with. Can you direct her to that Peugeot? Tell her it's Priority One.'

The station officer looked surprised. 'You not stopping?'

'There's something I need to do.' Heck set off along the trampled pathway. 'But I'll be back ASAP.'

It was all very well Gemma saying he needed to stand guard on the felon's car, but this trail was fresh. A tracker dog would be perfect in this situ, but Heck didn't have one, and if he hung around and waited for one, the heavy rain would progressively weaken the spoor.

As he followed it, the trail wound through the bracken and joined a lower yard, probably an overspill car park, where he naturally lost sight of it, though from here he could see clear across the concrete and down an access ramp, which had long ago been fenced off at its lower end; this fence was a flimsy barricade made of ancient planking with a few coils of barbed wire along the top, and, by the looks of it, someone had kicked a man-sized hole in the middle.

Heck quickly descended the ramp and stooped through the hole.

On the other side, he found himself on a narrow road – if memory served, it was Norcliffe Avenue; beyond that lay a patch of wasteland covered in thorns and other deep scrub. From here, the fugitive could easily have been picked up by an accomplice in another vehicle. Just because Heck had suspected for some time that the Incinerator was a lone-wolf attacker, that didn't necessarily mean that he didn't have back-up. If that was the case, he was now long gone. Even if it wasn't, he could have run from here in almost any direction. And if that wasn't bad enough, the steadily intensifying rainstorm was again reducing visibility to the minimum. In the last half-hour, the sky had changed from slate-grey to purple and finally to the near-darkness of late evening. Shafts of sodium-yellow streetlighting only half-pierced the downpour, which got even worse the further out into the open he blundered.

Heck swore aloud. He was now completely saturated, hair plastered to his skull, clothing wet through to the skin. He stumbled across Norcliffe and onto the wasteland, blindly trusting that if the Incinerator was still on foot, he could not have got far – especially as at some point soon he would have had to stop in order to remove his armour. This patch of disused ground, with its straggling foliage standing in some cases almost to shoulder-height, would not have been a bad place for that. And in fact, no sooner had Heck begun looking around than he noticed a thread of stringy, blackish material snagged on a twisting clump of thorns.

When he rolled it between his fingers, the black – which was char – smeared his fingertips. The fabric beneath possessed a curious texture and was silvery in colour.

Almost immediately, he then spotted something else: a ground-level light glinting through the rain, some distance away but almost directly ahead of him. He knew what that was – the minicab office on the corner of Riverside Way. He hurried across the wasteland towards it, plunging knee-deep through more sodden vegetation. The rain still came down murderously, the wind whipping the greenery around his legs, so that he couldn't easily tell if a fresh trail had been kicked through it, but the flamethrowing bastard *had* to have made a beeline for that minicab place. He hadn't been picked up, so he needed wheels and he needed them quickly, and where else was he going to get some?

405

As Heck slogged on, the phone jarred to life in his pocket. He pulled it out and answered.

'Heck?' It was a short, sharp bark, recognisable immediately as the voice of DI Katie Hayes.

'Ma'am?' he shouted.

'You're supposed to be meeting me at the Lyceum. What are you doing now?'

'Pursuing a suspect across the open land to the northeast.'

Her tone changed. 'You got eyes on him?'

'Not quite. I'm tracking him.'

'You're tracking . . . who are you, Davy bloody Crockett?'

'Ma'am, the longer I chat to you, the further away he gets.'

'Give me your exact location and I'll catch up with you.'

'Negative, ma'am, if you don't mind. Someone's got to take charge of that Peugeot. It's the Incinerator's car.'

'Yeah, that's something you were supposed to have done!' she snapped back.

'Ma'am, I *had* to do this while there was still a chance. Take care of the car for me, will you – please? It's vital.'

She hesitated before replying: 'All right . . . *I've* got the car. But as soon as some support staff arrive here, I'm coming to find you, OK? That means you stay in bloody touch, Heck! Don't you dare ignore my calls again! I know that's what you were doing earlier.'

'Look, it's been a busy day –'

'Don't give me any bullshit either.' And she cut the call.

Past the wasteland, Heck took a footbridge over the River Pennington. The Pennington was now a boiling flood, surging along just a few feet beneath him, but he made it to the far bank without trouble, and there joined Riverside Way, on the other side of which stood a clutch of indistinguishable buildings. The minicab office sat in the middle of them, the light he'd seen penetrating dimly through its fogged-up glass door.

Bells jangled as Heck barged unceremoniously inside. Here, there was a small waiting area, comprising a damp, stained carpet and a bare wooden bench. On one side of the room stood a counter with a sheet of security glass on top, behind which an elderly, bespectacled woman sat next to a battered radio console.

'I'm sorry, darling,' she immediately said, her voice crunchy through a static-ridden intercom in the middle of the screen. 'We've no more cars for the foreseeable. They're all out, and a couple have even got stuck. There's flooding in some parts of town.'

'Someone's just been in here, haven't they?' Heck said, breathless.

'That's right,' she replied patiently. 'He took the last car available. The driver was Tim. But Tim's knocking off after this fare. So like I say, there's nothing I can do to help you.'

Heck approached the counter. 'I need to know what this last passenger was like?'

She eyed him warily, for the first time seeming to notice his dirty, bedraggled state. 'I'm not obliged to give information like that out. I'm sorry.'

Heck pressed his warrant card against the glass. 'Detective Sergeant Heckenburg. If you want Tim to be safe, you'd better tell me everything you know right now.'

The woman looked more than a little perturbed. 'What is this, please?'

'We don't have time for Q&As, love. You need to answer my questions.'

She worked her lips together, still uncertain. 'He was a foreigner – I could tell that much.'

'Foreigner how?'

'He had an accent.'

'What kind of accent?'

'I don't know . . . Eastern European maybe.'

'Eastern European?' Heck's scalp began to prickle. 'Russian perhaps?'

'Could be.'

'What did he look like?'

'Nothing special about his face . . . apart from it was red. From rushing to get out of the rain, I presumed. Normal height and shape, but short, bristly hair. Like a buzz-cut. He was wearing light clothes. I remember thinking that was a bit weird in this weather. He was soaked, of course.'

'What do you mean, "light clothes"?'

'Lightweight running top,' she said. 'Joggers, that sort of thing. No coat or anorak.'

Heck was bewildered. Surely the maniac hadn't ditched his whole kit. 'Was he carrying anything?'

She nodded. 'A big, grey-coloured sports bag. Looked really heavy, like it was full of stuff. Clanked too . . . you know, as if there were tools in it.'

Heck's thoughts raced as he tried to fit what few facts he possessed together. 'Tattoos by any chance?'

Another nod. 'Lots. Like I say, he was wearing light clothing. I mean, he had this running top on, but it was sleeveless.' Now seeming to have decided that she could trust Heck, she was starting to prove garrulous. 'He wasn't just wet from the rain either; he was all sweaty. I suppose, he could've been out running . . .'

'What about the tattoos?' Heck persisted.

'They were all down his arms and around his neck.'

'Would you remember any of them?'

'That'd be easy,' she said. 'They were spider webs. That's all they were. All over him.'

Heck gazed at her through the smeary glass. He'd been expecting this revelation for the last few seconds. But even so, it sent another chill through him.

'You're sure spider webs?' he finally said. 'There's no doubt in your mind?'

'I know spider webs when I see them, love. And like I say, he was covered. I mean, one time I wouldn't have given him a car, looking like that, but these days you see all sorts, don't you?'

'Where was Tim taking him to?'

'He just said to take him up the Old Town. Said he'd give him the exact directions when they got there. Listen . . .' She looked concerned again, probably because she could see the anxiety in Heck's face. 'You said Tim might be in danger? I hope not, because he's a lovely young fella and he's got a young family too . . .'

She left the point hanging, seeking reassurance. But Heck could provide none.

How did you tell someone face to face that there was no possible way their friend was going to make it? The Incinerator was Grigori Kalylyn, aka Nayka. The sort of brutal enforcer whom even the underworld walked in fear of; a certified crazy; a homicidal maniac who knew no limits, in fact who, as a *brodyaga*, would be expressly permitted by his paymasters, if not encouraged, to push the boundaries of violence to achieve his ends. That enough was reason to write Tim off. But there were other more valid reasons too: Tim would now know where Nayka was headed for. Tim would be able to identify Nayka. This latter applied to the woman behind the counter too; in fact, it was a miracle she was still alive, though in all probability the reinforced glass was responsible for that. Nayka had known the cops would be close behind. Taking time to silence this particular witness would have been a luxury he probably couldn't afford, though of course if he managed to elude his pursuers tonight, she might still be dead by this time tomorrow.

'Excuse me . . . Sergeant?' She interrupted Heck's thoughts. 'You said Tim might be in danger. Shall I call him on the radio, and tell him to come back?'

Heck still couldn't answer. He could picture the Russian assassin seated silently behind the innocent taxi driver, his terrible weapon and bundle of protective clothing all wrapped up in his sports bag; essential tools of his game, but a damning indictment if found in his possession.

No . . . there was no chance that poor Tim would live through this.

And no way for him to wriggle out of it, even if he was given a heads-up. Nayka would take no chances. Any curious behaviour from his driver, such as an unexpected change of direction, and that was the end of him.

'Does Tim have an earpiece?' Heck said. 'So you can speak to him privately? Or will the whole cab hear it?'

'The passengers hear our transmissions,' the woman said, increasingly looking and sounding alarmed. 'But what could we ever have done about that? We've never had this problem . . .'

It was the ultimate dilemma.

'Give me the registration of Tim's car,' Heck said. 'And its description.'

The woman did, and he moved across the office before phoning Bradburn Comms and passing the info on, at the same time supplying Nayka's name and description as a suspect in the Incinerator murders.

'I want you to call Tim,' he then said, turning back to the frightened woman. 'Just ask him how he's coping with the weather, where he's up to. We need to know where he is at this moment. But make it sound chatty, casual . . . you understand?'

She nodded, twisting the microphone up to her mouth.

'*Casual*, yeah!' Heck reminded her, one palm flat on the glass.

She nodded again, licked her lips, and hit the transmission button, enquiring about Tim's location and his ETA. The response that came back was broken because of a weak signal, but it sounded chirpy enough.

'*Yeah, Glad . . . I'm on Maldon Hill. Slow going in this bloody rain. I've never seen anything like it, over.*'

'You're having no other problems though?' she asked.

'*No,*' the driver replied. '*We're on high ground here, so no real trouble.*'

'All right, take care,' the woman said. 'Keep me updated, over.'

'*Wilco.*'

She glanced hopefully at Heck. 'Everything sounds like it's all right . . .'

'Everything's all right because Tim's passenger needs to get somewhere. That's the only reason Tim is still alive.'

'Oh, my God . . . look, I feel awful not warning him, not giving him some kind of –'

'You warn him and it's his death warrant. You understand?' Heck met her gaze through the grubby glass with his best interrogation-room stare. 'What's your name?'

'Gladys White.' Her mouth trembled, the top lip moist with perspiration.

'Listen to me, Gladys . . . you warn Tim, you warn the killer too.'

'The *killer*?'

'Yeah. Sorry, but I'm not going to sugar-coat this for you.'

'We can't just do nothing.'

'I don't intend to do nothing. But I need to borrow a car.'

'What?' Despite everything else, she looked stumped.

'I know the Old Town, and I know the quickest way to Maldon Hill,' Heck said. 'But to get there fast I need a set of wheels.'

411

'But how did you get *here*?'

'I ran, chasing miladdo.'

She still looked uncertain. To Heck's mind it was astonishing that she could dither over something like this – as if the whole thing might be an elaborate charade to enable him to pinch a taxi. Heck flipped open his wallet to show her his authority again.

'And if you still don't believe me –' he dug a scrap of paper from his pocket '– you got a pen?' She passed one under the safety glass and he scribbled down a number. 'I'm entrusting you with a lot giving you this, Gladys – it's the personal number of Detective Superintendent Gemma Piper of the Serial Crimes Unit. Ring this number and ask her about me. She'll confirm everything I've told you. But if you value Tim's life, you'll need to do it fast.'

He thrust the notepaper under the glass, but Gladys clearly decided that she'd seen enough. Without bothering to call anyone, she rummaged in a drawer and produced a key with a green plastic tag, which she slid through to him.

'It's a turquoise Honda Civic,' she said. 'Parked in the yard at the back. You can get round to it down a passage at the side.'

'Thanks,' he said. 'Call that number anyway, please. Tell Superintendent Piper what I've told you, and make sure you give her the last location of Tim's car, OK?'

'Yes, of course. But listen – if you get stuck in one of these flooded areas, I can't help you.'

Heck clattered back outside. 'If I get stuck, no one can help us.'

Chapter 40

Heck staggered round to the rear of the minicab office. Only one vehicle, the Honda he'd been told about, was waiting there. He leaped in behind the wheel, and it grumbled to life. Rain pounded on the roof as he slid out onto the main road. Despite the conditions, he made reasonable time. Foot to the floor, with full-beam headlights forging through the downpour, he reached the foot of Wardley Rise, which led up into the Old Town, within a few minutes. Already, though, it was increasingly difficult to imagine that whatever was going to happen to Tim the taxi driver when he reached his destination would not by now have happened, which prompted a new train of thought.

Nayka . . . the Incinerator.

For some reason it hadn't sent Heck reeling with surprise.

The Russian mafia were no one's friend. The idea that they'd come over here to make an alliance among equals with Vic Ship and his Manchester mob was in some ways laughable, but a ruse along those lines was more than plausible. If the Russians wanted a controlling influence in this region, it would have paid them to be clever. They were looking for new territory, but it would have made no sense to get involved in a full-blown shooting war with the Brits. So why not send a single operative over here, a commando, someone whose arrival they could pay for through the promise of cut-price, bulk-load fentanyl, but someone whose real purpose was to sow discord among the native factions? If Britain's home-grown gangsters destroyed each other in a civil war, that would make it a lot easier for the Tatarstan Brigade to move in afterwards.

'Is that what you were really tasked with, Nayka?' Heck wondered aloud.

It wasn't an especially ingenious plan, but it hadn't needed to be. Britain's organised criminals were way too cosy with their easy earnings from the dope business, and far too greedy for more to take an especially hard look at anyone guaranteeing them an even bigger slice of the toxic cake.

Except possibly for Vic Ship.

He'd retaliated once against his unknown enemy, almost spontaneously, recruiting a freelancer, John Sagan, to torture and kill Calum Price and Dean Lumley – most likely to get information out of them. But after that he'd held off. Did he suddenly smell a rat?

Heck progressed onto the gentle rise that was Maldon Hill. The going got slower, his wheels spinning in the surface water without gaining real purchase. The terraced houses to either side were little more than ghostly outlines in the gloom.

It would have cost Vic Ship nothing to strike back at a piece of trash like Lee Shaughnessy. The underworld would have expected it, maybe demanded it. But of course when all this started he was being watched by the same Manchester police team who'd taken apart the Wild Bunch. That was another reason for him to have brought in a mercenary to do his dirty work. But then, if he'd eventually developed some doubts about Shaughnessy's involvement, he might even have put his gun-for-hire on hold . . .

Before Heck could speculate further, his headlights fell on a blockage ahead.

A beige Toyota Yaris was sitting askew across the road, as if it had skidded to an abrupt and crazy halt. Heck jammed his own brakes on and slewed forward about fifteen yards before stopping and climbing out. The woman called Gladys had told him that Tim was driving a Toyota Yaris. This was clearly it, because there was a minicab licence disc in its back window.

Heck hastened towards it on foot, tottering around to the car's offside. There was no sign of Nayka; clearly the bird had flown – but the front door, the driver's door, hung open, and a bearded body was draped out of it headfirst.

'Shit!' Heck sank to his knees.

Even as an experienced officer, he was not qualified to pronounce death, but it was pretty obvious in this case. Tim – for that was surely who it was – sported a cut across his exposed throat, which extended from ear to ear and had sliced clean through his windpipe. The front of his quilted anorak and the floor around him would have been patterned scarlet by the arterial spray, had the rain not washed it away.

Heck checked the carotid artery. As he'd expected, it was a lost cause.

'Fuck,' he said under his breath, standing up and dragging Kemp's phone from his pocket. But before he could place a call, it rang.

'Heck!' It was DI Hayes again. 'Whereabouts are you?'

'Maldon Hill – at a brand-new murder scene, I'm afraid.' He bent and glanced inside the Toyota. 'It's a minicab driver –' he consulted the licence under the windscreen '– name of Timothy Mulholland.' He again had to shout to be heard above the deluge. 'Cause of death looks like a fatal laceration to the throat.'

Hayes sounded astonished. 'Is – is this connected to –'

415

'Yeah, yeah, I'm sure it's our Russian friend Nayka. Also known as Grigori Kalylyn.' He passed on the details as best he was able, rounding off with a request that some kind of armed protective detail be attached to Gladys White, who worked at the minicab office on Riverside Way.

'Just in case we don't get the bastard tonight,' he said. 'She's seen him face to face, so –'

'Fine, I'll sort that!' Hayes said, interrupting. 'Listen, Heck, we're getting up there as soon as we can. I'll come myself. But full support's going to be delayed. The Pennington's burst its banks in some places, and a couple of bridges are out. Traffic's bottled up in the town centre, and parts of the suburbs are under water. On top of that, we've still got half the team on the stakeout at Hunger Hill. The main thing is . . . Heck, are you listening to me?'

'I'm listening,' he grunted.

'We've started searching the Peugeot at the cinema. There's an awful lot of stuff in there that's relevant to the Incinerator's mission.'

'Good.'

'Such as several spare cans of petrol. A pile of tools, a thick steel bar that's been improvised into a Halligan by having an adze and pickaxe welded to one end of it . . .'

'Excellent,' he said. 'That means we've got him for the Blaymire Close murders.'

'Also a heavy triangular plate with chain attachments. Some kind of homemade wheel-clamp.'

'A clamp!' Finally, Heck understood why Shelley Harper had abandoned her car the night she died.

'Heck, there's something else. Are you listening to me?'

'Yeah, course I am.' He wondered why she suddenly sounded tense, even nervous.

'There's also –' Hayes hesitated. 'There's also a number

of diagrams and street-maps of Bradburn's Old Town. Plenty of Russian handwriting on those, as if he'd been working to identify certain locations and such.'

'Yeah, and . . .?'

'And photographs. They look like surveillance shots.'

'Anywhere in particular?'

'Try 23 Cranby Street.'

He stiffened. 'That's my sister's address.'

'And that's where you're lodging at the present time, isn't it? Looks like you're on Nayka's radar yourself.'

'Obviously,' Heck said. 'Why else was he waiting for me at the cinema?'

But her tone remained terse. 'There's something else too – among these photos, I mean. It's St Nathaniel's Church . . . and the presbytery. There are even shots of your uncle. I believe he's the parish priest there, yes?'

'What are you talking about?'

'Heck . . . these are surveillance shots too. And there's not just a few of them. We've got your uncle talking outside the church to parishioners, going in and out of his front door. You know what I'm saying?'

Heck stood ramrod straight. 'My uncle's just a harmless old guy!' But he was thinking aloud rather than responding to her. He certainly wasn't seeking an explanation for this, because suddenly it was all too clear. 'Christ almighty, that sodding bastard . . . in case he couldn't get me, he had a secondary target lined up.'

'*Heck, listen!*' Hayes tried to sound stern and authoritative. 'This is a direct order from Superintendent Piper – you are *not* to go up there alone. You are to wait for support, which is already en route. Do you understand?'

'The hell with –' Heat surged down Heck's back.

'I repeat, Heck – support is en route. It won't get there immediately. Like I said, we've got roads blocked and bridges down. But you are to wait for additional units to arrive. Now that's a direct order.'

But when Heck spoke to DI Hayes again, he'd already jumped back into the turquoise Honda. 'No disrespect to you, ma'am, or to DSU Piper . . . *but the sodding bloody hell with that!*'

Chapter 41

'How are you feeling, Kempy, mate?' Vic Ship asked through wreaths of cigar smoke.

He was on the private balcony in his nightclub in Castlefield. As with all such establishments these days, a no-smoking policy was strictly enforced in the club's public access areas, but Ship's balcony was also his ornate and spacious private office, and sealed off by a wall of reinforced glass which, brightly reflective on its exterior, also served as a one-way mirror, enabling him to chug on his King Edward without anyone even knowing. The glass was so thick that it was also soundproof, so though on the other side of it stroboscopic lights dazzled the throng of revellers below, and dance tunes boomed at multi-decibels, it was quiet enough in here for the boss to have heard his mobile chiming in his pocket.

'Ahhh . . . poor old Kempy,' came a heavy, urgent voice. 'And *stupid* old Kempy too. Forgot to report he'd had his phone nicked, did he, Vic?'

Ship frowned and jammed his cigar between his teeth while re-checking the number on the phone's panel. There was there no question about it; he was being called from the mobile belonging to his associate Tony Kemp, who currently was hospitalised.

'Or is it just that he's too knackered to even have thought about that?' the voice wondered.

'Who the fuck is this?' Ship asked, his voice so taut that his two minders looked curiously around from the bar in the corner.

'Who do you think?' the voice wondered.

'I think you've got the wrong number, pal. I don't know any Vic –'

'I've not got the time for stupid games, Vic. Nor the patience. If you don't know who this is, you're not as clued in as I thought. It's DS Heckenburg, Serial Crimes Unit. You can't have forgotten already. Kempy's probably still wrapped up like an Egyptian mummy thanks to me.'

The heavies got to their feet, but Ship signalled them to stay put. He stubbed his cigar in an ashtray. 'You've got some face, pal, I'll give you that.'

'Well . . . you're right to call me "pal",' Heck said. 'I did you a big favour the other night and I'm doing you another one now.'

'Sounds to me more like you're running for your life,' Ship chuckled. 'Can hear an engine revving away back there. Pissed someone else off, have you?'

'It's the other way round, mate. Remember the Incinerator? The one-man army who's been making a total monkey out of you in the land where once you were king? I'm not very far behind him. But I'm on my tod . . . and likely to be that way for a little while just yet. Bad weather stopping traffic and all that. You wouldn't by any chance have any firm in the area who can assist, would you?'

Ship's expression tightened, but again he signalled his colleagues to keep their traps shut. 'You wasted your time before,' he sneered. 'You're wasting it now. I have no clue what you're talking about.'

'I'll make it easy. I'm talking about Nayka.'

This time Ship said nothing. His right fist slowly clenched into a rock of flesh and blood.

'Yeah, I know,' Heck said. 'Just like you suspected, eh? But when you think about it, it's the obvious answer. It was never going to be Lee Shaughnessy, was it? I mean, the Britannia Boys are pretty good at dealing dope to the desperate, I'd imagine, and battering the occasional everyday punter who happens to be in the wrong place at the wrong time. But when it comes to something complex, something that requires planning, I doubt there's one of them could tell you his arse from his elbow. What do you reckon, Vic?'

Ship's nostrils quivered. His cheeks had flushed a livid blood-capillary red.

'It's Nayka, my old pal,' the taunting voice added. 'But you've really got no one to blame but yourself. I mean, you've been bulk-ordering China White, haven't you? Well, that's a bit naughty, but it's not my case at present. The main thing is, it gave the Tatarstan Brigade an entry point to the drugs market here in the Northwest of England, didn't it? I don't know the exact terms of the deal you made with them, but I reckon it went something like this: you get lots of discount deliveries in return for showing a few of their lads the UK ropes . . . perhaps with the promise of some kind of power-sharing arrangement in the near future. Is that right? Trouble is, Vic, the Tatarstan Brigade don't share. Ask the crew who used to run St Petersburg . . . if there're any who aren't at the bottom of the River Neva. Anyway, that's it for now . . . oh, except where you can find this lad who's been giving you so much trouble. Try St Nathaniel's Church, Bradburn. There, or somewhere in the vicinity. But you'd better be quick if you want a piece of him, Vic. Because I can't guarantee I'll be leaving much.'

*

Heck shoved the phone back into his jeans pocket as his borrowed motor slid to a halt on the lower road alongside St Nathaniel's. He leaped out and scrambled up towards the church via the steep slope of the graveyard. The soaring height of the religious building was lost in the rainy murk, but up close a dull light was visible through its windows.

Heck knew he was heading into a trap. If *he* was removed from this equation, the only solid evidence that the Tatarstan Brigade were behind the Incinerator murders was poor old Gladys White, who wouldn't be much of an obstacle on her own if Nayka managed to eliminate Heck first. But there was no choice in the matter. This *had* to be done.

Again, the phone buzzed angrily in his pocket. In the brief time he'd been chatting to Ship, it had registered two missed calls. Heck knew they'd be from Gemma, so he ignored them, letting them shift to Kemp's voicemail.

The church's main door loomed in front of him. He threw himself at it and grappled with the ring-handle. Ordinarily he'd have gone first for the presbytery, but he'd distinctly seen lights inside the church. He twisted the handle – but no access was possible.

The doors wouldn't budge.

Heck flung his shoulder against the wood. It shuddered, but there was no give. Then he heard what sounded like a prolonged, wailing groan – abruptly curtailed.

He backed away, ears straining – and thought he heard a muted sob.

Heck slammed his ear to the wood.

It came from inside.

Along with a jabber of harsh, hyena-like laughter.

He dashed away, careering around the corner of the church. There was a rear door just off a passage running between the presbytery garage and the sacristy. The presbytery itself came into view in front of him. There were no lights inside;

it was dark, gloomy, its windows dead. Mrs O'Malley would long have gone home, of course. Father Pat would have been here alone.

However, before Heck reached the sacristy passage, he saw something that brought him to a sliding standstill. The church car park was on slightly lower ground, and at present there were only two vehicles there. His uncle's blue Volvo and a van of some sort.

A rather dingy van, with distinctive green-and-white livery.

Heck trod over there, incredulous, trying to see more clearly, checking that he wasn't mistaken. It was the same van that had been parked outside the Empress Britannia earlier that afternoon. Before he could work out what this meant, a nub of cold steel pressed into the back of his head.

'Hands where I can see 'em,' came a voice with a thick Manchester brogue.

Initially Heck froze, but then did as instructed.

His captor frisked him, taking the phone, switching it off and stowing it in his own pocket, but finding no weapons, circling around to the front. He wore a black waterproof over his bulky frame, and orange woollen gloves. The face under the hood belonged to Marvin Langton, his eyes like points of metal, his white-toothed grin a glinting crescent in his ebony face, that single gold denture gleaming in the middle of it.

At first Heck didn't know what to say. He'd been expecting to find Nayka here, not one of Lee Shaughnessy's firm. What this now signified he couldn't immediately fathom. Had the Incinerator not arrived yet because he was on foot, which might give him the opportunity to flee unnoticed? Or was he already here and biding his time, determined to see things through?

Which was the worst of those possibilities?

Langton meanwhile grinned all the more, pointing his gun

directly between Heck's eyes. It was a Beretta 92, a highly efficient and easy-to-use weapon, especially in close combat.

'So, you finally shook your tail?' Heck said.

'Not so easy to keep tabs on me in this weather,' Langton replied. 'Park up and turn their wipers off, they can't see through the windscreen . . . leave 'em on, I can spot the surveillance car from way off. No biggie to sneak away on foot. Anyway, move your arse . . . that way.' He pointed his free hand along the church wall. 'There's another door round the back.'

'Funnily enough, that's where I was going.'

'Excellent. You'll only be a little bit late.'

Heck trudged along the path. By the heavy thud of his boots, Langton was close behind. Heck could sense the Beretta trained on the back of his neck. He glanced left, looking towards the nearest houses, but in the torrential rain there was no sign even of those, let alone any cavalry units charging to the rescue.

There was no sign of Nayka either.

Heck wondered where exactly the Russian had secreted himself, and what his plan was.

'Don't know what you're thinking, Heckenburg,' Langton said. 'But I advise you not to try it. I'm not one of these Bradburn scallies. I've seen it all.'

Chapter 42

Gemma climbed in behind the steering wheel of her command car, flinging back her drenched hood as she visibly seethed with frustration.

'I've tried higher ground, I've tried further down the road . . . I can't get through.' She tossed her mobile onto the dashboard. 'You'd have thought that on an exposed hillside like this I'd have no problem getting a signal.'

Ron Gibbshaw was slumped in the front passenger seat. 'Don't worry, ma'am, you'll be getting a signal. Heck's probably turned his phone off – pulling his usual stunt of going it alone.'

Gemma sat tensely, staring through her window. Technically speaking, her lying-up point, tucked away in a semi-flooded layby some thirty yards up Hunger Hill Road from the main entrance to the French & Sons Auto Traders vehicle compound, was an ideal position from which to watch the comings and goings. But she was now torn with indecision about staying put. It was unclear how much support she personally could give Heck, while if she went back into town now to try and assist him, it would mean leaving Gibbshaw in charge here, which didn't feel like a great idea either.

Everything seemed to have gone askew; suddenly there were no easy options.

There was no telling when things would start happening here. She might vacate her post just as it was about to kick off. She'd instructed Katie Hayes and her team down at the cinema to provide Heck with all the necessary back-up. They ought to be able to manage that; they were much closer than she was. She'd even authorised those AFOs among them to draw firearms – though of course that procedure would take time, so most likely Hayes and a few select individuals would be heading up there unarmed.

'Mustn't be too hard on him though,' Gibbshaw said, sipping coffee, his bearded features saturnine in the blueish glow of the dashboard light. 'He's doing his job after all. Pursuing a murder suspect.'

'Yes, but he's alone,' she replied, aggravated that Heck's fate clearly wasn't a great concern for the Organised Crime Division man, whose main priority was still the apprehension of John Sagan. 'And this Nayka's killed at least seven people that we know about.'

Gibbshaw sniffed. 'If this guy's ready and waiting with his fireproof suit on, and his helmet, and he's got his flamethrower fully fuelled, I'd say that even Heck isn't stupid enough to tackle him head-on. But I'm not completely convinced by that. Especially if this priest fella's already been hurt. Funny thing . . . I heard a whisper among the team that Heck doesn't have any family left in Bradburn. At least, none that he cares about.'

Gemma gazed through the streaming windscreen. 'I suppose now he's learning differently.'

*

Heck plodded into the passage between the garage and the church. Scaffolding reared above, planks forming flimsy

426

walkways overhead, plunging them into shadow, though firelight now shone from the open door to the sacristy. Langton shepherded him into this, pistol muzzle jammed into his spine.

The sacristy, which was little more than a stone ante-room to the church itself – a preparation chamber for the Mass – stood in half-darkness. On the other side of it, an interior door connected to the north side of the altar. This too was open, firelight flickering beyond. The usual combined odours proliferated: incense, candle-wax and polish, along with new additions thanks to the building work – creosote, damp plaster, dust. But now an agonising groaning was audible too, as well as more coarse, drunken laughter. Heck almost ran forward, but Langton snatched him by the back of his collar and frogmarched him through the internal door.

The interior of the Roman Catholic Church of St Nathaniel's had always possessed a tranquil beauty, its altar and alcoves ablaze with candles, the carved ends of its pews garlanded with flowers in spring and with holly at Christmas, its statues of saints and angels peering serenely down from their plinths, its many pillars soaring up to a vaulted roof now painted eggshell blue and scattered with gold and silver stars, to create Father Pat's image of Heaven on Earth.

Now unfortunately, it was exactly the opposite.

Because of the refurbishments, a mass of scaffolding clad the north wall and the rear of the altar, and there were dust sheets over several pews. Behind the baptismal font in the northwest corner stood a clutter of brushes, rollers, tins and bottles.

But all this was normality; all this was perfectly acceptable.

Less so were those statues thrown down and smashed, including the Virgin Mary and Christ as the Sacred Heart. Less so was Lee Shaughnessy and his crew, about twelve of them in total, now dotted across the nave with tins of beer in hand. One had a spray-can and was busy decking each Station of the Cross with a grinning demonic face; two others were lighting joints from the candles in a side-chapel. Shaughnessy himself slouched in the front pew, drinking from a cheap bottle of wine – the Communion wine no doubt – and between gulps filching sacred hosts, several at a time, from a chalice on his knee, cramming them into his mouth like crisps.

More shocking still, Father Pat was also present.

Heck didn't spot his uncle straight away, because they entered the church to the right of the altar, and his attention was only drawn belatedly to the rear of this by a series of ape-like sniggers. The first thing he saw when he glanced back there was the weirdo who liked staring at people, Eyeball. He sat cross-legged on one of the altar servers' stools, like a demented gargoyle. Again, bizarrely, he was bare-chested, having stripped to the waist. In his right hand he held a broken beer bottle, and in his left something Heck couldn't quite identify – mainly because he was distracted by the sight of his uncle, who was also stripped to the waist, and now stretched upright against one of the legs of the scaffolding, his hands lashed to the crossbar above his head with rope.

Father Pat had been cut repeatedly, bloody lacerations zigzagging across his pale, bony torso. He was grey in the face, his eyelids closed.

'*YOU FUCKING MANIACS!*' Heck bellowed, his voice thundering down the nave.

Surprised, several of the gang immediately drew pistols and cocked them. Langton jammed his Beretta into the side of Heck's head and wrapped a brawny arm around his chest.

Shaughnessy meanwhile looked delighted by the intrusion.

'Well, well, well,' he said. 'If our party isn't complete. Detective Heckenburg.'

'He'd better still be alive, Shaughnessy.'

'We keep checking to find out.' Shaughnessy nodded at Eyeball, who reached out with his left hand. Heck now recognised the vinegar bottle they'd used with their fish and chips in the presbytery only two days ago. Brown fluid splashed over the gaping wounds. Father Pat twisted in agony, eyelids fluttering.

Heck lurched forward, but again was hauled back. Langton forced him across the front aisle, and shoved him up against the pews.

'Shaughnessy, you're off your bleeding rocker!' Heck spat. 'Who do you think you are – the Mexican mafia? You're not just gonna walk away from something like this.'

'Oh?' Shaughnessy sidled out of the pew and strolled down the aisle, still drinking wine and eating bread as if he was on a picnic. 'And who's gonna stop us?'

Heck was about to blurt out that there were more cops on the way, but he resisted – why give them a heads-up? As far as Shaughnessy knew, Heck was here on a family visit. The hoodlum would probably be in no rush to do whatever he was planning – and that might just save them.

But it wouldn't be easy.

Heck gazed at his uncle, agonised by the old man's pain. The priest hung there like a tortured martyr, his wounded flesh pale as ash, his dark trousers slick with blood. Frantic thoughts raced through Heck's head: exsanguination, shock, infection . . . the ridiculous notion that any of these would matter, because neither he nor the priest was likely to be spared. In which case he had no option but to try and keep the bastards talking, and buy themselves as much time as possible.

'Some crimes are too unforgivable, mate,' he told his tormentor, who now stood directly in front of him.

Shaughnessy smirked as he placed the chalice and bottle

down on the altar rail's marble top. 'And so what happens next? Righteous fire comes down from Heaven?'

'You never know.'

'But I do know.' Shaughnessy drew on a pair of heavy duty gloves; thick leather, with extra padding on the knuckles. 'There *will* be payback here tonight . . . but strictly of the mundane variety.'

Heck said nothing.

Shaughnessy flexed his hands inside the gloves. The padded leather creaked.

'We were just discussing that, as a matter of fact,' he said. 'Your uncle and me. I suddenly had this overwhelming desire to know where I could find you. Why do you think that was, detective? Something to do with this afternoon, maybe? When you –'

BANG!

The left hook that caught Heck in the face was ferocious in its power. His head rang.

'– royally overstepped the mark?'

BANG!

A right hook this time.

'You really thought I was going to be your bitch?'

BANG!

An uppercut.

Heck slumped in Langton's grasp, head hung low, blood streaming from his nose and mouth.

Shaughnessy leaned down alongside him. 'You seriously thought you were going to play your two-bit games with *me*?' He placed a finger under Heck's chin and levered his face upright. 'You're looking puzzled. Hmm . . .' He stepped back. 'I suppose you're wondering how I knew Father Pat here was your uncle. Well, guess what? It took five minutes. You see, our lads weren't always bad uns. Azzy, let's be having you, son.'

Heck's scrambled senses tumbled back into place and he managed to straighten up, just as another of Shaughnessy's creatures came ambling along the aisle. This one looked older than the others. He was tall but overweight, with long ratty hair, a grizzled chin and sunken eyes. He wore a dirty old Wrangler jacket over a stained white T-shirt, and leaned a sawn-off pump shotgun over one shoulder.

'Azzy here used to be an altar boy,' Shaughnessy said. 'Doesn't look the part now, does he? People change though. I think he'd got to a state where he'd even forgotten what the inside of a church looked like. And then that business today in the Britannia. He's watching from the corner, you see . . . watches you come in, hears your name . . . gets some idea there was once a priest here in the Old Town who had a nephew called Heckenburg. A young rugby player, bit of a schoolboy superstar. Well . . . wasn't hard after that. We went through the phonebook. Rang around the local churches. Not many left, are there? You Catholics are a dying breed, I'm sorry to say. Each time we asked if we could speak to Detective Heckenburg. No dice the first couple. No one knew what we were talking about. But then, when we rang St Nat's presbytery, we got this mouthy Irish cow, who seemed irritated we'd rung. Think she thought we were coppers too. Anyway, she says she doesn't know where you are but that your uncle's around somewhere and she'll ask him. We say, "Nah, it doesn't matter. We'll catch you later." And look . . .'

BANG!

Another monstrous right hook. Heck was knocked dizzy again.

'. . . we *have* done.'

BANG!

A stinger to the nose. Heck felt the cartilage crack, but somehow kept his feet.

'Where's the fucking Makarov?' Shaughnessy asked. He

reached under his own jacket, and pulled out a different pistol, a Ruger semi-automatic, its grip encrusted with gold, jewellery and other ridiculous bling. 'I mean, as you can see, I've got my own piece, my own pride and joy . . . but I have a vested interest in the other one too.'

Heck spat more blood. 'Somewhere you'll never find it. Somewhere no one'll find it.'

'Oh, dear . . . that's no good.' Shaughnessy tucked his gun out of sight, turned and walked away. 'Have your share, Benny. You're owed it.'

Yet another of his crew stepped forward. Heck spotted the bruised and swollen face of Stardust, who grinned dementedly as he swept in with several vicious punches of his own: body, head, body again. Fleetingly Heck was nowhere; all strength and awareness hammered out of him. When the aisle's tiled floor hit the side of the head, he realised he was lying curled at their feet. Stardust and Langton stood one to either side, grinning as they kicked his face and ribs.

'You enjoying this, old man?' Shaughnessy shouted up to Father Pat. 'Apparently this pig's your nephew, yeah? Well, the sad truth is we're having to do this because you lot didn't. You know, spare the rod spoil the kid and all that.' He turned back. 'OK, that'll do.'

They hoisted Heck back to his feet. His legs half-buckled.

'I'll ask you one more time,' Shaughnessy said, drawing his gloves off. 'Where's that Makarov pistol that you so casually boasted you were going to frame me with?'

Heck shook his head feebly. The offending weapon sat in the glove compartment of his Megane, of course, which at present was out of their reach. But the moment he told them its true location, it was all over for him and his uncle.

Shaughnessy glanced at Eyeball, who swung round with his broken bottle and scored another deep gash across the priest's ribs. Father Pat rolled his head in agony, mewling aloud when more vinegar was poured onto the open wound. Eyeball imitated him, pulling weird monkey faces as he vocalised dramatic *oohs* and *aahs*.

'Sure you don't want to tell me?' Shaughnessy wondered.

Heck looked groggily up. 'I was wrong about one thing, Lee . . . you and the Britannia Boys are no bunch of tiddlers. You're as bad as they come.'

Shaughnessy nodded approvingly as he picked the chalice up and crammed more wafers into his mouth. 'Well, if recognition from an expert like you is all we get out of this, it's been worth it just for that.' He turned to Langton. 'How much blood do you reckon's left in that old coot, Marve?'

'Couple more cuts should do it,' Langton said.

Shaughnessy sighed. 'Bad news, that, detective. You see, we don't really need your uncle as much as we need you. And well, we have to start getting serious at some point . . .'

But Heck was no longer listening. His attention had been captured by the chalice in Shaughnessy's hand. A goblet of polished gold and silver, it reflected various exaggerated images: the firelight from the candles, the distorted shapes of the gang members – and now a hulking black form emerging from behind the choir screens at the very back of the altar.

'Sorry.' Shaughnessy held the chalice up, scraped out the last two Communion hosts and gulped them down. 'Will *this* send me to Hell?'

'No.' Heck glanced across the altar. 'But *he* may.'

Their heads turned.

The Incinerator stood there: char-black armour and helmet, new-filled tank strapped in place, flamethrower levelled, finger tightening on the trigger.

Chapter 43

'What now, Gary?' Gemma asked, not disguising her irritation that this latest phone-call was from one of her own observation posts rather than from Katie Hayes. She was also testy because it was an exhausting struggle working her way back around the exterior of the vehicle pound on foot; rain still hammered unceasingly down, and she was ploughing through quagmire upon quagmire.

'Ma'am, there's movement in the compound,' Quinnell said breathlessly. 'Difficult to be sure in all this crap . . . but it looks like one of the vehicles is pulling out. And it's drawing a caravan.'

Gemma stopped in her tracks, pulling her hood back despite the rain. 'Is it Sagan?'

'Dunno, do I?' He sounded frustrated. 'We haven't had a close look yet.'

Gemma had just completed a half-circuit of the vehicle pound, which was no mean feat in these conditions, given that its overall diameter was probably about a mile and a half. The purpose had been to check on her various OPs, most of whose personnel, lying out in the muddy ditches or under wet bushes, were naturally having a miserable time of it, and if possible to free some of them up so they could head back into town and join the forces converging on St Nathaniel's. She'd now decided that she was going down there. But if Sagan was on the move, that changed everything.

She started running, as much as she was able to.

'Gary . . . are you still on the west gate?' she asked.

Quinnell's post was one she had not been able to visit, as it was located on the far side of the compound. He and Sally Gorton were on a rise of tree-covered land, which didn't just overlook the whole west side of the pound but also a single-lane exit on that side, a little-used cart-track which was already deep in mud when they'd arrived here. It was only a small exit, but on earlier examination the chain on its gate was found to have been hacksawed through and the gate unfastened, which suggested this might have been the way Sagan had originally entered.

'Affirmative,' Quinnell confirmed.

'Gary – you need to intercept him right now!'

'Ma'am! It's been chucking it down for hours. I don't know how easily we'll get down there! We're parked off-road.'

'Gary, I told you to find a decent lying-up point!'

'We did, ma'am!' he protested. 'But this weather's a bugger, isn't it?'

If Gemma was honest, that was the truth. Just to get near the west gate and avoid the swampy exit lane, Quinnell and Gorton had parked on Hill View, an adjacent road further down the hill, and then had ascended the slope on foot over rough ground until they could find their OP. Hill View connected with the exit lane about eighty yards south of their current position; in normal circumstances, even during ordinary rainfall, they'd have been able to scramble back, jump into their car and move it out in time to create a

435

blockade at the junction. But the incredible intensity of the storm had dumbfounded all of them.

'What if we're stuck?' Quinnell said. 'I'm up to my ankles just walking around up here.'

'You'd better bloody not be!' Gemma staggered on, rounding the northeast corner of the vehicle pound. 'I told you all to keep an eye on that.'

'We were doing,' he said. 'But it's been coming down for bloody hours . . . *shit-bollocks!*'

'What's the matter?'

'It *is* Sagan. It's a beige Discovery. He's passing through the west gate now.'

'Gary . . . just calm down! These conditions can't be easy for him either. He's hauling a caravan, for God's sake.'

'Yeah, but he's in a four-wheel drive, isn't he! Talk about prepared for every eventuality.'

Which we quite clearly were not, Gemma thought as she stumbled on. 'Just get back to your vehicle and follow at the first opportunity!'

Gemma clambered through a ditch that was knee-deep in foul water, and found herself back on Hunger Hill Road, a hundred yards or so away from her own lying-up point. She started running again, at last gaining speed. It seemed incredible to her that, with officers covertly observing every conceivable exit and entry point, no one had noticed Sagan come back here for his vehicle. Even if he was on foot, someone should have spotted him. Unless . . . and this was a particularly ugly thought; suppose he'd been residing *inside* his caravan? They said it was a torture chamber in there, though from what they knew of this guy he'd be right at home.

But none of that mattered now. Hunger Hill Road connected a mile further down the hillside with Hill View, so that was no problem. Even though the bastard was driving a Land Rover, Gemma was determined to overhaul him before he gained any distance. And when they did that, it was possible he'd give them a fight. She wasn't sure what she felt about that, but inside her anorak the Glock was holstered snugly beneath her left armpit. She'd had all her SCU personnel draw pistols before coming up here.

There'd be no more unarmed coppers shot dead on her watch.

All she needed now was for Ron Gibbshaw to have moved her Merc onto the actual road to ensure it wasn't bogged down, as she'd ordered him to do before going for a walk, and the chase would be on. But a moment later, when she came in sight of the vehicle, it was still parked on the layby, now sunk almost to its wheel-arches in thrashing water.

Gemma raced forward and yanked open the front passenger door.

Gibbshaw jerked awake.

Clearly the ultra-long shift, the lulling drone of the rain and the luxurious warmth inside the Merc had been too much for him.

'*Christ's sake, Ron!*' she shrieked. '*What the hell are you playing at!*'

'I . . . erm . . .' He was sallow-faced, pop-eyed. 'I wasn't asleep!'

'The hell you bloody weren't! I told you twenty minutes ago to get us out onto the road. Now look where we bloody are!' She hurried around to the driver's seat and threw herself in.

The car started easily enough and crunched into gear, but when she tried to reverse it out, she found herself grinding muck and slurry. The chassis shuddered, but the Merc gained no traction.

'Ma'am, I –' Gibbshaw began sheepishly.

'Shut up, Ron!' She grabbed her radio from the dash. 'All units, this is DSU Piper . . .'

*

Eyeball was the first of Shaughnessy's hoodlums to specifically catch the Incinerator's attention. His mouth dropped open as the newcomer drove a roaring wedge of flame across the altar, completely enveloping him. The bare-topped gangbanger stood rigid, before cavorting away, a living torch.

A dozen things then happened at once.

Shaughnessy and the bulk of his crew staggered backwards, the leader leaping over the pew behind him. Dropping to one knee, he tried to take cover. He pulled his jewel-hilted Ruger, intending to pop a shot at the advancing figure – but instead he had to shield his face against the unbelievably intense heat. Inevitably, he ducked his head.

Meanwhile, Heck rounded on Langton, slammed a knee into his groin and, as he doubled over, clenched his fists together and bludgeoned the back of his neck. But Langton's ox-like frame was sturdy, his aggression instinctive. He kept his feet and clung to his pistol as Heck wrestled him for it. Their struggle took them over the altar rail and onto the altar itself, where they fell to the floor. They rolled back and forth, each with one hand clamped to the weapon.

The rest of the crew began shooting as they backed down the aisles. Sporadic cracks of gunfire and staccato muzzle-flashes filled the church. The Incinerator had to be well armoured because he came on regardless, bypassing the hanging priest, ignoring Heck and Langton too as he stepped down from the altar into the front aisle, but looking left and right as he decided which of the other, more dangerous elements to go after first.

On the altar, Heck used his left hand to try and wrest the

gun free, which meant that his stronger right hand was available to bombard Langton's head and face with punches. Langton tried to gouge Heck's eyes, even to bite his throat. Heck head-butted the bridge of Langton's nose. They scrambled back to their feet, Langton bloodied but clinging to his gun, before crashing into the solid slab of marble that was the altar table. Heck slammed Langton's gun-hand down on it several times. The pistol came loose and skittered out of sight. Langton responded by grabbing Heck's throat in his orange-gloved hands.

Some twenty yards away, the Incinerator took the north aisle first. He jetted an arc of fire at the knot of figures retreating down it, sweeping it left as some straggled across the nave through the pews. Two or three, including that big, dopy-looking character, Azzy, were engulfed; they staggered and toppled, screaming and blazing. One shucked off his burning jacket, and attempted to clamber up the scaffolding on the north wall. Two others had already scaled this. All three turned their pistols on the invader as he tromped down the aisle. The pistols discharged, those slugs that didn't hit him ricocheting from the tiled floor, whining and screaming.

With a fresh *WHOOSH* of flame, he swept his arc upward. It roared through the steel framework, embracing all three as they clung to their perches. Pistols clattered to the floor as hoarse screeches filled the smoky, stinking air.

A fusillade of additional fire now struck the Incinerator from the south side, where Stardust had managed to marshal a few more troops. They pumped shot after shot at him. He spun around, and let loose another searing torrent. It snaked across the nave, exploding through the wooden pews, falling on them like infernal rain.

Still on the altar, Langton was in the process of throttling Heck, having bent him backward over the marble table. His spade-like hands applied crushing force to Heck's windpipe.

In return, Heck went for the bastard's eyes, which were already bloodied and puffy. Langton clenched them shut and drove his head down, cracking it against Heck's jaw – once, twice. The pain was dizzying. Heck felt consciousness ebbing away. Frantic, he clawed out across the table, and found a heavy brass candlestick. He grabbed it and swung it over. There was a massive *clunk*, as it connected with Langton's skull. The grip on Heck's throat lessened. Langton slumped slightly. Heck coiled his legs and kicked him backward. Langton reeled away. Heck jumped up and landed another blow with the heavy piece of metal. This one was two-handed, a roundhouse, like he was swinging a cricket bat.

The impact was colossal, the sound like meat smacking stone.

Langton dropped to his knees, head wobbling, eyes rolling as blood spilled over his face.

The third blow was the hardest yet; it sent him nose-down to the altar floor.

In the south aisle, Stardust ran towards the back of the church. Those of his troops not already burning were so mesmerised by the demonic shape barging across the nave, passing through fire and smoke unscathed, that they barely realised their clips had run empty. Another of them tried to flee, but the Incinerator caught him in a crosswise blast, lighting him head to foot.

With shrieks, the remaining two took the first door they came to – it stood directly behind them, but it led to the ultimate dead-end: a confessional box. The Incinerator kicked his way in after them. They howled like babies as he blasted them with flame.

Heck meanwhile, swaying on rubber legs, made his way to the scaffolding at the back of the altar. Father Pat hung insensible. His lean torso and belted trousers were caked with clotting gore. Heck checked for the priest's vital signs and found that he still had a pulse. He reached up, tore at the knots and yanked them open, before catching the tortured body as it sagged down.

At the other end of the church, the last four of Shaughnessy's soldiers struggled to escape the building, but the main door had been locked. They kicked and punched the heavy timber, but to no avail. With relentless footfalls, their nemesis came on. Sobbing, screaming, they attempted to reload. But he was only yards away.

As Stardust fled, the others collapsed like waxen figures in the roaring, white-hot spume.

Stardust sped for the church's northwest corner, where the font stood beneath a window from which the glass had been removed and where only paint-stained canvas hung in its place. The font, which was made from intricately worked metal, and roughly the size of a child's bathtub, was penned in by wooden railings, but Stardust vaulted these with ease and leaped up on top of the structure. The window's lower ledge was only seven feet overhead, but with the canvas hanging lower, he knew he could reach it – until he heard feet close behind.

Stardust's handgun of choice was better adapted for urban warfare than many: a Smith & Wesson Model 500, with shortened barrel. His knowledge was better too. This maniac might be wearing Kevlar under his fire-retardant suit, but up top it was only a motorbike helmet.

Stardust went for the head.

His aim was poor – he was in the process of climbing the canvas and firing one-handed. Of the three shots, one missed, but though the other two only clipped the Incinerator's helmet, the effect was huge. The fifty-calibre rounds smashed the headpiece apart, the faceplate flying loose, the rest of it torn clean off, revealing a grey canvas hood and the sweating, smoke-stained features of Nayka underneath. The force staggered the Russian, knocking him down to one knee, his aim slipping downward, hosing the footings of the font, which, thanks to the paint and spirits stored there, literally exploded.

Soaring flames licked at Stardust's soles, driving him up the canvas like an ape. The window ledge was almost in reach when the fabric tore. He plummeted back, landing full in the font, though it now more resembled a cauldron, the water bubbling, hissing. He struggled and kicked as he boiled, but could gain no leverage, his suffering only ending when the Incinerator strode up through the flames, now wielding one of the others' discarded handguns, from which he pumped four heavy shells into Stardust's chest.

Much of this macabre scene was obscured from the front of the church by swirls of oily smoke, but Heck kept one eye on it as he hauled the inert form of his uncle to the rear of the choir screens. The priest's face was cadaverous grey; his cheeks had sunken. When Heck whispered to him, he showed no signs of life.

A few yards away, Lee Shaughnessy finally raised his head, wild-eyed, drenched with sweat.

All around were burnt relics of his crew: blackened, semi-melted forms hanging from the high scaffolding; twisted travesties of humanity sprawled on the pews or in pools of seething fat. The nave was filled with smog and a foul stench of sizzling flesh. But the way to the sacristy, and the open outer door beyond it, was clear. He clambered over the pew into the front aisle, and scampered across the northeast corner of the altar.

'Shaughnessy!' Heck shouted, appearing around the choir screens.

Shaughnessy turned and pegged a shot at him with the Ruger, but it went wide. Heck ducked out of sight anyway, because now heavy footsteps echoed down the church. As

Shaughnessy glanced over his shoulder, the Incinerator advanced along the north aisle. Even without his helmet, he looked no less a monster, the familiar deranged face under the canvas hood blackened and blistered, a tongue of flame flickering at the end of his device.

Shaughnessy raced blindly out through the sacristy.

Nayka followed, tramping past the altar.

Heck watched from around the choir screens, before retreating to his uncle, who, by his low moaning, was gradually regaining consciousness.

'Uncle Pat,' Heck whispered into his ear, having now stuffed an altar cushion under the guy's head. 'You've got to lie still, all right? And keep it down. We're not out of this yet.'

Not sure if the priest could even hear him, he glanced back down the church to check that the fire wasn't spreading. Though cloying smoke hung everywhere, what little there was that could actually burn was no more now than ashes and embers. Reassured by that, he moved to the sacristy entrance. From somewhere beyond that, he heard the cough and snarl of an engine as it ground to life.

For half a second, Heck went groggy. He'd taken quite a beating earlier; both sides of his face were crusty where blood had trickled from his busted eyebrows. But this was no time for calling in sick. He swayed through the sacristy to the outer door and then into the passage between the garage and the church, which he edged along until he'd reached the first corner. From here he could see down onto the car park, where an amazing sight met his eyes.

Almost as quickly as it had started, the deluge was suddenly losing its intensity, but even so the church car park was flooded to a depth of several inches. Lee Shaughnessy, who had got back into his green-and-white van, now skidded and slid as he tried to negotiate his way across it towards the entrance on the main road. Nayka was also out there on the open lot, stalking almost casually after him, aiming the flamethrower one-handed as he jetted spears of flame at the clumsily moving target. The van had been struck at least twice already; it was seared black along its offside, two of its tyres alight. Shaughnessy pulled a desperate righthand turn in an effort to angle away from his tormentor, and the damaged vehicle slipped completely out of control, turning 360 degrees as it slewed away.

It came to a rest facing Nayka, though with about seventy yards between them.

The van growled to life again, Shaughnessy clearly seeing his chance, hitting the gas hard. It juddered forward, picking up speed despite the fire eating away at its flanks and under-carriage. Nayka levelled his weapon in both hands, but held his ground as it barrelled towards him – twenty miles an hour, thirty miles an hour, almost reaching forty before he drove another massive cloud of flame into the front of the van, engulfing it entirely: its engine grille, its bonnet, its windscreen.

With a yowl that was almost like pain, the blazing vehicle swerved sideways, caroming off Father Pat's Volvo and skating along the car park kerb, before hitting a raised manhole lid, which flipped it over onto its roof with a shattering impact, though it still slid another thirty or so yards before coming to a halt. During the course of this collision, the deeply puddled rainwater surged up and over it, which accounted for most of the flames. That could only be a good thing; the van had a petrol tank of its own, after all. But given the force of the crash, it seemed unlikely that Shaughnessy would have survived. Even so, Nayka strolled idly towards it, intent on finishing his work – at which point he spotted Heck in the entrance to the sacristy passage.

Again he veered away from his chosen target, but halted

by the kerb. Even from forty yards or so, Heck saw the Russian's smoke-grey features split apart in a big toothy grin.

'How you doing, cop!' he shouted up the slope. 'You pansy English motherfucker. Here I thinking . . . this English cop, this Detective Heckenburg, he better than others. He good cop. But today I go to Britannia . . . I spy, my plan to kill Shaughnessy and *bratva*. But what I see? Heckenburg . . . beating him? *Da!* You beat Shaughnessy. Get good intel, *da*? So, I follow . . . Shaughnessy later, you first . . .'

'Yeah, and how did that work out for you?' Heck shouted back. Now, with the rain easing off, their voices carried on the chilly night.

Nayka laughed raucously. 'It work out in end. Here we are, *nyet*?'

'You think you've done a job of work?' Heck retorted. 'You fouled up, Nayka. You were supposed to get these Brit gangsters to destroy each other.'

Nayka shrugged, still grinning. 'Hey . . . we do what we can.'

'They know it's you. The Manchester mob . . . they know you're the Incinerator, that you've been burning their associates. This latest massacre might show that it's nothing personal, but it won't do much else. The Tatarstan boys will never be welcome in the Northwest of England now.'

Nayka hooted with mirth. 'You think we need Vic Ship's permission? Vic Ship . . . I say Vic Shit! I hunt him next, *da*?'

'What?' Heck tried to sound scornful, but nonchalant though the Russian's attitude was, Heck could tell the guy was being absolutely serious. After all, Nayka could hardly go home without some kind of result. He was another who'd finish up in the River Neva – if he was lucky.

'English gangster fags!' Nayka laughed. 'Pansy chickenshit fucks. I hunt them too. Whole Vic Shit gang! You think they stop me? You think cops stop me? You not know Nayka. But – you will, *da*?'

And flamethrower still in hand, he came yomping up the slope.

Stumbling back down the passage, Heck was half-minded to duck inside the church. There were several semi-loaded firearms lying around in there, but – and he paused briefly at the sacristy door – his uncle was in there too, only half out of sight behind the altar screens. The cavalry ought to be arriving soon; if he could find somewhere else to hide . . . so he stumbled on past the open door, towards the rear of the church.

The graveyard back there was no longer in use. It hadn't been used for almost a century, and it looked the part, the forest of decrepit tombstones still possessing an eerie atmosphere.

Heck blundered to the edge of it, glancing left to right.

Jumbled ranks of rotted stone ranged away on all sides: eroded statues, leaning crosses, Victorian obelisks. He fled blindly into it, veering crazily through the ranks of monuments, until he planted his left foot on the flat top of a rain-wet tombstone and skated across it, pulling the splits as he landed hard on his back.

The wind was jolted from his lungs.

Heck gasped aloud, and for a second was in so much pain that he briefly wondered if he'd be able to get up again. But now his sixth sense kicked in, telling him to man up, to lie still. So he bit down on his agony and held his breath, staring dumbly at a sky of glacial black, stars spangled across it where the rain-clouds had broken apart.

He listened intently.

But suddenly there was silence.

Stealthily, he turned onto his front and wormed his way along a narrow path between the headstones. OK, Nayka might not be able to see him . . . but now Heck couldn't see Nayka either, which might not be completely to his advantage. Keeping as low as he could, he crawled leftward from the path before lying still again, listening, hearing in lieu of the storm only a steady dripping and trickling from branches and stonework. Long seconds passed, the chill of the wet ground seeping through his already sodden clothes. He was unsure whereabouts in the graveyard he was. Directly in front, the decayed statues of two children in Dickensian clothing stood on a pedestal, the taller figure of an angel with folded wings behind them, a hand on each of their shoulders. When Heck tried to slide forward towards this, the level ground underneath him gave a hollow thud. He was lying on the grave itself, he realised; probably one of those nineteenth-century tombs, the dead laid to rest directly beneath its eroded concrete lid.

Warily, he shifted off it onto a firmer base of gravel – just as the Russian's voice came floating across the burial ground towards him.

'You find your last resting place, English cop. That good. No need for funeral, uh?'

Heck glanced left to right, but from this prone position it was impossible to tell which direction the voice was coming from.

'Some say I let you live, yeah?' the Russian teased. 'You bring all Shaughnessy's pigs to me . . . to their slaughter. But I think no . . . you fuck my plan. And more bad still, you fuck with me. You crack my head, you put gun to me.'

He fell silent again.

Heck lay perfectly still. It was too easy to imagine the maniac skulking towards him.

A soft thud sounded in the darkness behind. Heck spun around, but still saw nothing.

After an ear-straining moment, he rose to his knees,

seeing more crosses, more leaning obelisks. But no movement. When he heard another thud – a footfall maybe – this time to his left, he spun again – and briefly was transfixed by the sight of a figure standing some fifteen yards away. With relief, he recognised it as a traditional death-statue. The Grim Reaper: hooded, only the lower part of its face visible, scabrous and grey with age.

At least . . . this was what Heck thought.

Until he spotted an orange glint of flame at its midriff and realised that it was pointing a flamethrower at him. Those terrible grey features split apart in that familiar grin.

'No one do that to Nayka.'

Heck made a dash for it, a jet of fire spurting after him, only to trip over the rim of another Victorian tomb, and fall headlong across it, striking the flimsy lid with such force that it boomed like a massive drum, the six-foot obelisk of engraved stone at one end of it juddering violently.

Though winded, Heck threw himself over onto his back and tried to crab-crawl away.

The ash-grey figure grinned again as it advanced until it was about ten yards short, at which point it lifted its device to chest-height, training it on him squarely.

'This part where I offer you job, English cop?' Nayka wondered. 'Come, work for us, I say. Earn easy money, yes?' He chuckled, shook his head. 'Nah . . . this part where I kill you.' And he yanked back on his flamethrower trigger.

But nothing happened.

There was a *clunk*, but no flame burst from the muzzle. In fact, the tiny starter-flame at the end of it had also gone out.

'Ahhh . . .' Nayka sighed with mock frustration. 'Fuel gone. No matter.'

He casually unbuckled his harness, the petrol tank sliding off his back, and discarded the flamethrower. Among the

448

various items on his tool-belt, Heck spotted a pistol, a Walther P5. But the Russian didn't go for that. Instead, he drew that big, guard-hilted fighting-knife that Heck thought he'd divested him of in Longsight.

'So . . . I fillet you like taxi guy,' Nayka said. 'Like fish in market.'

Heck scrambled to his feet, backing off as the Russian came at him, knife at chest-height, shoulder turned – the classic combat posture.

It was probably too much to expect that Nayka didn't at least have some kind of military training; he'd handled the flamethrower with aplomb, after all. In addition, Heck was out on his feet; still dazed from the earlier beating, wet through and cold. The best he could do was try to keep moving, playing for time, hoping to God that at some point a support unit would show up, though of course, how they would know he was back here in the depths of this forgotten necropolis was anyone's guess.

He stumbled left, trying to keep the six-foot obelisk between them. It again shifted on its base, from which age and weathering had clearly loosened it.

Nayka grinned, catlike, as he circled around it.

'Not so tough now, uh?' he gloated.

'You drop that blade, pal,' Heck said. 'We'll see who the tough guy is.'

'Hah! You want I give up advantage? Sure . . . why not? This sport, after all, not real thing.'

Nayka lunged, steel flashing as it swept at Heck's throat. Heck ducked backward, again circling the obelisk, feet drumming on the hollow tombstone.

'Truth is . . . Nayka like Heckenburg. You got balls, my friend . . . so I take them as trophy.'

He lunged again. For all that he was encumbered by his heavy, flame-retardant coveralls, he moved in a blur of speed.

Heck only just evaded the thrusting blade, and half-tripped, tottering. Sensing that his foe was weakening, Nayka leapt forward again, seeking to grapple with Heck if not stab him, and landing hard with both feet on the tomb's rotted lid – which collapsed beneath him. As Heck stumbled away, Nayka crashed down into the recess below, a cloud of dust and decay exploding upward.

He cursed volubly in Russian. He'd only dropped six feet or so, but aware that he'd lost the advantage, he threw his knife away and drew his Walther. Heck ducked behind the obelisk as the first shots rang out, two slugs caroming from one side of it, blowing off chunks of aged stone.

'*Soo-keen sihn!*' Nayka screamed, shooting again as he attempted to climb out, both slugs again ricocheting into the night.

Heck could have taken his chance and run for it. But he hadn't come all this way for that.

Instead, he put his shoulder to the obelisk that was loosened from its foundation.

It wasn't an easy decision to do that.

Not much it wasn't.

He gave it everything he had left, straining every muscle.

Already undermined, a half-ton of carved granite now toppled remorselessly forward. Nayka shrieked, shooting madly up at it, as if that would do any good – before it landed full length in the grave, crushing him downward with a huge and reverberating *CRUMP*.

Still vaguely dazed, Heck limped around the pit as the dust floated.

It was too dark to see much, but the obelisk, despite fracturing in at least two places, completely filled the rectangular hole. Nothing stirred underneath it.

He teetered there, before slapping absently at his pocket and trying to remember where exactly Kemp's phone had gone – and so was barely prepared for the metallic *click* behind him. He sagged with disbelief, but not before a massive blow, delivered with a hard, angular object, struck him on the right side of his neck and his right shoulder.

Stunned, he slumped down to his knees, the world spinning, before tilting over and falling sideways next to the rubble-filled grave. At first he was so stupefied by pain that he could barely see the ragged figure circling around into view, let alone work out who it was.

There was a low cackle – a crazy but familiar sound.

It was Shaughnessy, though he looked distinctly the worse for wear.

No longer the elf prince thanks to the congealed blood streaked down his face from a gash across his forehead, he was now more a demonic goblin, especially when his V-shaped smile exposed a mouth full of broken, bloody teeth. His left arm hung gory and useless at his side, but his right was fine; and in his right hand he clutched his bejewelled Ruger pistol, which he trained squarely down at Heck.

'I know what you're thinking,' he said. 'I should be far away by now, eh? It's all gone. My friends dead, my gang kaput. Well . . .' he shrugged, 'I *am* thinking about leaving town . . . but if I'm gonna start somewhere else, I have to salvage a bit of rep. And what would that be worth, eh, without getting at least some payback to brag about?'

Heck was so groggy that he couldn't even move, let alone respond.

Shaughnessy cackled again, cocked his firearm, took careful, one-handed aim – and then ripped the air with an astounding, ear-splitting shriek.

Heck watched through bleary, confused eyes as a third party grabbed Shaughnessy from behind, looped one arm around his throat and yanked his head backwards, at the

451

same time giving something that he'd already stuck into the middle of the young gangster's back a savage twist.

This third party wore gloves and a heavy anorak, its hood pulled up, thin breath issuing from it, along with a penetrating ray of light. Shaughnessy's scream dwindled to a bizarre, non-human gurgle as he sank to his knees. His one good arm rigidified; the Ruger fired off two harmless shots before dropping from nerveless fingers.

Almost gently, the newcomer lowered him to the ground and laid him flat.

Heck was still too stupefied to work out what was happening. Until he heard the voice: low, relaxed, neutral – Middle England all through – and yet eerily sibilant.

'Wondering why you can't move, Mr Shaughnessy?' it whispered.

The figure knelt down alongside the young hoodlum. Heck saw that whoever he was, he carried an open haversack on his left hip, into which he placed something: a blade that glinted red.

'That's because I've just severed your spine below the fifth cervical vertebra . . . which means you are completely paralysed from the neck down. Though you are still able to breathe, have a pulse and are fully aware of everything around you, you're basically just a living head. In the past, I've left certain individuals at this stage, the future looking pretty bleak for them, of course. But alas that isn't in the contract where *you're* concerned.'

The figure rummaged in his haversack.

Heck tried to move, but managed no more than a few helpless twitches.

'The good news, Mr Shaughnessy, is that you'll no longer feel pain from the neck down,' the newcomer said matter-of-factly. 'None at all. The bad news is that I intend to go from the neck up.' He produced his next tool, which looked like a hacksaw, and placed it crosswise at Shaughnessy's throat. 'In fact . . . I intend to *remove* you from the neck up. And I'm in no hurry to get it done quickly.'

Terrified gargles emitted from Shaughnessy's inert form.

'It's also part of the deal that I make you a film star in the process.'

The figure drew back his hood, revealing that underneath it he wore a small helmet-cam strapped around his forehead, from which the beam of torchlight issued, but also, more crucially – to Heck at least – revealing a very familiar face.

His hair was now black, and his glasses square-lensed and horn-rimmed, but there was no mistaking John Sagan.

Shaughnessy's gurgling wail rose again, with one last huge effort transforming itself to an horrendous, beseeching shriek. '*HECKENBURG!*'

Using everything he had, Heck managed to croak a response: 'Sagan . . . wait . . .'

Sagan looked sharply up, spearing his torchlight towards Heck's prone form.

If it was possible for that bland, unemotional face to smile, it did so now – albeit fleetingly.

'Conscious after all, Sergeant Heckenburg?' Sagan raised his voice so that Heck could hear him properly. 'I don't suppose I should be surprised. Quite the badass down in Peckham, weren't you? And you've certainly had a fun time up here. But this changes things, of course.' He glanced down again. 'Seems we haven't got as much time as we thought, Mr Shaughnessy . . . fortunately for you. This is compliments of Mr Ship, by the way.'

With two deft but purposeful strokes of the hacksaw, its steel teeth grinding through gristle, he sliced the paralysed hoodlum's oesophagus wide open, gouts of dark, claret-coloured blood venting out.

As the mangled, dying victim choked and gagged, Sagan

stood, shoved his saw back into his haversack, strode across the graveyard and produced another item, this from his coat pocket. It was the inevitable pistol, but a huge thing, with a big, triangular barrel and massive muzzle. A Desert Eagle 50-calibre semi-automatic, no doubt loaded with hollow-points for an even more spectacular killing effect.

'It doesn't have to be as nasty in your case, Sergeant.' Sagan stopped about five yards away and removed the safety. 'As I say, you gave me a shitty time in London, but I'm strictly a pro. I do what I'm paid for and nothing more. For you it's a simple case of lights out.'

He cocked the weapon and made to lift it – but the shot that tore the night came from somewhere else entirely.

Sagan jumped violently, taken by surprise. And then froze rigid.

Heck craned his neck around, though it hurt to do so. A fourth party was advancing from the direction of the church, framed against a swirling blue light now filling the sacristy passage. This one too was armed with a pistol, and having fired a warning shot in the air, was now levelling that pistol squarely at Sagan.

'Raise that shooter another inch, you sadistic fuckhead, and I blow your brains out.'

It was DI Hayes. She wove up through the gravestones towards them. 'You alive, Heck?'

'Just about,' he groaned, levering himself painfully onto one arm. 'Be careful.'

'Don't worry about me.' Her eyes never left the target. 'John Sagan!'

'Talking to me, officer?' he asked quietly. He was about twenty yards to the left of her.

'I mean it, my man . . . I've got you dead.' She clasped the pistol in her right hand, the left cradling it training-school fashion. It was a Taurus 9mm; not police-issue, so she'd probably lifted it from one of the corpses inside the church. 'I'll give you a count of three, and if you don't drop that weapon, I'll drop you. One . . . two . . .'

Sagan's gloved hand opened, and the Desert Eagle fell.

'You're under arrest for murder,' she said. 'You don't have to say anything. But it may harm your defence if you don't mention when questioned something you later rely on in court. Anything you do say may be given in evidence. That's just so no one can say we aren't doing things text-book . . .'

'As if anyone would,' Sagan replied. He looked amused as she approached, gunsight fixed on his chest.

'Just be careful,' Heck said again.

It was all too familiar: Shawna McCluskey advancing on Sagan, pistol in hand, thinking she had him, but getting an inch too close, her attention slipping for half a fatal second.

'*Hands where I can see them!*' Hayes barked.

Sagan raised them obediently, spreading them out wide – just like the last time.

She was now only two or three yards from him. 'Oh, and get that stupid helmet-cam off. You look like a fucking cyberman.'

Sagan's smile faded. 'My helmet-cam?'

'Get it off!' she hissed. 'Now!'

Puzzled, he reached up with his left hand, hooked his fingers under the strap and tugged it loose.

'Throw it!' she said.

He did as instructed, tossing it into the darkness.

'Good man.' And then she flew at him, like a cat.

Her first punch thudded into the side of his jaw. Sagan looked startled rather than hurt, but the second one was under his chin, an uppercut *wallop* that echoed through the night. His glasses flew off and he hit the ground like a sack of potatoes, but remained conscious – just about. She dropped

455

to her knees alongside him and jammed the gun muzzle hard into his throat.

'Don't look too despondent, John,' she said. 'At least I didn't use a knuckleduster.' She risked a glance over her shoulder. 'You all right, Heck?'

But Heck was already tottering back towards the church.

Epilogue

Heck watched the morning rise through the big window, a beaker of cold coffee in his hand.

The ICU waiting room was a typically drab affair, the floor made of scuffed linoleum, rows of plastic chairs arranged along either wall and bolted to the floor just in case someone ever fancied stealing one, a lone table in the middle, scattered with dog-eared back copies of the sorts of magazines and periodicals that he couldn't imagine anyone wanting to read.

At least it was on the hospital's third floor, so the window looked over much of the town – and the view out there wasn't too dispiriting. The sun was up, and not a scrap of cloud clogged the pearlescent blue sky. The rainstorm the previous night had caused utter but only temporary chaos. Its effects were already dwindling. Everything still sparkled out there, wet through and dripping, but traffic was on the move, commuters were on their way to work. Once the April sun reached its midday zenith, there'd barely be a trace of rainwater left.

As Heck pondered this, Gemma entered the waiting room, pink-cheeked, fair hair damp and stringy. It made her even more beautiful, he thought. Not that any of that mattered at present.

'OK, how you feeling?' she asked, joining him by the window.

'Beaten but not bowed.' He didn't intend it to be an ironic response, even though both his eyebrows were plastered, as was the bridge of his nose. He also had a cracked rib and a stiff right shoulder.

'And how's your uncle?'

He gazed out through the glass. 'Still in IC. Sedated.'

'What's the prognosis?'

'They say he should pull through. But he won't be modelling any beachwear for a while. He's had nearly nine hundred stitches.'

She grimaced at the mere thought.

'How's DI Hayes?' he asked.

'Over the moon, naturally. She's just made the arrest of her career.'

He nodded, but said nothing. For several seconds, the only sound was the growing hubbub of Bradburn Infirmary waking up beyond the doorway.

'She saved my life,' he finally said.

'She's a good cop. With luck, she'll get everything that's due to her.'

'Speaking of which – how's Sagan?'

Gemma was po-faced. 'Hinting that he wants to make a deal.'

Heck half-smiled. In the wan morning light, his hollow eyes and unshaved jaw complemented his multiple cuts and bruises. 'The cheek of the bastard, eh?'

'Says he can name dozens of big-time hoodlums who've paid him to punish their rivals.'

A second passed before Heck glanced round at her. 'He seriously thinks he can witness for us?'

She shrugged. 'It's a tempting offer.'

'You can't be serious?'

'Ultimately, it's not my call. But well . . . it's not like we haven't got the upper hand at present. We found the Pain Box a couple of streets from the church. It's a horror story inside, as you'd expect. At first glance, more like a mobile butcher's shop, all hooks and hanging blades and chains. But then you see that X-shaped cross, and the medical equipment as well. Course, it'll be a treasure trove in forensic terms. It's already been towed in and they're going over it in microscopic detail.'

Heck pondered that, envisaging the numerous DNA samples they'd likely lift in there. 'Evidence of missing persons?'

'By the bucket-load, with any luck. We recovered his head-cam too. Apparently he made some comment about Vic Ship hiring him to kill Shaughnessy.'

'Yeah,' Heck said, remembering. 'So that's it for Ship, eh?'

'It's a start. In addition, we've got Sagan's laptop.'

'Nice.'

'Encrypted obviously, but we're working on it.'

'Electronic accounts book maybe?'

'Hopefully.'

Heck sipped his coffee, indifferent to its tepid foulness. 'So it might not just be Ship who's sweating today.'

'It's certainly got the potential to go a lot further than Manchester.'

'Not a bad week's work,' he replied, though he was too numb and weary to feel as elated about it as he perhaps ought to. 'Could've been a lot worse.'

'Something of an understatement,' Gemma said. 'We've stopped two multiple murderers in their tracks, we've put the biggest firm in Manchester under bone-cracking pressure, and Shaughnessy's crew are finished – mostly dead, in fact.'

Heck snorted. 'Couldn't have happened to a nicer bunch.'

'Course, *they* didn't actually murder anyone.'

'That's a moot point, ma'am, if you don't mind me saying. They were running Vic Ship's dope in Bradburn for years. Then they branched out on their own. It's anyone's guess what their actual tally of deaths comes to.'

'Well . . . they paid a higher price than anyone.'

'And we should let the world know about it.'

She glanced curiously around at him.

'We should make sure the photos from inside the church get publicised,' he said, his tired voice thickening with emotion. 'Because the truth is, at present we've got way too many Jesse James wannabes running round in neckerchiefs and shades, packing six-shooters. We need to give them a glimpse of their future. We should plaster it on the front pages . . . the Britannia Boys hanging on the scaffold, burned.'

Gemma mulled this over. 'As making examples goes, some might consider that a bit, I don't know . . . Tudor.'

'It's *their* justice, not ours. It's out on the streets where it all goes wrong for them. Or alternatively –' he shrugged '– we could just lie. Tell them to keep doing what they're doing because they've got great days ahead.'

'On a not unconnected matter,' she said, consciously opting to change the subject, 'we've still got the Russian angle to consider. At present, the Tatarstans probably don't even know their man is dead, but I doubt it'll set their plans back by much. He was once in the Russian military, by the way – Nayka. Served for eight years in an elite flamethrower unit.'

Heck almost laughed. 'Might have helped if we'd known that earlier.'

'Eric only found out overnight. But to be fair to the St Petersburg Criminal Investigations Directorate, they'd only just learned that we were looking into a series of flamethrower murders. We need to talk to each other more.'

'Nayka was more than just a blunt instrument, of course,' Heck said. 'His primary job was to get our native gangs to liquidate each other.'

'I realise that now.'

'He was frustrated in that by Vic Ship's natural caution. First Ship used a private contractor – Sagan – rather than risk getting his own hands dirty. He wasn't even that keen to use Sagan. He wanted more information about what exactly was happening. I'm guessing that's why Nayka tipped Shaughnessy off about where Sagan was hiding – told him he was up at Woodfold, to try and get Sagan killed and draw Ship into the battle himself. When that failed, Nayka kept his nerve. Continued to play along with Ship. He was an arch-pro. He'd already familiarised himself with Bradburn and the Bradburn underworld, so he thought he'd eliminate a few potential witnesses as well: Sonja Turner . . . me . . . Didn't go right for him ultimately. So he took the next best option: tried to wipe out the opposition all on his own, starting with Shaughnessy's crew. And he made a pretty impressive stab at it. Worrying thing, eh, when homicidal violence is both your passion and your profession? One sure way to get very good at it. And there'll be more like him, ma'am. Ship had other Russians in his crew, to start with.'

'I wouldn't give much for their chances now.' Gemma had a think. 'Or yours, for that matter, Mark – when Nayka's bosses learn you were responsible for his death.'

'It had crossed my mind,' he admitted.

She glanced over her shoulder, checking there was no one loitering in the doorway, before adding, 'Which is why you *aren't* responsible for his death.'

'Ma'am?'

'You know me, Mark.' She adopted her most serious tone. 'I don't like shades of grey in the job. Creates a fog that can hide a wealth of sins. But if Nayka's bosses in St Petersburg

461

find out how he died, you'll never be safe again. So I'm giving it to the media that he died in his battle with Shaughnessy's crew. There are none of them left to deny it. That will become the official line, and we will never, ever veer from it.'

Heck nodded as he contemplated this.

'You could at least pay me the respect of looking surprised that for once I'm not playing a straight bat.' Her tone was sharp, as if this was a big sacrifice on her part.

'I always knew you were flexible, ma'am.'

'It's a case of needs must.'

'It is when I do it too.'

She threw him a look, wondering if he was trying to be clever. But he was peering through the window again. Bright sunlight glimmered on the wet rooftops beyond.

She sighed, weary herself, having been up all night. 'We're all learning new stuff about ourselves, I suppose. Not least you.'

'Me, ma'am?'

'Who'd have thought you still loved your family?'

Heck was puzzled by that. 'I *always* loved them. It's just . . . it was my dad I resented, really. He was the reason all this happened.'

He rubbed at the back of his neck and tried to roll his shoulder, which made him wince.

'You sure that joint's OK?' Gemma asked.

But Heck's thoughts were elsewhere. He gazed through the window again, but it was distant, unfocused. He wasn't seeing Bradburn in the present.

'I was his golden boy, you see,' he said. 'My dad's, I mean. I was the sports star, the one who was going to bring pride to the family while the older one, the one they'd invested so much hope in academically, turned into a druggie dunce. But . . . after Tom killed himself, well, everything changed.

I mean, obviously it changed. And indirectly, I suppose, that part of it *was* my fault.'

Perhaps sensing that he finally needed to discuss this long-lasting hurt, and, despite her fatigue, adopting a patient, near-parental tone, Gemma asked: 'How was it your fault?'

He shook his head, as if the answer should have been obvious to him all along.

'My dad went through a kind of breakdown. I mean, I realise that now. At the time I just thought he was being a pillock . . . he suddenly got guilt-ridden, you see. All he'd ever done when Tom was getting into drugs was punish him, bollock him, tell him what a waste of space he was. He hadn't actually tried to help him. And then he suddenly got guilty about that . . . when it was all too late, of course. And that guilt, because I guess it was intolerable and just wouldn't go away, eventually forced him to pass the buck. He started to whitewash Tom's memory, decided that in reality Tom had been the one who'd been going places . . . while I'd wasted my time concentrating on sport, hanging out with my mates, being a lad around town. All the things he'd previously thought were pretty cool. As a result, I packed the rugby in before I even got a sniff of playing profession-ally.'

He shrugged as if it was no biggie, but the glaze on his eyes told her differently.

'It was voluntary, of course,' he said. 'I didn't want to be the cause of any more friction, so I gave up my dream.' He smirked, trying to make light of it, but there was no humour there. 'Some dream, eh? Rugby League players don't get paid that well even today. Instead, I got stuck into my studies, managed to get a few half-decent grades, whereas beforehand it would have been failures across the board. But even that wasn't enough for Dad, you know. By then he'd completely flipped.'

He moved across the room to the vending machine in the corner, shoved change in and drew himself another thin, watery coffee as though on auto-pilot.

'As far as my dad was concerned – or so he told me – the wrong one of us had died.'

Gemma couldn't respond to that. Her own late father, himself a police officer, had been an unyielding character, a firm man who let his role in society temper the affection he showed even to his loved ones. But she'd idolised him all the same, had seen no evil in his clipped, no-nonsense persona, had wanted to be just like him – an ambition he'd tacitly if not warmly encouraged, because deep down he'd sought the best for her: the best job in the world, as he'd called it, the worthiest career. He could be strict and cool, but underneath there was much fondness there. It was impossible to imagine her own father ever making as tactless and damaging a comment as that.

'So you see, Gemma,' Heck said, still in his semi trance-like state, 'my joining the job was actually nothing to do with me wanting to show the world how police-work should really be done. I know I've often said that, but that was bravado, bluster. In reality, I became a copper as an act of revenge. Pure and simple. Against my dad. Oh . . .' Even though he'd been speaking to her, only now did he seem to notice that she was standing there. 'Do you want a brew, ma'am? Sorry, that was rude of me.'

'No, it's OK, Mark.'

'Don't blame you really. This is pretty crap stuff.' He trudged back to the window. 'At the time it never occurred to me that it would alienate me from so many people. That isolation probably wouldn't have lasted if I'd only stayed in the job a couple of years. But we Heckenburgs . . . unfortunately, we dig our heels in. Especially when it's a war situation, which that became . . . I mean it wasn't just my

464

family. Soon it felt like everyone I knew hated me. Felt like the whole town hated me. So then I was *determined* to stay a cop. On top of that, I was pretty good at it. I think.'

'*Pretty* good?' She allowed a hint of a smile into her voice. 'You're so good at it you've only gone and saved the town that hated you. If it *did* hate you . . . which I don't believe.'

Heck looked uncomfortable with that. 'I wouldn't go as far as to say I saved the town.'

'Maybe not, but, thanks to your instincts and efforts, we've removed some pretty unsavoury elements. And we'll be removing more in due course, not just from Bradburn but from all across the Northwest, and further. The dominoes are falling, trust me.'

'Good day at the office then.' He sipped his coffee.' Even if it doesn't much feel like it.'

'It was never going to happen without casualties.' She put a hand on his shoulder. 'Mark . . . you look tired and famished. You need some sleep, but first let me buy you breakfast.'

Gently and politely, he moved her hand away. 'No, thanks . . . ma'am.'

'OK . . . why not?'

He peered through the window again. 'I'm sorry I came on to you a couple of times.'

'A couple of times? It happens *all* the time.'

'Yeah, I know . . . and I should've got the message by now. It's selfish, inconsiderate and rather ungallant of me.'

'All right, fine, good, I'm delighted you realise it . . . but why does that mean we can't have breakfast?'

'I should stay here.'

'Mark, your uncle's under sedation and stable. What more can you do here?'

He shook his head. 'I need to get the house shipshape. Dana's due back on Friday.'

'Today's only Wednesday. I can help you get the house

465

shipshape in time for that. Let's have some breakfast, eh? If you insist on keeping it professional, we can sit and discuss the case.'

'No. We should discuss the case in the office. Make it formal.'

'Mark . . .' A faint sting had crept into her voice. 'Are you fishing for reasons why I can't buy you breakfast?'

He glanced at her, surprised. 'Don't take it to heart.'

'Don't take it to heart? I sat on John Sagan for hours last night during one of the worst downpours I've ever known, and still someone else got the collar.'

'You were only a minute too late to arrest him.'

'Our other main target was dead several minutes before I even arrived. And now I can't even take you to breakfast! Are you for real?'

He fidgeted awkwardly. 'Well, if it means that much to you . . .'

'It means plenty to me. I *like* breakfast.'

'OK, but I want to go back to the family grave first and put some flowers on it.' He took his jacket from a chair, seeming certain about this at least.

'You realise the whole church and the churchyard are a crime scene?' she said.

He edged to the door. 'I'm sure if *you're* with me, ma'am, I won't have a problem getting through the tape.'

'Great.' She followed him out. 'At least I'm useful for something.'

466

Get back to where it all started with book one of the series, where Heck takes on the most brutal of killers...

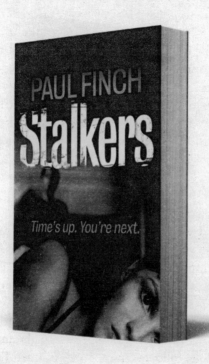

Dark, terrifying and unforgettable.
Stalkers will keep fans of Stuart MacBride and M.J. Arlidge looking over their shoulder.

A vicious serial killer is holding the country to ransom, publicly – and gruesomely – murdering his victims.

THE #1 EBOOK BESTSELLER

Sacrifice

PAUL FINCH

Who will be next?

A DETECTIVE MARK HECKENBERG THRILLER

A heart-stopping and unforgettable thriller that you won't be able to put down, from bestseller Paul Finch.

DS Mark 'Heck' Heckenburg is used
to bloodbaths. But nothing will
prepare him for this.

Brace yourself as you turn the pages
of a living nightmare.

Welcome to The Killing Club.

As a brutal winter takes hold of the Lake District, a prolific serial killer stalks the fells. And for Heck, the signs are all too familiar...

The fourth unputdownable book in the DS Mark Heckenburg series. A killer thriller for fans of Stuart MacBride and *Luther*.

Heck needs to watch his back. Because someone's watching him...

Get hooked on Heck: the maverick cop who knows no boundaries. A grisly whodunit, perfect for fans of Stuart MacBride and *Luther*.

A stranger is just a killer you
haven't met yet...

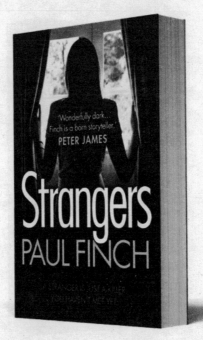

Meet Paul Finch's new heroine in the first
of the PC Lucy Clayburn series. Read the
Sunday Times bestseller now.